Who
We
Are
Now

ALSO BY LAURYN CHAMBERLAIN

Friends from Home

Who We Are Now

A Novel

LAURYN CHAMBERLAIN

DUTTON

DUTTON

An imprint of Penguin Random House LLC
penguinrandomhouse.com

LIBRARY OF CONGRESS CATALOGING-IN-PUBLICATION DATA

Names: Chamberlain, Lauryn, author.
Title: Who we are now: a novel / Lauryn Chamberlain.
Description: 1. | [New York] : Dutton, [2023]
Identifiers: LCCN 2022049861 (print) | LCCN 2022049862 (ebook) |
ISBN 9780593182840 (paperback) | ISBN 9780593182857 (ebook)
Classification: LCC PS3603.H33675 W56 2023 (print) |
LCC PS3603.H33675 (ebook) | DDC 813/.6—dc23
LC record available at https://lccn.loc.gov/2022049861
LC ebook record available at https://lccn.loc.gov/2022049862

Printed in the United States of America

1st Printing

BOOK DESIGN BY DANIEL BROUNT

To Arvin Ahmadi,
who is the best parts of every character I write

Who We Are Now

PROLOGUE

DECEMBER 2018

At dusk the mourners pour out of the chapel, spilling down the steps in a black current. They sweep over the narrow sidewalks of Norfolk Street, unsure of whether to stay, go somewhere and drink, or go home and disappear.

"So many people came," a man comments. "Hundreds. It was nice to see."

"So young, though. It's tragic," a woman in a black pillbox hat and a heavy wool coat says, and there are nods and murmurs of assent.

"Who are the organizers?" the man next to her asks, his breath visible in the air. The weather is uncharacteristically cold for December in New York, the spindly trees frozen in a way that feels apt. "I want to pay my respects."

The woman points up at the top of the steps, where three figures stand, unmoving, silhouetted in the doorway.

"Them, up there. They were all friends in college, I think."

The man nods. He turns and approaches the stairs. But before he can reach them, one of the shadows in the doorway drops to her knees and sobs. It is a distorted, guttural kind of sound, animal and ugly.

The man looks away, not wanting to intrude on her grief.

It could have been any one of us, he thinks.

He is guiltily grateful that it was not.

He looks at the stairs one more time, but the figures have disappeared inside. All he can hear is a wailing from behind the shuttered doors.

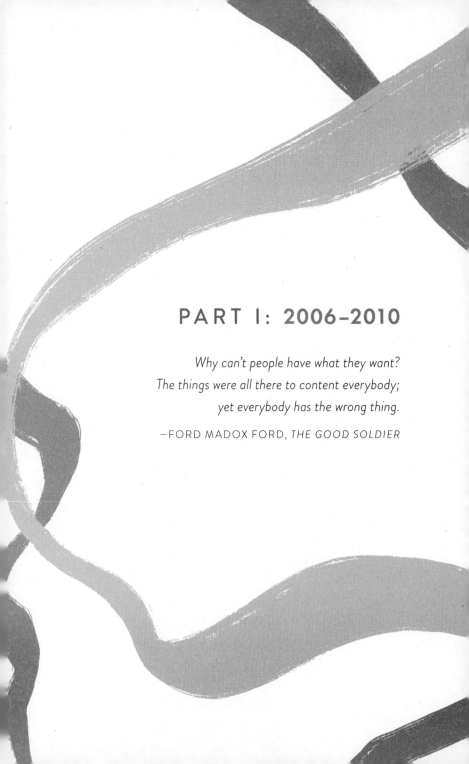

PART I: 2006–2010

Why can't people have what they want?
The things were all there to content everybody;
yet everybody has the wrong thing.

—FORD MADOX FORD, *THE GOOD SOLDIER*

On the night before the last day, Nate slept until four in the afternoon.

He woke up to the sound of someone pounding on his bedroom door. The knocks came in quick succession, one clipping the heels of the other, no attempt on the knocker's part to listen and discern if he might be getting out of bed or if he might prefer to be left alone.

It had to be Rachel, then.

"I'm up," he groaned, rolling over carefully in his twin bed to look at the bedside clock: 4:02 p.m. He had a vague recollection of stumbling into his room around dawn. His head throbbed with a steady, painful pulse that seemed to exist separate from the rest of him, with a mind of its own. His Radiohead poster was blurred by his double vision.

"You're not 'up'; you're waiting for me to leave so you can go back to sleep." Rachel threw open the door and bounded over to his bed. She hopped up and sat squarely on top of the spot where his feet were nestled under the covers.

"Ow."

"Sorry." She pouted, batting her eyelashes.

That was all it took; his hangover haze be damned, he grinned at her. "S'all right," he said, rumpling his sweat-matted hair in a way he hoped looked attractive. Despite—or perhaps *because of*—her utter lack of respect for his personal space, Rachel was undeniably his favorite of his housemates. Not that he would ever have told her that.

"Good, because I'm not really sorry. It's the last night before graduation, and there's no way in hell I'm letting you sleep through it."

"Easy for you to say. You left the party last night by one. I stayed out until five."

"I needed to conserve my energy for *this*." Rachel made a sweeping gesture indicating her outfit. She was already dressed for a night out: a top tissue-paper thin, like something Nate wanted to unwrap. Flimsy straps, a short black skirt. He had to look elsewhere so he wouldn't stare.

"Can you believe it's the last night we'll all be here? It's so weird."

Nate shook his head, then massaged his aching neck. No, he couldn't believe it. The last night of college? Four years of midterms and Easy Mac and tapped kegs and a blur of evenings like the one he had just passed had all culminated in . . . *this*? It seemed both too incredible and too ordinary to be believed.

"Get dressed." Rachel reached over and smoothed his hair. "We need you in the living room at five."

He glanced at the clock again. "Five? I need more time."

"But we missed you so much all day!"

"I don't believe you."

"Fine, we want you to drive us to go pick up vodka for the pregame."

"Ah, bingo."

"Thanks, Natie," Rachel said as she stood up. "I'm going to finish getting ready. The last Friday night!"

Nate leaned back against the wall at the head of his bed, trying to will himself to get up and get in the shower. *The last Friday night.*

Every preceding Friday night for the whole of their senior year had started in pretty much the same way. He and Dev would hang out in their shared room—he was still annoyed the girls had won the battle for the separate bedrooms upstairs— reading for their Joyce seminar, messing around on the guitar, or napping off the effects of a too-wild Thursday night. At some point in the evening, they'd hear the squeak of the stairs, glance up at their sloped ceiling, and wait for the clacking of Rachel's high heels and the stomping of Clarissa's boots as the two of them bounded downstairs. Then the girls would burst into the room, announce the plans for the night, and start needling the boys, making fun of them, dressing them, offering them vodka shots like intrusive collegiate fairy godmothers.

It never occurred to Nate or Dev to make any Friday night plans. Every weekend, they waited for the girls to plan their adventures. He would miss that when he moved to New York, he thought, but he decided he had to assume that his "real life" would work itself out. What was the sense in getting maudlin over the unremarkable end of the four-year headache of university? Sufficiently galvanized, he heaved himself up off his bed and headed to the shower, towel wrapped around his waist.

He ran into Dev in the hallway on the way to the downstairs bathroom. Dev wore sweatpants with no shirt, and he held a slice of cold pizza in one hand. He raised the other to fist-bump Nate.

"Dude," Dev said. "We should've gone home last night when Rachel and Clarissa did. I'm fucking wrecked."

Nate shrugged noncommittally, deciding not to let on how bad he felt. No matter how "wrecked" he claimed to have been, Dev never seemed to throw up or look hungover or embarrass himself. Nate had been trying to carry off this kind of casually-put-together nonchalance ever since he had been assigned to room with Dev freshman year, but by now it was starting to seem like the kind of thing you were just born with—like height, or a fast metabolism (both of which Dev had as well).

"We have to rally. Last night of college! Rachel already came in to berate me."

"Well, after tonight, it's just the *first* night of our real lives, right? Even better."

"Maybe." They padded down the narrow hallway to the kitchen, where Nate stopped in front of the fridge. He found Dev's broad grin energizing, as he often did, but he also needed something with stronger medicinal powers than optimism. "I need a shower beer. Hair of the dog, take the edge off."

Nate popped the can, took a long sip, and exhaled.

Dev shook his head and laughed. "Better?"

"Better. What am I going to do without you in New York?"

Nate meant this as a jovial sign-off to their conversation, and he started back toward the bathroom. After a shower and a full beer to clear his lingering hangover, he'd be ready to have a genuine conversation. But Dev had other plans, it seemed; he followed Nate out into the hall and toward the bathroom.

"Actually, I've got some news." He raked a hand through his thick black hair, cocking his head. "I think I'm gonna move to New York, too."

"Okay, yeah, you're shitting me." Nate laughed, assuming this was a typical Dev joke. "Now, get out, I have to shower. Rachel thinks we're going to take her to get liquor."

"I'm serious."

Nate turned back to face him. *Is this for real?* With Dev, you never knew. He was always threatening to do things like start a band or organize a protest, but then he would abandon the idea as suddenly as he'd taken it up. The rest of them had already determined their postgrad plans: Nate would be an analyst at Lehman Brothers; Rachel had taken an editorial assistant position at *New York* magazine; Clarissa planned to stay in Chicago and wait tables or bartend while doing the "comedy thing" on the side. Dev was the only one who hadn't settled on a plan yet, characteristically laid-back even about this most defining decision.

"Really? You found a job in New York?"

"I mean, I didn't find a job *yet*," Dev said. "But I will, right? I'm applying to a few communications things out there, and I can always temp. Or maybe teach. I'll figure it out. But it just feels like New York is the place to *be*."

Nate didn't say anything. Until this very moment, he had felt sad at the idea of leaving Dev behind in Chicago. Now something about the idea of Dev coming to New York seemed less than desirable. He sensed that the night suddenly had the potential to become entirely about Dev moving to New York, in the way that Dev's spontaneous adventures often became the focal point of, well, everything.

"Come on, what do you think?" Dev raised his eyebrows. "I mean, my parents would be more into it if I were moving out there to work at Lehman Brothers with you. But screw it. You going is enough for me."

With that, Nate's mood changed. He thought of their years of shared houses, their shared adventures. He was being an idiot; *of course* he wanted to move to New York with his best friend.

"Hell yeah, man." Nate smiled, clapping Dev on the shoulder. "Let's do it."

Dev grinned back. "Okay, I'll get out of here so you can shower. Alcohol run at five sharp."

"Five. Got it."

Dev broke the news of his move to Rachel and Clarissa in Nate's car on the way back from the liquor store.

"Oh my God, yay," Rachel shrieked, throwing her arms around Dev's neck to hug him from her perch in the back seat of Nate's Camry, and Nate wished he could say something that would invite the same kind of physical response.

"Ow, release the choke hold," Dev joked. "I regret calling shotgun."

"Where are you going to live? Move to the West Village! That's where I'm looking."

"I can't afford the West Village. I haven't sold my soul for the big bucks like Nate here."

"Hey!" Nate objected, hoping he sounded jovial, but the comment stung, even though he usually felt relieved to have added a somewhat last-minute economics minor to his English major, thus opening a door toward financial security. Three months ago, he'd been forced to make the big decision: to take the Lehman Brothers job offer, or to pursue a graduate school acceptance at Columbia. He'd wavered for only a moment before choosing the chrome and flash of Wall Street over the green-leafed idyll of academia. After all, ever since he had decided to apply for investment banking jobs, Lehman had been his dream: He wanted the very best. Still, every now and then, when his roommates talked about their creative dreams, a part of him wondered if he'd done the right thing.

"That's not an insult, by the way," Dev clarified. "I'd sell my soul immediately if I had any takers."

"Well, wherever you live, this is big news," Clarissa said evenly, always the more pragmatic one. "Is Nate helping you move? Are you going to get a place together?"

"Um, we didn't talk about that yet," Nate said.

"Wow, you guys always have the most detailed conversations," Rachel mocked. "Dev, why'd you tell him first?"

"Because he's my best friend, dude."

"Your *best* friend? Ouch! And don't call me dude."

"Settle down," Clarissa said, putting her hand on Rachel's shoulder. "I can't relive the argument over Dev's MySpace Top 8."

As Nate pulled up to the curb in front of their ramshackle house, he gave a silent thanks for Clarissa's moderating influence. Without it, Rachel and Dev could be a little bit . . . much.

"Okay, everybody out," he commanded. "Grab the booze from the trunk. Pregame and then Cody's party on Hamlin?"

"Roger that," Dev said.

Cody was a friend of Nate's who would also be going the investment banking route in New York after graduation, and they had recently signed a lease on an apartment in Murray Hill, a place Nate had heard of but never seen. Nate had known Cody since freshman year, but he was more useful for when you wanted to shotgun a beer before the game and less useful for providing details on lease negotiations and managing paperwork.

As he reached the front door of the house, trailing Dev with the final case of beer, he heard the click of the answering machine and his mother's distinctive "Hi, Nate," the "hi" an octave higher in pitch than his name. "We can't wait to see you at commencement tomorrow—nine o'clock sharp, remember."

"Leave it," Nate commanded Rachel and Clarissa, who were likely to pick up the house phone and talk with his mom for twenty minutes before passing the phone to Nate. "She's sentimental about graduation. If it's anything urgent, she'll call my cell."

"Be nice and talk to her," Rachel, who talked to her own mother every single day, ribbed him. "She's excited for you."

"Nah, he's right," Clarissa said. "Love her to death, Nate, but I'd rather not listen to your mom wax nostalgic about how you were in diapers just yesterday while we're trying to pregame."

Rachel shrugged and busied herself setting up bottles of chasers for the vodka on the Formica countertop of the outdated rental kitchen.

Nate felt a flash of guilt, even though he'd see his parents first thing the next morning. Throughout college he'd complained about them hovering and about what he derisively called their "midwestern prudishness," but he knew he owed them for everything he had. Anyway, their only crime was to be middle-class and middle-aged, different from Rachel's Manhattan sophisticate parents and Clarissa's Chicago-born, Poland-bred extended family. But he shook his head to clear it, finding his way back to a more productive train of thought. He couldn't magically go back in time and seem more grateful for them throughout his college years; he'd start again tomorrow. Wasn't that what growing up and graduating was for anyway? Finally realizing everything your parents had done for you. Screw regrets; screw nostalgia; there would be plenty of time for those. For now, it was time to get drunk.

Rachel quickly poured out four shots of vodka. "Remember when we used to pregame together in the dorm during freshman year?" she said to them as Dev walked into the kitchen to join in. "We were so much crazier back then."

"What do you mean, we were crazy *back then*?" Dev interjected, passing shots around. "Speak for yourself. Nate and I PR'd at the keg stand last night."

"We did?"

"You blacked out? No wonder I had to wake you up at four. Hey, Clarissa, Nate and Dev think they're so much crazier than us."

"Let them have it. I'm an old lady now. I'm taking two shots, max."

If there was one thing he would miss, Nate thought as the first shot settled in his stomach, it was listening to his housemates talk over one another like this. It was an endless cacophony in the house almost all the time: Rachel reading Joan

Didion essays aloud, even when no one was listening; Dev and Clarissa telling jokes and trying to outdo each other as their stir-fry burned, forgotten, in the kitchen. But now three of them were going to New York. Maybe it would be a lot like this, Nate thought, at first optimistically and then with a strange acid feeling in the pit of his stomach, like he'd eaten something that didn't agree with him.

"I have an idea," Rachel announced as Clarissa began fiddling with the CD player, starting up their pregame mix. "Everyone tell your best story from college."

"We need another shot for that," Dev said, reaching around her for the bottle to pour them each a second round. "But I'm game. I'll go first, obviously."

"Because you think you're the best storyteller?"

"I don't *think* I'm the best storyteller. I *am* the best storyteller."

"Let's hear it, then." Rachel raised her eyebrows at him. "Bottoms up."

Dev started to talk, waving his hands and holding court, and Nate felt the warm rush of drunkenness starting to creep up his neck. He smiled. He looked around at his three roommates; his eyelids heavy, it seemed like there was an actual rosy glow to his vision.

Maybe they all felt as sentimental: Rachel leaned her head against Clarissa's shoulder, her silky brown hair—she had about four products in their shared shower that Nate couldn't identify—layering over Clarissa's light strands. He had a foggy, drunken thought that he didn't fully understand the girls, maybe never would, not the way he felt he understood Dev. The two of them smiled at each other knowingly, like they possessed the answers to questions Nate didn't even know to ask.

Then Clarissa handed one more shot to Dev, who grinned and raised it in Nate's direction.

"This is cheesy, but fuck it." Nate raised his glass, too, and looked at all three of them. He found Rachel's eyes last and kept his gaze on her. "To the rest of our lives, yeah?"

"To the rest of our lives."

AS SHE RAISED HER SHOT GLASS TO TOAST HER THREE BEST friends, Rachel remembered with disbelief that she hadn't wanted to go to Northwestern. She had almost missed all of this, she thought, incredulous. She had almost never met the most important people in her life. Four years ago, Rachel had applied to Northwestern as a backup school—an admittedly cocky decision given its admission statistics, but Rachel had been raised to aim high. She'd had her heart set on her parents' alma mater, Princeton, but her wait-list acceptance had never come through. She remembered sitting on the floor of her bedroom in her parents' Park Avenue apartment and crying for a full hour before boarding her one-way flight to Chicago.

But that was the day she met Clarissa. She had walked into Allison Hall to find her already sitting on one of the twin beds in their shared room. Clarissa had all of two suitcases compared to Rachel's ten boxes, and she had unpacked alone—Rachel was flanked by her parents throughout the entire process. And yet, despite their apparent dissimilarities, they had ended up talking for three straight hours their first night, lying only a few feet apart in their twin beds, their closeness immediate. The next night, they went to their first college party, and Rachel held Clarissa's fine blond hair back as she threw up jungle juice in the sticky communal bathroom. By the third day, they were best friends, and Rachel remembered having a distinct thought that it felt like meeting a part of herself that she had never known existed.

By the time they met Nate and Dev in a creative writing class the next month, she couldn't believe she might have chosen a different school and never met them. How could she have ever wanted a different life than this one?

Rachel shook her head, willing herself not to get too nostalgic. At least not until they were all drunker. She downed her shot and slammed the glass down on the counter.

"Let's get out of here," she told her roommates. She turned toward the door, happy in her confidence that they would all follow.

They had timed their arrival perfectly. When they walked into Cody's party, it seemed like every one of her friends was there: her sorority sisters who lived down the block, the enigmatic Australian twins from her poli-sci lecture, their suite mates from freshman year.

"Oh my God, hey!" she screamed at one of the twins—Asher, she thought—pulling him in for a hug. Dev slapped five with Christian.

"It's the Rachel and Dev show," she heard Clarissa scoff, but she knew she didn't mean it unkindly. "Nate, do you know any of these people?"

"*You* know these people, Clare." Nate slung one arm around

her shoulders and the other one, a bit awkwardly, around Rachel's. "Cody lived in our hall freshman year."

"I know *Cody*, you idiot. This is his house. Oh good, I think I see one of my friends from sketch comedy class."

Then Clarissa split off, because that's what she did: At any given party, Rachel could find Clarissa congregating with a few girls in the corner, contentedly sipping a beer even if it was flush with foam from the keg and carrying on the kind of conversation that could have just as easily taken place at a coffee shop. Rachel could admit that she, on the other hand, preferred to be the life of the party, the center of attention. Strangely, this had made the two of them closer, rather than driving them apart. They could appreciate each other's style instead of wanting to compete in the same scene.

Dev, on the other hand, worked the room. He said hi to everyone, slinging inside jokes and fond insults—at least until he found whatever girl would hold his attention for the evening.

Though Rachel feigned either annoyance or disinterest whenever Dev talked about his many flings, she had to admit, if only to herself, that she understood exactly what everyone saw in him. It wasn't only his looks: His thick, eternally messy black hair and dark eyes were striking enough, she supposed, and it didn't hurt that he was six two, or that he had a very specific, independent swagger, but it was more than that. Every time his popularity, his need to be at the center of things, bordered on obnoxious, or entitled, he countered it with something unexpected. In the second year of their friendship, Dev had consistently partied six nights a week—except for the time he'd spent six nights in a row sleeping on the floor of Rachel's room her sophomore year when her mom had been diagnosed with breast cancer. She'd been terrified and alone, but Dev had folded himself into her life in a way that made her feel as if he'd always been there to keep her safe.

Suddenly warm with feeling, she walked up to where Dev stood sipping a drink with a few guys in the kitchen and put her head on his shoulder, not saying anything.

"Oh, so this is Krista?" Cody asked, gesturing at Rachel with his beer while staring pointedly at her chest. She bristled, jerking her head from Dev's shoulder.

Cody was better friends with Nate than with the rest of them, but he certainly knew who she was. He wasn't confused, Rachel knew; he was making a joke at her expense, suggesting that she was just one of Dev's "girls." That any woman hanging around Dev had to be sleeping with him, and that all of said women were interchangeable.

"Maybe lay off being a dick for just one night, Cody, huh? Rachel's my best friend," Dev defended her. He reached down and laced his fingers with hers, and then he flashed her a lopsided smile, and she realized he was drunk, and she also realized she didn't care and let him keep holding her hand.

Cody held his hands up in surrender. "Just giving this guy some grief. He deserves it from time to time."

"Well, that we can agree on," she acquiesced, forcing a smile.

"Anyway, Rach," Dev said, grabbing her a drink with his free hand. "We were just discussing how we'd rate this party on a scale of one to ten. What do you think? Take a minute."

Rachel glanced around. That J-Kwon song thumped from the speakers in the living room, the bass strong enough to knock over a beer. *Everybody in the club gettin' tipsy.* A few couples were dancing—drunkenly grinding, just swaying, really—but most weren't quite drunk enough for that yet. Instead, they talked in groups, yelling into one another's ears over the din. Some of them were taking photos to post on Facebook; others were probably telling secrets, making last-night-of-college confessions, but more likely, most were trading the kind of gossip common to all Northwestern senior parties: who had made out with whom, who got a job offer where, who might be doing drugs in the bathroom.

"Eh." She shrugged, shifting her weight from one foot to the other and feeling the sole of her shoe stick to the beer-covered linoleum. "Like, a five."

"That," Dev said, stabbing a finger in the air like a professor, "is exactly the perfect number. That's what I just said."

"It's still early." Cody shrugged, defensive. "Plus, that girl from my discussion section with the great tits is here."

Rachel rolled her eyes, twin feelings coursing through her: annoyance at Cody's gross comment and a paradoxical desire for her breasts to be viewed as better than those of this anonymous girl from discussion section, whoever she was. She rolled her shoulders back, her chest emphasized.

Dev simply chugged the remainder of his beer and shook his head. "In any case, the last night has to go out with a bang. We will accept nothing less. And a five out of ten is definitely less. Rachel, any ideas?"

She did have an idea. She knew what she wanted to say, and she knew Dev would go along with it. But as everyone turned to her, hanging on her words, she also knew she wanted to prolong the moment. She wanted them all to stay eager, expectant; she wanted them to look at her exactly like this.

She raised an eyebrow. "I do have an idea. But we're going to have to get a lot drunker first."

An hour and several drinks later, the three of them stood outside the padlocked gates at the entrance to the beach. The light from the moon illuminated the unblemished sand, the breaking waves, the empty lifeguard stand.

"How do we, like, get in?" Cody asked.

Rachel raised an eyebrow. "You've never skinny-dipped at North Beach before?"

"It's a Northwestern rite of passage. Good thing we got to you, and just in time, too. I don't think they even let you graduate if you don't do it." Dev slapped Cody's shoulder. "We'll boost Rachel up and over and then she'll grab the key—she knows where they keep a spare in the beach shack."

Climbing up on Dev's shoulders, she made it over the iron gate easily enough. She retrieved the key and handed it to the boys through the slats. They fiddled with the padlock on the chain holding the gates together, and then soon enough they were all running out onto the sand of North Beach in the pitch-darkness. They were away from the streetlights, away from everything except the soft sound of the waves lapping against the shore. Dev came up next to her and slung an arm around her shoulders.

"Beautiful, right?" she asked.

"To look at. Cold once we get in there, even in June," Dev reminded her. "You ready?"

When her friends from Dartmouth or Cornell or University of Michigan came to visit Northwestern, they were always shocked that the school owned a strip of the Lake Michigan coastline. "You have a private beach?!" they'd exclaim, and Rachel would smile and nod, ignoring the fact that it was too cold to enjoy it seven months out of a nine-month school year—and seemingly closed every other time. They made good use of it during finals week in early June, but the gate swung shut promptly at 10 p.m. to prevent, well, exactly what she and Dev and Cody were trying to do right now. Students getting drunk and going for a swim on school property was a liability nightmare for the university—hence why Rachel had to befriend a lifeguard and flirt her way to hidden key access.

"We're fucking done! Do you hear that, Chicago? We out!" Cody whooped, whipping his shirt off over his head as he bounded toward the water. He dropped his boxers on the wet sand near the shoreline and staggered in, waves breaking at his knees and his ass on full display.

Rachel shielded her eyes in faux modesty and turned toward Dev. "Maybe I didn't think this plan through. That's really more of Cody than I ever needed to see."

"But not more of me than you want to see, right?" He wiggled his eyebrows as he pulled his own worn T-shirt up over his head, stripping down to just his baggy shorts.

Rachel shoved him. "Ew, as if," she said, but, her vision blurring from the beer and the adrenaline and the starlight, what she really thought was, *Wow, what if?* She raised an eyebrow in a way she hoped suggested she was calling his bluff, and then nonchalantly shrugged out of her silk camisole, daring him to look.

She drew a deep breath and broke into a sprint, catapulting down the sloped sand toward the water, stumbling over herself and barely able to keep up with the downhill motion of her own legs. She couldn't see him, but she knew Dev was just a beat behind her, over her right shoulder, and before she knew it, the water was upon them, stinging her shins, then her knees, and then her goose-bumped thighs.

"It's so cold," she screamed. "Why is it this cold in June?"

Cody splashed Rachel playfully, and she winced, crossing her arms in front of her chest, suddenly feeling every bit as naked as she was. The only thing to do was go under. Drawing a deep breath and steeling herself against the stabbing pain of the cold water, she arched her arms above her head and dove under a breaking wave.

It worked. She was still cold, she knew, but holding herself there in the bubble of silence under the surface, she felt everything equalizing, like she and the water had become the same temperature. At first, she held her breath just to see if she could do it, and then she kept holding it when she realized that she could not remember the last time she felt such a profound sense of calm. Quiet. This was the best kind of isolation.

Rachel did not, in general, like to feel isolated.

She had meticulously planned her life after graduation to avoid that exact problem. While Clarissa had decided to strike out on her own in the Chicago comedy scene, Rachel would board a one-way flight back to New York, the city of her birth, and stay at her parents' apartment on the Upper East Side until she could sign a lease of her own. She had a job lined up as an editorial assistant at *New York*, and it was exactly the kind of position she had hoped to land by majoring in journalism and minoring in creative writing. It would be a stepping stone to—hopefully—bigger opportunities in the magazine industry, and, in her mind, the perfect job to have while finally working on her novel. "Actually, I write fiction on the side," she could already picture herself saying at cocktail parties and book launches. She would be right in the middle of the city, in what she had always seen as the chaotic, noisy heart of life itself. She would be surrounded by all her friends from childhood: friends from her summer camp upstate, girls from her high school. And Nate. And now *Dev*.

It was the perfect plan, and she was . . . terrified. Terrified? It didn't make any sense, but suddenly she could feel this dread tangibly, snaking its way around her core and tightening. No, wait. It was something else she felt coiling around her. Something solid. An arm around her waist. Her waist! Rachel had almost forgotten that she had a body. But then she felt cool air hit the top of her head, then her face, then her shoulders. The lake; she was in the lake, and someone had yanked her out. She whipped her head around to see Dev holding her. Naked. Keeping her afloat.

"Jesus, Bergen! I thought you were drowning," Dev said, loosening his grip as they both started treading water. "You were so still under there for so long."

"I wasn't drowning." She giggled, bobbing in and out of the water to waist height, thinking that she no longer cared if he saw all of her. "I was just . . . thinking."

"Thinking? While holding yourself under water?"

"Hey, assholes," Cody yelled. "Sorry to interrupt your

'moment,' but I'm freezing my balls off. I'm out of here. Going to get some more beer."

"Let him go," Dev whispered in her ear, surprising her. "Let's go home."

"The roof," she said, meaning the flat part of the roof right outside her bedroom window, the spot over their garage where she and Clarissa would lie out every Saturday, reading books and sipping wine coolers.

"Perfect."

Later—sometime later, who knew when, the gradually lifting alcohol haze made it difficult to tell—Dev and Rachel lay shoulder to shoulder on the roof, their backs flat against the still-warm shingles.

"Okay, next one: What was your biggest mistake in college?" Dev asked her. They had been asking each other questions, trading silly and sarcastic answers as they often did, competing to make each other laugh.

"Um, I don't know. Getting a B in our Joyce seminar? I'd read parts of *Ulysses* in high school. I thought it would be easy."

"A B? Getting a B is your big mistake? Way to have a wild college career, Bergen."

"You're just mad because *you* got a C-minus in that class."

"Touché." Dev laughed, turning his face toward her. "'Think you're escaping and run into yourself.'"

"So you did read it."

"Enough to get the idea."

"Your favorite moment?" she asked, staring straight up at the sky, not meeting his gaze. Something about the way he was looking at her made the right side of her body tingle, as if she could really *feel* his eyes on her. Dev looked at her all the time, always had, and it never made her feel much of anything. Now she had goose bumps all up and down her arms, and she had to physically restrain herself from doing something completely stupid and girlish, like curling toward him and saying, "I'm cold."

"My favorite moment? I don't know, tonight?"

"Try harder."

"Yeah, okay," he said. She waited for him to tell a crazy party story or recount a tale of some improbable academic triumph. But then she heard him sigh, and when he spoke again, she could've sworn his voice had changed. Like it was stripped of an edge. Dev, but different.

"Well," he said. "It's weird, but thinking about it, maybe when I stayed in your dorm all those nights sophomore year. When your mom was still sick? Shit, maybe that's messed up to say."

"You think?"

"No, I mean. I'm not happy she *had cancer*, obviously. But that was the first time I felt like I had a friend here. Or, I don't know, like I really *was* a friend to someone." He shook his head. "Go ahead and make fun of me for being corny, I'm ready."

But Rachel didn't have anything to say. She remembered the exact feeling she'd had on those nights, too, the deep sadness inside her but the way she felt cocooned and safe with him there, like nothing else bad could happen if he was around.

"I know exactly what you mean," she said, and then she finally did turn to him. Somehow, to her surprise, he was leaning in toward her at the same moment, and their lips collided. Almost like it was an accident, but she was almost certain it wasn't, and the kiss melted onto her lips, strange and yet familiar, wrong, all wrong, yet so, so right, and suddenly she was sure that he could feel it, too. They kept kissing, several minutes longer without breaking to say a word about it, as if they did this sort of thing all the time. They stopped suddenly, in seemingly mutual agreement that they should go back inside the house, and Dev took her hand gently and led her through the window. As they climbed into her dark room together, Rachel didn't think about what it meant to kiss her best friend. The only thought in her head was that familiar refrain, once again: *What if I had never come here?*

Was her life going to be a series of near misses like that? Was everyone's? And how did she almost miss *this*, right now, with Dev?

"I think I've wanted to do this for a long time," she murmured as they sat down on her bed and leaned in to kiss each other again. She breathed in the scent of his neck, a mixture of the Acqua di Giò cologne she knew he wore and something mustier, a T-shirt on a repeat wearing, maybe, but that somehow still didn't smell bad. Dev had probably always smelled like this, but it had never seemed so . . . sexy.

It was now.

"You *think* you've wanted to?" He stopped kissing her for a minute, laughing. "You really do know how to make a guy feel confident, Bergen."

"I don't think you need any help in that department." She pulled at the bottom of his shirt, clumsily yanking it off over his head. "And don't call me by my last name."

"Rachel, Rachel, Rachel, Rachel," he joked as he fumbled

with her bra, and for a moment her head stopped spinning, and the smell of him faded a bit as she pulled back to look at him, and she wondered if, actually, this was a terrible mistake.

She was about to ask it, to say out loud, "Is this a terrible mistake?" but then her bra was unclasped, and suddenly he had his hands in her hair, pulling her toward him, hard, and this time he whispered her name, said it right up against her lips as he kissed her again, and she felt a warm feeling deep in the pit of her stomach, and then lower still, and she decided that this was actually a very, *very*, good idea after all.

He moved his hands down onto her breasts, and it surprised her how lightly he circled them, teasing her in exactly the way she liked, and she determined that this wasn't a result of all his famed "experience" with women—he was doing this because it was her he wanted, and he *knew* her, and it felt exactly right, as familiar and inviting as slipping into your own bed at the end of a long night.

Then finally, finally, after long enough touching the skin of her breasts and her shoulders and her back, he slipped off her skirt and slid his hand into her underwear, and he asked her, "Yes?" as a question and she said back, "Yes, definitely, yes."

CLARISSA KNEW THE ENTRANCE TO THE STADIUM HAD TO BE somewhere in front of her, but she couldn't see a damn thing.

She squinted into the morning sun. The Ryan Field parking lot had transformed into a sea of purple. Northwestern purple, that deep, plummy purple of the flag that flew in front of the Norris student bookstore, and which was now the purple of more than a thousand oversize graduation gowns. Sleeves and tassels fluttered around her as her fellow students stamped their feet and pushed past one another, trying to locate their friends before proceeding into the football stadium for the commencement ceremony. At five one, Clarissa was mostly at eye level with unfamiliar purple shoulders. All her housemates were late, as usual, and at this rate she would probably never find them. She should have waited for them at the house, instead of coming early to hold a good spot in line.

"Oh my God, Clarissa!" she heard a familiar voice shout above the low roar of the crowd. At last, the gowns parted like the Red (purple) Sea and Rachel materialized, her graduation cap in one hand and an open lipstick in the other.

"You made it. I was starting to wonder."

Rachel pulled a pocket mirror out from somewhere in the recesses of her gown and started applying a coral lipstick. "Ugh, I'm so hungover. Is this too bright for nine a.m.?"

"You know I have literally no opinion on that," Clarissa said, feigning annoyance, but really, she felt her heart leap up into her throat. How many times had she and Rachel had these same dumb exchanges, bickering back-and-forths that seemed like nothing but actually served to show her that maybe she could truly *know* someone, and be known in return. God, she was going to miss Rachel.

"I know, I know, 'makeup is a tool of the patriarchy,' or whatever." Rachel elbowed her and then pointed ahead. "Hey, I think we're moving. We'll never find the guys; let's just go."

"It's not a tool of the patriarchy if you're wearing it for yourself." Clarissa linked her arm with Rachel's as they shuffled forward toward the entrance to the stadium. "But I know you're just asking because you're worried *Lisa* won't approve of the color, and I have to say, I don't really care what she thinks, either." Lisa was Rachel's mother, and she had opinions on things like which makeup was too bright for daytime and which floor-length dresses were *really* appropriate for a black-tie dress code, and all sorts of other things that Clarissa would never have thought about.

The mob of students narrowed to a four-abreast line, and then the arched entrance to Ryan Field swallowed them up and spat them out into the end zone of the football field. A sunbeam felt like it was shining directly onto Clarissa's head like a laser, roasting her inside the heavy gown and black graduation cap. She started to sweat.

"Having graduation in June sucks," she said, trying to wrangle her hair under her cap. "I'm going to sweat to death before I ever get my diploma. Nice knowing you."

"Seriously. And we're, like, the only school on a quarter system, so everyone in the world already graduated. All my friends from high school are already in the city, and we're still here."

Unlike Rachel, most of the people Clarissa had grown up with hadn't graduated, and they weren't going to. Northwestern had been a phenomenal reach for Clarissa; her dream come true made possible through a combination of the labor of her parents, a generous scholarship, and a heap of student loans. A lot of her high school classmates hadn't gone to four-year universities at all. Some had gotten scholarships to places like the University of Illinois, but it seemed like most were pursuing classes at community college while working back in her predominantly Polish neighborhood on the southwest side of Chicago.

This was not something she frequently brought up to Rachel.

They found seats at the end of a row. No one walked across the stage at the Weinberg College of Arts and Sciences graduation; there were too many students. Instead, they would sit patiently, their attending friends and family in the stands behind them, and listen to speeches from the dean and whomever had been chosen as the year's "inspiring" graduation speaker. Then they would march out the exact way they came in, and Clarissa would—thank God—probably never have to set foot in a football stadium ever again. Their diplomas would come in the mail.

Rachel raised her camera to take a photo of the speaker onstage, which she would probably upload to Facebook later. (Clarissa had refused to create a profile and would never see it.) She watched Rachel as she stowed the camera away in the folds of her gown: her chemically relaxed hair was the opposite of Clarissa's curled blond strands, just as her platform espadrilles were the opposite of Clarissa's beloved vans. But then at the same moment they turned to each other and—

"Congratulations, class of 2006—we did it!" they shrieked together, half quoting *Legally Blonde* and poking fun, half genuinely celebrating. Wordlessly, they were in sync, once again. Could your opposite also somehow be your twin?

Clarissa was about to say this, to stop joking around and being sarcastic for once and say something sincere. "You know—"

"Okay, I have to tell you something. I can't keep it in anymore!" Rachel blurted, and they both stopped paying any attention to what was happening onstage. "I slept with Dev last night."

Of course.

Of course they got together, was Clarissa's first thought. She didn't know whether to laugh or sigh, and she ended up somewhere in the middle, emitting a sort of coughing exhale. She sounded like her mom, recognized it as exactly the noise Magda used to make when Clarissa would try to push back her curfew in high school. That exact laugh, followed by a shake of her head and a "You know better, córka."

Clarissa missed that. She wished with a burning feeling in her chest that surprised her that her mom could be out there in the crowd behind them, sitting right next to her father and sister and babunia. But Clarissa had messed up—again—and told her the wrong date for graduation back in January. By the time she realized her mistake, her mom hadn't been able to get someone to cover her shift at the hospital.

"Clare, hello," Rachel said. "I'm freaking out. Say something."

"Something."

"Seriously?"

"I'm just." She shook her head. "I'm not exactly surprised, Rach. Well, I'm surprised it took until last night, I guess, but it was only a matter of time. All of us together in that house, come *on*. You, Nate, and Dev are the weird *Three's Company* love triangle I never asked for."

"But you love us."

"So much." She smiled at Rachel, who was nervously biting her lip, clearly waiting for Clarissa's approval. Clarissa sighed. Whether or not the will-they-or-won't-they dynamic had ever interested her, or that Dev had always been the Ross to Rachel's, well, Rachel, this was clearly a big deal. Perhaps a *really* big deal, depending on how it had gone. Clarissa pivoted to interrogation mode.

"Details, now," she said. "Tell me everything. Who kissed whom? Did he make a move after the party? Where did you two go, by the way?"

"So, when we left the party, we went skinny-dipping on North Beach, and then—"

"Oh, so this was premeditated. The physical stuff, I mean. One of you invited the other one skinny-dipping as a pretense."

"No, it wasn't like that. Cody had never been, and I don't know, we were drunk. Said we had to do it before graduating."

"Still think it was all planned. The old, 'take a girl to the nearest body of water and—whoops! I forgot my suit' routine."

"It was my idea, actually." Rachel smiled, seeming a bit proud of herself.

"Oops, we gotta walk." Clarissa grabbed Rachel's elbow as the rows on either side of them started to stream out into the aisle, getting ready to proceed out of the stadium.

That was it. They had done it. *Congratulations, class of 2006*, she thought. *Here's a diploma, an overpriced class picture, and a six-month heads-up that your student loan payments are coming due.*

"Anyway," Rachel continued as they crossed under the shadow of the tunnel out of the stadium. "So, we had, like, a moment on the beach? I guess? But then it happened when we got back to the house. We went up on the roof with a bottle of wine, and I asked him about his best moment of college, and then he . . . we just started making out."

"That's hot." Clarissa did her best Paris Hilton impression, making Rachel giggle. She pulled out a cigarette and flicked her lighter as they entered the parking lot, taking a long, desperate drag; she would need to finish and pop a piece of gum in her mouth before her family found her. *The good Catholic daughter facade.* She thought about her babunia, who would probably be wearing one of her 1950s floral-print shift dresses, which she lovingly hand-washed and starched. They made Clarissa think of running in circles around her grandmother's kitchen when she was only waist-high, when she would stay at her house every afternoon while her parents finished work. She pictured her father emerging from the crowd in his best suit, and her older sister, Maria, holding her son, Joey, Clarissa's nephew. She did not want to disappoint them. Not with her cigarettes, and not with her secrets.

"You and that Nate looked . . . cozy," her sister had teased the last time she visited Clarissa at college.

"It's not like that," she had wanted to say, but she didn't. If only her family knew how *not like that* it really was. That it wasn't ever going to be *like that* with Clarissa and any guy.

Her housemates knew. She was out at Northwestern, had even started to date a little bit, but Northwestern's campus and her home felt like two completely different worlds. Her heart beat faster, throbbing with nervous energy, as she imagined what might happen if she ever tried to merge the two.

"Stay here, by gate H, so my parents can find us." Rachel laced a manicured hand with hers, grounding her. "Anyway, now I don't know how I feel about what happened with Dev. He was gone this morning; he went to pregame graduation with Nate and Cody and the guys before I got up. Like, is it a thing, or isn't it? Do I want it to be?"

"Lisa, ten o'clock," Clarissa hissed. "We'll talk about this later."

"Oh God, thanks for the warning," Rachel said under her breath before changing her tone entirely, entering a higher register that Clarissa had only ever heard her use around her family. "Mo-ooom! Hi!" she shrieked, arms outstretched as Lisa walked toward her. "Can you believe it?"

Then Clarissa was ensconced by the Bergen family, Rachel's parents, her brother, her two aunts, and an uncle closing in around them. In total, six of her family members had flown out from New York for the weekend.

Lisa slipped a porcelain, Pilates-toned arm around Rachel. "No, I can't believe it. My baby girl, a college graduate. David, take our picture."

"I can take it," Clarissa volunteered, just so she could have something to say. "You know, so you can all be in it."

"Perfect," Lisa chirped, gesturing for the rest of the family to get into the shot as David handed Clarissa the Canon digital camera. Clarissa waited as they arranged themselves, Rachel's aunts angling their left sides closer to the camera, Rachel adopting the skinny-arm pose favored by her sorority sisters even though her graduation gown swallowed her petite frame anyway. She might as well have been wearing a freaking circus tent, and here she was, still voguing.

"Say 'graduation,'" Clarissa said.

"Graduation!" they echoed as Clarissa clicked away.

"You know, this is a big day for Clarissa, too," Lisa said to the family as she took the camera back and stowed it inside a purse Clarissa couldn't identify but that she was sure cost as much as her annual work-study income.

Duh, I graduated, too. See the cap and gown? Not just a fashion statement.

"She's the very first person in her family to graduate from college! We're so proud of you, too, Clarissa."

Clarissa recoiled, taking a half step back. *Rachel told them?* She silently cursed herself for being embarrassed, even for a moment. She crossed her arms over her chest. She was proud of herself, proud of her family, and if anyone should be embarrassed it was Lisa, who had functionally pointed at Clarissa like she was a creature in a zoo—"Wow, look, a first-generation college student in the wild!"

"Uh, thanks, Mrs. Bergen," was all she said. Maybe she was being unfair; maybe they really were just proud of her. After all, Rachel's family had been good to her, sending her snacks in Rachel's care packages, asking about her when Rachel called home. Some people were just a little bit tone-deaf.

"Call me Lisa, please."

Clarissa squinted as the sun beat down harder, her watch ticking toward noon. "Well, Lisa, I have to go find *my* family before they get totally lost out here. We'll see you back at the house for the barbecue?"

"Of course. Congratulations again," she said, and everyone smiled at Clarissa. Rachel caught her hand and squeezed it, and something about the gesture felt wistful, already nostalgic somehow, but Clarissa told herself it was nothing, and she slipped off to find the people who actually belonged to her.

SIPPING HIS THIRD BEER OF THE DAY, DEV SURVEYED THE backyard, lazily contented, his eyelids heavy. He had slept maybe eight hours total over the whole weekend, but that was fine. He had the rest of his life to sleep.

He leaned back in his lawn chair and breathed in the scent of the grill. Nate's and Rachel's dads were cooking up hot dogs, and veggie burgers for his parents, who were currently occupied yelling at his sixteen-year-old brother, Sumeet, for trying to nick a beer out of the cooler on the deck. As the oldest of three, Dev had always taken most of the heat in the family. But now he was a verified college graduate and—poof! He wasn't their leading problem anymore.

Good kid, though, Sumeet, Dev thought. He would sneak his brother a shot of something later.

On the other side of the backyard, he saw Nate's mom tying CLASS OF 2006 balloons to their picnic table. On the table sat bottles of wine, a decorated cake, melting fast in the heat, and . . . Rachel.

Dev watched her take a sip of rosé and blink her eyes closed. He looked at the spot, half-hidden by her inky-dark hair, where her white graduation dress dipped toward . . .

He shook his head. Rachel was one of his best friends, and if he thought she was beautiful, well, that's because she was. It was a fact, not an opinion, but he had managed to keep from acting on it until last night. Logically, he knew this to be a very good thing. If anything had happened sooner, given his track record, it probably would have ended in one of them breaking their lease and moving out of the house angrily, never to be heard from again.

Rachel looked up and made eye contact with him, and he hoped he hadn't gotten caught staring. He didn't want her to think what happened between them had meant something— and at the same time, he didn't want her to think he thought it meant nothing. What *did* it mean? Something or nothing? If only they weren't at a fucking graduation party surrounded by every single one of their family members. If they weren't, then he could—what? Probably still do nothing, but it was comforting to *pretend* like it could be going better.

He rubbed his temple. This line of thought made his head hurt. *But why worry?* he told himself. They'd probably look back on last night nostalgically as exactly the kind of silly, harmless mistake that made them love college. As he stood up to force himself to join Rachel at the picnic table, the patio door swung open. There was Clarissa on the deck, still in her graduation cap, brandishing a platter of her mom's Polish pastries.

Saved by the bell.

"Clarissa!" Dev shouted, grateful for the distraction from a potential one-on-one conversation with Rachel. Now that all four of them were together, he knew what they needed to do. "Stay there. Nate, Rachel, come here. Parents: Can you excuse us all for a minute?"

Everyone chuckled and acquiesced, and Dev felt victorious. He ushered his roommates up onto the deck and back through the door into the house.

"What is this about?" Rachel asked.

Grinning, Dev reached into the hall closet and pulled out . . . the shot ski.

A chorus of groans erupted. The shot ski was exactly what it sounded like: an old, banged-up ski with shot glasses glued to the top. Up to four people could raise the ski to their lips in tandem and take a coordinated shot of alcohol—or, more likely, spill cheap vodka down their shirts when they got out of sync. Dev couldn't remember who had first acquired it, but it had become a tradition during their snow-day parties; anytime Northwestern had classes canceled or delayed due to snow, he would say, "Let's go skiing," and pull it out of storage.

"I object." Clarissa shook her head. "Seasonally inappropriate. Try again next winter."

"Oh, come on. Just one last time, on the roof. Somewhere we can be out of Grandma's earshot—no offense, Clare."

She held up her hands. "None taken. And fine. God help you if any of you take the Lord's name in vain in front of Basia."

"Like you just did? We all know you're the worst offender," Dev needled her, but in truth, he appreciated the commonality between them. He loved his parents, he supposed, but he didn't think of them as his friends, not the way, say, Rachel did. He knew Clarissa felt the same way about hers.

They filed upstairs and, one by one, climbed through Rachel's bedroom window and out onto the garage roof for the last time. The last time? No more lying up there passing joints, half reading Dave Eggers, watching Clarissa and Rachel try to get tan? No more long afternoons sipping out of Solo cups, calling to friends passing by on the sidewalk below and inviting them to come up. This was it, Dev realized, and though he was tempted to shrug it off as nothing—he knew there would be other roofs, other joints, even other friends, maybe—he somehow suspected already that this was a time and a place that would loom large in his memory whether he wanted it to or not.

Dev poured alcohol into each of the shot glasses, trying to look at each of his roommates equally, to not make heated eye contact with Rachel again by accident. *Especially not in front of Clarissa and Nate.*

"Well, that was college, I guess," Clarissa said.

"To the most excellent four years," Dev joined in loudly, getting back into the celebratory spirit. "Better than anything young Dev could have imagined when he arrived here a scrawny, undersexed dork in the fall of 2002."

"So now you're just a . . . scrawny dork?" Rachel raised her eyebrows. *Touché*, he thought. The innuendo stirred something below his belt. He liked it.

He raised his middle finger at her in reply.

"To the best four years, and my three best friends," Nate said, already sounding buzzed. "If that's cheesy, fuck it."

"To the best four years," they all echoed.

"But may they be worse than any set of four years that any of us will live for the rest of our lives," Dev added. "Now, before we drink, tell me: Where are you going to be four years from now?"

"I'll be an assistant editor at *New York*," Rachel said immediately. Dev knew that she spent several hours a day thinking about this exact question. "My first novel will be coming out in the spring. Then I'll start writing full-time."

"I'll be writing and doing comedy, I hope," Clarissa said.

"Think bigger," Dev said, aiming to inspire. "You're going to make it." Clarissa was by far his funniest friend. Without knowing anything about the inner workings of comedy, he believed in her in a way that felt borderline religious, in that it did not require facts or evidence.

"Fine. I'll be on *SNL*. That's my secret dream."

"It will happen," Rachel said. "You're the funniest person I know."

"Then you might need funnier friends," Clarissa deadpanned, then softened. "But thanks."

"Am I allowed to say *rich*?" Nate asked.

"Shallow," Dev joked, though of course he hoped the same. To do better than his parents, to help them, to pay back a debt, perhaps. He looked at Clarissa, who he knew felt the same way, and she nodded back, a tacit agreement.

"And I'll be famous, of course," Dev announced, because he didn't mind shooting too high and being wrong. Why not hope for the best? "Hopefully, I'll also be surrounded by a lot of alcohol and my three best friends, just like today. Now, let's drink."

They lifted the ski to their lips, flipping it in tandem. The vodka burned. He swallowed quickly.

"Perfect execution," he said as they set it down. "A ten." Rachel leaned against him on one side and Clarissa on the other as the four of them gazed out at the town of Evanston, across the frame houses and yellowed backyards that held their entire collegiate experience, the whole of their collective memories. They surveyed the neighborhood without speaking, the only soundtrack that damn Vanessa Carlton song Rachel and Clarissa loved, the one from their junior year, blaring from a backyard CD player. *Maybe you'll remember me. What I gave is yours to keep.*

Clarissa put a cigarette between her lips and flicked her lighter. In the quick flash of the flame, Dev felt like he saw it: everything they were moving toward rather than what they were leaving behind. The outline of his future life, illuminated for the very first time, like the distant skyline of Chicago. It was out there.

The afternoon stretched ahead of them, hot and languid. It was June 10, one of the longest days of the year, and right at that moment, Dev Kaur's life felt infinitely long, too.

RACHEL

2007

I t was strange, Rachel thought, how quick and slippery the passage of time could be.

Through an entire life spent in school, she had always been waiting to level up: to pass from one grade to the next, to acquire one credit and then another. The time clearly demarcated, one simply had to have patience, and then be rewarded for reaching the next milestone. *Congratulations on graduating high school. Congratulations on graduating college.* Now? One week could become two, and two weeks could become four, with deceptive ease, each moment blurring into the next with no more grades or final exams or graduations to measure up against. Just the totality of life itself, stretching over an unspecified distance and leading to no horizon line.

Not that it was all so dramatic. The beginning had been exciting: For Rachel's first weeks at *New York*, even the most mundane tasks had felt like a revelation. She marveled that she,

Rachel Bergen, could be trusted to fact-check a real magazine article! She loved walking to the printer to pick up a copy of a story for the next issue, then walking back to her desk (her own desk!) with the printed sheets in one hand and a vending machine Diet Coke in the other. She loved using a pink highlighter to segment out the hard facts in each story, from the height of the Empire State Building to the age of a quoted source, so that she could conduct research and check every detail for accuracy. Even the office culture fascinated her: *New York* felt different from *Elle*, where she had interned in college; it had much more of a downtown, newsroom feel. People wore either slouchy pants or skinny jeans; they talked loudly on the office phones. They sat on the industrial-carpeted floor of the Fact Department eating empanadas on late nights at the end of the week when they had to wait to close copy. Then, afterward, they would all decamp to a bar nearby in Soho to celebrate the end of another week, another issue sent to print. Over cheap beers, they bantered about the *AngloMania* exhibit at the Met, or argued over their opinions on Jerry Saltz's new piece, and Rachel listened closely, trying to adjust her mind to this specific kind of cultural consciousness, to pick up the right things to know.

It was the perfect job for an aspiring writer—if you ignored that the job did not, technically, include any writing. Rachel had been assigned to the Fact Department, and so she spent her days fact-checking other people's stories instead of writing her own. After a few months—who could say where they'd gone—there was no highlighter color that could distract her from the fact that she needed to figure out what she wanted to do for herself, creatively speaking.

Still, this was fine for the short term, she reasoned, because it would give her time and energy to focus on her novel. She could spend Friday night Shabbat dinners with her brother and parents at their apartment, and then wake up early the next morning, walk to a coffee shop, and get to work. She believed in the theoretical sensibleness of this plan, and she spent six months telling everyone she knew that her Saturdays were for writing—but all she *actually* managed to do on weekend mornings was spend $10 a day on overpriced espresso drinks while combing through sections of an outline of her "novel" with a red pen, changing next to nothing, trying to see straight through her hangover.

On New Year's Eve, on vacation with her family, she made a promise to herself, a resolution: 2007 would be the year. She stood on the white sand beach in Anguilla, tipsy and full of desire, and looked out at the fireworks exploding over the ocean.

"I'm going to publish a book!" she shouted at the waves.

"You're so pathetic," her brother teased, but she didn't care. The surf roared back, pounding the sand with a resounding "yes, yes, yes."

IT WAS ELEVEN O'CLOCK ON A LATE MARCH NIGHT, THE FIRST signs of spring sparkling in the New York City air.

Lights glowed from every storefront and apartment window, thousands—millions—of little cells, a honeycomb of vibrating activity. Or at least that's how it looked to Rachel from her vantage point on the balcony of the apartment temporarily shared by Nate, Dev, and Cody, located on the eighteenth floor of a high-rise building in Murray Hill. The noise of honking cabs and a stream of late-night twentysomething revelers swarming Thirty-Fourth Street beneath them swelled. She imagined describing it in her novel, which was, of course, set in New York.

Rachel took a sip of her drink, a lukewarm vodka soda in a Solo cup. She listened to the thrum of the party behind her back inside the apartment, the pulsing beat of a Lil Wayne song and the shouts over the beer pong table. She had spent the first part of the evening in the center of the action, pouring drinks in the kitchen and then creating a makeshift dance floor with her high school friends Isabelle and Nicole. But now she wanted some air.

If she was honest with herself, she wanted something else, too. Some attention after walking out here alone. She turned to look over her shoulder just in time to see the sliding door open, and it turned out that her plan had worked after all. There he was.

Dev.

Dev had finally arrived in New York two months after her. Cody and Nate had slapped up a flex wall in their apartment and moved him in. On his first weekend in New York, Rachel had felt as apprehensive as she had before her first kiss in the sixth grade (Joshua Greene, a game of spin the bottle, an unwelcome amount of tongue). She had refused to let her nervousness show, so she'd marched over to the apartment with a bag of Levain cookies and a bottle of vodka to welcome Dev. Even though she'd been agonizing over seeing him through the eight weeks of June and July, Rachel worked deliberately to spend equal time talking to him and Nate, deciding to play it cool and show him that the night before graduation hadn't meant anything to her.

Except that it had, of course. Looking back on it, she realized that maybe she had miscalculated; when she was standoffish, Dev had withdrawn, and while he'd acted the same around her as he always had at group dinners and parties in the months that followed, he never asked her on a date, which it hurt her ego to realize she had been expecting. Or at the very least, wanting. In the end, she'd backpedaled, putting herself back into the rhythm of attempting to be "one of the guys."

The truth was, a part of her still wanted more than that. But her pride dictated that she refuse to be the first to admit it.

Dev stepped out onto the balcony, coming to stand beside her and lean his arms on the balcony railing.

"Nice . . . skulls," he said, picking up the end of her paperthin McQueen scarf and running it through his fingers. "Seems a little hard-core for you, no?"

"It's called style? Not that you'd know," she tossed back. Before she could decide on a follow-up remark, Dev pulled out a cigarette and flicked a lighter.

"You smoke now?"

"You don't? I thought that was part of your whole Carrie Bradshaw thing." Rachel owned the *Sex and the City* DVDs and had forced Dev to watch a marathon of the show leading up to the finale, which aired during their sophomore year.

"Only on special occasions," she said, grabbing the cigarette from his hand and taking one deep drag. "Which this could be, I guess. Every Saturday night in New York can be a special occasion. So, the party: How would you rate it?"

"Eh . . . honestly, a four or five. The usual music, usual drinking games." Dev blew smoke out of the side of his mouth, seeming coolly relaxed. "But it's still early. I just came out to get some air."

He hadn't followed her?

"Getting air works better without smoke, you know."

"Noted."

"Seriously, though. I don't think I've seen you go somewhere alone at a party . . . ever?"

"Well, I'm just wondering if all this"—he sighed and gestured vaguely, sweeping a hand across the skyline, something melancholy in his voice—"was my brightest idea." He let the cigarette hang off his lip, the expression on his face making him seem faraway.

"Oh, just that?"

He laughed. "Yeah, you know. If coming to New York right now was a smart move."

"You're worried you won't find a job?" she ventured. Dev had searched for a period of months and found only temp work before landing a back server position at Nirvana, a mid-priced Indian restaurant in Murray Hill. It wasn't the kind of job any of them had imagined taking with a Northwestern degree.

"No, I know I'll figure it out." He exhaled again, and Rachel shook her head, half-moved, half-annoyed by Dev's eternal confidence. "It's just that . . . you and Nate have stuff like business cards and expense accounts. You know the passwords for speakeasies and shit like that."

"If speakeasies are the problem, I can introduce you to the door guy at Milk & Honey."

Dev bit his lip and shook his head, chuckling lightly. Rachel tried to keep her attention on the fact that Dev was clearly going through something, and not on the fact that, well, he looked very attractive biting his lip like that.

"Rach, that's exactly what I mean. I have no doubt I can get a job in New York. But am I the kind of guy that really *wants* to spend time getting to know the doormen at clubs and speakeasies? Is that my purpose in life?"

"Point taken," Rachel said, sipping her drink, though she couldn't exactly imagine why he *wouldn't* want to possess the kind of information she had to offer. New York was all about finding the city beneath the city, not the shiny tourist trappings but the underground experimental restaurants, the art, the all-night parties that didn't advertise. The, yes, speakeasies. *Is it possible,* she wondered, *that Dev is having a crisis of confidence?* Rachel could help him with that, she thought, and her chest felt warm at the idea that maybe she would be the one to lead Dev, to show *him* the adventure in life for a change.

But it didn't seem like Dev to care about that, not really, not in the way that it sometimes seemed to bother Nate. Dev shook his head, smiling slightly, the way he looked when someone had made an illogical point in a debate but he had decided to let it go without a counterargument. She sensed from this that he was struggling with something else, something connected to life in New York, but not because he was scared or intimidated by it— rather, because he was genuinely questioning if he wanted it. *But who* wouldn't *want this?* Rachel wondered as she gazed out at the sparkling Midtown lights. *What else could there be?*

"Listen to me. Am I boring tonight or what?" Dev said, reaching out to grab Rachel's drink and take a sip. "I think all I need is a little more alcohol. And . . . maybe some time away from this apartment." They both looked in the window in time to catch Brad-something ripping his shirt off after yet another beer pong victory with Cody.

"I see what you mean."

"I just need to figure out what I really want to do next. It'll come."

He sounded confident enough but still seemed a little bit sad. She wanted to help, she realized. Even more than she wanted to grab him and kiss him, she wanted to be his friend. Or she must have, the feeling must have been strong, because for years to come Rachel would look back and wonder why she did what she did next.

She started to say how glad she was that Dev had come to New York, and, as if on cue, he finally leaned forward slowly to kiss her. Her heart beat faster; her skin tingled. Rachel felt the moment freeze in suspended animation, and she hovered just inches away from his lips. What should she do? She could give in to the impulse and kiss him back. She imagined the two of them walking inside, disappearing from the party, hiding away in his bedroom. It could be the start of something, she thought. Or it could just be one night of sex that left her wallowing in uncertainty and worried about their friendship for months afterward.

Again.

She considered the other option. They could walk back into the party together, friends still, just friends, but only for now. The rest could come later.

She took a deep breath and placed a hand on Dev's chest, stopping him.

"Shit, did I misread that?" he asked, but without seeming too self-conscious.

"No, it's just . . ." She paused. Part of her body was screaming for him to kiss her, of course. But, in a way, simply *knowing* that he still wanted to was enough for that night. "We're both still getting our lives here sorted, and our friendship is so important to me, and . . ." She trailed off before saying that it seemed like he needed a friend, that maybe they both did. She still wanted *more*, of course she did, but maybe once they got their feet under them a little bit.

"Right." Dev ran a hand through his hair and gave her a crooked smile. "I was thinking the same thing."

"You're just saying that because I said it first."

"I know a good idea when I hear one."

Then they hugged, swaying slightly, and Rachel realized that they were both drunk. There would be time for everything else later, she assured herself. Because she was still young enough, new enough to this city not to know the way certain types of moments could slip through your fingers like sand, unrecoverable. She looked back in through the window as someone high-fived her friend Isabelle after a beer pong shot. To their right, she saw Nicole leaning heavily against Nate's shoulder, the two of them slowly making their way toward his room. She raised an eyebrow at Dev, and he shrugged, smiling. Then he stepped through the doorway, back into the throbbing heat of the party. Rachel downed the rest of her drink and followed.

Stepping through the doorframe, she locked eyes with Cody,

who gestured to her from behind the beer pong table, waving her over with enthusiasm, and she went to him.

"You're empty?" he asked, looking at her glass. Then he appraised her with the gaze she remembered from skinny-dipping at the beach, his eyes focused just a little too intently below her collarbone. She just stared back at him, blankly, not remembering when she had finished her drink. "Let me refill you."

He returned with a half-filled Solo cup of what he said was vodka, mixed with a splash of something pink, cranberry maybe. As she sipped, the vodka strong and sour, her stomach swirled, and she had a fuzzy thought that she should dump the drink out and just go home. Cody sidled up right next to her and dropped a heavy arm over her shoulders, sticky with sweat, and she forced a smile and let him leave it there.

"You good?" he asked, and she realized through the haze of too many drinks that he was flirting.

"Better now," she responded, her flirting a reflex more than a desire, her tongue heavy.

Across the room, she watched, stunned, as Dev pulled a petite blonde toward him, his arm around her shoulders. Her stomach turned. Nate and Nicole had disappeared.

"Good." Cody squeezed her shoulder. She flinched but didn't move away.

Isabelle walked over and joined them. "Everything okay?" she asked Rachel.

"Fine," she responded, pushing aside any doubt. "Now, let's remind these guys who taught them how to play beer pong in the first place."

The edges of her vision blurred as the next wave of vodka hit. Her knees felt liquid, like Jell-O that hadn't set. She wondered when she had gotten so drunk. She wondered if she was going to be sick.

Rachel leaned against the table, unsure if she would be able to throw the ball. She felt Cody slide his arm around her again, and she wondered why he wasn't crossing to the other side of the table to begin the game. He tightened his grip around her ribs, squeezing her to him, a gesture of ownership she wanted to stop but couldn't. She closed her eyes, just for a second. This already felt like the kind of night it would be better to forget.

It took Rachel exactly seventeen minutes to get from her West Village apartment to the *New York* magazine offices on foot. Twenty-three if she stopped for a bagel and a coffee; eight in a cab if she had woken up late and had to rush. Not that the fact-checking department did much rushing around; since they stayed late at night to close issues, lingering at the office until 9, 10, 11 p.m. on Thursdays, as a result, no one came in until after ten most mornings. Still, Rachel believed in timing her life to a T. It made her more productive, she thought, this ability to account for every precious minute. It was also something she could control. There were many things, she now knew, that she could not.

As she walked along Sixth Avenue, she forced herself to turn her attention to the story she wanted to ask to check that week. As a new hire, she didn't often get the opportunity to check the hard-reported feature stories. This week, the magazine would be preparing to run a feature on female ambition, anchored on an examination of high-profile women's careers, including that of Katie Couric. The topic mattered to Rachel, and she knew she could do it. She would speak up in the editorial meeting, plant her flag in the ground, become serious, work late if required.

Less partying, she told herself. *No more nights like last weekend; you will not fuck up like that again.*

She spun through the revolving door into the office lobby, checking her watch—10 a.m. on the dot, twenty-three minutes exactly—and rehearsed in her head on the way up in the elevator. She reached her cubicle and opened both her Outlook email and a blank Word document, ready to list significant articles she had checked recently, anything that would support her case for being given the lead assignment of the next issue. But before she could start, she found herself furiously typing an email to Clarissa. They had a habit of emailing throughout their days, Rachel sneaking a note to Clarissa in between work emails, and Clarissa writing her back from her desk at home, where she did her writing and her stand-up material before heading to her shifts at the bar at night.

Clare, I feel like such a fraud sometimes, Rachel typed. *An impostor? Like I don't know why anyone would have given me this job, or if I'll ever be a "real" writer, and in the meantime, I just have to wear this serene mask of the person who knows what's going on, who has a perfect plan, who knows where she's going. But do I, really? Do I know where I'm going?*

I'm scared.

Anyway. Do you ever feel like that?

Rachel sighed, then took a sip of her latte. She stared down at her desk, perfectly stacked papers on her left, color-coded highlighters and Post-it notes on her right. If it were possible to conquer doubt through organization, she would have achieved it by now.

Her email dinged.

I feel that way pretty much all the time, the first line read.

But if this is about the feature story, it's going to be fine. You're going to get it, okay?

"Okay," Rachel said without meaning to, as if Clarissa herself had the power to make it true.

Walking into Mercer Kitchen the next week after work, Rachel should've felt like she had *arrived*. Her pitch had gone perfectly; in the end, she had won the assignment. But as she descended the chrome-and-glass staircase into the belly of yet another trendy Manhattan restaurant, the beat of the music throbbing around her, she felt more tired than she expected, and overstimulated. The modish, subterranean Soho spot thrummed with low bass and loud conversation, and as she slid out of her coat, she watched more than one man give her a once-over, taking in her silk dress, which bared the tops of her shoulders. She stiffened and turned away.

"Rach, over here," Isabelle called from a corner banquette, raising a martini in salute.

She put her blazer on the back of a chair and sat down across from Nicole and Isabelle. She looked at them, their familiar smiles lifting her own like strings on a marionette. She remembered when they all used to sneak downtown in high school with their fake IDs, drinking their water bottles full of vodka on the train. Now here they were, adults at last with real IDs, real drinks, real jobs. That was something to celebrate, at least.

"So, how was work?" Isabelle asked, leaning forward interestedly to rest her chin on her hand. Her gold bracelets glimmered in the candlelight.

"Good, actually." She gestured to a nearby server and ordered by pointing wordlessly at Isabelle's martini. She told them about the assignment to fact-check the feature story, and why it was a step up from her usual work, which consisted of verifying the details of smaller front-of-book stories, checking to see if a particular handbag really cost $195 or calling around to confirm the year a certain Madison Avenue storefront had been built.

"But what we all really want to hear about is your date with Josh last night," Nicole jumped in, changing the subject. Isabelle worked in finance and her cutest coworker on the trading floor had finally gotten up the nerve to ask her out.

"It was . . ." Isabelle took a sip of her martini, enjoying holding the group's attention. "Ah-mazing."

Nicole clapped excitedly, and Rachel took another big sip of her drink, then forced herself to chime in.

"So, where did he take you? Tell us everything."

"Balthazar, then drinks at Pegu Club. Then we took a car back to my place, and we made out the whole time, but I didn't let him come upstairs. That was the right call, right?"

"Absolutely."

Rachel listened as Isabelle detailed the evening, reciting all the staples of dating in Manhattan—well, dating *investment bankers* in Manhattan—from oysters at the start of the night to a Lincoln Town Car at the end. Without meaning to, she started thinking about Nate and Dev. Nate had quickly learned the expected routine of New York dating, maybe even copying his coworkers a little too much with the excessive cologne and liberal use of his expense account. She thought, unbidden, about Cody, the heavy scent of his Drakkar Noir cologne, which sabotaged her appetite.

She turned her thoughts to Dev instead. He, on the other hand, would never cruise around in a town car like a parody of Mr. Big—or order an overpriced plate of oysters. Rachel loved oysters, but the last time she'd ordered them in front of Dev he'd made fun of her for "spending thirty dollars on tepid salt water," and she'd laughed until she almost snorted red wine mignonette up her nose.

As if on cue, the server deposited a plate of oysters in the center of their table. Nicole reached for one.

"Speaking of dating," Isabelle said, downing an oyster and turning its empty shell facedown on its bed of ice. "Rachel, what's going on with you and Dev?"

Absolutely nothing had happened with Dev since the night of the party, and now she didn't know if it ever would. Rachel had told Nicole and Isabelle that they'd slept together on the last night of college, and now that they had met Dev, they understood her attraction to him—he was cute, they said, even if they agreed that the working-part-time-in-a-restaurant thing was not. Rachel didn't care about that; she cared that Dev was someone she could trust. She had made a mistake; that much was clear. But which time? Which decision had been the wrong one?

"Nothing's really 'going on,'" she finally replied, shrugging. "Set me up with someone."

Her phone vibrated against her thigh.

Dev.

"Drink later tonight? I have interesting news."

"At dinner but meet you after. Somewhere near soho/village?" she typed back quickly on the keypad.

"Ear Inn @ 10," Dev responded immediately, and that was it, likely because he had run out of texts for the month.

"Who was that?" Isabelle asked.

"Dev." She took a sip of her martini, avoiding eye contact as Isabelle and Nicole exchanged a knowing look.

Two hours later, Rachel passed under the old neon sign reading BAR and crossed the threshold of the Ear Inn, flushed and tipsy and more eager to see Dev than she wanted to be.

With its pockmarked wooden bar and an older crowd who seemed like they had been perched on bar stools since it opened as a shipyard watering hole in the 1800s, the Ear Inn was more Dev's kind of place than hers. She spotted him leaning against the counter, already three-quarters of the way through a beer. His hair stuck out at odd angles, uncombed, and he wore an old black Northwestern hoodie and jeans, his typical off-day uniform. It made for a marked contrast to her silk dress and bag. She walked up to him, ready to rib him about his bedhead.

"Sorry, I should have told you, this is a *dive bar*," he said, beating her to the punch as he looked her up and down with a smirk. "*Not* the Carlyle. You see, a dive bar is a place where people who can't afford fifteen dollars for a drink sometimes hang out when—"

"Oh, so sorry that I came from a restaurant, instead of emerging from under a pile of dirty laundry after sleeping until eleven."

"All work and no play makes Dev a dull boy."

"Exactly." She dropped an affectionate kiss on his cheek and took the stool next to him, feeling better than she had at dinner. This was the way they always were with each other, sharp and snarky, and she loved it, loved the way it kept her mind sharp, the way they could spar and say anything to each other.

Dev took a long sip of beer, then turned to face her. "So, guess what."

"I have absolutely no idea." Had he gotten a new job? she wondered. Had he met someone, maybe the blonde from the party? She resented this thought an unfortunate amount.

Then Dev said the last thing she ever expected. "I'm writing a book."

Her ears rang, as if Dev's words had detonated a bomb that left her shell-shocked. She watched his mouth move without comprehending a word, as she thought, with both disbelief and a sting of jealousy, *But I'm supposed to be the one.* She made herself nod coolly, then tried to say something encouraging, like "Oh really, wow, tell me more."

She dug her nails into her palms, forced herself to calm down. What, did she think she was the only person on earth entitled to attempt to write a novel? She and Dev had met in a creative writing class, for God's sake. He was sharp and witty; he had a unique voice. Of course he should pursue something that interested him, she thought, something more fulfilling than working at the restaurant. She felt a flash of guilt. Besides, if anyone knew that having an idea for a novel didn't amount to even a tenth of what it took to write one, it was her. After returning home from her New Year's trip, she had written fifteen pages in a burst of inspiration, tapping into a flow she hadn't experienced since early in college. But since then, she had struggled. In the past month, she had opened the document only to move sentences around or add adverbs. *Thought* became *thought resentfully*. It was slowly becoming clear that she didn't know what she was doing, or maybe she simply had a lack of grit, neither of which could be solved by adding *ly* to the ends of words. Her book was ostensibly about a young woman in New York, working her way up the corporate ladder while wrestling with both society's limitations and her own, a sort of literary, pop-feminist deal about women and ambition in the new millennium, Candace Bushnell meets Meg Wolitzer for the twentysomething set. It seemed trivial now, somehow. She hoped Dev wouldn't probe her about her progress.

Instead, she decided to ask about his.

"I'm about a quarter of the way through? Maybe? I don't know, I've never written a book before. But I have about eighty pages."

Rachel thought about her unpolished twenty pages, which lived lonely on her desktop. She thought about how she had joined writers' groups in college, workshopped short stories, while Dev sat at home with Nate drinking beer and strumming the guitar. She grabbed Dev's beer and took a long sip.

"By all means, help yourself." Dev shook his head, then waved to the bartender to order her a drink.

"What's it about? The book," she asked.

"I kind of need to figure that out for myself." Dev shrugged. "I mean, I know what I'm working with: New York in the early aughts, coming-of-age, post-9/11 politics. But you can be the first to read it when I finish. You are, I must admit, my most talented writer friend."

Rachel felt her shoulders unclench. The compliment spread through her, a softening effect, and it embarrassed her how much she needed it. She leaned off her bar stool to give him a hug, and as she pulled away, she could see he was smiling.

Then he asked how her day had been, and she told him, going into far more detail than she had with Nicole and Isabelle. Dev knew about her subtle rivalry with the fellow entry-level editorial assistant, Laura. He understood her pride at being assigned to check a feature story. He nodded sagely as she spoke, keeping his eyes on her the entire time. As much as he sometimes made fun of her, Dev always took her seriously, she realized. A heat spread through her core, bleeding out to her limbs and warming her body.

"Anyway, I don't know exactly how long I want to stay at the magazine," she concluded. "It's an amazing place, and there's so much I love about it. But I'm starting to think maybe I want to eventually get my MFA." This was the first time she had said this out loud, maybe the first time it had truly occurred to her. Maybe Dev's book would be the match that lit the fire for her, the thing that propelled her forward. "Or maybe not. But I've been at *New York* for nine months now. I want to move up, somehow."

"Well, here's to that," Dev said, raising his glass. "To big plans."

"So, what's it been like for you, writing the book?" Rachel wondered if he ever felt frustrated, stuck, like her. She needed him to say that he did.

"Ask me when I've finished it. No, I don't know. Some days it's like there's something inside me that just flows out effortlessly, as if it literally needs to exist in the world—like it always *has existed*—and I'm just the vessel for it. Then other days, it's like I'm the biggest fucking idiot to ever string two words together." They both laughed at that. "More days than not, I hate it, and then I remember no one's doing this *to* me; I'm doing this myself. No one gives a shit if I write a book or not. On those days, I write three words and then give up and play *Halo*. So, as you can tell, I am an artistic genius."

Rachel nodded, comforted by the similarity between them, and suddenly eager for them to help each other. Maybe they would write their books together, launch them in the same season, a literary duo. A twenty-first-century Bret Easton Ellis and Donna Tartt.

"James Joyce definitely took breaks to play *Halo*," she joked. "I read that somewhere."

"And Toni Morrison, for sure."

"Definitely." She knocked her head against Dev's shoulder.

The bar's low light muddied her vision, but she looked up at Dev for a moment, examining his profile, wondering if he might angle his chin down, just a centimeter or two, and maybe, just maybe, they would kiss. This time, she thought, she would say yes. She felt him take a deep breath—was it about to happen?—but then something changed, and he shifted his weight away from her on the stool. She sat back up, unsure, nervous, a hollow feeling in her chest.

"You're my best friend, Bergen, you know that?" he said, a faraway look in his eyes that she didn't completely understand.

She could tell him now, she thought. She could say that she had thought about him, did think about him, *like that*. But then something inside her froze up. It was not nothing to have someone in her life whom she could truly trust, someone who wanted the same things she did, a platonic relationship she could feel safe in. She knew this was rare, rarer than she had once hoped.

"I think my best friend is probably . . . Clarissa." She mustered a smile and winked, copying his trademark gesture. "Kidding. You're my best friend, too. Tied, at least."

***

One whole year.

Three hundred sixty-five days, 8,760 hours, 525,600 minutes. She started humming that song from *Rent* under her breath, which she and Clarissa both loved. It had been that long since she'd set foot in Chicago, the place that had held her entire existence for four full years. Just over a year ago, leaving had seemed unimaginable. Now the particulars of the place had begun to recede, like a mountain that had once towered over her life shrinking slowly in her rearview mirror as she drove away.

As she stepped off the Jetway at O'Hare Airport on a hot July morning, bits of memory flooded back. She would need to either take the Blue Line toward the city center or direct a cab east to Clarissa's apartment at the border of Andersonville and Uptown. Because Chicago didn't hold just memories, she reminded herself. It held Clarissa, and Clarissa's whole life. Present tense. She was not just a line of text in an email. She was not just a tinny voice on the phone, a phone Rachel would press against her ear in hope of making Clarissa's voice louder, bringing her closer.

Rachel decided to take a cab. Expensive, but faster that way.

When she stepped out onto the curb on Lawrence Avenue, she saw Clarissa sitting on the cracked front steps of her building, holding a small bouquet of bodega flowers in one hand and a tumbler in the other.

"I missed you so freaking much!" Rachel shouted as she sprinted toward Clarissa as fast as her kitten heels allowed. As she said it, she realized that it was true. She had spent weeks wondering what it would be like to be with Clarissa again, how the time that had passed might have changed them, but as soon as she saw Clarissa's broad smile, and her familiar half-moon tattoo below her collarbone, she knew that all the months apart didn't matter.

"You, too," Clarissa said, burying her face in Rachel's shoulder and embracing her.

They stepped back to look each other up and down.

"I like your haircut," Clarissa said, checking out Rachel's long, angular bob, which brushed her collarbones. "Very chic."

"I like yours, too." Clarissa had cut her hair short, almost a complete pixie cut, with just a few longer blond locks remaining on top. She had sent Rachel a picture, and while she thought the look was a little severe, she had to admit that Clarissa could pull it off. "And I like those flowers. For me?"

"No, but this is," she said, handing Rachel the tumbler. "Coffee. I know your flight left early, and you'd better be ready to stay up late tonight."

"Thanks. Wait, this is half-full."

"At least you didn't say half-empty." Clarissa smiled. "I drank some; I had the closing shift at the bar last night." She fit a key into the front door lock and swung the heavy door open. "After you."

"Which floor?"

"Just the second. And by the way, someone's in there who I . . . yeah, I want you to meet. She's who the flowers are for."

Rachel took a beat and then she realized exactly what Clarissa meant. *At last.* She gasped excitedly. "Oh my God, Clare, is it . . ."

"Yes, fine, it's my girlfriend. Be cool, okay?"

Rachel nodded solemnly, but she could see Clarissa barely concealing a grin as they reached the second-floor landing. She swung the door open, and there in the hallway stood a petite and beautiful brunette, exactly Rachel's height, clad in a wrinkled silk slip dress. She had attractive, angular features, a wide smile, a slightly crooked nose.

"Hi, I'm Rebecca. Wow, it's so great to finally meet you. The famous Rachel!" the woman exclaimed, and Rachel rushed inside to hug her, because she knew it was what she was supposed to do. She tried not to let her mouth hang open in shock.

"Hi, Rebecca. It's great to meet you, too!"

"Clarissa didn't tell you, did she? I knew it." Rebecca rolled her eyes and gave Clarissa a knowing but affectionate glance. Rachel watched them make eye contact, and the look suggested deep intimacy, a greater knowledge and closeness than she would have expected from two people who had been dating, what, a month? Or had it been longer, and Clarissa just hadn't told her? That would explain Rebecca's remark, which sounded a little like an attempt to let Rachel know that she understood Clarissa—Rachel's best friend of *five years*—better than Rachel did.

Rachel took a deep breath and sat down across from the two of them in the bohemian-style living room, in a tattered, clearly thrifted wingback chair. "No, she didn't tell me. But I'm not surprised," she said with a smile that she hoped communicated that she, too, understood Clarissa's penchant for last-minute announcements—as well as her tendency to play anything emotional close to the chest.

"Because who wants to hear about my mushy feelings over the phone?" Clarissa rolled her eyes. "Please. I knew you were going to come visit, and so I just wanted you to meet her and hear everything in person."

"Well, then, let's hear it." Rachel smiled. This was a big deal, she knew. Clarissa's first real relationship. Who cared if she felt a little left out? She wanted to be happy for her friend. No, she *was* happy for her. Actively. She took a sip of the coffee

Clarissa had made just for her. "Tell me how you met, how long you've been together, everything. I want to hear everything."

The storytelling session started with coffee and then graduated to wine, because why not, and by the time the late afternoon sun streamed through the curtainless windows, they had cracked a second bottle of sale-rack pinot grigio. Rachel winced at the sickly-sweet taste but kept her mouth shut, feeling the warmth of intoxication flooding her veins—and feeling a lot warmer toward Rebecca, too. She and Clarissa shared a caustic sense of humor, but Rebecca seemed a bit more measured, more mature in her approach. Maybe Clarissa finding someone who somewhat resembled Rachel wasn't a bad thing—wasn't her trying to *replace* Rachel, but instead a recognition of the kind of person she did best with, the kind of dynamic that brought out the best in both of them. Viewed that way, Rachel understood it. She thought it was a great idea. Maybe the three of them would all be best friends.

Suddenly excited, she jumped into a conversation between Rebecca and Clarissa, something about the weekend timing for some sort of food co-op. "Let's go out somewhere nice for dinner tonight! I want to celebrate this." She gestured at the two of them. "Pump Room. I'll call for a table."

Rebecca and Clarissa exchanged a look. "That sounds great, but I actually bought some stuff for chicken piccata to cook for us? We were thinking we'd have dinner here before we take you out to a few of the bars. Andersonville's best, I promise."

"She's a great cook, Rach, I swear. Nothing like me almost poisoning you with half-cooked chicken junior year."

"Pump Room would be my treat," Rachel added quickly, backpedaling, hoping she hadn't caused offense. After a year away, she had forgotten that Clarissa didn't always have the money to go out to restaurants. This had been an issue a few times early in their friendship, but then it had mostly been forgotten. After all, college was about house parties and cheap beer, no matter how much money you had. But now, after countless dinners with Isabelle and Nicole, and a year of sponsored media lunches, something had shifted.

"Oh no, it's not that," Rebecca insisted, sounding a little surprised. "Hey, I'm new here, though; it's whatever you two want."

"Rach, we planned a whole thing, damn it, don't be an idiot." Clarissa crossed the room and boffed her affectionately on the head, then refilled her wineglass. "Eat the chicken piccata. If you insist on treating us to your precious Pump Room tomorrow, we'll talk about it. But you don't need to. Rebecca is a marketing exec, actually." She smiled proudly.

"I'm sorry. I didn't mean to . . . imply anything. I just missed you is all," Rachel said, meaning it more than ever.

"It's fine," Clarissa said, looking away. "It's fine. Tonight is going to be awesome."

The night turned out to be as fun as promised. Rebecca was indeed a great cook, especially when helped along by a strong wine buzz and a hungry crowd. The bars were fantastic, too: From a quiet dive around the corner where they played their favorite hits on the jukebox to the extravagant camp of neon-light-filled gay bars in Boystown, Rachel had never been happier to be away from home. Being with Clarissa allowed her to access a different side of herself, a side she hadn't even known existed before college. Clarissa had invited her to her parents' house to make her first pierogi; she had always egged her on to go skinny-dipping. Around Clarissa she felt freer, somehow, able to tap into a space so unselfconscious, so transcendent, that it almost felt as if she had meditated her way there. Drunk and grateful and, for once, unworried about what she looked like or if a man might hit on her, Rachel whipped her hair back and forth all night as they danced to old Madonna hits. She threw her arms around both Clarissa and Rebecca, and they embraced her in return, the three of them melding into one another on the dance floor.

When they finally got home—at 3 a.m., and after late-night burritos in Edgewater, which Rachel typically wouldn't have allowed herself to eat—the three of them brushed their teeth together over the cracked sink, drunk and harmoniously happy.

"This was so great," Rachel mumbled through her toothpaste.

"What?"

She spit sloppily into the sink. "I had the best time ever, you guys."

"You're drunk," Clarissa teased. "And I am, too."

"Drink some water." Rebecca handed her a glass.

"Do you have an extra pillow? I can crash on the couch," Rachel volunteered, realizing, somehow for the first time, that Clarissa and Rebecca were clearly living together most of the time, even though they hadn't explicitly said so. Earlier in the day she might have minded, but not anymore. They made sense together, the two of them. Rachel was glad to feel like she wouldn't be abandoning Clarissa when she left, leaving her all alone as the rest of them from college had moved away, moved on.

"You can sleep with us." Clarissa giggled, sounding drunk now. "Like old times, remember?"

She did remember. Sometimes during senior year, the house-mates had all crawled into Rachel's queen-size bed together, drunkenly recapping the night, and they would end up all passing out together.

"I will if you will." Rachel raised an eyebrow at Rebecca, who dutifully flirted back with a wink, even though they all knew they would be out cold in just a few minutes.

With that it was decided, and they all crawled into Clarissa's double bed, shoulder to shoulder with Clarissa in the middle, underneath the old quilt, which Rachel knew her grandma had knitted for her years ago. Rachel felt a little bit hot, still flushed from the alcohol and dancing, and she knew that none of them would sleep very well, but somehow it didn't matter. She felt like a punch in her gut that someday, and probably not very long from now, they would be too old for this. They would have to grow up, get married, stop having sleepovers and sharing a bed with their friends. Maybe they would enjoy it, maybe there would be some appeal to that phase of her life that remained as yet unseen, but it certainly wouldn't be *this*—this kind of cramped, close love that you could physically curl up into. She turned her head toward Clarissa.

"I'm so glad I came," she whispered, sensing that Rebecca had already fallen asleep.

"Me, too, Rach," Clarissa breathed. "Me, too."

"Clare?" she asked, her heart suddenly beating up in her throat. "Can I tell you something? Something weird happened to me. With Cody."

"Of course, tell me," Clarissa whispered.

And then she did.

The email arrived two months later, while Rachel was out at lunch with Nate.

The two of them had formed a routine at the start of the summer: Once a month, they made the trek to meet for lunch on the west side, between Rachel's Tribeca office and the Midtown headquarters of Lehman Brothers, where Nate worked. Since Nate couldn't escape his managing director for very long, they ordered things like chopped salads or preboxed sandwiches from Pret a Manger, affordable and easy to scarf down quickly—but Nate always paid for both of their lunches, an unnecessary but sweet gesture she appreciated. They would catch up for twenty minutes, and then Nate would rush back to his desk on the subway. Rachel took her time, walking down along Eighth Avenue and enjoying the afternoon sunshine.

On that day, by the time she returned to her cubicle, she had been gone for an hour and a half. A bit long, but hardly a deal breaker on a slow Tuesday when they weren't closing an issue. But there was the email: a last-minute meeting scheduled by Rachel's boss's boss, Lex Winter, a long-tenured senior editor who both oversaw the Fact Department and served as an editor for writers on the editorial side.

Rachel froze. Her pulse raced. Had they seen her cubicle empty? Was she going to be fired, just over a year into her first job?

She entered Lex's office with trepidation. Lex was a relic from another era, a grizzled '70s-style reporter who wore a sweater vest, who sipped black coffee at all hours, and whose office still occasionally smelled of cigarettes despite the strict indoor smoking prohibition. Rachel felt an equal mix of admiration and intimidation: She had only been called to meet with Lex one-on-one once, in her first month at the magazine, when she had fact-checked a music retrospective and failed to verify the year of Mick Jagger's birth (1943, not 1941). Lex dressed her down for the mistake for five minutes, let her squirm and apologize, then nodded curtly and sent her back to her desk.

"Hello, Lex," she ventured, looking at him over the towering stack of papers on his desk. He typed furiously for several minutes before acknowledging her.

"Rachel Bergen. Our Fact Department ingenue," he said, and then Rachel knew she was not there to be yelled at. She smiled, wary but interested, expectant.

"I've noticed your work," he continued. "You've spoken up in editorial meetings, taken on checking features, pitched great story ideas that someone else gets to write."

"Thank you."

"I have an opening for an assistant editor. Front-of-book stuff, someone who writes short pieces on a quick turnaround. It's not glamorous, but neither is verifying people's names for 'Party Lines.'" Lex shrugged, referencing the magazine's weekly "party highlight" section, which featured New York celebrities-about-town. "Is this something you'd be interested in?"

Rachel paused. Of course she was interested! She was flattered, elated to be noticed. She wanted to be a "real" writer, whatever that meant. But before she spoke, she remembered what she had said to Dev the last time they talked about their novels. She had told him she needed time to write, that she might want to get an MFA. Did a part of her *enjoy* not actually writing at the magazine, leaving her creative energy for her own personal projects? Over the summer, she had added twenty pages to her draft.

But she wasn't sure if they were any good. She had no idea when she would—if she would?—have created anything publishable, worthwhile. If she took this job, she could see her name in print the very next month. *In* New York *magazine.* She took a breath, the pause thick with possibility.

"Yes." Rachel nodded. "This is absolutely something I'd be interested in."

Two weeks later, she became Rachel Bergen, assistant editor, *New York* magazine. One month later, Nate and Dev took her down to the newsstand. Each of them bought a copy of the issue with her first byline. They all took their copies to a coffee shop, to pore over them properly, and Rachel sat there, mystified, running her fingers over her name, printed in black ink, permanent.

2008

The printer lurched into motion with a low-pitched groan. Dev hovered over it, his arms crossed in satisfaction, watching with unblinking focus as it spit forth its sheets of paper, white tongues from a mechanical maw. Ten pages, fifty, one hundred. Finally, page 348: THE END.

He had done it. He, Dev Kaur, who had never been strong at following through on anything in his life—who had quit piano lessons after a year, guitar lessons after two—had written a novel.

"Yes!" he exclaimed to no one, triumphant, as he lifted the pages. They felt so significant like this, their heft indicating that he had finally accomplished *something*, at last. He looked around, searching for a sign to mark the momentousness of the occasion. The other patrons of OfficeMax simply continued to punch buttons and make copies as if it were simply any other Tuesday, but

Dev knew it was not. He swung his backpack onto his shoulder and strode out onto Twenty-Third Street.

Back at his apartment, he put the pages into a desk drawer and left them there for a full week before he was ready to consider the volume of work still ahead of him.

IN AUGUST 2006, TWO MONTHS AFTER GRADUATION, DEV HAD moved into his flex-walled "room" at Nate and Cody's, an eight-by-eight corner of the living room behind thin plaster. His share of the rent for this space, they informed him, would be $900 a month.

"It's a sick deal with three of us," Nate explained, and apparently, he was not joking. "As a true two-bedroom we would have each been paying thousands."

Dev needed to find a job, posthaste.

In his first three months in New York, he went on fourteen job interviews. *Fourteen* interviews, one numeral higher than the number of dollars left in his bank account ($13.07) by the end of the ninety days. Maybe they were the wrong interviews; maybe he didn't know the right people; maybe it really *was* as difficult to get hired with an English degree as his parents had told him. Whatever the reason, on the ninety-first day, Dev walked into Nirvana, an Indian restaurant in Murray Hill on Twenty-Eighth Street, one that seemed to him just upscale enough not to be embarrassing. After twenty minutes of confidently exaggerating his experience working at his uncle's restaurant in high school, he walked out with a job.

The first months had been a slog: late, loud nights at the

restaurant followed by later nights out drinking, commiseration over entitled customers, a kind of restaurant-world camaraderie he vaguely remembered as a cross between familial closeness and a version of Stockholm syndrome. It had culminated in a strange, disaffecting New Year's break at home in Virginia, crammed back into a bedroom with his brother Sumeet, while his parents repeatedly announced, apropos of nothing, that they were not pleased that Dev was using his Northwestern degree to pay New York rent while waiting tables at the kind of restaurant he could have worked at back home. They suggested that maybe he move home for longer, suggested grad school, suggested anything other than staying in New York indefinitely while making minimum wage.

It certainly wasn't the grand postgrad adventure he had imagined for himself, either. By March, he had found himself uncharacteristically drunk, standing out on the balcony at a party, confessing to Rachel that he wondered if he should have moved to New York in the first place. He then compounded this humiliation by trying to *kiss her*—and she rebuffed him, something that, admittedly, almost never happened to Dev where women were concerned.

He needed to get his shit together.

But as winter began to thaw into spring, his weird, wasted first postcollegiate year slipping away, a notion occurred to him, a lighthouse shining to him from the shore, and he wondered why it had taken him so long to see it: He was going to write a book.

It wasn't like Dev had never thought of this before. He had majored in English and minored in creative writing, after all, and attempting a novel had long held a spot on his life bucket list. But he had never been like Rachel, he thought, who enjoyed being able to reference Nabokov offhand in conversation and liked to jot down book ideas in a little notebook at the coffee shop. Dev did not write down ideas in Moleskine notebooks; he wrote them down on scraps of paper and promptly lost them. But then an idea finally came to him, an idea too good to ignore, and he understood at last what people were talking about when they described lightning-bolt-like moments, divine flashes of inspiration.

It happened like this: One day, Nate had walked into their apartment and set a Rolex box down on the granite counter with a heavy, self-satisfied thunk.

"Check it out," he'd said. "Finally got around to using my holiday bonus."

"Cool," Dev had responded, barely looking up from his copy of *The New Yorker*. Watches weren't his thing, but he knew they were a big deal at Nate's work. He started thinking about how it was interesting that every group of people, every subculture, possessed its own set of disparate status symbols. Finance guys from the East Coast liked watches, he had learned. Most of the guys on the restaurant staff with him were into sneakers. The very definition of *success* seemed to vary, too: Dev's parents seemed so impressed when one of their friend's kids became a lawyer or a doctor, yet Cody and his finance friends had recently said to Dev over dinner that doctors "didn't even make any money any-more," which seemed false and ridiculous, but it just went to show the imprecise nature of success, and that who had it and who didn't would never be the same in everyone's eyes. Like, if

Nate hadn't told him that the new watch was a Rolex, he wouldn't have even known to be impressed, and then Nate's flex wouldn't have worked. Buying the watch was a calculated move designed to appeal to a specific set of people.

Then, somehow, Dev started imagining himself in Nate's place. He imagined that if he had abandoned the arts and gone into investment banking, like Nate, there would have been a whole set of cultural touchstones, certain references and aspirational symbols that he would have needed to learn in order to succeed. He understood Excel and he hadn't pulled horrible grades in the AP calc classes his parents had forced him into in high school, but that wouldn't have been quite enough. The finance world was rich, and, at the executive level, it was largely white. Dev had grown up NoVa cool, played sports, pulled good grades, but when he imagined himself at Lehman Brothers, he knew there would have been just a slight disconnect he'd have had to work to overcome.

Suddenly, right in front of Nate, he was lost in a daydream so vivid that it almost felt like watching a movie in his head. He saw a Brown kid like him learning the ropes of the finance world in New York, working his way up in the start of the decade, only for 9/11 to hit. And then, all at once, Dev imagined, this character would find himself in these two worlds. He would be in solidarity with these bankers, who would be his coworkers, and with this American Wall Street image—but he wouldn't be white, or Christian, so suddenly people who don't know him but are buying into the racist media frenzy of the early 2000s are looking at him like maybe he could be a threat. Never mind that he's *Indian*. Dev had experienced a version of this phenomenon himself, stopped by TSA twice as often and looked at sideways when he walked around Arlington at night without shaving. So, he imagined, this character would experience all this and end up in an identity crisis, reckoning with how much all the highbrow success and the money and the "fitting in" hadn't been quite enough to change the way people see him in Bush's America. That was the serious part, but this type of story could be fun, too, Dev thought. There could be girls. Early-twenties shenanigans. All of it.

It really felt like being struck by lightning. Dev felt a spark of electricity zap through him, a purifying conviction. He realized that this story was *a book*. And he had to write it.

"Dev, did you hear me? What do you think?" Nate asked.

Dev had no idea what Nate had just said.

"Sorry, I was just . . . thinking. I just had an idea."

"About what?"

"For a book? I'm going to try to write a book."

He looked at Nate to clock his reaction, but Nate's Black-Berry had buzzed, and he already looked far away.

For several weeks, Dev worked on the project in secret. It was fun that way, he thought, to have something that was just his. As part of a chaotic family of five and then a crammed collegiate house of four, Dev realized it had been a while since he'd kept much to himself. Since he'd really had the space to listen to himself think.

He posed questions in his head as he carried appetizers to

table two, or when he took long midnight walks home along the East River. *What firm would Damian work at when he started his career?* he wondered. (He had been calling his protagonist Damian, wondering if it would stick.) *What kind of music would he listen to? What details would matter?* It was fun to do this, to conjure a person from thin air—even if, in the end, Damian ended up being quite a bit like Dev himself.

Dev had spent years allegedly studying writing, but in college, he had stopped spending time on it outside class. It shocked him to find out just how much he enjoyed creating without a deadline, or a prompt attached, how much it captured his imagination. He was relieved to find how badly he wanted something, at last.

A few weeks later, he told Rachel over drinks at the Ear Inn. He didn't understand why he needed her to know, exactly, but as soon as the words were out there, it lit a fire under his ass. Dev knew his friends would not expect him to finish a novel. He knew he had been the slacker of their group, accepting Bs where he could have gotten As because he was simply too busy enjoying his life. He didn't regret it, but something inside him had started to kindle, something that burned to prove someone—everyone—wrong.

He powered through the draft. He finished it in the winter of 2008, less than one year after he had picked up his pen.

DINNER THAT FRIDAY NIGHT, THE FIRST FRIDAY NIGHT IN months that Dev did not have to work, was at Lil' Frankie's, an affordable, just-cool-enough downtown Italian spot. Rachel did not like coming over to the apartment they shared with Cody anymore, calling it "a frat house in a high-rise," and so the three of them, he and Nate and Rachel, had started going out for meals instead.

Tonight, the pizzas and pastas were house made, but the real draw was the carafes of red wine and the pitchers of sangria that came as cheap as $15, cash only. With its rickety wood tables and red-checked plastic tablecloths, it almost felt like the kind of neighborhood place you'd find on a side street in Rome. Or at least Dev imagined it could be, having never been to Italy. Another item for his bucket list that he hoped to be able to afford one day.

They were seated in the back room, designed to feel like a garden with its glass-covered skylights and plants hanging from wooden beams in the ceiling. Dev glanced across a neighboring table of twelve—Lil' Frankie's was always chock-full of tables, groups of twentysomething friends just like them downing glasses of the cheapest red wine before wandering across Houston to the nearby bars—and looked at the faded, framed photos on the wall. In one, a man smoked a pipe in a field, somewhere in Italy in 1910, according to the date in the bottom right corner. *What was his story?* Dev wondered absentmindedly, then caught himself. Maybe he was slowly turning into a *real* writer, he thought, not without a bit of smug self-satisfaction. He had been trying to think about—to notice—details that had always escaped him before. It was apparently becoming habit.

"Dev, hello, are you even listening?" Rachel waved a hand in front of his face.

Right. He was not noticing *all* the details. Maybe his mind was just doing its own thing, like it always had.

"I'm a multitasker." He smirked. "I'm always listening."

"In that case, repeat what I just said."

"Easy. 'In that case, repeat what I just said.'"

"You idiot." Rachel rolled her eyes and they all started cracking up as she poured them more wine.

Nate grabbed his glass and took a sip. "Rachel was just asking how it was going at the restaurant."

"Really good, actually," Dev said, because admitting dissatisfaction felt like it would be admitting defeat. He decided to spin the positive. "I like a couple of the guys I work with. Good tips, good place to meet people. Nate met Arjun, my coworker. I'm moving into his spare room since Nate's getting his own place." Nate's new apartment would be a one-bedroom, $3,600 per month, in a high-rise near Union Square. By contrast, Arjun had offered Dev a $500-a-month room in an Alphabet City apartment with one sink and a shower in the kitchen.

Dev *really* hoped he could sell his book. He would miss Nate, and he would be glad to be free of Cody, but what he really wanted most of all was his own place. One day.

"He seems like a cool guy," Nate said. "British, into soccer. We're watching the Arsenal match with him at some bar on Sunday."

"British, you said?" Rachel batted her eyelashes flirtatiously. "Is he single?"

When Dev had first arrived in New York, he had been so glad that Rachel hadn't wanted to have the "what are we?" conversation. He'd been relieved not to get dragged into the kind of drama that had occasionally plagued him in college, where he'd go out with a girl once or twice and then, if he didn't call, somehow end up cornered by one of her friends at a party asking what went wrong. He didn't want to be a jerk—he didn't want a girlfriend and he always, always, said so up front!—but he knew that his intentions were usually a bit more principled than his actions. So, with Rachel, he'd been worried. But then, on that night when she had rejected his kiss, his relief had quickly morphed into . . . embarrassment? Disappointment? Eventually, he'd settled down and concluded that she was right, that the potential of a few weeks or months of (great) sex wasn't worth trading in what they had: easy familiarity, a similar passion, a working relationship centered around their writing. He felt confident about working on his book, and happy with how easy it had been to meet new girls like Shivani, a host at the restaurant and an NYU student he had been out with several times. But after a few glasses of wine the whole thing was bubbling up and, okay, maybe starting to bother him just a little.

Which was possibly why he got annoyed at her asking about Arjun, and why he spoke up at that exact moment to say, "Actually, I have some news. I finished my book. I printed the whole thing off this week. Capital-*D* done."

"Dude, congrats," Nate said, leaning across the table to give Dev a fist bump.

"Thanks." He shrugged, aiming for humble, and then he looked expectantly at Rachel, who had not yet said anything. Was it his imagination, or did she, now looking very intently down at her half-eaten plate of pasta, seem disappointed? Jealous?

After only a second or two, she looked up, a broad smile plastered on her face. "Dev, wow. I'm so proud of you."

"Thank you," he said again. Then he realized he didn't just want to show off. He needed their help: Nate and Rachel had paid far more attention in their creative writing classes than he ever had, and Rachel certainly had media and publishing connections. "But honestly, I'm not sure what to do next. Other than to have you read it."

Rachel shook her head. "Now, why doesn't that surprise me?"

"Don't look at me." Nate shrugged. "I switched to finance for a reason."

"You need multiple beta readers before you do anything," Rachel informed him.

"Like the fish?" he joked.

"Critique partners. Like we had in class. I want to be one of them, of course."

"Only if I can read what you're working on, too."

"Soon," she said, looking away, then taking a sip of her wine. "Just not yet."

DEV DECIDED TO SEND THE COMPLETED FIRST DRAFT OF HIS novel to three friends from his creative writing program at Northwestern. He also gave a copy to Rachel. It seemed like the right number. Five would be too many conflicting perspectives, he thought, but one or two too individual, too myopic. A part of him felt a little nervous at the idea of sharing his most personal work with Rachel—he had based his protagonist Damian's off-and-on love interest on her, in a way he hoped wasn't overtly obvious—but the other part of him felt too proud of himself not to let her see it. He brimmed with it, sometimes, the pride of having accomplished something; he felt taller somehow, as if he were striding across a movie set as he walked down Twenty-Eighth Street to work at Nirvana.

Within a few weeks, all three of his critique partners responded. Two offered only minor line edits, and the other added one larger structural revision about where the novel started. Dev had begun with his protagonist, Damian, moving to the city after his college graduation and getting swept up in the finance world. The structural feedback was that he should try starting in medias res, with Damian on the day of 9/11, then flash back a couple of years, and then take the story linearly all the way into its "present," which was set in 2004. Dev agreed with the note, and then promptly gave himself a figurative pat on the back for being the kind of writer who could accept criticism easily.

He was putting the final touches on the new final scene at a coffee shop in the West Village, pushing himself to finish before he was supposed to meet Nate and Arjun to catch a late-season NBA game. He looked up from his clunky Lenovo laptop, staring off into space like he might somehow see inspiration wafting at him through the air. Instead, he saw Rachel.

"Are you following me?" he joked by way of hello, getting up to give her a hug.

"I was going to ask you the same thing." She sat down in the chair across from his. "This is *my* block. You're just hanging out here and you didn't text me?"

"I'm revising, and you know we always end up talking when we work together."

"True." She took a sip of his cappuccino without asking. "But I was going to call you anyway. I finished your book."

"Yeah? And?" His emotional mix hovered somewhere between eager and preemptively annoyed.

"I loved it," she said, and Dev grinned wider than he meant to. The praise felt like a caffeine rush.

"But . . ."

"There it is."

"Look, you know Damian is literally just a composite of you and Nate, right?"

It was typical of Rachel to stumble upon something and then immediately decide she was the first person to have thought of it. Or that she always had a way to make something better. A few weeks ago, when she dragged him shopping, she stepped into a store called Intermix and then spent five minutes suggesting to the floor associate how she should rearrange the window displays. He ignored the small voice inside him that told him Rachel was technically a stronger writer than him—she had published a short story in *Epoch* in college, a byline he truly envied—and decided that she wasn't an expert on finishing a *novel* because she hadn't yet managed to do it.

He shrugged. "I mean, yeah, Rach, I know. I wrote him. I used inspiration from Nate's work life, and then kind of transposed myself onto it, imagining what would be the same and what would be different if that character weren't white. How the industry would respond—or not respond—to that." He was glad she liked the book, but it wasn't like she could tell him anything about his characters that he didn't already know. "Anything else?"

"Don't be a snob. I mean that I love the character—how could I not?—and I think you're doing something important.

But it reads too much like putting you, putting Nate, on the page. Damian reacts to the events in the book like *you* would react to them—in a way that's kind of, I don't know, glib? I think he *should* be funny, but also, you didn't live through all that stuff, Dev—9/11." Rachel took a breath and blinked her eyes closed for a beat. She looked walled off, faraway, as if she were remembering things Dev couldn't imagine. Then, in an instant, she shook her head, picked up the coffee cup, and looked him in the eyes. "I know it impacted you. I don't mean to say it didn't. But not like people who were living in New York at the time. That tragedy in the moment is going to be different from the way you see it now, at a distance of seven years."

Even though it was completely obvious, Dev had somehow forgotten until this conversation that Rachel had been in Manhattan during 9/11. Her dad had been downtown and had lost many of his friends. *Shit.*

"Well, you're right about that part. Sorry if it seemed like I was making light of anything," he said, and she smiled in a way that told him it was okay. "But otherwise, I don't think it's a problem that the character is kind of me. Isn't that how all first books are?"

"Yes and no." Rachel shrugged. "But I think there's a difference between being inspired by you and *being* you. If you're revising anyway, I just think you should keep in mind that the character is older than you, has different experiences. I think it would be more genuine—and more interesting—to create a little bit more distance. To really try to get inside his head as someone separate from you."

"Thank you, Madame Editor."

"Whatever, don't take my advice."

"I'll think about it."

"Do you have agents in mind?"

"I can't just send it straight to the publisher? Like Fitzgerald?"

Rachel raised both eyebrows in an "are you kidding me?" expression.

"Give me a tiny bit of credit; I know better than that. I know I need a literary agent," he said, although, admittedly, it was the first time he had bothered to do any level of research before diving into something. He remembered the time he had presented on *Love in the Time of Cholera* in Spanish 301 without reading a word, waxing on about the themes from his SparkNotes reading and embellishing with his own takes. He had gotten an A-minus on the strength of his bullshitting alone, which he still thought might be more impressive than if he had gotten an A by actually reading the material.

"Well, if you haven't thought of who to send it to, I have a friend, Mel, who's a junior agent at—"

Rachel had a friend who was a something at every single place. Dev equally longed for this connection and wanted proof that he could succeed on his own. He took the last sip of his cappuccino and gestured that they should get going. "No, no Bergen-family-connections help." He shook his head, shrugging into his jacket. "I'm going to search online, make a list of agents who might be into it, mail it out."

"Good. And speaking of exciting opportunities," Rachel said, following him closely out of the coffee shop, "did you hear about Clarissa's audition?"

"Something for HBO, right? A special featuring a lineup of

new comedians?" Dev asked. After a long time—Dev could admit that he was terrible at remembering to return a phone call—he and Clarissa had talked on the phone earlier that week. This was her first opportunity for a big break. She, like Dev, was still relying almost entirely on shifts at the bar to pay the bills.

But that could all change for her, this very week. Dev willed himself to believe it could change for him, too.

Rachel nodded. "Mm-hmm." She paused, as if weighing what to say. "It has to be competitive."

"She'll get it," Dev said, flicking his lighter. He had no idea if this was true—had not even had the time or disposable income to bother seeing a comedy show since he last watched Clarissa perform in college—but he wanted to believe it could be.

"I hope so." Rachel stopped at the corner of Bleecker Street, ready to turn in the direction of her apartment. She dropped a kiss on his cheek. "I'm busy at work this week, editing a new writer—but good luck with the agents. And if it doesn't work out this round, remember what I said."

"Yeah, yeah." Dev resolved to send the book out as it was to at least three agents. Partially for his own reasons, but partially just to prove her wrong. Damian made perfect sense as he was.

"I'm just saying." She threw her wispy scarf over one shoulder and twirled away.

Dev headed north to meet Nate and Arjun for the game, watched the Knicks beat the Hornets, and mostly forgot the conversation. But he managed to keep his resolve, and he sent the first twenty-five pages of his finished manuscript to five agents the very next week.

THREE OF THE REJECTIONS WERE SWIFT, POLITE, AND unspecific. The fourth query languished for months, with Dev having no idea if it had ever found its way to the intended recipient. The fifth resulted in a response that said the agent had loved the sample pages and asked Dev to send the full manuscript? He felt coolly confident as he sent it off, but sure enough, he received a rejection three weeks later, this time with a longer note attached.

The rejection didn't bother him; there were hundreds—thousands—of other agents in New York. The feedback was a different story. Dev sat down at his desk and scanned through the notes, phrases jumping out at him: "loved the voice, but difficulty connecting to the main character deeper into the draft"; "struggled to relate"; and the like. The possibility that Rachel had been right irked him unexpectedly.

Dev was happy to take the compliments. They liked his voice, they had read the full manuscript, and he felt sure someone else would, too—and next time, it would be someone who would sign him and represent him. But he didn't know what to do with the notes. Should he keep sending the book out as is? Should he listen to Rachel's feedback and rewrite his main character? Would that also fix the unspecified relatability problem, or was "unrelatable" simply code for "no one is jumping to buy stories from an Indian kid's perspective"? Would it ever happen for him? he wondered. Would he ever see the day when he got to call his parents and say, "Look, it wasn't a waste of time, they're going to publish it"?

Screw it, he thought. He'd figure it out later. For now, he needed to get drunk.

He headed into the living room, happy to find Arjun sprawled out on their new sectional sofa and sipping a beer.

"Got another of those?" he asked.

"Be my guest." Arjun pointed to the fridge and chucked a bottle opener in Dev's direction.

Dev's phone vibrated. He popped the bottle cap off with one hand and grabbed for his phone with the other, flipping it open to find a text from Shivani.

After they had slept together for the first time, back in the fall following a shared shift at Nirvana, Dev had told Shivani that he wasn't looking for anything serious. Surprisingly, she agreed readily, with no attempts to convince him otherwise or faux threats to break things off. She was still in college, she reminded him, and if she could find something simple and easy that would fit into her life and still leave her time to go out with her friends and study for the MCAT, all the better. They'd continued seeing each other off and on, and while she'd become friendly with Nate and then Arjun when she slept over at his place, they hadn't integrated their friend groups or their lives, which seemed to work out for both of them. He didn't want to get involved in anything before he knew where his life was going. Which, with his present literary agent success rate, might be back to NoVa to live at home while he looked for a "real job."

Which was why Dev was surprised to see her text reading, "Hey! Drinks for my best friends 21st at Tortilla Flats tonight, wanna join? Going out after."

She wanted him to come meet her friends? Join her best

friend's birthday dinner? Maybe it was his lingering bad mood from the manuscript rejection, maybe it was the implication of seriousness that "meeting the friends" implied, but Dev decided that he could not deal with it right now. He shot off a quick "busy tonight, sry" text and closed out of the message.

She didn't respond.

Dev took a big swig of his beer, flopped down on the couch, and reopened his phone to message Clarissa. He realized he had forgotten to check in to see how her audition for the HBO show had gone. Clarissa didn't have Facebook, which was something he loved about her, but it also made the notion of long-distance friendship harder and more abstract. Especially for someone as forgetful as, well, him.

"Audition update?? Sry, been busy and forgot to ask."

She wrote back right away. "Didn't get it. Fuck me, right?"

"Just got rejected by another agent for the book, so. We're in it together."

"Keep fighting the good fight," she sent.

Dev smiled. He and Clarissa were the curt messengers of the bunch, unlike Rachel and Nate. Whether via AIM or email or text, Rachel had always sent paragraphs. Nate sent a few words at a time, meaning that he might send ten separate messages before getting his point across. He and Clarissa were simple, no-nonsense, one-liners. He missed her.

"Miss you Clare."

"Miss you too," she shot back right away, and Dev felt lighter, capable of remembering that he didn't really have anything to worry about at all. He would figure things out. Starting by telling Rachel that he wanted an introduction to her "junior agent" friend after all. Why pretend he didn't have connections? Standing on principle wasn't going to get his book published. Besides, all the old, dead, white authors had used connections, probably. Why not him?

Satisfied, he picked up a video game controller and joined Arjun in blasting zombies into oblivion.

A MONTH LATER, A FRIDAY NIGHT IN JULY. MIND-MELTINGLY hot, typical New York summer humidity hanging over the afternoon and evening with no precipitous drop in temperature even after the sun sank below the Hudson. All of them—Nate, Dev, Rachel, Arjun—were having dinner at yet another nameless mid-priced, dimly lit restaurant on West Tenth Street. They were belatedly celebrating Nate's promotion from analyst to associate, or else associate to analyst. Dev always mixed it up, despite having written a whole novel centered on the finance world. It meant more money, was the main point. It meant things weren't as bad as the ominous rumblings in the news. That was all Nate seemed to want them to know.

"One more bottle, on me," Nate said loudly as they finished up their pesto pasta, their chicken cacciatore. He asked the server to bring them something nice, a Barolo, whatever that was. Nate looked to him for approval on the choice. Dev shrugged. If it was alcohol and Nate was paying, that was good enough for him. "Should I text Cody to come meet us after?"

"No," Rachel blurted quickly, before the words were even out of Nate's mouth. They all looked at her. She composed herself, then said, "I mean, I'd just rather not have to watch him hit on everything with a pulse all night. Including me. He can be . . . a lot."

"Jeez, okay." Nate rolled his eyes, then softened. "Point taken."

Rachel signaled for Dev's attention; she seemed to want to say something to him. But as Dev looked back at her, his phone started to ring.

"Party foul," she said, shaking her head at him.

"I'm just shocked it's not mine this time." Nate chuckled. His work BlackBerry went off in the middle of everything they'd done for the past two years.

"Hello?" Dev said, plugging one ear to block out the noise of the packed restaurant. "Sorry, having trouble hearing you. This is Dev."

"Hello, Dev. This is Laurel Hartwhite, from the Thompson and Miller agency. I'm sorry to be calling a bit late, but I just finished your manuscript and I had to get in touch. Is now a good time?"

Dev practically burst through the restaurant's glass door like the Kool-Aid man. He bounded out onto the sidewalk. "Yes, absolutely. A great time."

"Well, I picked up your manuscript in the middle of this week on the high recommendation of my assistant." *Rachel's friend Mel.* "I read pretty much straight through to tonight, and I'm calling to offer you representation. I just loved your novel, Dev. Loved it. It's unique, honest . . . a new voice for a new millennium." She gushed for a bit longer, and Dev just let the words rush over him, grinning.

"I know I may have some competition, but I'd love to throw my hat in the ring to represent you."

When Dev would recount this story later, he would say he was stunned. Awestruck. He was: He hardly knew what to say, a rarity for him. Should he play it cool? he wondered. Or should he admit the truth, which was that he wanted to sign with Laurel, and he didn't need to hear any competing offers? Dev thought of the late nights at the restaurant, of turning down his dad's offer for an entry-level office job in D.C. How would his life change if he said yes to her now, tonight?

"Laurel, I'd love for you to represent me. Thank you. I accept."

He heard a surprised laugh from the other end of the line. "You don't need more time? Any questions? Anyone to inform?"

"No. I'm not sure if I'm supposed to say this, but Thompson and Miller is my top choice. Any other questions I have, I can ask you when we meet in person. We'll figure it out."

Laurel laughed again, and Dev realized that maybe he should play this more professionally. But hell, she was going to represent *him*, which meant that she was going to get to know him eventually.

"Well then. Let's set up a meeting for sometime next week? I have a few notes, a couple minor revisions to discuss, but I think we're quite close to being ready to go on submission."

"Notes?"

"Simple things, nothing you have to undertake if you don't want to. Mostly just some ideas about fleshing out Damian's character a bit more, making him real in a few ways that might differ from your experience. You said in your query letter that 9/11 very much affected your family, but that you were still in school at the time, correct? Damian is older."

Damn it, Rachel was exactly right, he realized. He was never going to tell her. "Yeah, that's right. All makes sense."

"Anyway, I'll email you with a few dates and times we could meet. Then we can make it official with the paperwork. Looking forward to this, Dev. Really, I'm so thrilled!"

"Same here. Thank you so much, Laurel. I'll talk to you soon."

When he walked back into the restaurant, all eyes were on him. He relished the moment, loving the expectant looks on his friends' faces, loving that last second of sameness before he announced to them that his life was, just maybe, about to change for good.

"Looks like we have two things to celebrate tonight." He grinned, sauntering up to the table. "Thompson and Miller called. I just got an agent."

NATE

2009

For Nate Davis, 2008 careened into 2009 like a boulder crashing down a very long, very steep hill. For months, he had woken up every day wondering just how far they might fall. He was now a *former* associate in equity research for Lehman Brothers, but he had no illusion that this was rock bottom. Not yet.

One day in January, he came into his office to discover that, yet again, he had been assigned a new supervisor. This hadn't been entirely unexpected: They had all spent a long and depressing year watching the collapse of Bear Stearns and then Lehman itself, their bosses telling them it was impossible right up until the moment when the mountain slid into the sea. The impossible became possible after all. Nate lived panicked weeks thinking that he would lose his job, then weathered the sale of the equities division to Barclays, and then one day there he was: Dale Richardson, the new boss.

Dale had the background you'd expect, Harvard and Wharton, and the kind of firm handshake that seemed like he was both trying too hard to assert confidence and also actually asserting confidence. Nate decided that he would try to like him. A few days in, he heard two of his female coworkers talking, praising the way Dale had handled a first department meeting, and then one of them said, "He's clearly smart, but it's something else, too, you know? He just has *it*."

Nate easily recognized that Dale did have *it*. He didn't even know exactly what *it* was—was it the tailored but unflashy suits? a certain type of charisma? living like you had a right to be at the center of things?—but he knew it when he saw it and, apparently, so did everyone else.

"Let's push through and get this deck done by dinner, huh, man?" Dale asked later that afternoon, swinging by his desk to drop off a Diet Coke and fist-bump him, which was nice, but Nate just thought, *Man? Man? Are you kidding me?*

Nate did not think he had ever had *it*, and he had started to wonder if he ever could. Dev had *it*. A certain cool nonchalance, a projection of certainty in everything he did or said. The ability to land on his feet no matter how far he'd fallen. Nate felt stupid for letting it grate on him; Dev didn't do it on purpose, but it did feel like he *had* gotten slightly more annoying in the months since he'd gotten an agent. They were revising his book together now, apparently, and Dev seemed excited by the progress. Unfortunately, this meant that he would frequently leave the room for phone calls and come back all "sorry, that was my agent," and Nate would think, *Come on dude, just call her Laurel.* All while Nate's life was going to shit.

So no, it wasn't entirely about Dev, he reasoned, but more about the turbulence in the industry in general and the horror of Lehman's dissolution and the sale of his department more specifically. They'd been sold off "like scrap" after the bankruptcy in September—at least that was how Cody liked to tell it, even though that wasn't the full story. The equities division at Lehman had been making money for the business all year, even during the collapse, and it was considered a valuable asset. As young associates who had relatively small salaries when compared with the managing directors and big-bank execs coming under fire, there was no reason for the company to get rid of the Nates and Codys—they would go on working, which was lucky when you thought about it in perspective, when you looked at the crushing tidal wave of the guaranteed recession. But there was still some justification for Cody's bitching, Nate thought: While life under Barclays—under *Dale*—might be objectively fine, there *had* been a series of subtle changes on the floor that hadn't gone over well. In addition to the new management and the attendant cultural shifts, Barclays had decided to redesign the office. This shouldn't have seemed particularly important, but their use of new colors and slightly lower-quality office furniture seemed like it rendered everything just one degree uglier, like a dial turning at an eye exam and bringing the picture just one notch further out of focus. The change was small, but it underscored an important point, one that everyone seemed to feel without explicitly having to voice it: Everything was just a little bit worse now.

Nate could almost feel himself spinning out. He could almost hear Clarissa telling him to gain some perspective, that working at a top ten bank instead of a top five bank wasn't what qualified as a real problem. Then again, who was she to tell him what a real problem was? He had made his choices and made his sacrifices: He'd changed his minor, and he had gone into his field with the long hours and the endless demands because of his affinity for numbers, yes, but more so because he wanted the life. He wanted the security of the money, the opportunity to be self-reliant, and he also wanted the coolness factor. He, Nate, could admit it! He wanted to be at the *best* place, at the center of the action, the most respected, and he was willing to work hard for it. Why did he have to apologize for that? Clarissa and Dev had made their own compromises, giving up financial certainty for creativity, for the chance to pursue an artistic dream. If they were allowed to do that, why wasn't Nate allowed to go after exactly what he wanted? And what he wanted was to be at the best firm, and at the top of his industry. That wasn't where he was now, not with the changeover, and he refused to be shamed as an out-of-touch, privileged monster for making calculated evaluations about his career. This wasn't his fault; it was just exactly Nate's kind of luck that he would go into finance fewer than two years before the biggest collapse since the Great Depression.

He glanced away from his computer and over at the newspaper folded on his desk. From *The New York Times*: FOR JOB LOSSES, NO SIGN THE WORST IS OVER. Nate slumped in his chair, deflating as his righteousness escaped him.

Maybe all this *was* a little bit his fault. The fault of people like him. But what could he do about it now? Nate crumpled a piece of paper and threw it at his desk trash can, hard, then watched it bounce out. He pulled out a pen, black ink, his preferred type. When he had started at Lehman, he had learned that no red pen would ever be allowed on the trading floor, because red is the color used to write losses.

One superstition of many that had ended up making absolutely no difference. He was fucked.

Two years ago, things had been different.

Nate's first year in New York had been . . . well, maybe not perfect, but the craziness of work aside, pretty damn close to perfect, he thought. On his very first weekend in the city, before they even had any furniture in their apartment other than the couch, he and Cody had thrown a huge party. Rachel and her friends came, and they danced around him all night. The boom box in the corner pounded Lil Jon, everyone drank and rapped along, and then shortly after midnight they all went to a bar—Joshua Tree, back when that had seemed novel—and Nate had been thrilled to discover that it didn't close at one thirty or two like all the Evanston bars: It stayed open until *4 a.m.*, and when they all finally stumbled out the door near dawn, the streets were alive, full of young and happy and drunk twentysomethings just like them. They all bought pizza slices—only 99 cents, and none of that midwestern deep-dish shit—and then Nate passed out in his own bed, in his own room, feeling better than he had in a while. He woke up with two girls' phone numbers in his pocket, and he knew moving to New York had been the right decision after all.

The following months were dominated by work, punctuated by meeting Rachel for lunch, where he easily picked up the check, and he marveled at the fact that he'd ever worried about "selling out," worried if going into finance had been the right choice. Could he have been a journalist like Rachel? A writer like Dev? An English professor? Maybe, but at the end of the day, work was work, no matter what you were doing; the gleam faded, in everything, and Nate would be happy to have the money to fall back on when it finally did. He bought his parents their first flat-screen TV that Christmas, replacing the clunky black box of a set that had sat in the corner of their living room for more than a decade. They seemed proud of him. Hell, *he* was proud of him. "College is the best time of your life," Nate's parents and their friends had once said, but it had turned out that they were wrong. Real life was just like college but with *money*, which made it altogether better. He loved using the money to do things for the people he cared about—and then for himself, too.

Two years later? With the economy crumbling around him? He didn't feel that thrill anymore.

Nate looked out the window, the early spring sunshine indicating warmth, suggesting life and optimism that did not penetrate the hermetically sealed office building where he spent the vast majority of his days. But tonight, at least, there would be something to break the monotony: Rachel had invited him to Soho House for a pop-up event, some spirits brand launch that promised free alcohol, celebrity-adjacent guests, and attractive girls. Nate looked at his Rolex, feeling a flash of eagerness. Rachel would be coming directly from the airport to meet him and had promised to send a message when she was off the plane. He thought for a moment that maybe he should've asked for Rachel's flight information or something, but that seemed so . . . so *mom*-ish. Parents knew things like flight schedules of planes they weren't on, and the weather in places they didn't live. His mother, who lived in Cleveland, would call him up to say things like "I saw on *Good Morning America* that New York's getting a ton of rain this week. It's a wet summer, huh?" Nate vowed then that he would never, ever get old enough or boring enough to start conversations that way.

What had he been thinking about? Right, Rachel. Soho House. Nate rubbed his temples, his head hurting, his brain fried. He was burned-out. He needed something to take the edge off.

Mercifully, his phone rang, a call from Rachel. They arranged to meet at Soho House at 8 p.m. He looked at the clock, resigned, each ticking minute interminable.

———————

The Soho House rooftop *oozed* cool, from the lo-fi techno music pouring out of the hidden speakers to the string lights twinkling over the placid pool, where twentysomething creative types in summer dresses and pressed shorts lounged on striped chaises. Rachel had warned him not to wear a suit: When Nate heard "members club" he thought jackets and ties, but apparently Soho House was into a new model of exclusivity, admitting "creatives" only—musicians, actors, writers, and the socialites who loved them—and suits were seen as stuffy. He scanned the crowd and thought he saw John Mayer in a corner, wearing a fedora. He grabbed Rachel's arm and tried to point subtly, but that was all he could do, photos being strictly prohibited at the house.

"Holy shit, that's really John Mayer," he whispered in Rachel's ear as she passed him a drink.

"Yeah, he's here all the time. Don't *stare*."

"Dev's not gonna believe this. *Room for Squares* is in our top five desert island albums for sure."

"I know," Rachel said. "Be cool. Maybe we can say hey later."

Nate took a big sip of his drink. "I want to join. Soho House," he added weakly, as if that weren't obvious.

Rachel pursed her lips. "Well, we'd have to work on your résumé. Finance guys are usually guests, not members. Though I did hear they've started letting some in, which to me sounds like the beginning of the end of cool. You could definitely afford the fees, so that's a plus."

"I could have gotten in if I'd stuck with writing," Nate assessed, "but then I wouldn't have been able to afford it?"

"Something like that."

"So, Dev could join?"

"If he sells his book." Rachel pursed her lips. "Then yes, I guess so."

Nate thought about his parents saving up to join the country club in their Cleveland suburb, which wasn't even much of a country club at all; it just had a golf course and a snack bar. An uncomfortable, almost sickly feeling washed over him, and he hated it. Something about being at these kinds of places with Rachel always brought out a strange feeling of insecurity in him. It made him remember the kind of kid he had been, squeezed into the bottom of the middle class but never rich, not completely friendless but never cool, always just a step behind the conversation and never in possession of the right thing to wear or the right reference to drop. In a way, it should have put him off places like Soho House, and that was one side of the tension he felt. But on the *other* was a strange, almost gravitational pull toward this exact atmosphere, as if the only way to get rid of his sense of awkwardness or strangeness was to spend even *more* time at the "right" places, with the "right" people, as if an acceptance there would finally make him feel like he had arrived.

At that moment, emerging from the stairwell door and walking out onto the roof, Nate saw the last person he ever expected to see in New York. Someone who, after the anticlimactic Wilson High graduation of 2002, he hadn't ever wanted to see again.

Jake Matthews. Striding directly toward him. He'd been seen.

"Nate Davis? No fucking way."

Jake clapped him on the back, hard, with the hand that wasn't holding his picante cocktail. He looked almost exactly the same as he had in high school but filled out, extra muscle annoyingly visible through his Henley shirt. Bigger and tanned and smiling and slapping him on the back like they were old friends.

"Hi, I'm Rachel." Rachel extended a hand flirtatiously before Nate could think of anything to say. "And you are?"

"Jake. Jake Matthews. I went to high school with this one, if you can believe it. In Ohio."

"Of all the gin joints in all the towns in all the world." Rachel smiled.

"Huh?" Jake asked, confused for a minute before quickly recovering himself. Nate smirked, happy for the first time in his life that Rachel had forced him into repeat viewings of *Casablanca*.

"Good to see you, Matthews," Nate said, even though it wasn't, not at all. "So, you're in New York now?"

"Yeah, since school. Boston College, remember? Moved down here, got a place in Tribeca with a couple of my friends. Where'd you go to school again, FG?"

And there it was. At the sound of that stupid nickname, Nate felt acutely the sensation of falling, as if he were being sucked through a wormhole back to 1997.

Eighth grade, Tyson Middle School in suburban Cleveland, Ms. Bafonte's homeroom class. Nate could picture his younger self getting off the bus at one of those inane field trips to a historical village, spending a whole day kicking pebbles down a dirt road while feigning interest in a replica of a blacksmith shop and the painted facade of a general store.

Throughout his childhood, Nate had always been a step off socially, and he knew it. Knowing it was the worst part. He wasn't like Trevor Boxer, the kid who glued his fingers together and then *ate it* and yet still couldn't seem to figure out why he was always the butt of the joke. Nate was smart enough to know. He didn't have the right comedic timing, alternated between making awkward jokes and not saying anything at all. He also knew he was short and slight, his stride a half-length too short, meaning he often found himself trotting along the outside of groups, trying to catch up, inserting himself like an obnoxious younger sibling. (A sibling was *also* something he didn't have, and he sensed that being an only child wasn't helping his social standing, either.) No one put his head in a toilet or anything, but he had always been lightly bullied, called "shrimp," never got invited to sleepovers, and he wanted to fix it. But he could not magically give himself a sibling, nor make himself grow six inches overnight. He needed another way to improve his social prospects—without trying too hard, because it seemed imperative that he not try, or the whole enterprise would be a loss.

Then, on the historical village field trip, an opportunity had presented itself. In an antique farmhouse in front of a butter churn, no less.

Nate had been assigned to a chaperone group with Jake, Dan, and Kyle, three of the cool guys from the soccer team, and they had been matched up with a group of four girls. At the second stop on the tour, all eight of them were forced to take turns attempting to faux-churn butter, banging this wooden pole up and down. When Dan stepped up for his turn, Nate saw something, and he took a chance.

He elbowed Jake, gestured at Dan pumping away furiously on the butter churn. "Ha, looks like he knows how to work it. Pretty fucking gay, right?" he joked to Jake, but loudly enough for everyone to hear.

The room erupted in laughter, punctuated by gasps of "he said the f-word" and echoes of "gaaaay." The butter-churning instructor looked down at her apron while their teacher futilely attempted to quiet them by yelling "Boys, boys!" and "Nate Davis, principal's office! As soon as we get back!" It took a full five minutes to bring the room under control.

He knew instantly that it had been worth it all for every laugh, every high five. His subsequent detention didn't matter. He walked out of the principal's office like a Super Bowl–

winning quarterback out of the locker room, to Jake, Dan, and Kyle patting him on the back and calling him "FG," short for "fall guy." They had all been swearing on the bus, calling things "gay" left and right, but Nate had been the only one with the balls both to make the joke in front of everyone and to take all the blame. In retrospect, it seemed he had primarily been in trouble for saying "fuck" rather than "gay," a moral weighting that seemed to have subtly shifted by 2009. (Even if Nate didn't fully understand why it mattered so much, Clarissa had schooled him out of using "gay" as an insult—at least in her presence.)

Anyway, that was the moment Nate assumed he had joined the "popular" group. But in the end, he'd had no such luck: he still only scored invites to some of the parties, still heard that the guys made fun of him behind his back, Jake in particular. It felt as though he had tried to sell a part of his soul and there had been no takers. He'd had no way to buy what he wanted, even through base humiliation. When he left for Northwestern, he'd been determined to reinvent himself, determined to be *the* guy, the man, not the fall guy and the butt of the joke. It helped that he shot up six inches and filled out the summer before their freshman year. He'd left Cleveland behind. The person he'd been there? He preferred not to think about it. His *soul*? He'd sell the whole damn thing if he had to. For the right price.

But now Jake Matthews was here. In person. *God damn.*

"FG, right. I had forgotten about that." Nate shook his head and smiled, affecting good humor. He hoped he'd said it in a way that made it seem like Jake was still stuck in high school, whereas Nate had moved on.

"Meet my friends, Connor and Zach." Jake nodded to his

left, where two guys in similar Henleys and Patagonia vests approached, spicy margaritas in hand. Nate stood a little taller, glad that Rachel had told him to leave the vest at home.

"I thought you said they weren't big on letting the finance clones in here," he whispered into Rachel's ear. She muffled a laugh.

"She's cute," Connor or Zach said to Jake, looking appraisingly at Rachel. Nate couldn't tell if he was drunkenly pointing her out as someone to hit on or if he had been genuinely aiming for a compliment in the third person.

"She is, but she's with him," Jake said, gesturing to Nate. Part of him wondered if he should stop them from talking about Rachel like she wasn't there, but the other part, selfishly, loved when she didn't clarify that the two of them weren't together *like that*. He felt like he had won something at last, finished in first place after a lifetime as the underdog.

Rachel saved him, just like she always did.

"Nice to meet you all," she said. "But I'm overdue for a drink. Nate, bar?"

"Well, here's my card," Jake said to Nate, obnoxiously, like he was in *American Psycho*. "We should catch up properly."

"Sure, sure," Nate answered, striving for friendly but non-committal. Then Rachel linked her arm with his, seeming to understand exactly what he needed, and he had never been so grateful for her in his life.

"For real. It was good to see you, Nate," Jake said. It was the first time Jake had ever used his name. It stirred something in Nate against his will. Maybe things were different now. Maybe he was different. He imagined the glitz of the club, the halo of

Rachel's beauty, all of it having rubbed off onto him, making him glow by association.

"Good to see you, Matthews," Nate called, taking in just one satisfying glance over his shoulder at Jake's jealous expression as he escorted Rachel to the bar. The music soared louder, the beat energizing him. Someone sniffed a bump off a key in the middle of the bar crush, hardly discreet. Rachel's smile beamed, megawatt.

He had to find a way to join this damn club.

NATE WOKE THE NEXT MORNING TO A THROBBING HEADACHE and thought he'd lost his keys until he found them, still carelessly hanging in his front door. He experienced a quick flush of embarrassment at the fact that he'd gotten so drunk, then quickly absolved himself. Jake and his friends had clearly been partying even harder than he was, and Jake was a member. He dropped his keys in the entryway, said a prayer of silent thanks that he lived in a doorman building, and sat down at his desk to run a search for the Soho House application page. He might not have had the energy to shower, or cook himself food, but menial computer tasks sounded possible.

As he thought about how best to exaggerate his creative bona fides for the application—should he pretend to be an art collector? mention the Hopper retrospective Rachel had dragged him to?—his phone rang.

His heart raced as he looked at the caller ID, hoping it wasn't Rachel calling to tell him he'd made a fool of himself drunk at the end of the night. Instead, it was Dev.

"Yo, what's up?" he croaked. Nate typically prided himself on being one of the few people he knew who never smoked cigarettes, not even socially when drunk, but he now had a vague memory of bumming one from someone on the roof.

"Sounding a little rough over there." Dev laughed.

Nate cleared his throat. "I'm fine."

"Well then, guess what. I sold my book."

Through the haze of his hangover, it took Nate a beat to muster up the appropriate reaction. He sat for a moment in silence, just holding the phone.

"Hello?"

"Sorry, I'm here. That's incredible," he said, and it was. Dev had always put on a good face, like nothing bothered him, but Nate remembered the early days in their old apartment, when Dev had been trying to scrounge up restaurant work and dodging calls from his parents. Nate had felt a little awkward back then, alternately guilty about making so much money, about living extravagantly in front of Dev, and annoyed that Dev couldn't seem to get his shit together. Now Nate was both relieved and happy for him—more than enough to drown out any jealousy he might have felt. "Really. Congratulations. I'm happy for you, man."

Then Dev told him about his mid-six-figure advance, and Nate wasn't so sure of his dominant emotion anymore.

He said all the right things: He asked about the publishing house, the title, when the book would come out. (It would take more than a year, Dev informed him.) He remained cheerful, and a part of him was. Nate, after all, didn't lack for money, he reminded himself. Not anymore. He also didn't particularly want to write a book. But he remembered how he had chosen Lehman Brothers over graduate school, how he could have studied English, which had been his first love ever since his seventh grade language arts teacher had let him eat lunch in her classroom and pore over her personal collection of paperbacks. He had chosen the money, which had seemed like the sensible thing, but now Dev had made more money than Nate made in a year in one book deal. Had Nate chosen the safer trajectory? Sure, but he had also unwittingly chosen to work in finance during a once-in-a-lifetime recession.

"We'll go out and celebrate soon," Nate promised Dev, when he had finished sharing all the details.

"As soon as they give me the check," Dev agreed. "And no more cheap pasta and sangria. We'll go to one of your places, paint the town, do the whole thing."

"Sounds great," Nate said as he hung up the phone. It did sound great.

His stomach growled and ached, his hangover pounding with a renewed insistence like an impatient houseguest.

It sounded great, Dev's success. It just also felt, somehow, awful.

A month later, Nate invited Rachel to a comedy show. He thought that maybe he should try to spend more time with his friends one-on-one, and in a context that did not involve either work or screaming at each other over the music in a nightclub. He also hoped they might be able to stop for a drink at Soho House after, where his recently submitted application was languishing somewhere in digital purgatory.

Nate hadn't thought he intended the comedy show invitation to be a date, but then Cody invited himself along, and Nate's disappointment indicated that somewhere inside, he had been hoping it would lead to something more. And why couldn't it? He knew Rachel hadn't been seeing anyone seriously; on his side, a recent setup had fizzled out after three mediocre dinner dates, all of which he'd ended up running late for. Unfortunately, there was the matter of the fact that Cody had slept with Rachel, at a party during their first year in the city. Rachel had seemed to summarily dismiss Cody afterward—which made Nate happier than he'd ever tried to let on—but now he had to handle the awkward dance of seeing the comedy show as a threesome, and then trying to get Rachel alone for a drink after the show. It felt beyond his social capabilities, and he tried to convince himself to treat the night as a simple evening out with two old friends.

This worked until Rachel walked in the door to the Comedy Cellar, grinning at him from across the room while unwinding a long scarf from around her neck, revealing her cute, pointed chin—could chins be cute? hers was—and her lightly flushed chest peeking out of a low-cut sweater. Her smile fell as she took a seat at the table on Nate's right.

"You didn't say Cody was coming," she whispered, sounding somewhere between angry and worried. His heart leapt. He wondered if she had expected a date after all.

"Hey, Rachel, looking good," said Cody, talking across Nate from his left. Nate rolled his eyes, even though Cody was simply behaving like his typical self. He had seemed to get the message that Rachel wasn't into him after that one long-ago night, and they had not discussed her since.

"So, who's on the lineup tonight? Any idea?" Rachel asked, ignoring Cody completely.

"Not sure. Some locals, but I heard a rumor that Jerry Seinfeld has been popping up at the late shows." The Comedy Cellar was notorious for famous drop-ins, all-star comedians who were never on the bill but would come by for a set or two at the end of a night.

"God, I wish Clarissa were here."

"Me, too," Nate said, although he didn't, really. He wanted to remove other people from their night, not add them. He made a mental note to send Clarissa an email, though—it had been too long. She had started making YouTube videos, sharing pre-recorded segments of her stand-up routines, but he had so far failed to actually watch any of them. His guilt was fleeting.

"I just hope there aren't as many women on the bill as last time." Cody shook his head, taking a sip of beer. "No offense, Rach. I'm not sexist or anything. They're just not usually as funny."

"So, you think fifty-one percent of the population is automatically not funny?" Rachel said, an edge in her voice.

"I didn't say that." Cody shrugged. "I think they're usually trying to compete with men, trying to be as gross, or as shocking, and it just doesn't work. They end up overdoing it."

Rachel looked hard at Nate, clearly waiting for him to say something. He knew that Cody was being an ass, but he couldn't tell exactly what he was supposed to do about it.

"Come on, man, Clarissa's funny," he said, both indignant on

Clarissa's behalf and hoping this would be what Rachel wanted him to say.

"I meant straight women. Clarissa's funny. Oh, and Sarah Silverman, she's an exception. But hey, I'm not saying I'd be *mad* if there was a woman or two. Maybe they'll be hot."

"Well, I've never seen anyone at Comedy Cellar who didn't make me laugh. Hot or not," Nate said, hoping to both defuse the situation and shut Cody up. The emcee walked up to the stage, and the applause started. "Anyone want another drink before the first comic?"

"Just one for me," Rachel said. "I'm leaving early tonight. I promised myself I'd write tomorrow."

Nate's hopes for the night crumbled, quieting with the room as the emcee started talking. He wondered for a moment if he should just leave with Rachel. What if he finished his drink, then stood up, took her hand, and walked out? What would happen then?

Nate shook his head at this thought. He needed to get a grip on himself: He and Rachel were just friends. Tonight was the same as every other night they'd ever spent together. He would stay with Cody, enjoy the evening, reap the full benefit of the $20 cover, and then go out and blow off some steam. He needed it. He deserved it.

An idea occurred to him: Rachel wasn't the only Soho House member he knew now, after all. She wasn't the only person who could take him out. He reached into his pocket and fingered the edges of Jake Matthews's card. He held it as he took a long sip of his beer, then refocused his attention on the stage.

It was time for Nate to move on.

CLARISSA

2010

Ladies and gentlemen, we are second in line for takeoff. We'll be on our way to LaGuardia momentarily." The pilot's voice crackled over the loudspeaker. Seat belts clicked. A baby wailed.

Clarissa slipped on her headphones to block the noise. A new episode of a comedy podcast started to play. She recoiled as the voice of the week's guest filled her ears: It was none other than famed comedian Dawn Leiter. Clarissa stabbed angrily at the "next" button. She stared out the window, willing the plane to lift off, to take her away from Chicago for the first time in four years.

How much could Clarissa have avoided if she had never signed up for Dawn Leiter's improv class? She closed her eyes and thought about Dawn, then about Rebecca, and her heart squeezed, a painful throb.

Did she regret it? Clarissa did not usually believe in regret or second-guesses. But right now, today, she did.

The plane sped up the tarmac, lurching, and then it finally rose, carrying her toward New York, toward the people who had, four years ago, been her closest friends. She hoped that they still could be.

CLARISSA HAD SIGNED UP FOR A SECOND CITY IMPROV 101 class in her first year postcollege on a whim. Second City was famous and esteemed for sketch comedy—and as the launching point for Gilda Radner and Tina Fey, it seemed to be less of an old boys' club than most of the stand-up world—but the decision was motivated less by a clear-cut vision for her career and more by a sense of desperation.

On the day of graduation, Clarissa had felt eager to hurry up and get out of Evanston and into the "real world" of Chicago's city proper. While Rachel and Dev waxed poetic about New York, Clarissa had cultivated her knowledge of the comedy scene in the city of her birth. It had been a starting point for some of her favorite comedians, after all, and so why not her? "Why *not* me?" she had actually said, out loud, to her housemates. They had agreed, nodding solemnly, telling her that she was hilarious, that she had what it took. It could have been idle flattery from her best friends, but she had chosen to believe it, because Clarissa knew from her upbringing, which included eight years of Catholic school, that belief, faith, wasn't a birthright but a choice.

The reality of postgrad life had been less inspiring than she'd hoped. Most nights, she would lie down on her bed, shut her eyes, and pretend that she was back in their college house on

Maple Street. She listened to the rumbling of the el stopping at Lawrence every ten minutes with her eyes squeezed shut. The train tracks lay about fifteen yards behind her building, but she felt like she could touch them from her spot on her springy twin bed, which took up almost the entire room in her three-bedroom apartment, a sublet with strangers that felt very, very far away from the beautiful craftsman house she had lived in less than a year before with the people who had mattered to her most in the world.

Work wasn't much better. She had started bartending at a dive called Toby's Corner, and the rotation of late-night shifts and 1 a.m. open mics left her bone-tired. Rachel emailed frequently, asking how it was going, but Clarissa didn't know how to answer her questions, so even though they had seen each other constantly for the last four years, she was rarely fully honest with her best friend. She knew she had a decent sense of comedic timing. She had a "tight ten," honed in practice stand-ups around campus, which focused mostly on contrasting the culture of her Polish immigrant family with the Waspy, Ivy League–adjacent character of her alma mater. But she'd bombed at several Chicago open-mic nights, three nearly identical evenings of standing on a makeshift plywood stage in a bar backroom, in front of a few rows of skeptical faces sitting on metal folding chairs and sipping foamy beers disinterestedly out of plastic cups. She understood that this had always been part of the bargain—that she would play to half-empty rooms, join sketch groups that never did more than come up with a quirky name for themselves—but she was still plagued with doubt. She wondered, often, if she should look for an office job instead, and it guilted her how much she did not want to. It hurt every time she remembered that her sister gave her parents several hundred dollars each month out of her nursing paychecks, even though she never, ever shamed Clarissa about it.

Enter: the improv class. She needed a way to broaden her network, to improve her skill set. She needed something to do in her off hours other than listening to her roommates watch mind-numbing episodes of *Laguna Beach* through the wall while she attempted to astral project herself back nine months, to a time when she felt more like she was waiting for her life to begin, rather than making sense of what to do now that it had.

On the first night the class met, Clarissa slicked some berry-tinted ChapStick onto her lips, slid on her favorite jean jacket as armor, and whispered "go get 'em" at her reflection in the mirror. If only she had known whom she was about to meet. The *two* someones who were waiting for her.

The class was held in a nineteenth-century theater on Lawrence Avenue. As Clarissa opened the heavy door to the auditorium, filled with old velvet seats and a wide apron stage, a familiar smell of must and paint hit her nose. She breathed it in, an immediate anesthetic that made her calm and certain: This was the place she belonged. She took a seat in the first row, next to the other early arrivals. To her left, she saw two twentysomething guys in Converse, skinny jeans, and zip hoodies, the uniform of former "emo kids." *Definitely the typical comedy type*, she thought, though she guessed "lesbian in a jean jacket with patches on it" wasn't too far afield from her own performer stereotype, either. Two seats farther down, she glimpsed a petite brunette, her long hair tucked behind her ears, revealing diamond stud earrings. She was also, Clarissa couldn't help noting, incredibly pretty.

Before she could think about this too much, their instructor walked out in front of them with a flourish, her loose garments looking very Eileen Fisher by way of Salvation Army, in a typical drama instructor kind of way. But this one was different because this was—Clarissa realized—Dawn Leiter. *The* Dawn Leiter, a Second City alum and Chicago comedy fixture, who happened to be one of Clarissa's idols.

"Does anybody remember laughter?" Dawn crowed. "Sorry, a poor joke, but I can't resist a nod to my seventies heyday. I'm Dawn Leiter, and welcome to Introductory Improv."

Clarissa loved her already. She couldn't believe her luck.

After Dawn's introduction, the rest of the first class had consisted of the typical exercises: get-to-know-yous, drawing prompts out of a hat to riff on or act out. But by the time it was over, Clarissa decided she felt more optimistic than she had after the last disastrous "Laffs-a-Lot" open mic. She grabbed her backpack off a seat, said "see you next week" to the class, and headed for the stage-right exit.

"Hey, wait up," a voice called from behind her. "You can't leave without telling me where you got that jacket patch."

Clarissa spun around. It was the brunette, the petite woman who had introduced herself in warm-up with a surprisingly loud voice.

"What, the Bush one? 'A village in Texas has lost its idiot'?"

"Ha. No, but I like that one, too. I meant 'Andersonville is for lovers,'" she said. Clarissa's neighborhood, where she lived near the border with Uptown.

"You live in Andersonville?"

"I do. But it's more that I'm just a secret scene kid. You know, 'Ohio is for lovers'?"

"I don't really do emo." Clarissa raised an eyebrow, hoping she said it in a flirty, provocative way, not a confrontational one. "Old-school punk gal. With a few noteworthy exceptions, of course."

"Not into emo? With the eyeliner and the Converse low-tops? I'm not buying it." She smirked back, and was Clarissa imagining it or could she really, actually, be flirting back?

"I had a grunge phase in middle school, if that counts."

"No, but duly noted." A pause. "I'm Rebecca, by the way."

"Clarissa."

"Well, Clarissa." Rebecca paused and cocked her head. Clarissa tried not to look her up and down too obviously, but she did take in her fitted white T-shirt, tucked into a pair of dark-wash jeans, which were tight on her slim hips. "I don't know what you're doing now, but to be honest, I really started taking this class just to meet people. If you're not busy, do you want to grab a drink or something? I'm not a weirdo, I promise. Or, well, maybe I am—I'll buy you a drink and you can decide."

Clarissa smiled despite herself. She liked how fast Rebecca talked, as well as her subtle accent, the familiar midwestern vowels and softened Chicago consonants. She liked the round O of her pink mouth.

Clarissa couldn't believe she had to go work a shift at the fucking bar right now.

"I'm actually working tonight," she said. "Bartending at Toby's, right around the corner? But we're pretty slow on

Wednesday nights, so . . . nothing is stopping you from coming and having a drink at *my* bar."

"Good, then." Rebecca smiled, revealing a row of pearly white teeth. "I'll buy a drink, and I'll tip well. It will only cost you your life story."

"Sounds fair." Clarissa shrugged, slightly taken aback at her forwardness, but happy all the same. "Follow me."

Rebecca had been born in the Chicago suburbs, she said, on a quiet, tree-lined street in Skokie, with a twin brother—and with a stutter, which her parents had tried to cure by enrolling her in theater camp. She had liked it more than she expected, becoming a troupe member at a corny but welcoming local children's theater called Xpress Yourself. She told Clarissa this over a slow sip of her gin and tonic, while Clarissa tried—and mostly failed—to also pay attention to her two other customers. There was a lot of foam on the heads of her draft pours that night, as she barely watched the tap and kept one eye trained on Rebecca as she talked animatedly.

"Anyway, I fell in love with acting. I minored in theater but majored in marketing and communications, and now I just do the occasional class to meet new people, to explore new types of performing," Rebecca said, setting her glass down on the old oak bar. "It's just a hobby for me. I got the sense it wasn't for most of the people there tonight—like, those two guys in the hoodies were *way* too intense with their opening monologues. Comedy guys, am I right?"

Clarissa laughed and nodded.

"You, though. I couldn't tell. Hobby or profession? I'm guessing profession, because you were good right away. But also that you love it so much you'd do it for fun no matter what. Am I right?"

"Not about my being good." Clarissa smirked. But then Rebecca looked right at her with her soft, sympathetic brown eyes, and Clarissa decided to drop the self-deprecating schtick for once. "I'm joking. You're right. The goal is for it to be a profession, but I love it. I'd do it no matter what. We'll see. Right now, I have yet to get paid for a gig, so I'm *actually* a bartender, it appears."

"A great bartender."

"You've got to be kidding. That's just a gin and tonic."

"You'd be surprised how much you can mess up the ratio on a gin and tonic. My company—I'm at a marketing firm, so it's lots of events and stuff—hired a bartender who made every drink three-quarters gin. I mean, people had an *extra*-good time, but still."

"You work in marketing?"

"You do *not* have to pretend to be interested in that."

"But I am." Clarissa thought she would have been interested in anything Rebecca said, no pretending required.

"It's the usual: Fun events interspersed with typical office politics. The culture is a blend of creative and corporate, and our campaigns skew young, which I like. But it's funny, I try to have my 'cool' advertising persona, but I'm really just your average lesbian theater dork underneath." She gave a goofy smile, and Clarissa tried to keep her cool as five-alarm fire bells rang in her head chiming *lesbian lesbian lesbian lesbian.*

"But that's enough about me. I came here to hear *your* life story."

So, Clarissa told her. Leaning on the bar, she recited her

basic biographic information: her childhood on the southwest side of Chicago, her stint in Catholic lower and middle schools before successfully lobbying for a transfer, her first community center play, what it had been like meeting her best friends at Northwestern, her desire to make it in comedy—and something about the attentive, patient way Rebecca listened made her want to be way more open than she usually was with people she didn't know. The only other exception had been the first party she went to with Rachel, Nate, and Dev, but *that* bonding had involved copious amounts of grain alcohol. Now Clarissa was totally sober, but something about the low light and the late hour made her feel drunk anyway. They were the last two left in the bar, and it was almost closing time, but for the first night since graduation, she didn't want to go home.

"I wanted to stay in Chicago for a lot of reasons, but now it feels kind of strange being here."

"Because Nate, Dev, and Rachel all moved to New York together?"

"Ah, so you really *were* paying attention. Ten points to Gryffindor."

"I'll have you know I'm a proud Ravenclaw," Rebecca said, and something inside Clarissa swooned again.

"I'm a Gryffindor."

"Hmm. I see that, I think." Rebecca nodded and took another sip of her drink. "But anyway: It feels weird without your friends here?"

"That, yeah. But also because I . . . well, I had a really fucking different life with my family than I did in college." She shrugged. "Now that I'm here, and I go home every other weekend, there's this weird dichotomy between being the good Polish daughter and being the . . . well, lesbian theater dork. As you put it."

"See, I just knew you were . . . a dork."

"Shut up." Clarissa laughed, but the alarm bells were ringing in her head again. Now Rebecca knew. Who she was, what she wanted. "I'm not out to my family."

A pause. Rebecca traced the rim of her glass. "Well, I'm twenty-seven, and I just told mine three years ago. They took it about how I expected. A little disappointed, maybe, but accepting. They're your typical white liberals. Like, my dad might say 'Now, see, I just don't get *that*' if he sees a trailer for *Brokeback Mountain*, but they also like to pride themselves on being the 'accepting' type. We're fine now. I have Shabbat dinner with them most Fridays, that kind of stuff. But I know how it feels to think there's a part of you that the people closest to you don't know, what it feels like to hold that inside of you."

Their eyes met, and Clarissa, for once, didn't feel like she had to say anything. She didn't have to crack a joke or make an aside. Then, suddenly, she couldn't stop herself, and she leaned across the bar, her nose just about to touch Rebecca's. She paused for a second, just in case she had read this wrong, but she hadn't, thank God, she hadn't. Rebecca moved the last inch toward her, and their lips met. The kiss felt soft and yet solid at the same time, a declaration of everything she already knew about herself and a celebration of it as well, a kiss as both a period and an exclamation point.

"Well, that's good to know," Clarissa said as they pulled back to grin at each other.

"What? That I'm—"

"That the class was worth my hundred dollars." She winked.

"Oh, I am worth way, way more than that," Rebecca flirted back, raising an eyebrow. "You'll see."

"God, I hope so," Clarissa said, and then they cleaned up and closed down the bar together, and when they reached the door Rebecca slipped a hand into hers. She somehow knew they would be going home together that night and many nights to come, as certainly as she knew her own name.

Clarissa paused her iPod. The plane had reached altitude; in an hour she would be in New York for Dev's book launch. He, their Dev, had published a book. Equal parts celebratory, impressed, and jealous, she could hardly believe it.

She flipped open her phone, and she found herself scrolling toward Rebecca's name without meaning to. *No*, she reminded herself. *No*. She was grateful, suddenly, for the lack of cell service above the clouds.

Clarissa and Rebecca had never *officially* moved in together. But by early summer of their first year together, Clarissa had brought her grandma's quilt and half her wardrobe over to Rebecca's one-bedroom apartment, a welcome respite from Clarissa's crowded sublet. Rachel stayed there with the two of them when she visited over the years, and Clarissa felt the distinct warmth of being surrounded by the two women she loved most. It had worried her, the months of Rebecca and Rachel existing in different spheres, knowing different parts of her. Once she had seen them together, it felt as if her life made just a little bit more sense.

That left only one problem: Clarissa still hadn't found a way to come out to her family.

She went back to her parents' house in Garfield Ridge every other Sunday after church, eating an hours-long lunch and laughing over Joey's antics, and each time she felt like she was regressing into an earlier iteration of herself. But what surprised her was that it didn't feel oppressive; instead, it felt shamefully *comfortable*. It felt like having a blanket tucked around your shoulders after you fell asleep on the couch, or like waking up to the smell of someone already cooking breakfast in the kitchen.

When she had been young, Clarissa had chafed to escape, to move on to bigger things, to find success. Now when she came home to the house, she remembered it as a simpler place, representative of a time in her life before sex or politics or work. Clarissa's childhood hadn't been idyllic—there had often been too little money, too much noise—and yet every time she imagined herself disrupting the idyll of the long, lazy Sunday afternoons she spent with her family, she found that she could not do it. Wasn't life hard enough? Wasn't there so much to fight for? Rebecca and Clarissa spent most of their Saturdays working with Rebecca's friends, registering voters in preparation for the '08 election, or volunteering with the Sex Workers Outreach Project, before she had to rush off to a shift at the bar or a spot at an open mic. Clarissa had nearly everything in common with this group of activist women, and little in common, personally or politically, with her family. And yet she didn't want to lose them as a quiet space away from the rest of the world, the only people who knew the girl she had been instead of the woman she had been trying to become.

Rebecca came to her parents' house once, for Easter dinner. Clarissa had introduced her as her roommate. Rebecca allowed this; she said she understood. Clarissa watched the woman she loved across the table all night, appreciating her full-bellied laugh at her dad's jokes, admiring the way she gamely sipped a Polish vodka.

She didn't know how long this delicate equilibrium would last, but she hoped it would until she could figure out what to do next.

Then two years went by.

L adies and gentlemen, we are beginning our initial descent into LaGuardia." The pilot announced. "Weather on the ground is sunny and seventy-two, a beautiful September day."

It was Saturday morning. Dev's book launch would be on Tuesday; Clarissa had envisioned it happening on a weekend, with a lavish book party, tuxedo-clad servers balancing champagne flutes on trays. But that only happened in movies, apparently; in reality, book launches always took place on Mondays or Tuesdays, at bookstores, and they consisted of an interview, a reading, and a signing. So, their group of four had made plans for a bigger celebration over the weekend instead. Despite how low she felt, Clarissa was genuinely excited, as well as a bit nervous. Rachel's last visit had been before Dev signed with his agent; she hadn't seen Nate or Dev for a year before that. She thought back to the week she had found out about Dev's book deal. It had seemed to mark a subtle turning point, for all of them, and Clarissa worried about what it meant.

"SO, DID YOU HEAR?" CLARISSA HAD WOKEN ONE MORNING to Rachel shouting into the phone the second she answered, her eyes not even open yet.

Clarissa yawned and propped herself up against the bed's headboard, an uncomfortable wrought iron thing Rebecca had picked out when she'd moved into a new apartment in Edgewater that winter. She glanced at the clock. "Rachel, it's seven thirty in the morning here, and I work nights. I don't hear a damn thing except a ringing in my ears. Can you talk quieter?"

"Sorry, I'm on my way to work. I forgot it was an hour earlier there."

"Yep, as always." Clarissa paused and gestured to Rebecca, a pantomime exchange over coffee, and Rebecca left the room to go work her mysterious magic with the French press. "Anyway, did I hear what?"

"About Dev's book deal, obviously."

"I did. He called last night. Or this morning? At 2 a.m., I might add, and so that's both of you trying to interrupt my sleep cycle. Some things never change."

"You miss it."

"I do. Anyway, it's amazing news. It'll be interesting to see

Dev try to adhere to actual publishing deadlines, but I assume Laurel can keep him on track."

"Imagine being Dev's agent. It's hard enough to get him to a dinner with his friends on time," Rachel said, and they both laughed.

It had been several months since Dev had signed with his agency, a move that had made the book deal feel inevitable. But Clarissa understood, probably better than the others, why Dev still hadn't known if it would happen. Lots of books got agented and then didn't sell, or else they sold, but not in very lucrative deals. It had been the same for her. An agent had given her his card at a talent-stacked open mic on the west side, but then she had failed to get cast in an HBO special, and then few other offers had come her way. Dev's book deal, though, had turned out to be the kind of thing most creatives only dreamt about. *Nirvana*—a sort of ridiculous title, but apparently the powers that be in publishing saw no problem with it—had sold at auction to Random House for a $300,000 advance. It was more money than she had ever imagined in her life.

"Did you hear how big the advance is?" Rachel asked. Clarissa furrowed her brow, surprised to hear Rachel bring up finances directly, since Clarissa knew she had been taught by her family that talking about salaries and money with friends was rude. (Easy for Rachel to say, she who didn't really need salary transparency to ensure that she was making a living wage, to know that she wasn't being shortchanged.)

"Yeah, he told me." A pause. "It's incredible for him," she added, and she meant it. When Dev had called and said the mind-boggling number out loud, "three hundred thousand,"

Clarissa had actually *shrieked* on the phone she had been so purely happy. At the same time, she had felt embarrassingly relieved to find out that she was the kind of person who was capable of being happy for him immediately, rather than insecure or jealous. When the book had gone to the auction stage a week before, she had looked herself dead in the eye in the mirror and given herself a pep talk. Like, "remember that this isn't a competition, that Dev making it means *you* can make it—not the opposite." She had chipped in $200 for her parents to fix their plumbing just the month before, even though she barely had any money herself. So, she really didn't know how she was going to feel about Dev's windfall until she heard the words come out of his mouth. Somehow, the moment he told her, all his wildest dreams come true, Clarissa had genuinely felt like it was happening to both of them. *Dev is my friend*, she thought, without even having to force it. *Anything good that happens to him is something I would want to happen, a thousand times over.*

"Who expected Dev to be the independently wealthy one at twenty-five?" Rachel said, ignoring, of course, that *she* had always been the wealthy one. Though not independently. *I'd take any kind of wealth, dependent or independent*, Clarissa had thought. People with wealthy families always liked to go on about how it wasn't really their money, but it was, it fucking was, wasn't it? She walked out to the kitchen table and sat down in front of the mug of coffee Rebecca had made for her, told herself to calm down, to focus.

"I guess life is funny like that," she offered.

"I mean, *I'm* still making 50K a year," Rachel continued. "It's kind of wild that Dev got that in just one day."

"Well, not one *day*," Clarissa said, raising her voice a little bit. She wanted to ask Rachel where the hell she got off. "He worked on the book for over a year. And he didn't have any connections; he just did it."

"I know he did. That's not what I meant." A pause. "But, well, he did have a connection, technically. I introduced him to Laurel's assistant, remember?"

Clarissa plunked her mug down on the table hard enough to splash coffee over the lip.

"Watch the table!" Rebecca hissed over her shoulder.

"You are not seriously trying to take credit for Dev getting a book deal," she said, a hard edge in her voice, harder than she usually used with Rachel. But if she had really woken Clarissa up to needle at Dev's success *and* somehow claim that it was unfair that he made six figures to her $50,000—never mind her *fucking trust fund*, her parents' house in East Hampton—then . . .

"No, I'm not!" Rachel cut off her train of thought. A siren wailed in the background, then receded. "I'm sorry. I'm so excited for Dev, I promise I am. It's just a tiny bit weird to see someone else break out when you feel kind of, I don't know, stuck. You know I've always wanted to write a book. And I know it's my fault that I haven't finished it yet, I know that, but I'm saying this to you because I would never say it to Dev. I'm happy for him, but there's just this . . . tiny 'but.' About how *I'm* ever going to figure out what to do next. Personally, professionally. I believe in myself, but there's still just this, this thing. This doubt? Anyway, I called you because I just thought *you* of all people might understand that."

Clarissa opened her mouth to respond, indignant, but then felt herself soften. Rachel wasn't wrong. She *did* understand what it felt like to watch other people find opportunities, advance their careers, build wealth and access it, while you felt like you were standing still. She didn't want to judge Rachel for naming that feeling, however absurd it might be, any more than she wanted Rachel to judge her for calling to vent about someone else scoring an audition she wanted, or to complain about some stupid fight she and Rebecca had gotten into. Rachel never, ever judged her for these things, which made her more willing to return the favor, whether or not it was deserved.

"I do understand," she said finally. "But I refuse to feel bad for you about your salary. It's more than I make—probably more than my dad makes, actually."

"Sorry, that's not what I meant." Rachel sounded sheepish. "Really. It's just more that I think it's time for me to figure out the next step, career-wise. So that I don't feel like this anymore, you know?"

"I know. I feel the same way."

The rest of their conversation had been comfortingly normal, but a part of Clarissa had still bristled at Rachel's response. Later, she recounted the conversation to Rebecca.

"It's interesting, you're . . . ," Rebecca had said when she finished explaining. Clarissa looked at Rebecca quizzically, her head cocked.

"I'm what?"

"Just . . . unusually tolerant of her, is all. From what I've seen."

"I don't think I am," Clarissa responded defensively, even while she knew that she did this, that she forgave Rachel more easily than she did other people, simply because she liked her so much. But she didn't want to admit it to Rebecca. "'Unusually'?"

Rebecca raised her eyebrows. "Unusual for *you*, yes. You once gave a five-minute lecture about the evils of capitalism in a comedy class because someone made the mistake of saying they liked Starbucks. Also, Facebook."

"That's different. Facebook is evil and monopolistic, I'm telling you. Just watch."

Rebecca rolled her eyes, but she was smiling. "I'm saying that you are not the type of person who . . . you know, lets clueless remarks go by."

"I don't know." She shrugged. She wondered why Rebecca suddenly seemed so animated, why she cared so much. "Rachel's comments bother me sometimes, too, and I *have* called them out. You just haven't seen it. Also, we should try to be forgiving when someone's intentions are good, right? I know hers are."

"Okay." Rebecca nodded and kissed her on the cheek. "Oh-kay."

They sat in silence for a minute.

"Clarissa?"

"Yes?"

"It would be okay if you were jealous, you know. You can be happy for him, too; you can be both at the same time."

Was a part of her jealous? Of Dev? Of Rachel? Yes. Was she inspired? Happy? Incredulous? Certainly, she thought. She was all those things.

"I love you," she told Rebecca, leaning her head on her shoulder.

"I love you, too, baby. I love you, too."

THE PLANE LANDED AT LAGUARDIA, ON SCHEDULE. CLARISSA collected her luggage and then began the slow journey from the bus to the F train to Rachel's apartment near the West Fourth Street stop. She paused to collect herself in the hallway outside the apartment, listening to the roar of her friends' laughter through the door. She mustered her excitement, her best celebratory spirit. The details of her life could wait; this moment was for Dev. But before she could knock, she was overwhelmed with thoughts about what had happened just before she left.

About Dawn. About Rebecca.

A MONTH BEFORE THE TRIP, CLARISSA HAD THOUGHT THAT maybe, finally, something good was about to happen to her: She received a personal invitation from Dawn Leiter to audition at Second City.

One night, Clarissa came home late from a shift at Toby's to find Rebecca waiting up for her, a rarity.

As soon as she had closed the door, Rebecca blurted, "Guess who I ran into today?"

"Who?"

"Dawn."

"I've been meaning to email her, actually." Clarissa knew she needed to follow up with people she met, that connections were the key to the industry.

"Well, you should, because she said they're holding general auditions this month at Second City. For new talent. Understudies for the current corps, with the opportunity for it to become full-time. She wants you to audition. You, specifically. She said she had been trying to get ahold of you, but her emails are bouncing back."

Clarissa felt a unique pressure in her chest, but the kind from excitement, not anxiety. It occurred to her that maybe that was what people meant by the term *heart swelling*, which had always seemed hokey and imprecise to her before. "She said she wants me? Specifically?"

"Yes. You fit all the criteria anyway—you have to graduate from an improv or sketch program at one of the theaters, have performance experience. But yes, she said she thought that you, specifically, would be a great fit. And you would."

It's happening, she thought. *It is maybe, really, actually happening.*

"Holy shit." She threw her arms around Rebecca. "I can't believe it."

"Well, I can. Here's her number," Rebecca said, kissing her, then smiling happily. Clarissa had once wondered if things would ever become competitive between the two of them, but it turned out that what Rebecca had said the night they met was true: She really had taken the improv class on a whim, for fun. She had recently signed up for Intro to Pottery.

"I'll call tomorrow," she said, and then she rushed to the phone to call her friends in New York.

The audition fell on a Friday, three weeks before Dev's launch, her slot at 6 p.m. Clarissa had to bribe Rosa to trade shifts with her. Rosa, forty years old and with twenty-five years of bar experience, was not keen on picking up weekend shifts, and Clarissa had had to tempt her by offering up three shift covers for her one. But never mind, it would be worth it, she told herself as she walked up the steps and out through the black velvet curtains onto the stage at Second City. She introduced herself to the audition panel, which consisted of Dawn Leiter and three strangers, which made her unreasonably nervous. She drew in a deep breath and held it, like she was about to submerge herself in a lake, and then dove into her ten-minute opening routine.

She hit her first joke quickly, a reliable bit about taking her Polish parents to Whole Foods for the first time, when the Lincoln Park location had opened in the '90s. She paused a beat: no laughter. Maybe they didn't laugh during these kinds of auditions, maybe it was bad form. But shouldn't they encourage her? Clarissa tried not to look directly at the directors to gauge their reaction, instead confidently casting her eyes back up over their heads to the rows of empty seats.

She launched into her next section, pivoting away from the cultural material about her family—maybe they didn't like that, too niche—into some jokes about having missed everything good about Gen X but still having based her personality on *Reality Bites*. But she felt that her reeling thoughts had caused her to pause a moment too long, to break tempo. She pressed forward, but the room stayed silent, so she couldn't tell if she was doing well or not. All the guaranteed laughs from her open mic crowds landed with a thud. She hadn't known how dependent she had become on crowd feedback, didn't realize how poorly she performed when all she had in the room was a video camera or a judgmental casting director looking at her. Now she realized with a sinking feeling in her chest that her nerves were causing her to speak too quickly, and she had a terrifying image of a car in neutral sliding uncontrollably away from her down a hill with nothing to be done to stop it. The spotlight shone in her eyes, and the faces in front of her stayed grim, impassive. She had completely lost control.

She wrapped up her last bit with heat burning her cheeks, her heart deflating like a balloon inside her chest. She knew it already: She had bombed.

"Thank you, Clarissa," Dawn said after a beat, wearing the kind of half smile that looked like an apology. "We'll be in touch."

No mention of the next part of the audition process. She just nodded like a fool and darted out, stage left.

Exeunt Clarissa. Forever.

She knew that when she got home Rebecca would try to convince her it hadn't gone as poorly as she thought. "It could be all in your head, babe, you're so hard on yourself," she would say. Clarissa shuddered at the thought. She could not, did not, know how to convince Rebecca that she knew with certainty that everyone in that room had felt her discomfort, her awkwardness, and there would be no coming back from it. Second City did not give second chances. Three years of plugging away with nothing to show for it.

They never called. Rebecca feigned surprise and outrage, Clarissa kept her job at the bar, picked up all the extra shifts to appease Rosa, and waited for the sting of embarrassment to subside.

She tried to comfort herself with the knowledge that she still had Rebecca. She imagined the love between them as an ever-expanding thing, something that would grow in importance while her failures shrank in the rearview mirror. But as it turned out, their relationship would soon become another failure for Clarissa to add to her tally.

A week after the failed audition, Rebecca had invited her over to her parents' house in Skokie for dinner. The invitation had felt like a match sparking somewhere inside her. She liked carrying this flame around, this glowing proof of how Rebecca felt about her, and so she had almost understood Rebecca's point of view about what happened next.

"You know, I think maybe it's finally time I meet your family. For real," Rebecca had said on the train ride back downtown after dinner, lacing her fingers together with Clarissa's. "Do you think we could start planning that? We've been basically living together for years, Clarissa. This is getting ridiculous."

"You've met them," Clarissa had reminded her, being deliberately obtuse, because she did not like where this was going, even if it did seem strange that they had made it this deep into their relationship without her family becoming a major problem.

"I'm not trying to rush you," Rebecca said, and Clarissa knew this both was and was not the truth. Rebecca would never push her to come out to everyone before she was ready. She knew and loved and supported Clarissa in everything, just as she was. But at the same time, there was always this, this *thing* there between them. It was there when Rebecca spoke to her parents on the phone every Sunday, always giving them an update on Clarissa. It was there when they celebrated Rebecca's thirtieth birthday, a nagging reminder that she was a full five years older, that she might be ready for things that Clarissa was not. Suddenly, it was a wedge between them that had become tangible. And then, finally, there it was, in the near-empty train car on that late night, after they had just spent a wonderful evening with Rebecca's family. It was natural that Rebecca would wonder—would hope—that she could be part of Clarissa's family in return.

"You don't get it," Clarissa had said. "It's different. Your parents are Reform. Your mom went to Wellesley, for God's sake. My parents are not all-aboard-the-liberal-arts-school-lesbian-express. They think differently about this stuff." Clarissa hadn't wanted to reinforce the stereotype that coming out played different for a lot of immigrant parents, that they sometimes saw being gay as something "Americans" did, something that wasn't necessarily horrific but that just wasn't a part of "their" culture. But in her case, it was true. Her dad had once responded to seeing two men holding hands on Lawrence Avenue by muttering "American nonsense" in Polish.

"You'll never know what they think if you don't try talking to them about it."

"I don't think it's fair for you to ask me to risk my relationship with them."

Rebecca had let it go, but from then on, it had seemed like only a matter of time. Like a ticking bomb had dropped into the center of their relationship, threatening to detonate at any moment.

Clarissa had tried. She really had! She started imagining what it would be like to finally come out to her family, imagining speaking up over a plate of bigos some Sunday dinner, as they all talked over one another. She tried to steel herself, to stop caring about what they thought of her, to leverage the attitude she used with basically everyone else. "Who cares?" she practiced saying in the mirror when Rebecca was at work. "I hope you can accept this and be in my life, but if not, you can leave it. The choice is yours." But then she would imagine what it would be like to not be there to send Joey off on his first day of school. To not taste her grandma's signature gingerbread at Christmas. As someone who prided herself on being so outspoken, she didn't know how and why she continued to lose her nerve.

"So, you're really saying you don't think you can tell them . . . ever?" Rebecca had finally asked, just weeks before Clarissa had been set to fly out to New York for the launch. "Tell me honestly: Can you see me ever being invited to holidays? Being a part of things, with them?"

"Of course!"

"As your *girlfriend*, Clarissa. Not a friend. Definitely not a roommate. Your girlfriend. Your partner."

"Look, this is my private life, isn't it?" Clarissa had tried to reason, tears already welling up in the corners of her eyes, knowing already that everything was lost. "I don't talk to my parents about dating. It's not like I'm lying outright and telling them I'm going out with guys or something. We just. Do not. Talk about it. Can't that be enough?"

It had not, it turned out, been enough. When Clarissa

returned from New York, she would go back to her old sublet, alone, and haunt it like a ghost. Every time she pictured herself coming home—no Rebecca waiting for her with a tea, no nook to snuggle into as she fell asleep—it felt like a fucking knife in her heart. It made her want to pick up a phone and call her family now, today, to shout, "I'm gay!" and hang up, and then to call Rebecca not even five seconds later and tell her she had done it, that they could be together now. But a tiny, nagging voice inside her told her it wouldn't be enough. While her coming out had been the focal point of their troubles, the lightning rod that drew the activity, their breakup wasn't only about her parents. It was about Rebecca being in her thirties, at a stable place in her career, a de facto aunt to her friends' kids, while Clarissa was still bartending late-night shifts and struggling for a career in "the arts" that might never come. That was the part she didn't know how to fix. It stung, not knowing how to fix something with someone she loved so much. She kept waiting not to feel so wounded, but she suspected it might take a long time.

———

Now here she was, at last. With people who still loved her, if not the way Rebecca loved her, but it had to count for something. Clarissa took a deep breath and finally swung open the door to Rachel's apartment.

The instant they saw her, Rachel squealed and popped a bottle of champagne.

"I can't believe it. We're here!" Rachel shouted, rushing over to embrace Clarissa. She flushed with happiness, suddenly; that really *was* how it felt, Clarissa thought. Even though the rest of them lived in New York, now it felt like *they* were here. Not "you're here"—"*we're* here." That was the perfect way to put it.

"You know I couldn't miss the last weekend before Dev starts acting like a pompous asshole because he's a published author." Clarissa forced a joke, plopping down on the couch and grabbing a champagne flute off the coffee table. Hopefully the alcohol could help her access the appropriately festive spirit.

"It is far, far too late for that," Rachel said.

"Oh, you know me, I was born like this." Dev winked. He grabbed a champagne flute and then slung his arm around Clarissa. "We missed you, Clare."

"Careful with the flutes!" Rachel said, filling the last two for her and Nate. "Limited edition from Williams-Sonoma."

Clarissa stifled a laugh. Rachel had to be the only twenty-something she knew with a set of eight champagne flutes. She raised an eyebrow at Dev, and he shook his head, confirming that no, Rachel had not changed, either.

"We have so much to catch up on," Rachel gushed. Then she raised her glass in the air. "But first: To Dev. Congratulations. To your fantastic first book—but, to paraphrase you here, may it be the worst book you write for the rest of your career."

"I like how you actually believe I'll be able to do this a second time."

"Didn't you say your agent already wants to see the start of the next project or something?" Nate asked.

"Still, though."

"Really, congratulations, Dev," Clarissa echoed. The swarm

of their voices threatened to overwhelm her; she willed herself not to tear up. "We will love you even when you become more insufferable than you are right now."

Then she paused for just a moment and looked around at the faces of her three friends. Rachel beamed, a smile spreading across her heart-shaped face, and she seemed genuinely thrilled. Perhaps Clarissa had judged her too harshly on the day they found out about Dev's deal. Dev's smile was still bright and charmingly intoxicating, but his face looked more angular, and he had buzzed his hair short, shorn closer to his head than her own pixie cut. It looked good on him, but he also looked harder, somehow. Clarissa felt the weight of the years since they'd seen each other in person. Finally, she looked at Nate. He appeared reasonably happy but a bit puffy and pale, a side effect of late nights or perhaps a joint he'd smoked earlier in the day, as Clarissa knew this was one of his rare Saturdays away from the office. She felt the distance from Nate most keenly; she wondered where a conversation between just the two of them, alone, might lead. She knew he probably wouldn't be keen on her stance on the bank bailout, for one.

But maybe that didn't matter quite yet. They had a whole day of absolutely nothing ahead of them other than to celebrate Dev's good fortune. They raised their glasses to cheers. They talked about Dev's book, debating whether the ending to it was "happy." They made mindless conversation about his parents' visit for the launch, which acquaintances of theirs might show up, who they wanted to see, who they didn't. Then, when the alcohol in the apartment had been finished, Clarissa looked at the setting sun streaming in through the western window and remembered that there was a whole world of Manhattan outside, waiting just for them in the twilight.

She would tell everyone what had happened with Rebecca later, she decided. Tomorrow, even. The evening stretched ahead, the night wide-open, and Clarissa willed herself to be optimistic.

Two hours later, the four of them squeezed together around a wooden high-top table at a nearby sports bar, a nearly drained plastic pitcher of beer between them. They occasionally shouted jokes and observations over the din, but they were mostly trying to drink enough at the low-priced dive that they could continue to a club where Nate and Rachel had reserved a table for the "official" celebration. Clarissa's face flushed, her cheeks hot. She didn't usually drink this much.

"Rebecca and I broke up," she heard herself blurt out, apropos of nothing. She clapped a hand over her mouth, because apparently she couldn't trust her brain to control what came out of it anymore. *Well, fuck.*

"Oh my God, Clarissa." Rachel gasped. "I'm so sorry. Why didn't you say anything?"

"To avoid what is happening literally right now." She felt Rachel drape an arm around her, saw Dev and Nate looking at her with a pitying expression, maybe slightly uncomfortable. It was exactly what she didn't want today to be, even though mere moments ago she had thought she absolutely needed someone to ask her what was wrong.

"Are you okay?" Dev asked.

"Generally, yes." She stared down at the table. "That's a lie. No, I'm not. But what I do know is that I do not want to take over Dev's weekend with this."

"I don't care about that," Dev said. "What happened?"

"Maybe she's not ready to talk about it."

"What?"

"Can we get out of here? It's so fucking loud."

"Yeah, let's get out of here."

"Let's talk on the walk to the club."

Their words swirled around her, and Clarissa felt like she was receding into the background, fading away like a film dissolve. They walked out onto Greenwich Avenue, and the noise of the city—the chaos on the sidewalk, the honking taxi horns—felt like it couldn't even touch her. Clarissa had comforted her friends after their own breakups. She had read about heartbreak, acted it out in plays, pantomimed it. But the way it felt had still come as a complete shock. It was as if there were a thick barrier, like the kind at the bank in her old neighborhood, separating her from the sights and sounds of the world at all times. She felt like she was literally trapped behind plexiglass, numbed, disconnected.

"So." Rachel finally spoke. "Do you want to tell us about it?"

"Okay." She nodded, forcing herself to acknowledge how good it felt to have someone ask who really wanted to know. "But only for as long as it takes to get to the next spot. I'll tell you, and you can say you're sorry and I'll get over it, and that's it. Then this is over, and it's time to get drunk."

"That we can do," Nate said. Rachel linked an arm with hers, and she started talking. She told them the whole story, finishing only as they approached the red-velvet-roped line of the Jane.

"I'm going to come out," she said. "To my family."

"When you're ready." Rachel put an arm around her.

"No," Clarissa said, loud and forceful, and she couldn't tell if it was the alcohol making her brave, or her friends, or both, but somehow, it didn't matter. Something shifted inside her, a weight. "No, as soon as I get back. I've been recording some YouTube videos, putting bits of my comedy on there. You know, like that guy Tyler Oakley? Have you heard of him? He started making YouTube videos a couple of years ago to keep in touch with his friends, and they went viral? Now he gets money, and advertising deals, and everything."

She heard herself slur a bit, rambling. Her friends did not know any YouTubers, as it turned out, but they made supportive noises. Nate handed a bill to a bouncer, and a rope rose in front of them, by magic.

"Let's dance," Rachel said, grabbing her right hand, and Nate put a glass of champagne into her left. "To Dev," they all exclaimed again, and then Clarissa let herself be swept up and away by the music, the room, the money. It felt good not to fight so hard, just for a moment.

When Clarissa arrived home in Chicago, she did it. She recorded the video at her desk in her apartment, her room in the pitiful share house in Uptown, lonely without Rebecca. When the editing was finally done, she watched her finger hover above the mouse, the cursor floating above the "post" button in suspended animation. She had never understood why people would describe a pause as *pregnant* before, but she thought maybe she did now: This moment held potential, potential in the sense of birthing the next phase of her life.

Was she ready?

Before she could change her mind again, she clicked. She watched the upload bar chug along, bringing the video to life. The video in which she, Clarissa Novak, came out—not just to her friends, or even to her family, but to the world.

Clarissa stood up from her desk, slid on her backpack, and walked away. She would not watch for comments. She would not monitor the views, of which there had been steadily more of late. She decided that she would go to work, pull what would hopefully be one of her final pints at Toby's—God, four years there, three years and six months too long—and worry about it later.

She had titled the video "My Coming Out Story" and posted it to her YouTube channel, where she had about a thousand subscribers. She knew not to expect much attention: Her subscribers were mostly friends or friends of friends from the comedy scene, people who had only ever known Clarissa as out and proud. But still: Having her real self out there in the world, publicly, somewhere it could live eternally, or at least as long as the internet might live, which felt eternal? It made her feel something.

The video was ten minutes long, a wholly earnest confessional where she spoke directly to the camera. It was completely different from the typical comedy bits she shared on YouTube, and she wondered for a moment if it might be too embarrassing. But she had promised her friends, and she knew they would be proud of her.

Did she hope Rebecca might see it, too? Of course she did. She knew it would not magically fix the issues between them, nor bring them back together, but she still felt an odd cosmic debt, like she owed the first woman she had truly loved what she should have given her while they were still together.

Clarissa swung open the door to Toby's, ducked under the opening to the bar, and plastered on a smile.

"Hey, doll." She smiled brightly at the woman on the first bar stool, who had her dark hair in a pixie cut, late thirties maybe, but cute, *very* cute, actually, with a small sparkling stud in her upturned nose. "What can I get you?"

"Another gin and tonic, and a water." She sucked down the last of her remaining drink and flicked her hazel eyes up at Clarissa. "And if I'm lucky, your phone number?"

"I think that can be arranged," she flirted back.

Maybe it would be Clarissa's lucky day after all.

HIGH ON HAVING SECURED A DATE FROM A REAL-LIFE CHANCE encounter and from an easy shift at the bar, Clarissa stayed out all night for the first time since Dev's weekend in New York.

Toby's closed down at midnight on weekdays. Instead of throwing her mops and hurrying out the door, she turned to Ang, the new bartender and her new friend, and said, "So what are we doing tonight?" The answer turned out to be an all-night rave in Boystown, and after dancing herself clean to a mix of

Whitney Houston and electronic beats, she found herself back at a rambling railroad apartment in Ravenswood belonging to Ang's friends, who were twenty-three, sculpted like Roman warriors, and in possession of a good deal of cocaine and not much clothing. She politely declined a coffee table line, but she felt a contact high from being around it, from being part of passionate, rambling debates about the Obama administration to dancing on a couch until 6 a.m. and then, finally, sleeping on that same sofa.

She woke three hours later with a pit in her stomach and a throbbing headache. She left a note signed with *x*'s and *o*'s and let herself out without waking Ang or his friends, who were probably passed out in a tangle of limbs in one of the beds, which made her smile. She didn't go out with young gay guys, well, ever, and the ache in her neck reminded her of why as she padded out into the harsh sunlight on Damen Avenue. Still, it had made for the ideal celebration that night, the perfect antidote before she went back to her regular life of coffee shops and improv nights and editing videos and trying to, at last, eke out a living without Toby's—not that abandoning a steady gig while the economy still reeled from the worst recession in a generation seemed like a brilliant idea.

She turned her key in the lock and stepped into her apartment, eager for a real sleep in her bed and then a coffee the size of her head. She plugged her phone in at her bedside table—it had died while she was out dancing, another thing that hadn't happened to her in years—and watched it spring to life. Before she could climb under her quilt, the dinging started. Her phone buzzed and chimed, message after message, too much to deal with in her hungover state. She opened just one, from Rachel.

"Clarissa. Oh my God. I'm so proud of you!!"

"Are you seeing this? Where are you? Get online IMME-DIATELY."

Her heart beat harder. Almost afraid to look, she went to her desk, wiggled her computer mouse, and checked her YouTube. Her video had forty-five thousand views.

Clarissa had gone viral.

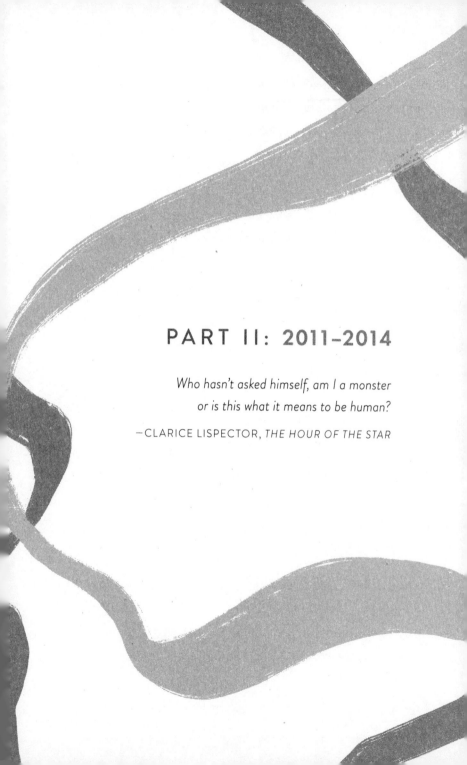

PART II: 2011–2014

*Who hasn't asked himself, am I a monster
or is this what it means to be human?*

—CLARICE LISPECTOR, *THE HOUR OF THE STAR*

RACHEL

As a lingerie-clad contortionist swung from the trapeze above her head, Rachel squinted at her watch in the dim light and wondered how much later she had to stay to seem relevant. She had the distinct thought that everything, no matter how purportedly unique or even debauched, had started to feel ordinary.

It didn't make any sense to her, this feeling. She was at a bar crossed with a burlesque club crossed with something far raunchier than that—something that, if it didn't shock the most jaded New Yorkers, it at least caused them to whisper to the person seated next to them. The Box had opened in a former vaudeville theater from the turn of the century, and it was considered "the place to be." But Rachel did not feel the celebratory zip in her veins that she usually experienced when she felt lucky to be somewhere, nor did she feel the urge to dance when Isabelle stood up on the velvet banquette to gyrate a bit nearer to

Leonardo DiCaprio, who was seated in the booth next to theirs. She was half dancing to the Avicii beat, half watching the show, overcome by a strange sense of ennui, a fatigue, as if she could fall asleep at any moment. Someone puffed an illicit cigarette and smoke hung lazily in the air, giving the room a hazy, dreamlike quality. Something about the scene reminded Rachel of the set of an opium den she had seen in a movie or on a TV show. She looked around and noticed that all the women in the club looked younger than her. She had never expected twenty-six to feel old.

She took a last swallow of champagne, set down her glass, and walked out without saying goodbye. The humidity hit her as she stepped out onto Christie Street, hot exhaust mingling with the steam heat rising off the sidewalk, even at 3 a.m. sweat dripped from her arm as she raised her hand to flag a cab. Three passed her, full. Rachel thought of the truth of the phrase *concrete jungle* to capture the essence of the city, its searing heat, its animal indifference.

She remembered another summer night, more than four years ago, when she, Dev, Nate, and Clarissa stood on the roof of their old house, the day of their graduation.

Where will you be in four years?

It had been five years since they graduated, and Rachel's unfinished novel—all one hundred printed pages of it—had sat in a drawer in her desk for months.

My first novel will be coming out in the spring.

In contrast, two hardcover copies of Dev's novel sat on her shelf. Lately, every time she logged on to Facebook, one of her acquaintances seemed to announce a book deal, or an engagement, or a series A, and she had to force herself to type some meaningless comment of congratulations.

But Rachel did have one thing, at last: an acceptance to an MFA program at the University of Michigan. Three rejections, one acceptance. It was less than she had hoped for, but it was not nothing.

WHEN RACHEL HAD ACCEPTED THE ASSISTANT EDITOR POSI-tion at *New York* more than three years before, she'd had no idea how much her days would change as a result. Gone were the late nights on the Fact Department floor—and so were the late mornings she'd enjoyed as a result. She often wrote or edited three short pieces each day, at first for the front-of-book sections, and then, increasingly, for *The Cut*, the magazine's online property devoted primarily to fashion and popular culture. The pace of people's internet consumption had sped up, necessitating ever more content to meet its demands—which in turn seemed to make everyone scroll faster, a feedback loop that just kept accelerating. Rachel sometimes felt like she and her fellow journalists were feeding the gaping maw of a beast she couldn't quite see or understand.

She adapted: She edited on a tighter turnaround; she learned how to position stories for different properties, different audiences. She was proud of her work, producing interesting stories from a feminist critique of school dress codes to a fun retrospective on *Sex and the City*. But none of it was particularly groundbreaking, and the volume of writing and editing that she did at work left her with less time and energy for her own projects. Stalled on the novel, she turned her attention to writing short stories, eager to produce some fiction, to prove to herself that she still could. By early 2011, she had several stories to her name. As rumors began to swirl about *New York*'s declining subscription numbers, as the tides of the magazine industry began to shift, it was with those stories that Rachel would finally assemble a portfolio and apply for her MFA.

Clarissa whooped on the phone when Rachel told her about Michigan, promising to take the train from Chicago to Ann Arbor often, something she could newly afford after the success of her YouTube channel, spurred by the following she'd gained as a result of that first video from nearly a year before. Dev had told Rachel that she didn't need to go back to school—he had become a card-carrying member of the anti-MFA debate, probably because he didn't have one—but he took her out for a group dinner and toasted her anyway. And Nate? He'd been absent more often lately, out with his colleagues, slow to answer his phone, but he had texted her congratulations and promised they'd get together soon.

Now Rachel just had to decide if she was going to say yes to U of M. What would it mean, to leave New York? To start over? And why, a small voice inside her kept asking, did she need to go to school for two years to write a book when Dev had been able to do it all by himself?

There was no answer to this question that didn't make her dizzy, sick with her own insecurity. She simply had to make a choice.

ON A GRAY, HUMID AFTERNOON THREATENING RAIN, RACHEL finally found herself sitting across from Nate at brunch in Tribeca, recounting all this. It had been a long time since they'd met for a workday lunch, a tradition that had slipped without her notice.

"I hate to be so 'goodbye to all that,'" she said, taking a long sip of her mimosa while Nate watched her attentively. "Am I done with New York? It's my home; part of me can't imagine leaving again. But is it wrong to need to leave for a little while? Is it normal to be this . . . bored?"

"What's 'goodbye to all that'?"

"Never mind."

Nate shrugged. "I think this is just what they call a quarter-life crisis, Rach. Which, I feel you. My work is shit."

Rachel nodded and thought, gratefully, that at least she didn't work in finance. The economy was still in the can; protesters were occupying Wall Street. The Nates of the world were at least partially at fault, that much seemed clear, but Rachel also knew how stressful it was for him, how uncertain his life felt years into what they were now calling the Great Recession. She imagined it was why they hadn't seen so much of him lately, why he surfaced primarily through 2 a.m. drunken texts and the occasional promise to "go get brunch." She wondered whom he was spending his time with. She knew it wasn't Dev and it definitely hadn't been her.

The server set two plates down in front of them. Spinach and

Gruyère omelet for her, eggs Benedict for him. The same thing they ordered everywhere.

"Can I get another mimosa?" Nate asked, mid-bite. He turned back to Rachel. "Anyway, what do you want to do about it? This quarter-life crisis. Buy a new Chanel bag?"

"That's rude."

"Just trying to think of the female equivalent of a sports car." A pause. "Is this about Dev's book?"

"No, of course not," she said, except that it sort of *was* about Dev's book, as much as she didn't want to admit it. It had come out in the fall of 2010, a "lead title," and it had done amazingly well critically. The sales had been a little less impressive, but Dev had left his job at the restaurant, and he had been hard at work on his next novel, though he had yet to show her any pages. He, their Dev, was an actual author. An artist, the way they had once talked about being back at Northwestern. But to say that this was "about" Dev didn't seem fair because it was "about" a lot of other things, too. Her uncertainty about the future of the magazine; her fear that if she allowed herself even just a few more years of nine-to-five stability, she'd never leave.

"What am I going to do about it? I'm going to say yes to U of M. I'm going to get my MFA and finish my novel." Rachel believed in manifestation; she had willed the acceptance into reality, and now she simply needed to do the same for the book.

"Well, there you go. Look at that—this problem was fixable in the time it took to consume one order of eggs Benedict. Can I trade my problems for yours?"

Rachel felt a twinge in her chest, a slight sting. Her favorite Nate was the one with the secret soft side, the friend who would watch *The Bachelor* and pick up her favorite snacks just because, the midwesterner with an occasional cluelessness about which shoes went with which types of pants. But then there was the other part, the finance bro who bought into the labels, who had told Clarissa she was "naïve" about the bank bailout, the one who took his own thoughts and struggles more seriously than anyone else's. But maybe he just needed someone to care.

"Nate, I should say—if you actually really need anything, or other job search connections, or—"

He waved a hand. "No, come on, I'm just complaining. I don't actually need any help."

This stopped the conversation effectively for a few minutes, but only until their server brought over a fresh round of drinks.

"On the house," she said, looking directly at Nate. Flirting. "Because the entrées were slow to come out."

Rachel started to say, "That's not necessary," as Nate blurted, "Thank you so much," and they all laughed, and the server did indeed leave them the free drinks. Nate had already burned through three to her one, and she wondered if this was something she should mention.

"See?" Nate said. "Who says we're not lucky? What more do we need?"

I'm lucky, she repeated in her head. *What more do I need?*

THE NEXT WEEKEND, RACHEL TOOK A CAB TO THE UPPER EAST Side for Shabbat dinner with her parents, like she had done every Friday of her life except during her four years at Northwestern. She would miss that, in Michigan. She couldn't wait to tell them: She had decided to accept. She would become Rachel Bergen, master of fine arts.

As the elevator doors opened to her parents' apartment on the twelfth floor, she noticed new details in their entryway: two porcelain vases emblazoned with the signature Dutch delft blue on the foyer console table, along with a hefty decorative book on Vermeer. Had her mom gone to the Netherlands, or just to Sotheby's? It didn't make much of a difference, but it did make her realize, with an anticipation that seemed to physically zip up her spine, that this wasn't her home anymore. One day, she was going to create her own.

She walked through the formal living room and into the dining room, surprised to find her parents and her brother already seated, silent.

"Am I late?" she asked. "I swear I left on time." She sat down in her chair. "Also, Mom. The new Dutch pottery stuff? Where's that from?"

"Rachel," her father said. "Honey. I'm sorry, but we got some news today, and we need to talk about it."

Somehow, she knew it right then. Her heart sank. As in, her insides felt so hollow that it seemed like her heart might really plummet out of her rib cage. She knew. This would not be the night she imagined. Everything—in one flash of a moment—was going to change. It would happen as soon as the words hit her ears, and a part of her almost thought about standing up and walking out, as if by refusing to hear what she already knew, she could make it untrue, roll back the tape and stop time. But, of course, she could not do that. She feigned normality; she made herself ask.

"What? Why are you all acting weird?"

"Well." Her mother spoke, staring down at her plate. "I had a routine scan the other day. A checkup, you know, as they do. But this time, well . . . unfortunately, it looks like the cancer might be back."

"Might? So, they don't know yet, or—"

"No, they know," her father said. "We will obviously get multiple opinions, but yes, it is back."

"Max, we don't need to alarm—"

"It's not an alarm, it's the facts," her brother jumped in. "Why are you always trying to protect Rachel from the truth?"

"No one is doing that." Her mother shot him a stern look. "We don't have all of the information yet. I told your father that we should let everyone know I'll likely be undergoing treatment again, and that will affect some things. But this is not something we need to panic about."

"Are you okay?" Rachel asked, tears welling in her eyes. *No. It couldn't be back. Her mother had beaten it. They had caught it early the first time; the outlook had been so good.*

"For right now, I'm fine." Her mother said this directly across the table, looking at her husband instead of her children.

"We will get the best doctors." Her father nodded. "No question about that."

They were all silent. She knew she needed to ask more questions, to find out where they thought the cancer had spread, what they wanted to do. But suddenly she couldn't speak, her chest tight like the time she had fallen flat on her back while Rollerblading as a child and gotten the wind knocked out of her. She flashed back to the stark, sterile walls of the hospital. The visiting hours. The pain of going back and forth from New York to Northwestern, trying to live one life as a carefree college sophomore and one as a girl who was terrified her mother was going to die. But she hadn't died. She hadn't. This time would be the same. She would beat it again. Right?

It's back.

Treatment again.

We will get the best doctors.

But. But what if?

Rachel thought about a lot of things as she sat there, quiet, wondering what to say. But the main thing that came back to her was a conversation she had with her mom three, maybe four years ago.

After graduating from college, the world had felt so wide, so open to her, like she might still do anything. That feeling had been dazzling, a kind of all-encompassing wonder. It made her feel like she had on the morning of her thirteenth birthday. But that's when she had realized: She still felt like a kid.

"Mom," she had asked, "when did you finally feel like a grown-up?"

"When I stopped using the term *grown-up*?" She smirked. She had been arranging flowers on the kitchen island, calla lilies. Rachel did not know why she remembered this.

"No, seriously, Mom. I thought it would happen as soon as I graduated and got a job, but it didn't. When did you really feel like an adult?"

Her mom paused, and she seemed to really be thinking about it. She tilted her head, her sleek brown hair—it had grown back so thick, so strong after the chemo the first time—flowing down over her shoulder. God, she had looked so beautiful then.

"Well, to be honest, I think probably when I had you."

"Oh no. Really? So not until you were thirty-two?"

"Shh. You know we don't say ages here," her mom mock-scolded, and then she laughed. Rachel's mom had not only forbade saying her present age, but she had banned saying the age she *had been* during important life milestones in case anyone bothered to do the math and calculate how old that would make her now. By now it was a joke between the two of them. Her mom had such a sparkling-sounding laugh, effervescent, bubbles in your mouth after the first sip of champagne.

"So, I won't feel like an adult until I have kids?" Rachel asked, concerned.

"Maybe, maybe not," her mom had said. Then, in a surprising display of affection, she wrapped her arms around Rachel, draping herself over her shoulders. "But even then, you'll still be my baby."

"Ugh, Mom." She had wriggled free, she remembered, even though she liked the hug. But she was in her early twenties, and resisting cloying parental sentimentality seemed like the thing to do. But then she had added something else, too: "Okay, but really. What if I never have kids? Or what if I do but still never feel like an adult? Can I still, like, call you to tell me how to fill in a check when I'm thirty-five?" She was joking, but with the tiniest grain of truth behind it. She wondered about the answer: It would be equally like her mom to tell her to buck up, that she was already an adult, or to indulge her in her concern completely. It could go either way.

"I really don't think you'll need my help for those kinds of things by then." She had smiled and walked back to her flowers. "But I promise I will be around for as long as you need a mother."

Rachel could only hope it would be true.

But how could she leave her now? She pictured herself saying it: "Mom, I'm moving to Michigan."

She could not say it. Not now. Maybe never.

Her mother's treatment started that very week. Sloan Kettering, the best in the country, where she had been treated the first time. Only five blocks from their apartment on Park Avenue, it made for an ideal home base.

"Nothing much will have to change," her mother promised. "This is just a blip. This is something we can deal with."

"Are you trying to convince us, or yourself?" her brother asked, snarky, how he always got when he felt scared. The whole family followed her into the chemotherapy suite, trailing her wheelchair like a procession.

The cancer had spread to her lymph nodes. It wasn't ideal, Rachel knew, but they still had a fifty-fifty prognosis. There was hope. But midway through watching her mother absorb chemicals through the port implanted in her chest all over again—her dark mane of hair still thick, her diamond tennis bracelets still adorning the toned arms that were sure to shrink in the coming weeks—Rachel felt her breath catch in her throat. Her heart throbbed, alive with an energy that seemed impossible when the rest of her felt dead, still. She pictured the driftwood on the beach by the house in East Hampton, withered, bleached white by the sun, and for some reason it was this visual that brought a wave of nausea.

"Just going to step out and get some air," she said. "I'll be right back."

As soon as she stepped clear of the doorway, she started running. She barreled down the hall, barely registering the doctors giving her concerned looks, and she didn't stop until she had found an exit. She sat on the curb on Sixty-Eighth Street, dizzy and breathless, wishing that she could leave her body altogether. After seconds or minutes, she wasn't sure, she picked up her phone and dialed Dev.

She hadn't told him yet. Telling him, telling all her friends, would make it real. Would invite it into every sphere of her life, would mean having to answer questions like "How's your mom doing, really?" when she would have preferred to talk about work or Zadie Smith's latest or even the weather. But she couldn't stop herself now. She needed someone. She needed him, needed him the way she had years ago, when he had been her newest friend but the one who felt the oldest, the one who showed up, the one who somehow knew what to say.

She called Dev. She was sure he would be there. But the phone rang and rang.

"Yo, it's Dev." The voicemail message finally crackled to life. "Talk to me."

"Honestly, Dev, change that voicemail message," she barked, and hung up.

At that moment, Rachel decided something. It wouldn't seem to her as if the thought had sprouted from Dev not answering his phone, or from her fear about her mother's treatment. It would feel like the idea had come to her, a spark of inspiration in complete isolation, and not as a reaction, not as an effort to replace someone—but it was, of course. But it didn't matter why it had come, simply that it came, and once it did, it had the power to put things she hadn't yet imagined into motion.

Rachel decided she was going to meet someone. She needed to put herself out there, for real. After years of ambivalence, and hookups, and waiting, maybe secretly waiting for Dev even, she decided she was going to meet the man she was going to marry.

O n my way to my third first date this month." Rachel typed a quick text to Clarissa a few months later as she crossed Hudson Street. "Not from OkCupid this time, so that's promising. Wish me luck . . . or probably just kill me and put me out of my misery already."

"Good luck," Clarissa shot back right away, which she hadn't done in a while. Lately, she took two or three days to respond. "Third time's the charm."

"But actually getting to a third date would be more of a charm. Text you later xo."

She turned the corner onto Eighth Avenue and crossed the street to the entrance of Anfora, a jewel-box-size wine bar. Opened by the owners of dell'anima, a fantastic Italian restaurant next door, it had a great wine list, but it was also a little bit of a lazy choice, being only four blocks from her apartment. She had picked it because she was done traveling out of her way for first dates where her optimism about the guy in question always faded even faster than she could finish her first glass of wine. She flipped through her mental Rolodex of the men she had casually dated over the past several years: Rod with the Hamptons share, who had lied and said he owned the house; Charlie, a visual artist so beautiful he'd actually lured her out to his barely furnished loft in Bushwick but then had never called her back; David, the investment banker whose dark hair and hulking frame had reminded her too much of Cody in a way that made her nauseated. Thinking about them had made her almost cancel tonight, but then it had turned out to be a perfect New York evening, the kind with a light breeze rattling the turning leaves, a crispness in the air that made it the perfect temperature for her favorite leather jacket. Autumn in New York. There was nothing like it, no matter how disillusioned she'd started to feel.

Rachel surprised herself by texting her date that she was looking forward to seeing him, and she would be there at eight.

She scanned the bar and spotted him at a cozy banquette table near the back. There he was: Aaron. Thirty-two, five years her senior, worked at a hedge fund. They had met at a hotel bar in Soho the week before, where they had worked out all the "Jewish geography": He had gone to camp with Isabelle's oldest brother, and they had plenty of people and places in common without him being *too* familiar. She had given him her number after a few vodka sodas but hadn't expected him to call; he'd surprised her by asking for a date only a few days later, which she accepted.

He was as cute as she remembered, with dark brown hair swooping across his forehead, the breadth of his shoulders unmissable in his fitted sweater. But he was surprisingly earnest-looking, too. He flashed her a broad smile from across the room and gave her a dorky but friendly wave as he stood up from the table. She felt a swell of excitement, hope, roll through her stomach.

Calm down, she told herself. *These things never work out anyway.*

"Hey." Aaron leaned down to give her a hug. "How are you?"

This is my third first date this month because neither of the other two went anywhere. My friend group has fallen apart. I think every day might be the day I get the news that my mom died.

"I'm better now." She tried to dance around the truth, flashing her flirtiest and most winning smile. She rolled her shoulders back, pressing her chest out subtly as she shrugged out of her leather jacket. She watched his eyes widen slightly. *Predictable.* Dating required a performance, and if there was one thing Rachel knew she could do, it was perform.

"Well, now so am I." Aaron smiled at her. "What are we drinking?"

She guided him toward her preferred cabernet, and they picked a cheese and charcuterie plate, the classic first-date staple. She wondered if her life was going to be a series of mildly awkward conversations over mid-priced cheese plates until she finally just . . . picked someone and settled. She watched Aaron as he ordered for them both and wondered if he even liked anything about *her* specifically, or if he was just another in a line of thirtysomething bankers who had decided they needed to find a wife, and any attractive girl in her late twenties who crossed his path would do. None of these men struck her as the kind of people she would like to be friends with, and yet she was ultimately supposed to marry one of them. Then again, the men she liked as friends didn't seem to be viable relationship prospects, either.

Rachel turned to Aaron as the server walked away to get their wine, and he turned the other way to discreetly check his Black-Berry. Not a great sign. She waited as he typed an email.

"Sorry." He turned back to face her. "I'm done. Now, tell me something about you."

"Well, I grew up in the city. I went to—"

"Dalton, I remember." The server set their glasses of wine down on the table, and Rachel took a welcome gulp. "Then Northwestern for college, back to the city with big plans for working in the magazine world. You're an associate editor at *New York*; you've been there a while."

She stared at him, a little impressed by his memory. She'd had quite a few vodka sodas the night they met, and she could barely remember the name of his hedge fund.

"Okay, so you *were* listening when we met. Touché."

"But I didn't mean your résumé. I meant, tell me something real about you."

"Okay," she said, taking another big sip of wine, hoping she could come up with an interesting answer. "Well, I've been thinking about going for my MFA. I love writing fiction—grew up doing it all the time, writing these silly little fairy tales mostly—but I think I'm ready to shift out of journalism to more of the creative writing side, to really invest in that. I hope."

"That's exciting." He nodded. "So what do you write—"

"Actually, no, you know what? That was a lie."

He furrowed his brow, confused. "So, you . . . don't want to write?"

"No, I . . ." Rachel wasn't sure exactly what she was doing, but it was like a dam had broken somewhere inside her and the words were just rushing out before she had time to think about them, unbidden, uncontrolled. "I write. I love to write. But I'm not going to go for my MFA. I've been saying I would for years. I even got accepted to a program, but my mom has cancer. *Had* cancer, like almost ten years ago, and then she relapsed earlier this year. And I was going to start classes this fall, but she needed someone—and maybe I was too afraid to make the move anyway, who knows—but I wanted to be around since I was at college the first time, and . . . now, well." She threw her hands up. "Surgery, chemo cycle, radiation. She's in a new trial that seems promising, but trials are trials, and she's not better yet. So."

Aaron was staring at her like she was . . . well, like she had just overshared some incredibly personal information to a near stranger. She started mentally berating herself for verbal incontinence, completely blowing a date for no reason. Didn't she want to meet someone? Didn't she want to stop going on first dates? Wasn't Aaron cute and interesting and *interested*? This wasn't the way to get what she wanted. She didn't even recognize herself.

"Sorry, that was . . . well, you said 'real,' didn't you?" She gave him a small smile, trying to backpedal while feeling like the damage she had done was probably irreparable.

Like the radiation burns on her mom's chest.

Stop.

"Hey, don't apologize." He reached across the table and took her hand, surprising her. "Actually, I understand. My dad was diagnosed with cancer last year."

Their eyes met, the contact between them intense, magnetic. She realized that his stare hadn't been one of judgment, but one of recognition. "I'm so sorry," she said. "How is he?"

"Completely fine now, thank God," Aaron said with a smile. "Prostate cancer, caught it pretty early, all that fortunate stuff. But it changed my life. I'm sure I don't have to tell you, but there were just . . . times it would consume me. Where I was so worried about him, or where all I could think about was trying to be strong for my mom. And then there were days where I would almost completely forget about it and be enjoying myself—because life has to go on, right?—but that felt weird, too. I almost felt guilty in those moments, if that makes sense."

"I know exactly what you mean." She nodded. For the first month, her mother's diagnosis had been the planet they all orbited. The longer it wore on, it had become more like a satellite circling Rachel's life rather than the other way around, important but tangential. In a way, it scared her that that could happen, that something so big, the very question of life and death itself, essentially, could make its way to the back of her mind so that she could . . . what, edit items for *The Strategist* about oxblood-colored bags for fall? She knew she understood exactly the kind of guilt Aaron had described. It ebbed and flowed, unpredictable.

"Anyway." He paused as the server dropped off their cheese plate, then thanked her. "Now I'm sorry if *that* was too much."

"Not at all. Thank you." She felt herself unclench as she

smiled at him, her muscles softening like someone had lifted a heavy suitcase out of her hands. She took a bite of cheese. "And this is delicious, by the way."

"Now try this one." He prepared a cracker for her, and she realized that he really wasn't judging her, nor was he going to let the rest of the date become some kind of cancer support group. She studied him again, this time noticing his kind eyes and his slightly crooked nose instead of his broad shoulders or styled hair. For a moment, unchecked, she let herself hope.

———

The next morning, she woke up to two voicemails. Her phone had died overnight, something she rarely allowed to happen—Dev made fun of her for being the kind of person who had to find a charger the minute her battery dipped below seventy-five percent. But she and Aaron had let a second glass of wine turn into a third, and after a tipsy walk through the West Village and a good—no, great—first kiss outside her door, she had run upstairs and fallen into bed with her phone in her hand, forgetting the charger completely. She felt like she had slept more deeply than she had in the past year.

The first voicemail was from Aaron. Seeing his name in her missed call log, she felt her heart do a strange stutter step, the kind of fluttering excitement she hadn't felt in a while. Certainly not since her mom had been back in treatment. If she was being completely honest with herself, she maybe hadn't even felt something like it since the early days with Dev. There had been other flings that made her feel validated or wanted, even those that had made her feel crazy turned on (once again, the Bushwick artist—why did the men who were the best in bed always have the worst apartments?). But it had only ever been Dev who inspired her to think about her feelings with romance-novel vocabulary.

"Hi, Rachel." Aaron's deep baritone voice spoke into her ear. "I think this might be a little too forward. Actually, scratch that, I know it is. But I couldn't wait to ask you on another date. Do you think I'm crazy? Don't answer that. But if you want to, too, call me back. I'd love to take you to dinner."

She grinned and stretched out in her bed, loving the feel of her soft Frette sheets against her back, loving that she now had the upper hand with Aaron, whom she really did like, loving the knowledge that she could call him back right away or that she could make him sweat it out a little bit. Happily, she clicked through to the next voicemail.

Dev's voice.

"Rach, sorry to call in the middle of the night." He paused and groaned. "I'm just so fucking blocked on this book. I've been up all night; I'm not getting anywhere. You always have the best ideas, so I just thought . . . I don't know. Call me whenever."

Rachel was surprised he had called, more surprised he had admitted something vulnerable, and she wondered if he had been drunk. Then she let the compliment settle over her for a moment; she knew she had given good feedback on his first novel, recommended changes that he had ended up making, even though he had never formally acknowledged this. She wished she could see her own work as clearly as she could see his.

She looked at the phone in her hand. She clicked from one contact name to the other, imagining.

Finally, she called Aaron.

DEV

S o, Dev: To start with, what inspired you to write *Nirvana*?"
That damn title. Dev had resolved never, ever to admit
how ridiculous he thought it was. Naming the book after the
restaurant? The trite wordplay? The suggestion had been a joke;
he hadn't expected his publisher to love it. But he had wanted
the industry to want him, and now, at last, it did.

At first, while the critical response to *Nirvana* had been favorable, the sales hadn't matched up—no bestseller lists, no mas-
sive royalty checks. But Dev's team had been strategic: They
believed in the book and had clearly put a good deal of money
behind it in terms of his advance, and his publicist continued to
push for press while his agent shopped the film rights in tandem
with the favorable reviews. Almost a year later, right around the
time of the paperback release, they succeeded in optioning the
film rights. It wasn't much money, and "optioned" did not mean
"made," so Dev thought of it as just a nice bonus, an extra cushion

to rely on while he tried (and largely failed) to draft his second book. But the news of the option in *Variety* had sparked something: Like one tiny match dropped into a pile of hay, the deal caught attention, which led to book sales, which in turn brought more focus and press back to Dev himself, and on and on in a perpetual-motion machine that spun itself faster than he could have imagined. Now, another year later, the book was firmly a commercial success. Not a number-one bestseller—he'd have to aim for that with the second—but a significant achievement nonetheless. To top it off, the film adaptation would begin shooting in a few weeks, here in New York. As a result, Dev now sat in a comfortable chair in the decidedly upscale Crosby Street Hotel, sipping a $6 coffee with a very pretty reporter from *New York* magazine, answering softball questions for a feature about the book and its journey to becoming a movie.

His publicist had assured him that there would be no questions about the next book. Dev felt an unwelcome wash of uneasiness, but he stuffed it down without much difficulty. Second-book writer's block was a tale as old as time, wasn't it? Just look at *Wonder Boys*. Dev told himself he would finish his next novel eventually; in the meantime, if TV and film were where all the money was, who really cared?

He flashed an easy grin and prepared to launch into his pre-rehearsed spiel. This was his moment, after all. He needed to appreciate it before it was gone.

"Well, in a lot of ways, it is a deeply personal story for me, Lucy"—using her name, *nice* touch, he mentally patted himself on the back—"and it's one that's partially rooted in my experience growing up as an Indian kid in D.C. around the time of

9/11. Bridged with, of course, the New York of my twenties. But it is also, undeniably, a novel of ideas." He liked that phrase, *novel of ideas*, and wanted it applied to his work. He hoped she'd quote it. In the beginning, Dev's work had drawn flattering comparisons to Mohsin Hamid, a contemporary of his, whose debut he'd loved, but now Dev not-so-secretly wanted to push a comparison to the older literary establishment. Someone like Michael Cunningham, maybe. Michael Chabon. Yes, the Michaels, he decided, would be ideal.

"I drew on what I was seeing and hearing in the pre-crash millennium," he continued, "the experience of the classic 'coming-of-age' against a backdrop of commodification, the evolution of Manhattan into a gated community for the über-wealthy . . ."

"You do live in Manhattan yourself, correct?" Lucy looked directly at him with her warm brown eyes, her expression serious in a way that could have been a playful challenge or a serious indictment. Had he gotten a bit carried away? He needed to be careful not to sound too pretentious, he reminded himself. He needed to be highbrow, not head-high-up-his-own-ass.

"Coincidentally, the book is also about how I—er, Damian—can be a hypocritical asshole. But don't print that."

She laughed then, flashing perfectly straight, white teeth, and Dev knew that she wouldn't. He sank back into the plush chair and relaxed into the interview.

THEY WRAPPED AFTER AN HOUR, FIFTEEN MINUTES OF PERSONAL conversation more than was strictly necessary, in which he learned that she lived with a roommate in Carroll Gardens, had grown up in New Jersey in a large Nigerian family, went for her master's in journalism at Columbia, and had known Rachel casually for several years, which was, in part, how the interview had come about. He asked for her number for personal purposes, but under the guise of in case he remembered any other useful anecdotes for the piece, and then they said goodbye on the corner of Mercer Street and he headed north to Nate's. He made a mental note to remember to thank Rachel for the connection later. It was generous of her, thoughtful, more than he really knew what to do with, especially considering how much time she'd been spending at the hospital with her mom over the past year.

And especially considering how things had been between them lately.

Dev hadn't answered the phone when Rachel first called him with the news of her mom's relapse. It had been a clear choice not to pick up, one he'd felt sure about in the moment, because he'd been in bed next to Sophie (or had it been Lilly?) and answering a call from another girl had seemed sure to put an end to what was happening there. Though of course, it had ended anyway. How could he have known what she was calling about? He'd felt guilty when he'd finally called back a few days later and heard the news, and he'd gone over to her apartment right away.

The sky had been threatening rain that day, and he remembered Rachel had worn an oversize scarf wrapped around her that made her look impossibly small. She had clearly been crying but had wiped her face clean, her skin smooth and pale, and as she stood there in her doorway, Dev was momentarily struck by how young she looked without makeup. Her hair was slicked back in a ponytail and her wet eyes looked big in her face as she looked up at him with a searching expression. It tugged at something inside him, that look.

"I'm so sorry," he remembered saying, uselessly. "I actually don't know what I'm supposed to say, and since you know me, you know I . . . usually have a pretty good idea of what I'm going to say every second. But I am sorry."

She walked into his arms then and he hugged her, a response he seemed to have no control over.

"I can't believe this is happening again."

"I know." Dev paused. "But also, 'again' means she already beat it once. That part could happen again, too." He recognized that he didn't know stats about this, didn't have any idea how often people beat recurring cancers, but it had to be possible. He also knew that, knowing Rachel, she was probably up to her ears in textbooks and first-person accounts and survival rates on cancer.org. She didn't need metrics; she needed confidence.

"And if it doesn't happen? If she doesn't get better again?"

"Then I'll be here." He cleared his throat. "Always."

"You will?" She looked up at him with the kind of pregnant hope that startled something inside him, made him rear back. She said it in a way of emotional expectation, and Dev felt a sudden need to discourage this. He knew he could lead a lot of women on, but not Rachel. He had resolved, years ago now, that Rachel and he would never happen. He admitted to himself that when he had first looked at her bare face and elfin ears he thought things that had very little to do with friendship. For just one moment, he had thought about going for it. For real, this time. But how much of a jerk, how self-involved, would he have to be to try to sleep with a friend whose mom had just been re-diagnosed with cancer? He pulled back.

"I meant, *we will all be here*," he corrected. "Me, Nate, Clarissa, Isabelle. All of us." He paused, not sure if that was too much of a platitude to be comforting, but Rachel gave him a wan smile. He smiled back, uncharacteristically tense, and then followed her inside.

That was when he had started trying to manage how often he saw her. He had to strike the right balance. The strange, swirling cocktail of emotions he experienced around her—unusual for him—was part of what kept him away. He didn't need to subject himself to this confusion, where he felt alternately pitying and grateful and guilty, and, yes, fine, attracted to her, too. He resolved to see her occasionally, to maintain their friendship, but he did not need to talk to her every day.

After all, he wasn't her boyfriend. He'd worked to make that very clear. Plus, after a few months of distance, he knew she'd started seeing someone new. That meant she required nothing from him, sometimes did not even respond to his texts about writing, or her mom, for a full day. Somehow all this was a relief and a slight in equal measure, a veritable Schrödinger's relationship for which, Dev suspected, he was completely responsible.

He shook his head, cleared the thoughts from his mind. He looked up, surprised to find himself already near Fourteenth Street.

NATE STILL LIVED IN THE GLEAMING HIGH-RISE NEAR UNION Square that he had moved into after their share in Murray Hill, outfitted with chrome appliances and sleek furniture. Dev preferred the laid-back feel of his own spot in the East Village, but it was hard to argue with Nate's sprawling sofa and his sixty-inch TV.

Dev reached into the fridge as soon as he arrived and tossed a beer to Nate, which he caught without taking both eyes off the screen. There were times when Dev wanted nothing more than for someone to ask him about his work that day, or about how the book was going—occasionally he would feel like he was almost bursting with it, brimming with a desire to talk about himself—but now was not one of those times. He and Nate settled into their default sports-watching mode, and he felt grateful for the silence. But when the buzzer sounded to mark the end of the first quarter, Nate put the TV on mute.

"So, want to tell me what you were doing earlier? Your text was super vague. Secret girl on the side?" Nate raised his eyebrows.

Dev grinned. He didn't like that he had become the sort of person who enjoyed telling people about press for his books as much as—more than?—he enjoyed writing them, but that was part of the deal, wasn't it? He had worked hard, and now he wanted to enjoy the perks.

"No, actually, I was at an interview. *New York* mag, maybe a mention on the cover, but I won't get my hopes up." His hopes were up.

"You and I probably don't belong in *New York* mag unless it's a mention in lowbrow despicable, but hey, here's hoping," Nate joked, referencing the magazine's infamous back page "approval matrix."

"You read *New York* magazine?" Dev asked, then groaned inwardly the second he said it. Rachel had worked there for years, so of course he did.

"How is Rachel doing, by the way?" Nate asked, following his thought process. "I've been a little AWOL."

"She's . . . okay? Honestly, I haven't seen her since she got me the interview. I should call." He paused, sipping his beer as Al Michaels droned on in front of them. He felt loose, the alcohol rushing in on his empty stomach. "She called a lot, when her mom first got sick, and . . . I didn't always know what to do, you know?"

"That's just kind of your vibe with Rachel, though, right? I feel like you're the one she calls in a crisis." Something about how he said it sounded off, or even annoyed, somehow, but Nate had said it as he pulled slowly on a joint, so maybe he was just high.

"I don't know anymore," Dev admitted. "Sometimes I feel like ever since we hooked up there's always been this . . . extra vibe, you know?"

Dev heard the glass of Nate's near-empty beer clanging against the glass of the coffee table. "You and Rachel." Nate cleared his throat, and in an instant, Dev realized his mistake. "You and Rachel hooked up?"

Shit.

Dev felt his heartbeat accelerate. He cursed his thoughtlessness and the beer rolling around in his empty stomach as he tried to figure out how big a mistake this was—though he was surprised that it hadn't ever come up in the past six years. He'd thought that they'd all laugh about it if it ever did. But from Nate's tone of voice, he could tell that absolutely no one was laughing.

As Dev took another sip of beer to stall before having to answer, he landed on what his tipsy brain was *pretty* sure would be the real problem. Nate would want to know that the group dynamics weren't at risk, and that this wasn't as big a deal as hiding it for years after the fact would make it seem. That was an easy fix, because their friendship, the friendship of the four of them, wasn't in jeopardy at all, especially not now. Dev exhaled, satisfied by this line of thought.

"Oh yeah. But it was a long time ago. Like, the-night-before-graduation long ago."

Nate didn't say anything, his eyes trained on the TV.

"I didn't mean for it to be a secret. At the time I just didn't . . . want to embarrass her? I didn't want to talk behind her back, and I didn't want you or Clarissa to think it was, you know, a 'thing.' But now it's been so long that I guess we can laugh about it. Right?"

"Right," Nate said weakly.

Dev heard his hesitancy and considered it. He guessed that Nate was still skeptical, whether it was about the fact that they had slept together or the fact that they hadn't told anyone, Dev wasn't sure. But while Nate was probably right to be suspicious—right that there had been a time when something like this could have spelled disaster for their friendships—they weren't twenty-two anymore. Everyone had missteps in their past: drunken nights, regrettable sex, white lies that only came out years later.

"Anyway." Nate cleared his throat. He tossed a bag of chips at Dev, a little hard, but it made Dev laugh. "Defense is laying an egg. I've got you beat in fantasy this season. Get ready."

Dev dug his hand into the chip bag, relieved.

ON THE NEW YORK CITY FILM SET OF THE *NIRVANA* ADAPTATION, Dev felt like a god.

He wouldn't say that out loud to anyone, of course, because he knew how it sounded, had learned the hard way how to watch himself for sound bites, especially with *Variety* prowling around all over the place. But what he meant by the godlike thought wasn't that he felt as if he himself were *perfect*. In fact, he had spilled a latte on his pants in the taxi that very morning and had to come to the set in athletic shorts from his gym bag, and he'd then been immediately mistaken for a courier, either because he had been wearing athleisure or because he was Indian, one of the two or both.

Anyway.

No, what he meant was that he had created these characters in his mind from thin air, back when no one had cared if he did or not, and now he got to watch them come to life right in front of his eyes, Damian with his dark hair and smirking scowl, Ray with his cocky banker's attitude and penchant for expensive status symbols. They now existed wholly apart from him, breathing and alive. He watched them walk around on set, watched them recite lines he had written, then improvise new ones that came from their own brains. The experience of watching his own creation exist separate from himself and with a mind of its own left him awestruck, because what, truly, could be more godlike than that?

Fortunately, Clarissa had come to visit him on set the week before, on the second day of filming, to provide a necessary dose of humility.

"Where's your trailer?" she asked, smirking, as soon as she arrived.

"I . . . don't have one."

"Can someone get me a coffee? Do you have an assistant?"

"Um, no. I'm an AP."

"So *you* are the assistant."

"*Associate* producer."

"And what does that mean in terms of what you actually do here?"

"It means that I . . . wrote the book and then my film agent negotiated well and conned them into giving me an AP credit," he admitted, trying to stay in good humor. "I mostly just visit the set to feel cool. Though I'm hoping if I hang around enough they'll let me make a cameo." He was only half-joking.

"Ah." A beat, then her radiant, slightly crooked smile. "Anyway, you know I'm just teasing you, right?" She put an arm around him, unusually affectionate. "This is incredible, and I'm so proud. That's just my job, keeping you humble."

"And you do it so well," he had agreed. But still: how amazing to watch the process of your ideas coming to life, your goals to fruition? When he put it that way, even Clarissa didn't disagree with him.

Clarissa also understood, to some extent: She now knew what it was to have the odd person recognize you on the street, knew what it was like to broadcast a public persona of your creative self that might or might not totally align with who was there underneath. They were both very, very slightly famous. Clarissa even more than him, probably, but just because of the visual nature of her success on YouTube. In any case, it was nice to have someone who could relate to him professionally, he thought, as he sipped a—self-procured—coffee on this, the third week of filming. It was even nicer that the person could be Clarissa. Their friendship had started as one of typical college hijinks and mutual connections, but she had ended up being the only one of his close friends who understood his relationship to his creative work, giving them something new to share in their postgrad lives. Dev found himself wishing that Clarissa would just move to New York.

Which, he realized, she might. Not only would it make sense for her work, but he knew, despite her caginess on the details, that she had been casually dating someone in New York, someone she had met when she came to the city for a gig last fall. Dev wondered who she was. He usually didn't like being introduced to friends' significant others in the early stages—or introducing his own, since they were bound not to last long—but he thought he might make a notable exception in this case.

He had granted one other recent exception, for Rachel. She had finally introduced him to her boyfriend, Aaron, over absurdly overpriced cocktails and sushi a few weeks earlier. He went to be agreeable, biting his tongue and resisting laughter when she instructed him "no sarcasm, no third degree" ahead of the date with a solemn expression on her face. She obviously liked this Aaron a lot. Against the odds, Dev had liked him, too: Sure, he was a bit older, a bit more serious, a "grown-up" in a way that underscored how much he still did not feel like he belonged to that category. No film deal or six-figure check seemed likely to change that. But Aaron had also been affable, almost irritatingly interested in Dev's writing, generous with the tip when he picked up the check, the quintessential "good guy." It all seemed perfect, except that Dev now found himself in an unexpected and undesirable position: He had spent a period of time thinking that Rachel finding a serious boyfriend could only benefit him, in that he would no longer be, say, the primary recipient of her late-night phone calls, making their friendship easier and less dramatic. It would also close that one percent of possibility that still occasionally shimmered between them like a mirage, but which he always denied himself. He would never let it happen because he knew Rachel, and Rachel wanted a boyfriend, and he was a notoriously shit boyfriend, and he refused to lead her on, refused to complicate things with one of the most important people in his life. But now he had found, much to his chagrin, that the definitive closure of that door made him *want* to swing it open, to bust right into that room of possibility. He didn't like himself for feeling that way, and so he had attempted to brush it off, but he didn't want to lose Rachel, nor did he want her to think he was at all bothered by her relationship, and so that was how he somehow found himself—three martinis deep—hugging both Rachel and Aaron goodbye and inviting them to stop by the set together.

Today.

Dev sighed and slumped into a seat in an open director's chair with ASSOC PROD written on it, his coffee in one hand and his phone in the other. He decided it would be better if he looked engaged with the preparations for the shoot, rather than as if he had been waiting for Rachel to show up, so he took a moment to casually survey the scene. Production had closed off a block of Vestry Street in Tribeca, a limestone warehouse building there standing in for a real apartment building uptown, where, he had been told, it would have been more complicated to block traffic. The scene in question was an important one, in which his protagonist, Damian, breaks down in front of his ex-girlfriend's apartment, finally allowing himself a moment to process both the trauma of the 9/11 attacks and the fact that he feels alone, unmoored, in a reeling city and a series of relationships with people who don't truly understand him. In the movie version of the scene, this would lead to a reconciliation between him and the on-off girlfriend, in which he reveals his true self, his estrangement from his family, his struggles over his identity, and then she accepts him. In the novel this moment had a less tidy ending, but, he figured, that's Hollywood. The film script wrapped it up in a way that leaned more romance than indie drama, and Dev wondered for a moment if he should be worried about that, if it might damage his reputation as a serious author.

Not that he was going to be a serious author if he couldn't string more than ten thousand words together on the next novel.

"Director's chair? Did they promote you?" he heard a loud voice call from over his shoulder. And there, wearing a trench coat, was Rachel, on his film set, next to a series of crew members adjusting lighting and backdrops for a scene featuring the very character that Dev had, at least in part, if he were being honest, based on her. She stood hand in hand with Aaron.

"I'll have you know that Clarissa already beat you to this mockery. She came last week." He pulled Rachel into an awkward hug with one arm, while extending the other to shake hands with Aaron. "Also, this actually is my chair, thanks."

He watched her take in the scene: the harried crew members, the movie cameras. A real film set. He waited for Rachel to say something about it, more eager for her to seem impressed than he wanted to be.

"You saw Clarissa? Did she . . . did she mention me at all?" Rachel asked instead, at the same moment that Aaron said, "This is cool, man," in a mild tone of voice, and both remarks felt somehow unsatisfactory.

"Say something *about* you? No, why would she?"

Rachel looked off into the distance. "No reason. It just seems like she's taking a long time to reply to me."

Dev shrugged. "She's probably busy. Work, dating, you know."

"Dating? She's seeing someone?" Her face brimmed with classic Rachel-brand eagerness. Aaron just stood there. Dev decided he knew better than to give Rachel a potentially juicy gossip tidbit when he himself didn't even know the full story.

"Ask her yourself. Anyway, you want to come meet the director?"

She pulled at a loose thread from the arm of her coat and didn't answer.

"Absolutely." Aaron filled the silence. "Lead the way."

They took a lap around the block, shaking hands with the director, rapping on the trailer door of Parth Patel, the up-and-coming twenty-two-year-old actor playing Damian. Parth chatted gamely with Rachel and gave her a lingering kiss on the cheek as a goodbye, which Aaron seemed not to notice or mind. Parth didn't say much to Dev, which irked him; would it kill everyone to remember that he was the writer, the reason for the project's existence? He wondered if he was bothered by the mood on the set, or the changes that had been made to the script itself, or perhaps even the next scene, which would involve Damian's family.

Apart from his brother, Sumeet, whom he called on the phone in short bursts or joined online to play *Call of Duty*, Dev's relationship with his youngest brother and extended family had dwindled to birthday Facebook posts and holiday greetings and an annual visit home. He sensed that the success of his book, and the surprise of the film adaptation, had given his parents something to be vaguely proud of—he didn't ever have to wait tables again—even if they still didn't fully understand his career choice. But his father hadn't been anywhere near as effusive about his pride as he had been with his disapproval during Dev's Nirvana days, and his mother, as she was fond of reminding everyone, had two younger kids to worry about. She still sent him handwritten notes every few weeks, detailing the weather and the state of the neighbor's yard and his youngest brother's college applications. They were sweet, and he felt sheepish guilt that he hadn't written anything back recently. Too busy showing his friends around his film set, he guessed.

He and Rachel still hadn't said much to each other by the

time he wrapped up the tour at the corner of Vestry and West. It looked like it would be a while until the scene started rolling, and he wished, once again, that he had a trailer of his own, somewhere to take them.

"How about I grab us some coffees from around the corner?" Aaron offered helpfully, and Dev experienced the sensation of being both grateful and annoyed, a feeling that also reminded him of his mother.

"Thanks, babe." Rachel squeezed Aaron's hand.

No sooner had he walked away than Dev started to say, "What the hell is up with you today?" at the exact moment that Rachel blurted, improbably, "What is going *on* with you?" and they both erupted into laughter. Rachel laughed until she sank all the way down to the gum-splattered sidewalk of Vestry Street, hugging her knees around her knee-high leather boots.

"Jinx, you owe me a Coke," she said, then extended a hand. "Help me up?"

"Make it a whiskey, and you've got it."

"That bad, huh?"

"No. Yes. I don't know."

"Is the poor tortured artist having a hard day on his movie set?"

He gave her the middle finger, then reached into his jacket pocket and pulled out his cigarettes. They sat down on a small ledge extending from the industrial building behind them, and he handed her one from his pack.

She shook her head. "I gave up completely for Aaron. Trying to be a healthier, better me. We're running the marathon in November."

He raised his eyebrows.

"Okay, one. Just one."

He watched her flick the lighter and close her eyes, pulling in a deep, slow drag. He had always liked this contradiction within her, Rachel as the healthy-living, end-cancer crusader and yet still a secret cigarette junkie. She nodded slightly, as if confirming her pleasure and approval, but she didn't turn to look at him.

"So, really. What's up?"

"The truth?"

"Only if it somehow involves praising the movie production." He took a drag. "No, I'm kidding. Of course. Shoot."

She nodded. "It does involve that, actually. Seeing you here, it's clear that you . . . you did it, you know? You're doing something you love, and that is totally right for you, and you are wildly succeeding at it."

He resisted mock humility and simply nodded, accepting this truth.

"That must feel incredible."

"It mostly does. But it's different than you'd expect, too. There's always a 'what's next?,' a 'what else?' It is somehow absolutely incredible and yet not as fulfilling as I expected." This, too, was true.

"I know, there's the ungraspable nature of success, the lifestyle creep. But being here, watching you do this, made me realize that it has been a long time since I've felt anything close to it. I have a good job, but I'm mostly editing puff pieces." Rachel shrugged. "I like it, but I've never loved it. They're talking about shifting the magazine to biweekly—don't tell anyone, but I think it's real this time—which means less chance to move up. I passed up getting my MFA because of my mom, and I swore I would channel that energy into writing fiction, but . . ." She paused. "It's not happening, and maybe it's time to just admit that if I don't think I have the drive, or the talent, it's time for a change. Time to do something where I can move up, do something I care about, be respected for what I do. Even if it's not as a writer."

Dev wondered how honest he should be. He didn't know if this was the moment when he told Rachel that he knew she had a book in her, that she had been a better writer than him back in college, that her short fiction showed promise. Or, instead, if he should tell her the *other* truth, which was that he now knew for certain that novels had as much to do with talent as, say, coffee had to do with milk. It was a nice additive for certain people or in certain situations, but when you thought about the novels that did best—as in, sold the most, were read the most widely—it was more about having a great idea and then the drive to put that idea down on paper. That, of course, combined with a healthy dose of luck and timing. Dev still loved to esteem his own talent, make no mistake, but the bursts of it that he did experience weren't what got the books written. And so, if Rachel thought she didn't have the ambition, or if she wanted a profession with regular hours and more guarantees, then she absolutely *should* leave writing.

Before he could say anything, she spoke again. "It's everything with my parents, too. My mom is doing better, actually. She just had a promising scan. But it's still day by day. And you try being in a new relationship with that happening, and even though Aaron understands, I wonder if it's—"

Just then, Aaron rounded the corner carrying a tray of

coffees and croissants. She stopped talking, flicked the butt of her cigarette to the ground. Whatever she had been about to say about their relationship, he would never know. He didn't know whether to be disappointed or relieved. But he did know that he had something else he could offer her.

"If you really feel that way," he said, "then I have an idea for you. My editor's team is hiring. For an assistant editor."

"Really?"

"They asked if I knew anyone in my network, and I thought of you."

"I'm flattered," she said. "But that's a reach. I haven't worked in publishing since my internship."

"But you *are* an editor."

"Magazines are very different. But yes, I am."

He could tell she was intrigued. He liked this feeling, of knowing he could do something for her. "They're different, yeah. But you have years of experience, and it's a more junior role, and if I tell them that you just have to be on the team, then maybe . . ."

"Okay, then." She smiled as Aaron arrived, handing them each a croissant. "Throw my name in the ring. Thank you," she added, but he was momentarily distracted. The actors playing Damian's parents had materialized on set; maybe someone had switched the filming order or the call sheets for the day. He watched as a facsimile of his own mother walked across Vestry Street, and then he saw Rachel watching him.

"And, Dev? Call your mom," she said, as if she could read his mind.

NATE

2013

Now, there were mornings, and there were mornings *after*—and more often than not, Nate had begun to think of sunrise as a signal to go to sleep rather than a natural alarm.

Not during the week, of course; he was still on the straight and narrow there. The "straight and narrow" meaning that he would at least get home by 2 or 3 a.m. and sleep for four hours before turning around and going back to work. This was typical in his profession, he reasoned, remembering when he had been a first-year associate, tasked with waiting around for some MD's deck until midnight and then turning edits around in a couple of hours. But he wasn't a first year anymore, and it had been a long time since he had been up until early morning *working on a deck*.

Weekends were a different level. He would have a few drinks on his own or with colleagues, maybe even starting Friday after-noon at a vintage two-martini lunch, and then continue through the evening as he finished up a little bit of work, finally texting whichever friend he thought would be most likely to want to keep the party going until the wee hours. Sometimes, it was Cody. Lately, it had been Jake Matthews. As much as Nate had simultaneously envied and resented him when they'd run into each other at Soho House for the first time, he had eventually come around to the idea that to cut Jake Matthews down to size meant to treat him the same way he would anyone else. That was, in no small part, why he had called him that first time: He wanted to prove to himself that Jake was just another guy, someone with a job similar to Nate's, a similar apartment, similar friends. There was nothing for him to be intimidated or impressed by. But then, that first night out together, Nate had had an absolutely amazing time. Maybe it was the above-average DJ; maybe it was the thrill of partying with the people who had mocked him in high school; maybe it was Jake's surprising generosity with his bag of (high-quality) blow. But whatever the reason, they had, improbably, struck up a friendship. Jake drunkenly apologized for "being kind of a dick to everyone" in high school, Nate ordered everyone another bottle, and they clinked their glasses to cheers a new friendship won, a new phase of their lives begun.

It wasn't the friendship Nate had once had with Dev or Rachel or Clarissa, of course. But it was fun and exciting and free of judgment, and anyway, he reasoned, who was Rachel to tell him what to do when she was busy with her boyfriend all the time? And where was Clarissa—somewhere in Chicago, immersed in her YouTube success, posting videos like clockwork but hardly answering their group texts?

The morning of New Year's Day 2013 found Nate in a

sprawling Bushwick loft, on a white mattress on the floor in the center of the room like a boxing ring. He lay next to a girl—Tess or Bess, though Tess seemed more familiar—who tickled him lightly, drawing circles on his arm, her feathery touch helping keep the nervous shake of the comedown at bay. They weren't alone; at least six of her friends were in the next room, continuing a stimulant-fueled after-party into the first hours of 2013.

He had met Tess at a warehouse rave, not his typical scene, but when Jake had suggested they get off the models and bottles scene for a night—trade Manhattan for Brooklyn, cocaine for molly—who was he to say no? He had danced all night, sweaty and loving it, the bass of Avicii songs pounding in his heart, rattling his rib cage, and he felt certain that this was the best anyone had ever felt, the most fun anyone had ever had. By the time Tess had materialized in front of him, he was convinced that 2013 would be the best year yet. The music (and, fine, the drugs) dulled the voice in his head that had been plaguing him lately, the one that nagged him with thoughts like *A third of your life is over* and *You spend seventy hours a week at your job and what has it gotten you?* In this, the new year, he would find a way to silence that voice permanently.

But now the pounding sensation had shifted from his heart to his head, which had started to feel like it was in a vise. He felt a growing awareness that he needed some water, and probably a bed that wasn't located in an apartment occupied by seven Bushwick twentysomethings. He listened to fragments of the racket of voices filtering through the wall with his eyes closed.

I saw him last year, in Berlin.

KitKatClub.

Fuck, my lighter.

Jesus, we've been up all night.

His eyes flashed open. He felt a sudden and pulsing need to escape.

"I'm going to go grab something to eat," he said to Tess by way of an excuse, hoping she wouldn't ask to come. None of them were hungry anyway.

"Sure, bye," she said lazily, her eyes still closed. "Happy New Year."

"Happy New Year," he said, and even though he had gotten exactly what he wanted, a part of him wished she had asked him to stay. He checked his phone, hoping to see something from one of his friends, but there was only one message: "Happy New Year, honey!" from his grandma, who had recently learned to text. He shoved the phone back in his pocket and threw open the metal door to the street, squinting into the dawn of a new year that now felt about as pointless as the last one.

AFTER A NAP, A SHOWER, A FULL NIGHT'S SLEEP, AND SMOK-ing half a joint in front of an *Entourage* episode on the DVR, by the *second* day of 2013, Nate's outlook had improved considerably. He stretched out on the couch and clicked off the TV, content. This year would be a great one; he could get a promotion, or, barring that, look at other firms. It could be time to make the switch to private equity. But before all that, there would be the ski trip. The four of them—he, Dev, Rachel, and Clarissa—had planned their first vacation together since the ill-fated camping trip at the Bonnaroo music festival in 2005, which had begun with Dev forgetting the sleeping bags and ended with Rachel crying over dropping her Motorola Razr in the mud after two days of near-constant downpour.

This trip would be much better. With money finally coming in from Dev's movie deal and Clarissa's YouTube ad revenue based on her surprising success as a vlogger, a luxury cabin had been reserved in Steamboat Springs. Nate would have preferred Aspen, but oh well. It would be a weekend of fresh powder, partying, and a return to their old shot-ski antics. Never mind that he hadn't seen Clarissa in more than two years. Never mind that *Dev and Rachel had slept together and never even told him.*

He shook his head. He could not—would not—keep thinking about that. It shouldn't bother him. Rachel had gotten into a serious relationship with someone new. Rachel and Dev had hooked up about a million years ago, and they were both still his friends, so who cared?

Nate cared. He had cared since the moment Dev had casually let it slip, truly by mistake or to taunt him, who could tell?

He stood up and started pacing around his coffee table, entertaining the thoughts for just a little bit longer. He imagined himself building a case for the defense: He cared only because he cared about the group dynamic! He cared because he and Dev had agreed early in freshman year—even before they knew Clarissa was gay—that they wouldn't get romantically involved with the girls, to avoid this exact problem. And, fine, he cared just a little bit because he had always assumed that if anyone were to break the pact, it would have been *him* and Rachel, not Dev. He was the one who had spent the Shabbat dinners with her parents when they all first moved to the city. He was the one who had watched all those hours of *The Bachelor* with her. Hadn't he made himself exactly the kind of man she would want? Wouldn't she have liked him better, given the choice? Clearly not. She'd had the choice, he reasoned. There was something so skin-crawlingly annoying about the fact that no one had ever told him, that they had probably been laughing over their own inside jokes, the inside knowledge of their shared nights together, while he just sat there, oblivious, as clueless as his mother when someone in a TV show would talk about smoking "herb" and she would ask, "What, oregano?" But despite this irritation snaking its way up his spine, it felt slightly unfair to stay mad at Rachel, at least at the moment—her mom had recently had a clear scan, but she was still in and out of the hospital—and so the remaining option was to be angry at Dev.

He ran a hand through his hair, which had dried from the shower matted and tangled, and sighed. The trip would fix things. It had to.

THE CABIN SAT ON THE SIDE OF THE MOUNTAIN, SNOW covering its sloped roof, which looked built into the earth in a way that reminded Nate of a hobbit hole. As the cab drove him, Rachel, and Rachel's four suitcases up to the house, he felt strangely hopeful about the place, about the weekend. He wanted to be here, ensconced in a snow-covered cabin, with his oldest friends. He wanted it even more than he wanted to be in bed with Tess or out at a club with Jake, a feeling he hadn't experienced in some time.

"I feel like I haven't seen you in a while," Rachel said softly as their car slowly stopped in the snow-covered driveway in front of the door. "I'm really glad you could come."

"Well, I've been busy." Nate shrugged, unsure why his first response was to feel defensive. Rachel was right; he'd just been having nearly the exact same thought. He had almost said no to this trip. Now, looking up at the cabin, warm light glowing from inside, and feeling a million miles away from his life, he saw everything differently.

"I know."

"Hey." He smiled at her. "I'm glad, too. I've been . . . I don't know where I've been."

Rachel nodded, apparently satisfied, and then she flung open the taxi door. "Look, it's magical!" she exclaimed. "Let's go in. Clarissa's already here."

Clarissa had flown in early to go to the grocery store and get the house set up. Dev, unchangeably frugal, had decided to connect through Minneapolis and arrive late—to save something like $25, probably.

The door swung open to reveal Clarissa in the small kitchen, wearing a bulky sweater the color of oatmeal and standing in front of the stove, the contents of a large stainless steel pot bubbling like a cauldron under her vigilant gaze. Nate swallowed a comment about how he'd been hoping they'd swing by Sauvage for dinner, because whatever she had simmering really did smell delicious.

"Oh my God, you're here! Hi!" Rachel exclaimed at Clarissa, at a pitch Nate thought should have been reserved for dog whistles. Her immense pile of bags kept her from running at

Clarissa, who trotted over with a wooden spoon still in her hand. "The celebrity vlogger herself."

He saw Clarissa roll her eyes, but she smiled, too, pleased. At last check, her subscriber count had climbed to more than 500K. Nate had heard she'd recently gotten an invitation to the *Vanity Fair* Oscar party. She'd equivocated about going, hating big events like that unless she was performing, and Nate felt a small spark of jealousy about the fact that fame always seemed to happen to the people who didn't want it.

"What, Rach, are you planning to crash a black-tie wedding while you're here?" Clarissa said by way of hello, grabbing a garment bag out of Rachel's hand. "Should we send a Sherpa for the rest of your stuff? And hi, Nate." She hugged him with her free arm.

"Hi, good to see you. Man, it's been too long," he said, starting to feel like it had, in fact, been too long, like they weren't going to know what to say to each other if years kept elapsing between their visits. After all, it wasn't as if they had common ground over work like he did with Cody, or over sports like he did with Dev; he didn't know anything about comedy, or You-Tube, for that matter, except when it came to sending around links to CollegeHumor videos. But then he looked at her, really looked at her, with her goofy grin and the sauce-soaked spoon in her hand, and he remembered that Clarissa had always been the one to hang back with him at a party when Dev and Rachel had rushed off to work the room, the one who had taken his side and lobbied for music festivals like the Bonnaroo camping trip when Rachel thought it would be "grody."

He could know her again, he thought. For real. He wanted to.

After all, a nastier part of himself added, *it wasn't like she was going to run off and leave him to sleep with Dev*. He picked up his bag, hefted it into the unoccupied bedroom, and returned to the kitchen to ask her about her latest video—and steal a taste of her tomato sauce. It was familiar, like his childhood. He realized that it had been a long time since he had eaten something that didn't come from a fancy restaurant or a takeout box.

DEV GOT IN THE NEXT MORNING, FLOPPING FACEDOWN INTO the twin bed opposite Nate at around 5 a.m. Nate pretended to be asleep. But when he woke for real around nine, he found himself weirdly eager for Dev to get up, his anger eased in the light of day. He wanted to hit the slopes with him, the two of them on their snowboards, even though Dev didn't really know what he was doing. Then Rachel busted into their room, already wearing a fitted ski suit.

"Get up, both of you. Do you know how bad the lines get?"

Nate bolted upright, while Dev just stretched and moaned. "Great to see you, too, Rach."

"See, this is classic him." She addressed Nate directly. "Flies in late to save twenty-five dollars, then sleeps through the first half of his lift ticket and wastes seventy-five dollars instead."

He felt less like playing along with their jokes than usual. He didn't want to moderate their faux arguments. His flash of desire to spend time with Dev melted away as fast as it had come on.

"Don't look at me. I'll be out the door with my board in five."

"And I'm just here for the . . . what was that, Rachel?" Dev croaked. "The ap-rez?"

"Après-ski. Say it after me: Ah-pray."

"I know, I'm just trying to piss you off."

Nate hefted himself up, grabbed his pile of ski clothes, and slammed the door to the bathroom. "See you out front in ten," he yelled back through it, not really caring if they heard him or not.

THE MORNING HAD DAWNED OVERCAST AND FOREBODING, weather that mimicked his mood, but against the odds, the day turned out to be beautiful. The clouds lingered just long enough to dump a fresh layer of powder, and the sun came out over the spun-sugar trees and gleamed brightly by the time they reached the top of the lift at ten. Nate and Rachel took a pass at a steep but short black diamond run while Dev hung back with Clarissa, teaching her how to shift her weight back and forth on her board, kindly remembering that she had never been skiing other than for some school-sponsored trip to an ant-size hill in the middle of Illinois. Nate told himself he would spend some more quality time with her at dinner, but for now he loved carving up the mountain with Rachel, tossing fond insults at each other as she complained about being stuck on a ski trip with three obnoxious snowboarders. Nate had to admit that she cut a cool figure in her tight one-piece snowsuit, her skis perfectly aligned mere millimeters from each other, but then remembered again that she had grown up skiing out west, because of course she had. He was glad he had joined the ski and snowboard club at Northwestern, giving him a leg up on the other midwesterners, allowing him to (almost) join the ranks of the east coasters who had seemingly slid out of the womb directly onto a ski slope. They turned onto a mogul run, more appropriate for skiers, but he was pleased to find that he was up to it.

They took run after run, pausing only for a quick break for lunch at the lodge. He tried to ignore how much he wanted to start drinking and failed. *One beer,* he thought. *Maybe two.* He told himself it was normal, they were on vacation, no problem. If he got tired, he could always pop one of his Adderall later.

THE ADDERALL TURNED OUT TO BE A MISTAKE. BY THE TIME they arrived at the bar at the base of the mountain for the après-ski party—which was less of the hot-chocolate-and-plaid-blanket vibe, more of the nightclub-on-the-slopes energy—he was tired from the beer (fine, three beers) and the physical exertion, his muscles limp, and yet also wired from the Adderall. But he resolved to get into the party mood; this was what they had come for. He ordered a bottle of champagne for the four of them, his treat.

"I don't know about you guys, but I'm not sure how into 'popping bottles' I am right now," Clarissa shouted over the dubstep beat pounding through the speakers. "I'm tired from falling on my ass all day."

"Actually, me, too," Dev said, shocking Nate. "I could do something chiller, actually talk to you guys."

"You would have had time to talk to us if you had gotten in on schedule. Instead of taking a Spirit Airlines cargo plane to get here." Rachel rolled her eyes and Nate gave her a fist bump. *Finally, someone making some sense.* But then she sighed, and he knew she was about to betray him. "I'll compromise: Let's finish this champagne here, and then we can go somewhere relaxing. Just for tonight."

Nate took a long chug from his glass and surveyed the room. There were cute girls everywhere, in various states of post-skiing undress, many of them wearing nothing but sports bras and overall ski pants, a look he found extremely appealing. He wanted to stay, wanted to party; this was probably the only vacation he would get this year—not that these three were likely to understand what that was like. His head buzzed with alcohol, or annoyance. Both.

"God, I knew I should have invited Cody and Jake." He shook his head. "I need someone to go out with when you all get soft."

"Enough"—Rachel slammed her empty champagne glass down on the table, jarring them all—"with fucking Cody."

"Rachel, come on," he said, sensing something slipping from his grasp, his control of the afternoon metaphorically plummeting down the mountain. He had a blurred memory of Rachel telling him something about Cody during a drunken night when they had celebrated Dev's book launch. Unfortunately for Nate, he had been more out of it that weekend than he had realized in the moment, and now he found himself grasping to make a connection. He knew that Rachel thought Cody had been creepy, but he figured it had been more in a sense of "I wouldn't go out with him again" than "never mention him to me again." Rachel stared at Nate, her arms crossed in front of her. His head buzzed. He wished he hadn't taken the pill. *Pills. Plural.*

"I didn't mean anything by it, Rach," he tried again. "We can have fun just the four of us."

"Never mind." Her eyes looked distant, glassy. "I'm getting drunk. I need something to eat."

"Fine, then. I'll say it." Clarissa shrugged. "Cody's a fucking asshole, and she doesn't want to tell you because you're, like, in love with him. There."

Nate jerked back in his chair like she'd punched him; getting scolded by Clarissa somehow always felt like disappointing his mom or his favorite teacher. But he collected himself, took his last sip of champagne. "What do you know, Clare? You've bothered to talk to him, what, twice?"

"I don't need to talk to him to know he sexually assaulted Rachel, and"—he saw Rachel recoil from the table, shaking her head furiously—"I'm sorry, Rach, but it's been years, and it's hard for me to believe Nate doesn't know, that he isn't covering for him, and I think it's time to say something. God knows you've said enough to me."

"I know, but it was stupid and—"

"I swear," Nate blurted. *How could they think this of him?* He knew Rachel had never told him this, not in these words. He wanted—needed—to believe he could not have overlooked this, forgotten something of this magnitude. The sharp sting of embarrassment gave way to anger. "I did not. Know. I knew they slept together once, not that long after graduation. Then we never talked about it."

Silence.

"Guys, that's it," he insisted. "They slept together. That's what she *told me*, to my face."

"Don't talk about her like she's not here."

"Clarissa, Jesus." Nate held his hands up, feeling under

attack. He looked around the lounge, hopeful that no one was staring. "Really, when did this happen?"

Rachel looked down at her lap. She picked at a fingernail. "That *was* it, that was the time. At your party, after we all moved to the city."

"What the fuck?" Dev was asking, and Nate wanted him out of there; this had nothing to do with him. But Dev would probably find a way to make it about him, as usual, Nate thought.

"But I . . . I saw you guys together, that night? You were all over him." Clarissa made a shocked expression, her mouth forming a perfect O, and he suddenly knew he had made a mistake. But what? "No offense, Rachel, I'm sorry. But you mean . . . *that* night? We were all hammered, and you seemed really into him, and then you left the next morning and everything was fine."

"She *acted* like it was fine. She tries to tell herself it was fine."

"Look, guys. I believe that this kind of shit happens all the time, obviously, and it's fucked-up, but just, like . . . I was there that night? I saw them together, and neither of them was trying to stop what was happening, trust me." He felt his mouth rumbling like an out-of-control freight train, but between the alcohol and the Adderall and how goddamn annoying they were all being, he couldn't stop himself.

"I'm not trying to defend Cody. I've said that before: If you don't like him, or you think he's a creep, fine! And good thing he's not here. Forget I said anything! But we don't need to make this"—he waved his hands wildly, hoping to change the mood— "we don't need to make it some big thing. Cody is forgotten— poof."

He looked around nervously at his friends. Dev, uncharacteristically, looked like he had nothing to say. Nate watched him shake his head and then look over at Rachel to see how she felt, which annoyed him. Rachel stared down into her lap, still looking like she wanted to disappear, and Nate wondered if he should apologize again. Clarissa looked furious.

"This, Nate. This is *exactly* why she never told you." Clarissa spat the last word—*you*—and then it dawned on Nate that maybe she *had* told the rest of them, and for some reason that made him angry all over again. This was such a big deal that they all needed to talk about it behind his back, but yet somehow not a big enough deal to actually tell him? He was now required to agree that Cody was a monster, but no one had ever pressed charges over it?

"She was embarrassed. Ashamed."

"Well, this is probably un-PC or whatever," Nate said, no longer caring about what happened, "but not all sex you're embarrassed about later is assault." He looked pointedly at Dev and Rachel. "Lucky for you two."

"What the hell, man?" Dev said. "Are you fucked-up? Let's take a walk, huh?"

"Clarissa," Rachel was saying, pleading almost, pressing the corners of her eyes, and some strange part of Nate wanted to comfort her, even though he was the one at fault. A part of him hated that he was hurting her, and a part of him hated how much energy he spent trying not to hurt Rachel when it was becoming abundantly clear that she hardly cared about him at all.

"This bothered me for years," Rachel said, tears in her eyes. "But there's a reason I didn't tell everyone. I didn't want to blow up my life over it. And now that I finally almost never think about it, you don't have the right to just trot it out like an anecdote because you're angry at Nate."

"I was standing up for you," Clarissa said, but she looked chastened. "But seriously, are we all just going to let what Nate's saying go by?"

"I will deal with him later," Rachel said, her voice suddenly as cold and sharp as the mountain air, a tone he'd never heard from her before. He knew, right then, with a hollow, sick feeling in his chest, just how big a mistake he had made.

"Rachel, I'm sorry," he slurred, but before he could finish, Dev grabbed his arm and hauled him outside, his head spinning. And the second they hit the door he vomited into the snow, heaving, as if his body knew he wished he could scoop out every part of himself and start again.

NATE HAD BEEN HAVING WHAT HE TERMED "THE PROBLEM" quite frequently: He would think, while partying, that he was in complete control of himself. In full possession of his faculties. Sure, he had a vague awareness of a feeling of . . . *enhancement*, let's call it, from whatever substance happened to be coursing through his bloodstream. He wasn't oblivious; he knew the coke was making him louder and happier, or that the booze was warming him up, but he could still think, and talk, and react, and his tolerance had increased a good deal over the past several years, so he had been finding himself, he thought, at the perfect level of fucked-up lately: enough to have a good time, but still completely in command, the way he had always wanted to be. The problem was that when he awoke the morning after, it became abundantly clear that his previous perception had been a lie, a trick mirror, and he had, in fact, said and done things that he would never have done in his right mind. So, when Nate woke up with a pounding headache, on top of the covers, all alone in his room at the cabin, he immediately knew that this had been one of those times.

It scared him. He had a thought that he finally understood what caused people to drive drunk, swerve their cars off the road, wrap themselves around trees. He had always wondered: *Why drive? Who would do that, when they could simply get a ride or a taxi or sleep the whole thing off?*

Now he knew: It wasn't that they knew they were drunk and were choosing to drive, choosing to chance it. It was that they *didn't realize they were drunk at all.*

But that wasn't him. It wouldn't be, couldn't be him. He could fix this, he reasoned; it was just one night of too much substance at too high an altitude. He could always rein it back in, could make sure he had only a few drinks, nothing else, no need for it. He would start by apologizing, though he wondered if he had really sounded as awful as he remembered. He couldn't let himself think about it for too long; he needed to lock it underneath a trapdoor somewhere inside him, somewhere it could not cause the start of a shame spiral that would knock him out for the rest of the day.

He rolled off the bed and immediately doubled over as nausea swept through him. On second thought, maybe his first step would be a Bloody Mary. One shot, maximum, he promised himself, but he couldn't very well mount an acceptable apology if he threw up in his mouth halfway through.

He stopped in the kitchen to mix his drink and then found Rachel in the living room, reclined on the oversize plaid sofa with a book in her hand. She looked up at him but didn't speak.

Nate took a big sip of his drink, then settled himself into the leather club chair across from her. He felt as if a spotlight was shining on him, and he did his best not to squirm in anxiousness. *Just fix it*, he told himself. *The sooner you apologize, the sooner this is all nothing.*

"Rach, I just wanted to say . . . I'm sorry," Nate offered, staring into his drink.

"For?" she asked coolly.

"For being a jerk yesterday," he said, hoping this would cover it, as his brain did not possess all the specifics. He also thought referencing sex directly might be in poor taste. "For not taking you seriously. For being an ass. I guess I . . . got a lot drunker than I intended."

"Shocking," she said, her tone biting at first, but then she rolled her eyes, and it seemed more like faux annoyance, the usual sarcasm she used to tease him.

"But I really am sorry. I didn't want to ruin the trip."

Rachel nodded. "It's . . . fine. You didn't."

Nate had hoped for more. But this was a start, at least.

"Where's Clarissa?" he asked. He imagined apologizing to her would help, too. "She seemed pretty pissed at me last night."

Rachel sighed. "You don't remember?"

"What?"

"She could only come for two nights. She just left for the airport."

"Shit," Nate said, half-ashamed, half-guiltily relieved. He sucked down another large sip of his drink, starting to feel better. "Already?"

"Her flight isn't until tonight, but I don't think she wanted to stick around much after last night."

"God, that bad?" Nate massaged his neck, his head cocked sheepishly. "I'll text her and apologize now. I didn't . . . do anything to her, right? She was mad on your behalf? And because I was a jerk about you and Dev?"

Rachel opened her mouth as if to speak, then looked like she thought better of it. After a pause, she said, "Just call her, Nate. Maybe when we get home."

Just the thought made him nervous. His hands shook as he pictured having to dial her number. He flashed back, unbidden, to the time he had called Jessica LePeer on the phone in eighth grade, heart beating in his ears as he asked her to the school dance. He had experienced one moment of pure elation when she'd said yes—followed by the crushing defeat of voices laughing from the other line, her friends listening in, the whole thing a prank—psych! She would never say yes to Nate.

That's how calling Clarissa and asking to be forgiven felt. Like a setup.

"I'll call her," Nate promised anyway, hoping he was telling the truth.

He watched Rachel stand up and cross the room. Dev waited at the entrance to her room, leaning against the frame. They went inside and shut the door. He could hear them talking in low voices, confiding in each other, and it somehow felt worse than if he'd overheard them together in bed.

NATE KEPT HALF HIS PROMISE. HE COULDN'T MAKE HIMSELF call Clarissa, but he sent her a text—one that went unanswered for two weeks, until he decided he couldn't worry about it anymore and deleted their entire thread.

After the awkward end to the ski trip, when the three of them said a chilly goodbye and flew home on different airlines, Nate spent a month back in New York on a bender. He knew it wasn't a good idea, but every time he stopped to get sober, he felt a queasy, sickly feeling in his stomach, the "everyone secretly hates you" notion he remembered from childhood. Nate didn't go out with Cody; he didn't know what to think about him anymore. Instead, he went to restaurants, replacing the two-martini lunch with the three-martini dinner with his fellow bankers, or skipped club lines with his DJ acquaintances from the nightclub scene. He took enough uppers to make it through the workday. He ignored a text from Dev saying he was "worried" and that they "should talk after things calm down with the movie publicity."

It wasn't much of a way to appeal to someone, Nate thought, saying you'd talk to them if you weren't so busy with your film production. He felt two dueling impulses, one to flagellate himself for being an asshole, to realize everyone was now too busy for him because he'd been neglecting them, neglecting his friendships for months—and another one to tell everyone to go fuck themselves.

But he couldn't think about that now. For now, inconveniently, he needed to go home.

DURING ONE OF NEW YORK'S SIGNATURE MARCH SNOW-storm, Nate boarded a flight bound for Cleveland.

The plane sat for thirty minutes at the gate, pushed back several yards, then stopped again. By the time the seemingly decrepit American Airlines connection shuttle finally rattled toward a runway through the swirling snow, Nate felt shaken, his movements jerky and uncoordinated. He shrank away from the hulking man seated next to him, unreasonably annoyed at the man's size and his ownership of the armrest, rude thoughts that he probably wouldn't have had, he told himself, if he had remembered to bring any of his Xanax with him so that he could sleep through the flight. But this was the weekend that he decided—perhaps too rashly—to "go straight," whatever *that* meant. Alcohol only, he supposed. Two drinks, maybe three at the event. If necessary.

The event in question was his mother's sixtieth birthday party. The thought of spending one of his rare weekends off from work in a hired banquet hall in Ohio surrounded by his parents' middle-aged friends, eating subpar canapés and answering their questions about "the market," did not seem like Nate's idea of fun. But he had missed his father's retirement party the year before, and his parents' thirty-fifth anniversary the year before that, and the time to use work as an excuse for shirking the hometown that held his least favorite memories had worn thin. He also decided that he sorely needed to take a weekend off from partying.

Every night for the last month, when he had come home at the end of yet another night out, his heart had pounded in his ears and he'd tossed and turned, alone, sleeping fitfully for the few hours between dawn and work. When had he, Nate, ever had trouble sleeping? No matter the event, no matter the drugs, he had always just passed out and woken up in the bright sun of the next day, ready to go. Now he had to take benzos to take the edge off, which didn't seem like a big deal—everyone had a script for everything these days—but it did start to make him wonder if his use might be more than recreational. It was as if he had looked up one day, surveyed the landscape from his familiar window, and saw that the seasons had changed without his notice.

Also, there was the mess he had made with his friends, of course. Both Rachel and Clarissa still weren't speaking to him, as far as he could tell.

Nate knew he had responded to the revelation that Cody had taken advantage of Rachel in the perfectly wrong way. He wished he remembered the exact moment better, but he only knew, with the kind of sickening, anxious feeling in his stomach that only a drink could quiet, that he had essentially told her that it didn't matter. He'd only *meant* to defend a theoretical "Cody," to defend a man's perception of the situation. To say, simply, that when you are drunk, and a beautiful girl is drunk with you, and she seems to want to go home with you, and so

you do, to later call the resulting sex a crime seems slightly unfair. He didn't know if this underlying point had gotten lost
somehow, but what he did know was that Rachel had been his
friend, a true one, in a way that Cody never had been, and yet he
hadn't listened to her or even really heard her. He'd been angry,
resentful of her and Dev. He regretted that, even as he didn't
know how to change how he felt.

But the thing was, he thought, making a case for himself as
the plane finally lifted under him, he *had* apologized the next
morning, and Rachel had said she'd forgiven him. They had
parted from the trip without any kind of dramatic fight. But
they hadn't spoken since.

This line of thinking did not have much else to offer him, he
decided. He stretched and yawned, then signaled to the flight
attendant and ordered a drink to quiet his mind. Just the one.

IT HAD STARTED ON THE PLANE, BUT IT HADN'T ENDED THERE.

Nate's hand had clutched a plastic cup of scotch like a talis-
man through the flight, but at first he felt sure that the liquor
was evening him out, bringing him back to himself. He stopped
feeling so annoyed at his seatmate and his mustard-stained tie,
stopped dreading the prospect of the birthday party. He even
had a smile on his face by the time his dad's old Buick swung up
to the curb, and even the fact that his mom stepped back from
their hug making a face as she sniffed the air around him hadn't
fazed him. He and his parents had had less to say to one another
over the past several years, but that was an expected consequence
of them getting older, of him building a life full of people and

cities that they had never seen and at this point maybe never would. Everything had started off well, he thought—well enough that he felt he had earned a glass of wine at dinner, just as a hedge against being unable to sleep later without the Xanax. He sat there, looking around at his parents' living room, at the boxy entertainment center, the stained, brown shag carpeting from his youth, which had already been out of style when his parents bought the house in 1985. Other than the new TV he had purchased for them, the house looked like it had been frozen in amber, a crystallized relic that perfectly encapsulated exactly why he had decided he wanted more from his life. He remembered sipping his wine, then charitably asking his mom if she was looking forward to the party tomorrow.

So, the dinner hadn't been the problem, Nate felt reasonably confident, even as his memory of it seemed like something he was watching play back on someone else's TV screen, through a dirty window, possibly from across the street. The problem had been after his parents had gone to bed, when he decided he needed a nightcap to sleep and had found the house completely dry. He had a vague recollection of grabbing his dad's keys out of the drawer under the old corded phone, curling them in his fist.

Then nothing. Not, at least, until the police found him asleep in the driver's seat of the 1999 Buick LeSabre in the parking lot of the local liquor store.

When they rapped on the car window, Nate had bolted upright, ready to explain that this had all been a mistake, to use the confident, convincing tone of voice he had perfected when he had to talk the door guy at 1 Oak into letting in just one more of his friends. He had a cover story ready: He planned to say that this was all just a big misunderstanding, that he had drunk a couple of glasses of wine at dinner with his parents, headed out in his dad's car to visit another family member in the area, and then—responsibly!—pulled over in the parking lot just as soon as he realized that he might have misjudged his own intoxication. He believed in the reasonableness of this story so deeply, in fact, that he felt confident even when the Cleveland police shone a light into his eyes, asked him to get out of his car, and gave him a Breathalyzer. He felt stone-cold sober now. He knew that he would pass the test, and then he would be on his way home, with his sleeping parents none the wiser.

But Nate did not pass.

Nate woke up for the second time to the cold press of steel against his cheek in the Cuyahoga County Jail.

"Nathanial Davis," a voice boomed from outside the bars. "I see you're awake. You ready for that phone call?"

His neck aching, his memory dimmed, he had one painful, grasping thought: He wanted to call one of his best friends, but he didn't have them anymore.

The officer escorted him from the holding cell and led him to a phone. With his one phone call, Nate dialed his parents, who had no doubt already awakened to find his room empty, their car missing. Shame liquefied his insides. There seemed to be no limit to his capacity to disappoint everyone, himself most of all.

"Mom?" he heard himself say, his voice squeaky and small. "Don't freak out. I can explain. But I . . . I need you to come get me. I'm at the county jail."

CLARISSA

The heat of the lights. The feeling of standing at the micro-
phone on the lip of the stage, like a figurehead on the prow
of a ship, the applause swelling in waves from the audience below. The sound of that applause crashing up against her, drowning out the memory of half-empty rooms and half-hearted
laughter. Clarissa swore to herself that she would never, ever
forget this. Success. Land on the horizon at last.

She didn't know why she kept thinking about sailing meta-
phors; she had only set foot on a boat once—and it had been a
Chicago River ferry tour in grade school. But something about
finding her way in her career—breaking 500K subscribers on
YouTube, finally performing a one-woman show for a sellout
crowd, having offers come to *her* instead of the other way
around—*did* feel like coming ashore after a long journey. At
times, she had given up thinking that she would ever make it

"there," wherever "there" was, but now she had. She had planted her flag on the island of success.

"There" to her parents had been America. It had been the tiny, crowded brick house in Garfield Ridge, the long night shifts, the very things Clarissa had looked at and said, "I want more than that." That wasn't lost on her, the sense that her parents had only wanted enough to get by in a new country, whereas she, Clarissa, had needed more than that. She'd burned for a captive audience, to be heard.

It had cost her something, of course.

Four years ago, Clarissa had spent about one day enjoying the fact that she'd made a viral video—and then she'd raced home on the el to finally tell her parents she was gay before they heard it from someone else.

Clarissa had thought using the video as a forcing function would make it easier to come out. Or she'd hoped that the nothing-left-to-lose feeling wrought by heartbreak would make her brave. But she still needed to steel herself in the kitchen of her childhood home for thirty minutes before she could force herself to walk back out into the living room and say, wholly ineloquently, "Oh, screw it. I'm gay, you guys."

No one had said anything, at first. She watched as her mom's mouth gaped open, fishlike. Her dad sank back into their ancient, squished, floral sofa. Her grandmother, mercifully, seemed to be completely asleep in the armchair, and her nephew, Joey, sat by her feet, repeatedly colliding two Transformers into each other with the laser focus of a surgeon.

"Autobots, roll out!" he shouted. Clarissa felt faint, her head spinning, the pause interminable, but somewhere beneath that, a quiver of laughter that the first response to her coming out had been her nephew yelling about Transformers. At least she could probably use that for a bit.

Her sister, Maria, stood up from her chair. "Well, what's important is that we love you, Clare. No matter what." She glanced around the living room, her steely expression that of the commanding older sibling ordering everyone to fall in line. Clarissa loved her so much in that moment. "Right? Everyone?"

"How could we not have known this?" her mom blurted in Polish, not answering the question. "I thought we knew you."

Clarissa tried to focus on the fact that she wasn't being excommunicated. That no one had shouted, "Get out of our house." But it hurt. She took a deep breath, her heart hammering.

"You do know me. But that's why I'm telling you this. So that you can know more of me."

"This is just a phase, maybe?" her dad suggested, sitting up excitedly, as if this were an original and important thought. "Sometimes dating is frustrating, but you can find the right man still. He is probably not in the *comedy* scene, but if you just—"

"Papa, no. This isn't about a bad date, clearly," her sister cut in.

The corners of her eyes tingled, tears welling. *You will not cry. You have nothing to cry about.*

"Mama, Papa," she tried again. She moved hesitantly to sit down on the couch next to them. "I don't expect you to understand right away, but this is not a phase. I'm still the same person. I love comedy, and eating dessert before dinner, and everything you already knew about me. I just . . . also like women, too."

"Clarissa, we love you. Of course we love you," her mom had finally said, and she felt one moment of relief.

"But this, this . . . lifestyle," she'd continued. "It's not accepted everywhere. Maybe it is okay to . . . experiment where you are. But think about our family, our community, think about what it means. This is something you will want to think seriously about, to pray about, okay? You can take it to God, he will tell you."

"Um. Okay."

"Now." Her mom patted her hand twice, then stood up, signaling the end of the conversation. "Who is ready for some pie?"

She took stock of the facts. They loved her; they hadn't thrown her out or told her never to speak to them again. But they also hadn't shown any willingness to discuss it further. They worried about what it meant for her life; they worried about their church. And that had been it.

Every time she thought about the conversation, it hurt in a strange way, a piercing feeling from her chest through to the center of her back, a dull ache. It could have been much worse, she told herself. Her parents had heard her; they seemed prepared to tentatively accept this fact about her as long as they didn't have to think about it for too long. But in a way, she felt much farther apart from them than she had before she had come out; she felt lonelier than ever. In pursuit of being "seen," she had traded away being understood. Her parents now knew slightly more about the intimate details of her life, but in exchange, they might never be comfortable with her again.

For several months, she leapt between sadness, anger, and denial. She spent Christmas with her family, and Easter, but while her relationship with her sister had improved—she gamely helped Clarissa make a dating profile on OkCupid, even though she knew little about online dating and less about dating women—her relationship with her parents remained that of remotely friendly acquaintances. *They're trying*, Maria told her. *Give it time.*

Time. It was a funny thing, slippery like a fish, days sliding into months into years. Four years after she had come out, everything had changed, and nothing had. Here she was at thirty, successful, a bright new decade ahead shimmering with possibility. Millions of people had now watched her videos; thousands of them left her comments, wrote to her for advice. Thousands more had seen her perform live.

Her parents still never had.

TWENTY FOURTEEN STARTED SPARKLING AND BRIGHT. ON A brisk January day, Clarissa found herself boarding a flight to New York, ostensibly for a hard-won gig at the Comedy Cellar. She filmed a bit of footage of herself in line at TSA PreCheck with her smartphone, thinking of the day-in-the-life video she would make about her trip.

She had been flirting with the idea of moving to New York for some time. It made sense for her work: She'd planned with her agent and gotten booked on the bill at the Comedy Cellar, the kind of opportunity that came around less often the more she focused on the confessional style of vlogging. The move made sense when she thought about Dev and Rachel—as well as, yes, the satisfying flings she'd had in New York over the years when she'd visited.

But that wasn't the real reason she wanted to go to New York this time.

Just two weeks ago, a Facebook update had informed her that a certain Rebecca Nielson had gone back to school to become a therapist. At NYU.

AS SOON AS SHE ARRIVED, CLARISSA TOOK A TAXI FROM HER hotel to a nondescript Irish pub in Chelsea, where she had asked Rachel to meet her. It was the kind of place Clarissa had always felt comfortable in: somewhere with an old wooden bar that perpetually remained slightly sticky, cheap drafts, and plenty of dark corner tables—the kind of place where you could relax, could hear yourself think. But when she walked in and watched Rachel appraise her, she knew that while her taste in bars hadn't changed, her style certainly had. Clarissa had on a pair of perfectly tailored black cigarette pants and a white button-down, half-tucked. She knew it made for a sharp contrast with her old style, all tank tops and shorts or old stone-washed overalls. Admittedly, she still wore the overalls pretty much every weekend, but she had a kind of glam-lesbian thing going on for her performer persona, and it seemed to be working.

"You look amazing," Rachel said as they embraced. She pulled back from the hug and looked Clarissa up and down. "You own Theory now? You, the girl who once wore the same Strokes T-shirt to three parties in a row?"

"Well, I have something a little more important than a kegger going on tonight." Clarissa raised an eyebrow. Then she checked her watch. She was glad to see Rachel, but she knew her mental energies were otherwise engaged. She wished they could have met for a drink after her set, but Rachel hadn't wanted to stay out past 11 p.m., citing Aaron, her now live-in boyfriend. Instead, she offered to meet beforehand, and then said she'd come watch the 9 p.m. show.

"Well, I should say congratulations. It's such a big deal, Clare."

"Congratulations on getting booked somewhere you've heard of, or on me finally having an outfit that doesn't make you want to give me a makeover à la Tai in *Clueless*?"

"Both." She smiled. They looked at each other, and Clarissa wondered if Rachel appreciated how far she'd come: the years of bartending in Uptown, all the late nights and half-empty rooms. The Second City audition she'd bombed, then the YouTube videos and the recent sold-out run of her one-woman show. She subdued a thought that came from the old Clarissa, the version of her that had imagined being a cast member on *SNL*, rather than a YouTube comedian mostly famous to people born after 1990. She didn't get "traditional" comedic opportunities often, and in order to get her a slot at the Comedy Cellar, her agent had needed to argue for Clarissa's comedic chops, to insist that she was more than a vlogger with a teen girl audience. She tried not to dwell on it. This, today, was a huge moment, she told herself. She was worthy of this opportunity.

They sat down together at the end of the bar, and Clarissa ordered a beer. Rachel asked for a scotch, neat, and drained half of it in one long swallow.

"Easy there." Clarissa took a sip of her draft beer.

"So," Rachel said. "Are you nervous? You must be nervous."

"Of course," she answered. "But it's more of an adrenaline rush than fear. I'm excited to be there—I want to be there."

"I wondered if you still got stage fright. You know, like the Second City audition."

Something about the dialogue felt oddly calibrated, almost as if Rachel *wanted* Clarissa to say she felt nervous. Clarissa ignored the intuitive feeling, and she answered honestly, breezily. "I'm not sure I ever did get stage fright, really. I've had bad performances, but only because I was inexperienced, or needed to work on my timing. Never because I felt nervous ahead of time."

Rachel nodded, and they were silent for a moment before Clarissa decided to change tack.

"So. How is everybody?"

"Good, I guess. Dev finally finished a draft of his second book. But I only know this because I work at his publisher now. He's been CIA-level secretive."

"I haven't read it yet, either. But I'm seeing him for lunch tomorrow," Clarissa said, and she looked forward to it, immensely. Something existed between her and Dev that felt like it was now missing with Rachel, and for the life of her she couldn't remember where along the line the dynamic had changed, when they had stopped speaking on the phone every week. Their closeness felt like a glass she had set down for only a second, then looked back to find it had been cleared without her knowledge.

Then again, maybe it made sense, she thought. She and Dev had a certain lifestyle in common now, the creative work, certainly, but also the publicity, the interviews, the obligations. People always talked about timing in romantic relationships, but how much of *friendship* was down to timing, too? Clarissa had always believed in forming closeness through ideals and personality, but maybe adult friendship was more about circumstance.

Or maybe she was getting too pessimistic. Clarissa had been born cynical, and turning thirty didn't seem to have helped.

"Oh, that's . . . nice," Rachel said, and Clarissa realized that she expected to be invited. "I'm going over to Aaron's parents' tomorrow for brunch, or I'd come with."

They drank in silence for a moment, while Clarissa resisted her typical impulsivity and swallowed a comment about how she wanted to see Dev alone, anyway. She checked her watch again. She was antsy about the show, and then even more eager for what she hoped was to come afterward. Trying to fit Rachel in beforehand had been a mistake.

But Rachel hadn't offered her any other time in the whole weekend, Clarissa thought. She was too busy with her boyfriend, her problems, her life.

"Speaking of old friends," Rachel said, "I haven't talked to Nate since the arrest. Has Dev told you anything?"

"Honestly, not really," Clarissa said, a bit surprised that Rachel had chosen to bring up Nate. Every time in the past year that Clarissa had tried to broach the subject, Rachel had changed it, firmly, which seemed fair enough. "Dev called me when he found out from Nate's family. He told me Nate was going to rehab, moving to Chicago so his parents could look out for him. Which, good. I hope he gets better. I'm sorry it happened, obviously, but I don't see how any of it is my problem."

"I know," Rachel said quietly. "But you don't ever feel . . . guilty? About what happened on the ski trip? I know I do. I had—I have—all the reasons to be mad at him, but I always wish it had gone differently."

"I wish all of it had, Rach. For your sake. But I don't think we're indebted to him in any way because of it."

"I know."

"Do you?" Clarissa asked, feeling herself soften toward Rachel for a moment.

"I do." She nodded. "But I don't know. He might be better now. Would you ever look him up in Chicago?"

"I hope he's better. But no, I can't say I plan to. Honestly, I'm not sure we were ever that close of friends. Even before . . . everything." It was funny, she thought, the way friendships faded after college. On graduation day, you had this naïve expectation that you'd all be best friends forever, that you'd live in a big house together for the rest of your lives. But it became clear, sometimes quite quickly, whom you had things in common with beyond housing assignments and partying habits, and whom you didn't. Someone could just forget to call someone back, and then suddenly it had been months and no one had noticed. The friendship had just outlived its usefulness, and that had been true even before Nate had made the asinine decision to defend Cody.

"That makes sense," Rachel said. "I think that's enough about Nate for tonight, anyway. Did I tell you that Aaron and I are talking about getting engaged?"

"No, you didn't, that's—"

"I mean, we've already picked the ring, basically," she interrupted. "And you should see his place I moved into. It's in Tribeca. It's huge, on Walker Street . . ."

Clarissa listened for a full five minutes. She was engaged as Rachel talked. And talked. And talked. About her life and her plans and her soon-to-be fiancé. It took five minutes without a single question about Clarissa for the thought to finally creep in: Was Rachel ever going to ask her about her show, or about her life? She'd wanted to tell Rachel about her nascent plans to move to New York, but she almost felt like she didn't have the energy to interrupt her monologue. How were they forty minutes into sitting here, their hour almost up, still making small talk about Aaron's apartment, anyway? Clarissa realized how much she wanted to tell Rachel—to tell someone—about her hopes to see Rebecca on this trip. She needed a moment to be vulnerable, because she couldn't be to her family, unlike Rachel, and she didn't have a partner, also unlike Rachel.

Instead of voicing any of this, she snapped.

"You know what, I think I should start heading down to the Village." Clarissa threw back the last of her beer. "I like to be early to prepare, you know."

"Wait, what? Already?" Rachel cocked her head. "Why? What's going on with you tonight?"

Suddenly, it was all bubbling up inside her: Rebecca's long-ago comments about how much she put up with from Rachel, the "first-generation college student" thing on the day of their graduation. When she opened her mouth, it was like breaking a dam; the words poured out, uninvited.

"Tonight? It's not just about tonight." She slammed her glass down again, harder than she meant to, and it clanged against the stupid reclaimed-wood bar. "Well, it's a little bit about to-night. Like, that you couldn't meet me later, or tomorrow, even though you know this is an important night for my career. And you're bringing up all the stage fright, my bad auditions—like you want to undermine me—I don't know."

"That's not what I was doing!"

"Maybe not. And I know the last couple of years have been hard on you, with your mom. I'm glad she's better now. But I'm sorry, Rachel, that can't be an excuse, because you were like this before. And you know what I think now?"

"No, but I'm sure you're going to tell me." Rachel stared at her, her face an unreadable mask, which worked only to make Clarissa angrier.

"It's easier for you when I'm in second place. When I look up to you."

"That's ridiculous."

"Is it? I think you took me under your wing. I think you liked being the one who got to be the expert on everything. Tell me everything, while I just listened. Teaching the first-generation college girl how to pronounce *prix fixe*, how to dress, how to order wine at Pump Room, but now—"

"So, you think I've been best friends with you out of pity? Or to make myself feel better? I've been faking it—faking this"—she gestured back and forth between them—"for twelve years? That doesn't make sense."

"No, I think we really became friends. Of course we were friends."

"We *are*."

"But that's not really the point I'm trying to make." Clarissa sighed, equally frustrated with Rachel and with herself. But she kept going. "I think you don't even realize it, but I'm not sure

I'm the kind of person you would be friends with as, like, an equal. Admit it: If we hadn't been assigned to room together freshman year, you would never, ever have talked to me."

"That's not true."

"It is. I think you know it is." Clarissa paused for a moment, making sure she was right. But it had to be true, didn't it? She knew she was nothing like the rest of Rachel's friends, the Isabelles and Nicoles of the world, the model-like women from Manhattan who populated Rachel's Facebook photo albums and her new Instagram feed. No amount of money, no amount of video streams, would make her a natural-born member of that world.

"Well, maybe you're asking the wrong questions," Rachel said, quieter now. "Yes, we did get assigned to room together. We did have to talk to each other. But no one made us be best friends. We didn't have to be, but we were. That was real."

"*Was* real?" Clarissa knew this wasn't fair, but she felt sparked like a live wire. Any comment would be enough to set her off. She sighed. "This is not how I wanted tonight to go."

"Well, obviously, me, neither," Rachel said with a sniff. "But I was worried going into tonight, to be honest. Clarissa, you're the one who takes days to respond to me now. Not the other way around." Her eyes watered, and having seen Rachel cry so many times throughout their friendship, Clarissa knew what was coming. It softened her, of course it did. She loved Rachel. But love was not necessarily enough anymore.

"Look, I am tense tonight. I have a lot on my mind, too. I know I haven't been perfect." *The show. My own family. A . . .*

certain New York woman whom I invited to meet me for drinks after the show, to "catch up." "But this isn't the moment to talk about it. And I really do need to head out soon. That wasn't a lie."

"Right, I know."

Clarissa waited to see what she would say. Resisted the temptation to jump in, to smooth things over.

"Anyway, go ahead. I'll skip the show tonight; I don't want to be a distraction. But break a leg. You will be amazing."

Clarissa drew in a deep breath. She knew that Rachel meant her decision to be kind, meant that she wanted to give Clarissa her space so that she could focus on her work, and that they could talk later. But anger rippled through her like a crack spreading across the ice. Rachel would miss her big night to go home and lick her wounds? Moreover, Rachel thought that she was the center of Clarissa's emotional life, like Clarissa couldn't see her in the damn audience without being distracted? *My mind is on someone else!* she wanted to shout. She needed to know if Rebecca had gotten her invitation, if she would be at the show tonight. That was whom she would be looking for in the audience. That was what she wanted to talk to her best friend about, but instead it had somehow become about past resentments and bitterness and then—as ever—Rachel's hurt feelings.

"That's fine." She snatched her purse off the table. "Look, we'll talk later. Have a good night. Get home safe."

CLARISSA HAD SENT THE FACEBOOK INVITE ON A WHIM, THE kind of thing you wish desperately will work but feels about as likely as buying a winning lottery ticket. And yet, even still, she hoped.

She waited at the bar upstairs above the Comedy Cellar after the show, nursing one pint of lager, and then a seltzer, just as an excuse to stay longer. Several fans—had she really become someone with fans?—had stopped by to gush about her set, and she smiled, thanking them, amazed. She should appreciate tonight as a moment of professional success, the kind she knew didn't come around very often. She should put the fight with Rachel out of her mind, and she should stop waiting for Rebecca, who would have sent her a message back if she planned to come. Clarissa closed her eyes briefly, picturing the laughter of the tightly packed crowd downstairs, the thrill of the moment when each joke hit, the joy in talking openly about dating women, making fun of herself, inhabiting her real identity and her real body in a way her twenty-year-old self had only ever dreamed about. It was enough.

But even that feeling didn't match the one she felt when she opened her eyes again and saw Rebecca. Wearing the fuzzy green angora sweater that brought out her eyes, her smile tentative, then full, the laugh lines around her mouth deeper than Clarissa remembered but somehow sexier, too. Joy crashed through her, unbridled.

"Well, fancy seeing you here," Rebecca said, taking the bar stool next to her and leaning over for a quick—much too quick—side hug. Clarissa realized that she was getting ahead of herself, that it was far more likely that Rebecca had come as an old friend and nothing more. "Sorry it took me a minute to get back here. I had to walk my friend to the subway after the show."

Friend—or girlfriend?

"It's great to see you," Clarissa gushed. "How did you like the show? Sorry, I'm fishing."

"Yes, you are." Rebecca laughed as she unfurled her scarf. "But you were phenomenal, Clare. I've kept up with all of your videos, but seeing you live is so different. You're so confident. And so . . . you. It's thrilling."

"Thank you. It means the most to me, to hear you say that." It was true. Clarissa had started to hear more and more often that she was funny, or creative, or inspiring. But few people knew her well enough to know when she was being herself. Authenticity, that was the thing she had felt change the most since the day of her first viral video. Clarissa had always known how to write a decent joke, but she hadn't always known how to be a real person up there onstage. Rebecca understood.

"Speaking of being yourself," she added. "I couldn't believe you moved to New York—and you're becoming a therapist? I want to hear all about it."

"Yes, let's pretend that's as interesting as being famous."

"It is to me," Clarissa said, and as their eyes met, she could swear she felt something there. Did Rebecca feel it, too?

"Well, you know I always enjoyed what I did in marketing, but I started to want . . . something more," Rebecca explained. "Early midlife crisis, maybe, but I thought about how much I love working with people, listening to their stories. Something kept telling me I wanted to make a change to doing something that would let me help people. I applied to just a few schools for a master's in social work, almost on a whim, it felt like—but now here I am. I'm working on getting my clinical hours now, and I should finish in about six months."

"That's incredible," Clarissa said. She remembered what an empathetic listener Rebecca was, how she had functioned as the de facto therapist for her friend group for years. For Clarissa, too, come to think of it. "I know you'll be great—if only because you were almost a therapist to me, sometimes. I'm sorry about that, by the way. I was young."

Rebecca considered her for a moment. "You have nothing to be sorry for. Really."

"Should we . . ." Clarissa hesitated, wanting to suggest that they move to a table, order another drink, but she still wasn't sure why they were both here.

"Get a table? Yes. I have plenty more questions for you, by the way. You know I want to hear everything."

"So do I," Clarissa said, steeling herself. No sooner had she made the decision than her hand was on Rebecca's knee, and Rebecca did not move away. "Can you stay for a while? I know it's late."

"For you," Rebecca said, "I have all the time in the world."

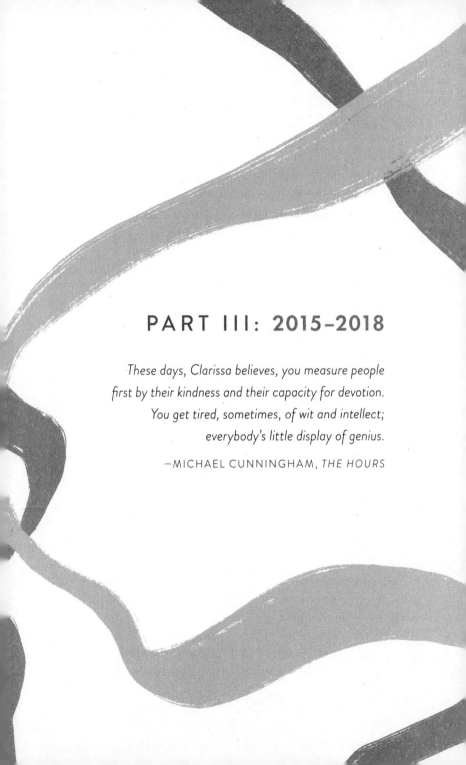

PART III: 2015–2018

*These days, Clarissa believes, you measure people
first by their kindness and their capacity for devotion.
You get tired, sometimes, of wit and intellect;
everybody's little display of genius.*

—MICHAEL CUNNINGHAM, *THE HOURS*

DEV

2015

I t had been an unseasonably warm December. Dev had worn shorts to the bodega on Christmas Day, where he bought a six-pack of beer to go with the Chinese food he always ordered. In the early years in New York, Rachel had come over to share it with him, both of them eating right out of greasy containers of lo mein and General Tso's. The Jewish Christmas tradition, she called it. This year they had just FaceTimed, even though Rachel and Aaron lived in Tribeca, only a stone's throw from his Thompson Street apartment. They had recently gotten engaged.

Dev had walked to their engagement party, ten minutes away in the upstairs space at Tiny's restaurant on West Broadway. He'd found the room decorated for the occasion with so many flowers and candles and heart-shaped trays of Dom Pérignon that it had felt like a wedding itself. *We found true love, and you didn't*, it all seemed to advertise. *Also, we are very, very rich.* In this tax bracket, which Dev was much closer to belonging to than ever before but of which he wasn't a native member, he had learned that it was important to never *say* the word *rich*, nor even imply that you thought about it, but you were allowed to project it through ostentatious displays staged around important events, like engagement parties.

Maybe, Dev thought, suddenly annoyed, he should just move to Brooklyn at last. He should save himself some money. Because what was the point of being at the center of things if your friends spent all their time with their fiancés, anyway?

Dev looked out the window. The unusually warm weather hadn't held, and January 2015 had rolled in like a storm, a dark and ominous month of snow. The winds were whipping up off the Hudson and blowing crosstown, the snow flowing almost horizontally in front of his third-floor window. He had only left the apartment once in the past three days, to visit his local independent bookstore under the guise of "browsing," but really to make sure the paperback edition of *Nirvana* had been shelved under the heading of "literary" rather than "commercial" fiction.

He stared out at the snow from the couch, and he had a momentary thought that he wished he hadn't agreed to go with Clarissa tonight. She was now a member of the board for New Dawn Treatment Center, an organization that provided holistic services for survivors of sexual assault. It was a cause they both believed in, but looking at the snowflakes hovering in the sub-zero air, he wondered if he had to believe in it *in person*. Couldn't he just send a check? (Had he become the kind of person who just sent a check?)

No, he should go. It was important, he reminded himself, and anyway, he *had* been hiding out in his apartment since New Year's, alternately working on a TV pilot and catching up on the final season of *Mad Men*. Mostly watching *Mad Men*, to be honest. And eating takeout.

He realized the irony of his student-like lifestyle: Here he was in a Soho apartment of someone's dreams—not his dreams, because *his* dreams had not originally included real estate, at least not until he finally had enough money that his financial adviser had told him he needed to put his cash somewhere, and that renting was money down the drain. Around the same time, it had swept over everyone he knew like a sickness, this sudden and insatiable need to talk about real estate. Conversations about open-concept kitchens and imported sofas ran rampant once you hit the age of thirty, and so he rebelled against this where he could: At thirty-one, Dev Kaur had a film adaptation of his first novel that had been nominated for a Golden Globe, a finished draft of his much-anticipated second novel, *The Family*, a series of flashy screenwriting credits, an *almost*-million-dollar apartment, and . . . a secondhand couch he'd been dragging around since 2008, which was currently littered with empty white containers of $8 Chinese food.

Dev heaved himself up off the sofa. He put the kettle on for a cup of tea and forced himself to amble over to the shower, so he'd look presentable for the night. He checked his phone and saw that Clarissa had texted him, writing that she'd swing by his place around six thirty and they'd walk to the event space together, which was nearby in Soho. He smiled at that as he stepped into the marble shower stall. Most people he knew in Clarissa's position—and he knew a lot of them, writers, actors, the general socialites who hung around at the events he seemed to keep getting invited to—would take a car. They'd want to avoid the crowds, or prefer to pull up in front of the event looking stylish and ridiculous in a limo or a town car, even if they lived only a few blocks away. But Clarissa wasn't like that. She and Rebecca walked everywhere; they took the subway. Rebecca had gone back to school to get a master's in social work, and she now saw her therapy patients in the spare room of their East Village apartment—and if any of them felt weird about the fact that they were technically also in the home of a celebrity, they never showed it. Rebecca and Clarissa were real, honest-to-God, down-to-earth grown-ups, Dev thought. Which scared one part of him, and then made another part of him almost . . . jealous? But he'd get used to it. For Clarissa, he'd make himself get over it.

Dev felt an ache in his neck as he contorted his head under the shower stream. Why did he keep waking up with random pains now that he had an expensive bed for the first time in his life? He'd slept on a mattress on the floor in a fifth-floor walk-up for most of his twenties and never had a problem. Maybe he was just getting old. He wanted that to be the problem, actually, because he couldn't think of any other explanation for why he felt so dispirited when everything in his life was objectively so great.

He tried to think about when he had been happiest, and he kept coming back to the same time, which meant it was probably true: at twenty-three, his second year in New York, when he was finishing the book, spending his weekends going out with his friends on the cheap, having absolutely no clue if any of it was going to lead anywhere. He liked thinking back on that time a lot, the period when he hadn't yet known if "it" was going to happen for him. Somehow, that had been the most fun part. The pursuit of the dream. He wished he could live it all over again: the same joyful uncertainty, but this time with more confidence.

He realized how ridiculous that sounded. He wanted to re-live his starving-artist years (an exaggeration, but that was his preferred narrative) but with the guarantee that one day something would come of it? Stupid, but that was what he wanted. Waiting to make it—almost making it—often seemed so much better than he had ever felt since having "arrived."

He had the same problem with women.

After another series of short-lived flings following his movie release, when he had, admittedly, been a bit full of himself, Dev had met a young and talented chef from Paris named Cleo. They hadn't met at some ridiculous press event, but instead at a local wine shop, when Dev had been agonizing about picking a bottle to bring to a dinner party at a well-known writer's Upper West Side apartment. He'd been wondering about the seemingly un-graspable difference between Corbières and Côtes du Rhône when Cleo had stepped up beside him and offered her opinion. She was beautiful—long dark hair striking against her pale skin, her face pretty and angular in a way that seemed distinctly French even before he heard her accent—and Dev had asked her on a date immediately. Now they had been out several times, but Dev had no idea how he was "supposed" to feel. There seemed to be a part of him that expected fireworks, expected a glowing neon sign announcing, "This is your soul mate." He wondered if it was because he had grown up expecting "love marriage" to be some magical, strangely ineffable thing, free of the mundanity and expectation that he imagined would have pervaded the kind of appropriate, family-arranged match his parents wanted to make for him. Or maybe it wasn't cultural at all; maybe he was missing some sort of love gene.

Or *maybe* he was simply like every other moderately success-ful thirty-one-year-old guy in New York City, and simply not in a hurry to settle down because he didn't have to be. Maybe it wasn't really that deep.

He would probably ask Cleo out again, though. She was sharp and funny. And she would make an ideal date to take to Rachel's wedding, if they could make it that long.

He was still thinking along these lines and wondering if he ought to feel bad about his commitment-phobic tendencies when Clarissa picked him up for the fundraiser. He watched her mouth move for several minutes as they walked before he recog-nized that he had not actively been listening.

"Earth to Dev. Calling Dev," Clarissa finally said, boffing him on the back of the head, but she didn't seem angry.

"Sorry. I was just . . . thinking."

"Well, stop," Clarissa teased, linking her arm with his as they turned onto Lafayette Street, heading north toward the restaurant that had been rented out for the event. Dev had for-gotten the name; he just knew that it was synonymous with *style*, a byword for fashionable, trendy. "Anyway, promise you'll make an effort to be a *little* bit more engaged tonight. They all want to meet you, the board members. Apparently there are indeed peo-ple out there who still read."

"I will," he answered.

Clarissa nodded, satisfied, and resumed talking to him about her work organizing the event, and the way she planned to use her influence to broaden the cause. He found himself unexpectedly glowing with pride, and he had to say something.

"You're the best person I know, Clare. And the smartest."

She snorted. "That makes me worry about the company you keep."

"Clarissa."

"Okay, thank you. It's flattering, at least."

Dev smiled, though he realized that perhaps he had said it partly to flatter himself, too, to indicate that he was the kind of person to notice and admire intelligence in his women friends and could point it out without feeling insecure. But he knew she probably knew this, too, and he also knew that he was still a little bit of a jackass, even when his intentions were good.

"Rachel would appreciate all this, I think," Dev said, not keen to broach the fact that Clarissa and Rachel were no longer best friends but somehow incapable of not mentioning Rachel.

"I know. Seeing how she was after Cody, how she never felt like she could talk about it . . . Well, it was part of the reason that I first got involved with the organization," Clarissa said matter-of-factly, in a tone of voice that served to both agree with him and declare the subject closed.

She reached over and straightened his bow tie, then grabbed his hand.

He watched her as they walked up the red-carpeted steps to the cavernous restaurant, noticing how polished she looked in her black jumpsuit, her blond hair cut into an asymmetrical short look that he had somehow only just noticed. It was still

Clarissa, but refined and distilled into her best self. He didn't mean that she looked more attractive dressed up—he didn't think of Clarissa in those terms, which was probably one of the reasons they were still such good friends—but he noticed that she wore this new glamour so confidently. He remembered Clarissa at college open mics in oversize flannels, her long hair hanging partially in front of her face, which sometimes looked relaxed and original, but other times gave the impression that she was trying to obscure herself. Without being able to put his finger on how he knew it exactly, he could tell Clarissa had finished with hiding.

They stepped into the main dining room, decked out with huge florals and enough candles to hold a séance, or burn down a building, the way these kinds of gala events always looked. They grabbed their name cards.

"You look amazing, by the way," Dev told her.

"Oh, stop hitting on me." She flashed a hand in front of his face, confusing him, but only for a moment until he saw the ring. "I'm a married woman now."

"Clarissa!" he shouted, genuinely shocked, his outburst causing a girl to snap a picture of them. It flashed, Clarissa rolled her eyes, and the silk-clad offender scurried away.

"Congratulations, then. I'm so happy for you," he said, and he was, though he still needed a sip of champagne to steady himself as they took their seats at their table.

"Thank you."

"But you should probably consider a backup career in the CIA. When did this happen?"

"Ah, but I've smoked too much weed." She shrugged. Her eyes sparkled mischievously. "The CIA would never take me."

"Come on, tell me. Enough jokes."

"Now, that's something I never thought I'd hear you say." She shook her head.

She and Rebecca had eloped two weeks ago, she told him, on a quiet and perfect afternoon at City Hall. Rebecca's parents and Clarissa's sister had served as the witnesses, they had done a photo shoot at home—because Rebecca loves photos; Clarissa rolled her eyes affectionately—and then the five of them had sat down to a long candlelit dinner at a quiet restaurant in an old carriage house in Williamsburg. It had been perfect for them, she said, and she wanted to enjoy the bubble of quiet peace for just a few more weeks before they went public with the news and the photos.

"And it only took ten months," Dev said. "You don't waste time, do you?"

"Only ten months." Clarissa smiled and shook her head. "Well, you know. Seven years and ten months."

"Right."

"But imagine, me. A person who has to 'go public' with things. Should I issue a press release?"

He elbowed her. "You always wanted that, don't lie. To be known."

"For my *work*," she reminded him. "I'm not like you, Mr. Film Set, Mr. Free Clothes at the *GQ* photo shoot."

Dev moved to retort, then stopped. He *did* love the Tom Ford suit he'd gotten to keep from a recent "creatives with style" spread he'd been tapped to participate in, and there was no point in denying it, so he just laughed.

"Really, I thought of the rest of my life as . . . separate." She sipped her drink. "You know that I'd do an interview here and there if I ever made a really big comedy special, or something. But that's not enough these days—I never expected the attention there would be on the original YouTubers. Or that I would have to be funny on Twitter."

"You are hilarious on Twitter, actually."

"Thank you."

"But you're happy?" he asked. *How?* wondered the small part of his brain he hated, which he always wanted to quiet. *Show me how.*

"The happiest I can ever remember." She paused. "You know, my parents even sent a card with my sister, actually. To the wedding."

Dev smiled. He hadn't wanted to ask, never knew how to bring up those kinds of things, or how to gauge what might be too sensitive, and so he preferred to just avoid it. But he felt a warm relief. "That's good to hear. A baby step, maybe?"

"Maybe. I mean, they didn't come, but they acknowledged it. They know I'm married, and they're not going to make me pretend I'm not. I think we might see them when we go back to Chicago to visit Rebecca's parents for Passover."

"That's great, Clarissa," he said, and she nodded, the conversation falling into a comfortable lull. "I'm going to visit my parents next week. Not even for a holiday or anything, just to see them on my own, without my brothers. I haven't done that in . . . ever," he told her, and saying it felt, inexplicably, like cracking open the door to a dark basement. It worried him, what could be down there.

She understood. "It's a good thing, Dev. I think you'll be happy you did."

HE TOOK THE TRAIN DOWN ON A FRIDAY, THREE RATTLING hours on the New York–to–D.C. corridor. It was the first time he had permitted himself the relative luxury of the Amtrak instead of the hours-longer, $80-cheaper bus ride. Despite his expensive apartment, and his newly acquired taste for pricey French wine, Dev considered himself loyal and unchangeable in his economically sound travel preferences. And then he discovered, with a shiver of irritation quickly followed by guilt, that he couldn't seem to talk himself into spending five hours on a bus to visit his parents. He reasoned that he could save himself time, as well as get some writing done, on the train, kill two birds with one stone.

He spent the entire journey pondering answerless questions. Why did he feel so avoidant? Why did it feel like there was a force field around the house he had grown up in, and he couldn't say what would happen to him or how he would feel if he breached it? Further, should he be worried about how much he'd channeled these feelings into his second novel, which was about an emotionally distanced family living in D.C. based on, not entirely discreetly, his very own?

His mom picked him up at the station, embracing him warmly and calling him "my son, my baby" in Hindi, which served to both embarrass and please him.

They made small talk about his latest screenwriting project and his youngest brother's studies at Duke as the city gave way to the suburban sprawl, leading at last to the cookie-cutter drive he had grown up on, populated on either side with boxy ranch and two-story homes built in the 1970s. Dev had spent some years wishing he'd been born in the city, that he could be truly *of* New York, instead of a place as generic as Rosemary Lane in Northern Virginia, but seeing it again, for the first time in more than two years, he felt differently. Fond, almost. He felt as though the place had given him more than he realized. In another life, he could have had his own version of this, Dev thought. It would have been so much *less* of some things. And much, much more of others. He remembered with a twang how close he'd come to calling it quits in New York during his early days waiting tables, living in an apartment with a shower in its kitchen. He watched the solid old trees lining the streets, the kind he never saw in New York, watched them sway, awash with the wind the way the sea is with the waves.

"So, is Dad home from work yet?" he asked as they turned up the drive, just to have something to say.

"He's actually not . . . he's not here this weekend, Dev. I'm sorry."

"What?" *His son, home for the first time in years, and he goes away?*

"You gave us so little notice about the trip." His mom shrugged, perhaps guilting him, or perhaps simply telling the truth. "He had a trip planned, with your uncles, a . . . guys weekend? They rented a cabin."

"A cabin?" When, in his life, had his father ever rented *a cabin*? And why did this disappoint him so much, after how much he had dreaded, avoided, the trip home? He wondered if he had subconsciously been hoping to show off for his father, tell him about the Golden Globe nomination, prove something to him. Put his success on display and hope it would be received well. That might have been part of it. But maybe, despite everything, he just missed him.

"He'll be back on Sunday, though. We can have breakfast before you leave."

Dev was quiet for a minute. He thought about being a teenager, when he would have tossed off a "whatever." He thought about complaining that his dad could have just moved the cabin weekend, could have put seeing Dev first. He thought about saying, *I don't care.*

"I'm glad," he said finally, putting a hand on his mom's shoulder as she turned off the car. "At least I can see him before I leave. I know I've been busy, but I have missed you both."

"And we've missed you," she said, smoothing his cheek with her thumb, a gesture that used to annoy him. "I miss all of you. Imagine! Me, here with no boys to ruin my house at last, and all I do is miss you."

"I'll come back again soon," Dev said, even though he knew he would find the house claustrophobic by the end of the weekend, even though he knew someone was bound to make an annoying comment about his lack of a haircut. Despite that, in this moment, he meant it.

"Good. Now, come in. I made your favorites."

"One second," he said, taking the last minute in the garage to send a quick text.

To Rachel: "Just wanted to tell you I took the Amtrak to DC. First time for everything."

Her response chimed back only twenty seconds later: "Wow. Maybe people really can change after all."

Despite the books he had written that seemed to show the opposite—despite all the times he had said, almost snidely, in interviews with literary magazines, "I don't think people really change very much, or if they do, it's almost imperceptible"—he did, in fact, hold on to just a tiny bit of hope that Rachel might be right. He did, he admitted to himself, want to believe that people could change.

RACHEL

2016

There is nothing like the East Hampton beach in the early morning, Rachel thought. The sun already shining down hard, glinting off the water and sparkling like the hefty engagement rings of the Hamptons wives who passed Rachel on her walk, lifting one manicured hand in silent greeting.

Although the beaches were marked as "private," they would be busy soon, a classic summer scene, but the veteran locals enjoyed walking them in the early morning, seeking out the momentary quiet. Rachel nodded to Mrs. Silver, who waved with one hand and held up the hem of her caftan with the other, trotting after her grandson down to the water's edge. Gulls flapped their wings; waves lapped gently against the shore. Rachel had known these sounds all her life but had taken them for granted. Now she closed her eyes and paused to listen. At the end of next week, she would be married. Her parents—both of them, together—would walk her down the aisle on this very beach. None of it, she now knew, had ever been guaranteed: Her mom had not gone into remission, but the trial she had participated in had appeared to slow her tumor growth almost to a stop two years before. No one knew the amount of time that had been purchased—months? years? decades?—and so they had to make do with what they had. Rachel was learning to live with uncertainty.

She took a deep breath and then opened her eyes. She turned toward the wooden stairs that connected the beach to their house and gazed up at it, its wood shingles and arched roof. Inside were the people she loved most in the world.

Almost all of them.

Rachel had surprised herself by forgoing a bachelorette party, and instead she had convinced her closest friends to clear their schedules at the same time and spend the week leading up to the wedding with her at the beach house. Now she, Aaron, Isabelle, Nicole, their fiancés, and Dev had decamped from the city for the last full week of August. She had been seeing more of Dev in the city than she used to, now that she worked for his publisher. She didn't work on his books directly—she edited primarily women's fiction and sought out debut authors, a great fit for her interests—but they crossed paths often enough in a professional sense. She felt closer to him than she had in years, and she was pleased with how well he'd fit in with Isabelle and Nicole this week, how he'd taken the time to really get to know their fiancés. Their group of seven had spent the past several days rotating between lounge chairs beside the pool and towels down on the sand. At night they alternated between grilling seafood on the deck and sipping wine, and then occasionally heading down to the Sloppy Tuna like they were still in their early twenties.

It made her think of Nate, but she had to push it away. Every once in a while, she missed him with a stab of longing sharper than she had expected after the way he had treated her, and she wondered what his life was like in Chicago, and if he was okay. He had sent her a letter, several months before. An AA thing, she thought, something aimed at making amends. He'd said he was sorry for what he did, for who he'd surrounded himself with. For the kind of person he'd been, trying to win the approval of people who didn't matter, losing everyone who did in the process. He said he had been sober for a while, that he wanted to live his life differently now. She had felt ambivalent on the first reading, then softened, wondering if she might respond. But thinking of Nate for too long had the unfortunate side effect of making her think of Cody, and her throat constricted, her heart sped up in involuntary panic, and she struggled to breathe until she remembered that she never had to see either of them ever again.

She *almost never* thought about that night anymore. *Almost never.* That's how she had phrased it to Clarissa and Dev on that night, years ago, in Colorado, after Nate had passed out somewhere, and it had been the truth: She *almost never* thought about Cody anymore. But it was the truth only on a linguistic technicality, because how wide was the gulf between *almost never* and *never at all*? Was it a chasm wide enough to swallow all her self-doubt?

And when she did think of that night—when it came to mind because she felt herself getting a certain sort of swaying drunk, maybe, or because someone reminded her of Cody—she'd take the chance to rewrite the story. How hard would it be to believe that she *had* gone after Cody all those years ago, that she found him cute enough to pursue, that she thought he might help her stop thinking about Dev? She had been drunk, certainly, but if she reoriented the memory, lit it and scene dressed it in just the right way, she could imagine that she had pulled him into the bedroom, rather than the other way around. She could imagine that the blurred memory of his weight pressing down on her, pinning her on purpose, refusing to let her move, and the way she'd squirmed, had been from pleasure, not fear. She could discount the blackout she had sunk into when he wouldn't stop moving above her and inside her.

Earlier that year, Rachel had opened her Moleskine notebook, the one she still kept next to her bed in case inspiration ever struck at night, and written a few lines:

If she could change anything about her past, it wouldn't be that night. To endeavor to change that night would be to admit that it mattered to her, and this was the double bind that suspended her life.

Maybe she would use these lines in a book one day, she thought. That way, she could turn those thoughts into fiction. She would stop them from applying to her reality.

But anyway, this week was *hers*, Rachel reminded herself. Hers and Aaron's. No person, no memory, would be allowed to take that from her.

As she swung open the patio door at the back of the house, she heard someone moving around in the kitchen. She hoped it wasn't someone's significant other; she hadn't showered or put on her makeup yet. She tightened her ponytail and drew in a breath as she rounded the corner to the kitchen, then exhaled with relief. It was just Aaron, who always woke early, like she did. She loved the way their schedules seemed to coordinate seamlessly: up for a run at six thirty or seven, even on the weekends.

"Hey, babe." Aaron kissed her on the cheek and then went to the fridge. "Want to run with me? Or did you already go?"

"I took an early walk on the beach, actually."

"Good." He smiled, pulling two green juices out of the fridge and handing one to her. "Anything you need help with today? What time does Cleo get here?"

It was Wednesday, two days before the "official" start to the wedding festivities, when the bulk of their guests would descend upon the Hamptons, but Dev's girlfriend, Cleo, would be arriving early. She and Dev had even offered to cook dinner for everyone that night. Dev, serving dinner to a group of eight people that wasn't spaghetti with ragù sauce from the jar! Apparently, Cleo was a chef. From Paris, no less. She had recently opened her own restaurant, a little boîte on a formerly NYU-bar-heavy block in the Village, even though she had only just turned twenty-seven. Rachel had recently celebrated her thirty-second birthday, so the whole "thirty-under-thirty" vibe irked her a little bit, but she tried not to let it show. She was not going to say anything. She would be nothing but friendly and gracious when Cleo arrived, the perfect hostess.

"Late afternoon, I think."

"Great. I might play a couple of sets this afternoon with your dad at the club, but I'll make sure I'm back by three."

"Perfect," she said, then pecked him on the cheek and headed upstairs to shower. *Perfect*, she thought, was exactly the right word: Could there be a more perfect man for her than Aaron? A brilliant doubles partner, chummy with her dad, committed and constant, the envy of her friends? They argued every now and then, of course, and sometimes she sulked, but the point was that Aaron was not only a good man, but the exact kind of man she had always thought she would grow up to marry one day. Most of the time, this made Rachel feel a profound sense of luck. But in her worst, most private moments of doubt, she worried it was a sign of a failure of imagination.

Not that she didn't love Aaron wholly and completely; she did. Sometimes she would wake up in the morning and look over at him, curled on his side with his arms hugging a pillow like a kid with a stuffed animal, and she would feel the purest swell of love inside of her, a bell ringing in her heart that had felt soundless for a long time. But then there were other moments, moments when they would be eating quietly at dinner or scanning new bath towels into their registry at Bloomingdale's, and she would wonder if this was . . . it. Forever. It was no fault of Aaron's, who had taken care of her through her mom's treatment before they'd even known each other well, who went running with her every single morning, who had given her a life back when she had thought she didn't even want one anymore. But it was still there, the question of what exactly made two people absolutely certain they wanted to share every moment of their lives, forever.

Rachel hadn't said this to anyone because she was sure it would make it sound like she had "cold feet," whatever that meant, and her feet were *warm*, damn it. She wanted to marry

Aaron because she had confidence that he was the best man she knew, and maybe that was all the certainty anyone could expect. And at the end of the day, she felt it was enough.

She shook her head to clear her thoughts, then stepped into the shower. A new part of their lives would begin here, amid the dune grass and the old, shingled homes, the cicadas, the sights and sounds she had grown up with. This would be the start of something.

RACHEL SPENT THE REST OF THE DAY WITH HER FRIENDS ON the beach, lazily passing the time and sipping at cans of Montauk Summer Ale. When Cleo finally arrived that night, late but with flowers and good French wine in her arms, Rachel, Nicole, and Aaron were in the kitchen rewarming the hors d'oeuvres.

Rachel heard a thump as Cleo dropped her bags. She tried not to enjoy it when she heard her hiss, "Putain," under her breath, clearly flustered. Dev rushed forward to kiss her on the lips, and Rachel smoothed the front of her dress, suddenly unsure about what to do with her hands.

"Cleo! So excited you could make it," she gushed, stepping forward to take the flowers out of her arms and then drop la bise on Cleo's cheeks. "How was the trip?"

"It was horrible," she said in the fully French way. *Or-ee-bul.* "I'm so sorry to be late, but the bus, the . . . jitney? It took an hour longer than I expected. And it is crowded, too, like a bus for a school trip, non?" She laughed, a pleasant trill that annoyed Rachel for no reason.

"Oh, the jitney isn't all that bad." She shrugged, suddenly

feeling the need to think the opposite of whatever Cleo thought, even though she agreed that the jitney could be terrible.

"Rach, you are, like, the mayor of complaining about the jitney, what are you talking about?" Dev said. "Now, come on, let's get some of this wine open."

After the introductions, they all poured glasses of wine and took their plates of finger food to the low-slung sectional sofa in the living room, the room with the glass wall that overlooked the deck and the walkway that led out to the beach. Rachel loved the fact that her mom had redone part of the house, blowing out the back wall to create the panoramic views while still preserving most of the home's older details elsewhere, like the fireplace, the shingles on the front.

"It is beautiful here, Rachel." Cleo smiled approvingly. "Your family has lived here a long time?"

"My parents bought the house a year before I was born, I think." Rachel took a long sip of wine. Saint-Julien, 2005. The woman had taste. "For a while, we couldn't spend much time out here, and they rented it out. It's nice to be back."

"Oh really? You—" Cleo asked, and then in a gesture so subtle she almost missed it, Rachel saw Dev place a hand on her knee and give the tiniest shake of his head. Cleo paused. "Yes, it must be nice for you to be back with both of your parents."

Rachel nodded, draping her hand over Aaron's leg. "We're thinking about buying our own place out here one day, maybe." Then she smiled warmly at Cleo for the first time. Some kind of invisible tension deflated then, which might have been obvious to everyone or imperceptible to everyone but her, but it felt like just a bit of air escaping a balloon, a slow release of pressure.

Because she knew now that Dev had talked to Cleo about her, about her mom's illness and her recovery.

Rachel knew it wasn't right for her to be protective of Dev and his relationships. She had no right to act as if she had some claim to him, just as it would have been equally wrong for Dev to be jealous of Aaron. But the possessiveness didn't come from the fact that they had slept together ten—*ten, had it really been that long?*—years ago. It came from the knowledge that their friendship would inevitably change when they both had serious partners. It would be couples trips, and double dates, and maybe brief one-on-one meet-ups for lunch or drinks. Their friendship would last, but it would become something else, because didn't it have to? Rachel knew enough married couples to know that they usually drew a veil around themselves and became a unit, an entity that was somehow impenetrable by anyone outside it ever again. But that one moment, that tiny shake of Dev's head, made her think that maybe this could be different. Maybe her marrying Aaron, and him being with Cleo, didn't have to mean the end of the individual bond between the two of them. Of their special consideration for each other. He would still talk about her to Cleo, still hold her in a special place that wouldn't belong to anyone else, no matter whom the two of them dated or married or became.

"These Brie bites are so good. Take them away—I think I just ate five." Nicole groaned, interrupting her thoughts, and everyone muttered their agreement.

"Amazing, Rachel. Maybe I should have you cooking for me!" Cleo said, sounding truly genuine.

"And I just love this, don't you?" Isabelle sighed.

"What?" her fiancé, Steven, asked.

Isabelle lifted her wineglass and gestured around the room. "All of this. Music, candles, good food. Wine that doesn't come from a jug." Everyone laughed. "The bar was fun the other night, sure. But I don't care if this makes me sound uncool: I'm so glad to be in the phase of my life where you don't have to *start* drinking at a pregame at eleven p.m."

"So, you're actually glad to be in your thirties, you mean," Dev joked. "And speak for yourselves—Cleo and I are going out after this." The roll of Cleo's eyes made it abundantly clear that they were not, in fact, going out after this.

"Here's to great nights with great friends . . . and me still getting eight hours of sleep at the end of it." Aaron laughed, raising his glass.

"Hear, hear."

Rachel laughed and clinked her glass with the rest of them, but the clink sounded hollow, and she felt a small ache inside. She remembered the night she had visited Clarissa in Chicago, not long after graduation, when she and Clarissa and Rebecca had stayed out dancing until dawn, then fallen into bed all together. She had known even then that that phase of her life wouldn't last forever, but it had started to taper off even sooner than she had expected. Now, tonight, everyone would sleep in their own beds, with their own partners, and wake up to cook breakfast and run and do yoga in the morning. Which was what she *wanted*, what she usually liked to do anyway, and so what was she sad about? But some small part of her still missed those other late nights, missed sleeping in a tangle of limbs, waking up with no plans for the day other than to eat a hangover brunch somewhere.

Or maybe she just missed Clarissa.

Clarissa and Rebecca would be attending the wedding, but Rachel had not invited them to spend the week. It had become clear, through the dwindling calls, and then the fact that Rachel had only been informed of their marriage via text well after the fact, that Clarissa and Rebecca did not consider her one of their closest friends. Not anymore. After the argument on the night of Clarissa's Comedy Cellar show, Rachel had privately thought that Clarissa owed her an apology. Apparently, Clarissa had thought the opposite—and neither of them had made the first move toward a deeper reconciliation. Rachel regretted this now, and a part of her wished she had apologized right away, even without knowing exactly what she was meant to apologize for. But perhaps it was easier this way, she reasoned. Clarissa had always been passionate, caustic, quicker to anger. Maybe time was the best remedy.

She hoped so, anyway.

She finished the rest of her wine and refilled her glass, a strong pour, and then sank back into the sofa next to Aaron.

AFTER FOUR HOURS AND FOUR GLASSES OF BORDEAUX, IT wasn't exactly clear to Rachel how she and Dev had wound up as the last two in the living room. The room had taken on a hazy, dreamlike quality, its edges blurred. She realized that she and Dev had somehow passed the entire week without ever being alone together, instead breaking off into same-sex groups to walk along the beach or saying good night when Rachel retired to bed early with Aaron. Rachel wondered how that could be possible, how she and Dev—who had once deliberately sequestered themselves alone in spare rooms and in the corners of bars and out on apartment balconies at every party—had wound up separated, even when they were sharing the same house for a week. She looked over at Dev and watched as he stood up from the far side of the sofa and came to sit in the corner next to her.

"So." He stretched an arm along the back of the sofa, behind her shoulders but not on them. "Now that we're finally alone, I know you're dying to tell me: What do you think of Cleo?"

"Wow." She snorted, not even taking the time to think over an appropriate answer. She was right back to responding by reflex; maybe the friendship, the intimacy between the two of them, was something she could tap back into whenever she wanted.

"'Wow' what? You cannot seriously have not liked her. And I see you sucking down that wine she brought. It's your favorite, isn't it?"

"I didn't mean 'wow' in a bad way," Rachel said, shaking her head. "I meant that it's very . . . not like you to even ask. When have you ever cared what I thought about your girlfriends?"

Dev stayed silent, staring straight ahead into the white-brick fireplace.

"Sorry, is 'girlfriend' too serious a word for what's happening? It usually is with you."

"Actually, no," Dev said firmly, surprising her. "It isn't. I think I do, in fact, want her to be my girlfriend. It was on and off with us in the beginning, but this time, I think it's for real."

"Well, now, that's *really* worth a 'wow.'"

"Your boy's growing up." Dev shrugged. "I don't know, we'll see. I'm trying it out. I'm starting to think maybe I'm missing the 'gene,' if I'm being honest."

"The gene?"

"You know, the thing that allows you to say, with one hundred percent confidence, 'this is the person for me.' That *this* is who I should spend the rest of my life with, and there's no chance I'm making a mistake. Maybe you can help me out there, Ms. Fiancée. What am I missing?" Dev slurred the last few words together and then took a long sip of wine. Rachel realized that he was a little bit drunk. So was she, come to think of it.

"You want me to tell you how you'll know someone is the one?"

"Bingo."

She paused, thinking, her head foggy from the wine. She looked down into her glass, the sediment settling at the base, wishing that she could read it like tea leaves, that if she stared long enough it could tell her what to do. Was this the moment to confess to Dev that she didn't know, either? That she loved Aaron, and that she had some kind of sense that he was the best at taking care of her, of loving her in return, and that that feeling was exceedingly rare, but that at the same time, she didn't "know" any more than anyone else did? That "when you know, you know" had turned out to be a lie, at least for her? Or would it be better to tell him that all the stories were true, that he shouldn't settle down until he found someone he was utterly convinced was his soul mate, whatever that meant, and that he would know it when he found it, or when it found him.

"Come on. I'm all ears, Bergen."

Her stomach flipped a little at the old nickname before she could help it. No one had called her by her last name in a long time. It would be her name for only a few more days. She would be taking Aaron's when they married. *Rachel Bernstein.*

"I think," she said finally, quietly, "that no one can tell you exactly how you'll know. That's why there's so much debate about the idea of soulmates: Some people genuinely feel like their partner is their soulmate—probably because they already believed in the concept or wanted to. So, they aren't pretending; their framework is just different. Then there are people who find the concept of 'one person for everyone' silly no matter how much they love someone. And if that's you, then you just have to decide."

"Decide what?"

"If you're with someone who's worth it. Maybe that was easier for me, because I *did* always want to get married. Unlike some people here." She gave Dev a pointed look, and he laughed. "But the point is, you have to know that you're with someone who supports you unconditionally, and who . . . who motivates you to do more, to *be* more, I guess. People talk about relationships as something you sacrifice for—you know, your alone time, or your money, or your sexual freedom . . ."

"Yep, pretty much . . ."

"But that's not all there is to it. A relationship should make you *better*, too. Stronger, or more loving, maybe. It should make you more of who you are."

"And you feel all that with Aaron?"

She thought of Aaron bringing her coffee in bed in the

morning. She thought about them running together, shaking off the miles. She thought, too, of the way he had looked at her on their first date, the way he had listened to her talk about her mom, and she just knew that he understood. That he *saw* her.

Then, unbidden, she thought about Dev.

She thought about him encouraging her to write her novel, and then, when that never came to fruition, spurring her to change jobs, helping her get the editor position that she now absolutely loved, at Random House. He had been right about her: She had acquired her first independent title by the end of her first year. She got to work with novels but was not required to write them, no longer punishing herself at every turn. It felt, at last, like the real start of something.

It had happened, in no small part, because of both Aaron and Dev.

She took a deep breath and chose her words carefully.

"Aaron is one of very few people I have felt all that with, yes."

"Mm."

"So," she said, her voice louder, disrupting the accidental intimacy that had descended over their conversation, "when you find that with someone—or find it again—then maybe you'll know."

"Maybe," he said quietly. Then, just a second later, he seemed like himself again. "But I have to tell you, I'm not in much of a hurry to get there."

She threw her head back and laughed, unchecked. "Now, why doesn't that surprise me?"

"Just don't tell Cleo. I do like her, so I'd like to keep her around to at least see how it goes."

"Thank you for . . . telling her about me, by the way. I saw what you did, when she was asking about the house."

"Sorry, I didn't mean for you to see it. Didn't mean to make it like we'd been talking behind your back about your mom or something."

"No, no." She put her hand on his knee. Friendly, just friendly, she hoped. "I liked it, that you had told her things about me. I like knowing you still do that, no matter how old we get, if we get married, have kids, even."

She paused to see if Dev might say something sentimental in return, but of course he didn't.

"Absolutely no kids." He shook his head furiously. "Kids are a no-go for me."

"I know," she said. "I want them, I think. But there's no rush."

Dev sighed. "So, you think I can try to make this thing work with Cleo? I can't afford to lose the discount at her restaurant."

"Do or do not, there is no try."

"Or, as she would say, 'Faire ou . . .' Damn it, the French language courses really aren't going well for me."

"You're taking French classes for her?" Rachel's eyebrows shot up. "You're right, then; this really is different. And it's 'Il n'y a pas d'essai,' Skywalker." She smiled, satisfied.

"Right, fancy prep school French classes."

"Oh, stop. And quit it with the 'I can't afford to lose the restaurant discount' shtick. I saw your book hit the list last week. Everyone at work was talking about it, of course. Congratulations. I'm sorry I didn't say it sooner."

Dev's long-anticipated second novel, *The Family*, had hit the *New York Times* bestseller list the Wednesday before. She knew how hard it had been for him to write it, the second book always an excruciating exercise in recapturing what had flowed so easily in the first. But finally, six years later, he had done it. The book had debuted at number seven. Pride had swelled up inside her as if Dev were her son, or her student. As if she had had something to do with it.

"Thanks. Though it'll probably be off in a week."

"When did you learn the art of self-deprecation?"

"I'm always evolving my form."

They were quiet for a moment, but Rachel felt the first sting of sobriety creeping into her head, and she knew she should go to bed before the spell was completely broken.

"You know, Aaron and I are thinking of getting our own house out here, one day." She yawned, forgetting she had already said this over drinks earlier. "Then, who knows? Maybe we can plan a beach weekend every year, all of us together. What do you think?"

"Big plans, Bergen," he said, sounding tired and a little bit far away.

"Bernstein, almost," she whispered. "Can you get used to it?"

"It'll always be Bergen to me," he said, and then he heaved himself off the couch and toward the staircase. "Good night, Rach."

THE CITY SEEMED TO VIBRATE BENEATH HER, THRUMMING with energy as she and Aaron drove back across the bridge two weeks later, heading home. She looked over at him, her wedding-band-adorned left hand laced with his right over the gear shift.

They were married, at last. It had been the perfect day, a Labor Day thunderstorm holding off until after the Sunday farewells, the sailcloth tent on her parents' lawn swelling with white flowers and filtered through by a light ocean breeze. But the best part, she thought, had been after everyone had left. She and Aaron had snuck back out onto the beach, her hair still up but her shoes kicked off, and swayed tipsily to their wedding song playing from his phone in the starlight. It was at that moment, and only at that moment, that she had finally known for sure: She hadn't needed the Dom Pérignon, the high-strung wedding planner, the fireworks. She needed—she wanted—the marriage. Not the wedding. Though the fancy wedding had been great. She was not *not* looking forward to the *Vogue Weddings* feature.

The next morning, her mom had found her sitting at their dining table with a mug of coffee, smiling, reflecting on the night. She'd draped her arms around Rachel's shoulders and hugged her tightly and wordlessly from above.

"Thank you, Mom," she heard herself say, words that she suspected had not come out of her mouth as often as they should have when she was young. *Thank you*, meaning, *for college. For the first apartment. For staying close, for giving me just enough space. For the wedding. For being alive. For everything.*

"It was an incredible celebration, if I do say so myself."

"It was."

"I can't believe it. My baby girl married." She smacked a kiss on Rachel's cheek. "All grown up."

"I've been grown up for a while." Rachel rolled her eyes, reverting, possibly disproving her own point.

"It's a different thing, though," her mom said softly. She

spoke more gently than usual. "Creating a new family. Having a new person—people—who are your own. You'll see."

Perhaps she would see. She wondered if it could turn overnight like that, if she would move from her parents feeling like her immediate family to feeling that Aaron, and their children if they had them, filled that role entirely. She suspected it might take time. She wondered what her mother knew that she didn't, about marriage, and life—countless things, probably—but she mostly felt a profound sense of gratitude that her mother would still be around to tell her about it. For a while, at least.

New York had a different pulse to it in September, she thought, as they finally turned down upper Second Avenue on their way home, rattling past the hot dog carts and corner parks and families playing music from their stoops. There was a live-wire energy like the first day back at school after summer break. She realized that not everyone left the city during the summer, of course, though it embarrassed her how late she had come to that awareness, and without meaning to, she thought of Clarissa rolling her eyes. Maybe it would be good to make new traditions, new ideas, she thought. Maybe they wouldn't buy a house in the Hamptons but somewhere else. The Hudson Valley, maybe. There were a lot of maybes in her life, something she did not normally like. She didn't feel completely at ease, but something about the weeks out east had changed things. It might have been the wedding. It might have also been her conversations with Dev and with her mom, which had both crystallized for her that she was entering a new phase of her life and she needed to open her mind, even just the tiniest bit, like moving a shade an inch to the side to let light in.

You just have to decide.

When they parked on their street at last and hauled the bags up into their apartment, Aaron went right to their bedroom to unpack; he didn't like to let things sit. Another thing she appreciated about him.

"Did you know that I love you?" she called into the bedroom after him.

"Well, that's a relief," he called back. "It's good to know the wedding wasn't just for show."

"Can we order food and talk about the honeymoon?" she asked. They had spent one night after the wedding at an inn out east, but they had decided to wait six months for the honeymoon so that they could rush less and look forward to it more.

"Of course," Aaron said. "Do you have any new ideas?"

They had discussed Bora Bora, where it seemed like every acquaintance of theirs honeymooned and stayed at the Four Seasons. They had talked about going the classic route, Lake Como and then Naples and Capri, where they had visited together while engaged. But what if they did something different? Rachel thought. What would it be like, she wondered, to surprise herself?

"Actually, yes," she said. "How do you feel about an adventure?"

2017

O ne day at a time.

That was how they phrased it in AA, an idea meant to break the looming months and years into manageable chunks, a way to make survival feel achievable when it might seem, to the program participants, like anything but. Nate had lived the last three years of his life exactly that way: one day at a time.

He woke up early each morning, 5 a.m., to fit in a gym session and a program meeting before work. "Work" now meant a boutique financial services company in an old limestone building in Chicago, not a private equity firm in New York. "Home" meant an apartment in Old Town, a place his parents sometimes drove to, to visit him on weekends. He lived down the street from Mc-Fadden's, the old, nondescript Irish pub where he had first tried his fake ID fall quarter of his freshman year. Now he only walked by it on his way to the bakery, where he channeled his urges to drink into the satisfaction of sweets. His sponsor, Jim, had gently suggested that he could find another, perhaps "less triggering" route. But changing which streets he walked felt like a failure of nerve, and so Nate pressed on. He had failed at enough already.

Three and a half years passed, like that. January skipping into June winding into September, as quickly as Nate spinning through the revolving door in and out of his new office. Sometimes—often?—he could not believe that this was his life. Other times, he was so profoundly grateful to have escaped New York without killing himself or anyone else that he felt distinctly humbled.

AA was also teaching him to embrace contradictions.

On a cold Tuesday in February, Nate trudged through the graying slush to cross Van Buren Street under the el tracks, the wind wailing in his ears as he made his way from the church that held his Tuesday AA meeting to his office in the Loop. He chose to take the stairs, all fourteen flights of them, hoping this extra exercise would combat the weight he'd started to notice appearing in his middle, the unavoidable result of going to a bakery every time he would rather have had a scotch at McFadden's. Lightly sweating under his suit, a smile plastered on his face, he offered a warm greeting to his executive assistant.

"Morning, Lucia," he chirped. "Is it especially bad out there today, or is it just me? I'm hearing it's going to be a long winter."

The *new Nate* smiled warmly at people. The new Nate had time for conversation with everyone.

"I think you were just away from Chicago for too long." Lucia smiled back, and the old Nate might have remarked on how nice she looked, with her dark glossy hair and her brightly colored sweater dress, but he knew that wasn't the right thing to do, and he stopped himself. "It's always like this."

"Fair enough."

"Oh, and Nate?"

"Hmm?"

"Happy birthday."

He smiled sheepishly and nodded his thanks, feeling somehow exposed that she knew and remembered. He, Nate, who had rented a private room at Babbo and bought a table at 1 Oak for his twenty-fifth birthday, slunk into his office, glad to be alone, but wistful, too. He looked forward to losing himself in work. But then he saw it: a cardboard box sitting squarely atop his desk. He approached it cautiously, as if it might need to be defused.

He looked first at the candy and a birthday note from his sponsor, Jim, which struck him as a bit corny and quaint, but that he found he appreciated nonetheless. Beside it sat the box. He took it gingerly in his hands, his leather gloves still on. The address of his building, *Attn: Nate Davis*, had been written on top in thick black Sharpie, and the distinctive handwriting could belong to only one person.

PUBLICLY, NATE HAD BEEN SOBER FOR SEVERAL YEARS. PRIvately, shamefully, he knew that he should have started his count again last February. On his last birthday, something had happened.

By the winter of 2016, Nate had managed to string together almost eighteen sober months, a surprise to everyone, but perhaps to himself most of all. His court-mandated stint in rehab—required to get the DUI, his first infraction, expunged from his record—had been embarrassing and anticlimactic. He had stayed in Cleveland for his sentencing, and then he had checked into an inpatient rehab center for two weeks, a real "no-nonsense" place, his mom had called it. He'd felt ridiculous in his twin-size bed, absurd in his group therapy sessions. He watched as the other participants detoxed, some of them suffering immensely from DT hallucinations and tremors. Nate never did, because if he even *was* an addict, he told himself, he wasn't one who had been using all day long. Nate already spent chunks of many days stone-cold sober, and so he didn't have any trouble with detox, could fairly easily go without a drink when he was so far outside the scope of his normal life. Who wanted to party in a fucking rehab center, anyway? It was hardly a beach club in Tulum.

If attending AA meetings hadn't been another court require-ment for his probation, Nate might never have gone. But it was, and so he did, and he realized for the first time that you didn't have to be wasted all day long for your drinking to chip away at your life. He confronted the fact that his drinking had landed him in jail, had forced him to take a leave of absence from his old job. Over the years, it had cost him his friends. He accepted these facts; he found his sponsor, Jim. He kept attending the meetings, even when he thought they were bullshit. But every time he told his pathetic story, he felt like a fraud next to his fellow members who had caused real tragedies, had killed loved ones while driv-ing drunk, had known real, bottomless pain. And who was he, some privileged finance guy who had once liked cocaine and bottle service and mediocre DJs a little too much? How had he ended up in a church basement in Chicago, time-traveled back ten years as if his life in New York had never happened?

One day at a time.

Then, his thirty-second birthday. February 12, 2016.

Nate had started the morning pleasantly surprised to receive a text from Dev. "Happy birthday, man," it read. "Let's catch up soon, hope you're doing well in Chicago." Unable to hide his excitement, Nate had tried to ring him immediately, but Dev hadn't picked up, even though he'd clearly had his phone in hand just a minute earlier. Nate burned with embarrassment at his eagerness, then resolved to dive into work and wait until the afternoon. When Dev hadn't called back by the evening, he hated how destabilized he felt, and he took a walk down the hall to see if the junior associates were still good for their offer to take him out after work sometime—an offer he'd spent months politely declining.

Why had he? he asked himself. He could tell them that he was sober and join them to watch a Bulls game anyway. But he had started to have a nagging thought, which was that it seemed ridiculous that he'd given up drinking altogether. After all, it wasn't as if he'd been showing up to work drunk every morning or beating people up while blacked out. He wasn't an addict; he'd just let himself get a little bit out of control and he'd made an idiotic mistake. He had learned his lesson.

"So, we got you to come out at last." One of the interns clapped his hand and then fist-bumped him as they made their way out of the building. "We thought you were dodging us."

"No." Nate shook his head. "Just been busy." He waited a beat, adrenaline flowing through him, the words he should say right on the tip of his tongue: *I'm sober. I don't drink.* But the promise of a night of normalcy tingled in his veins, as intoxicating as any drug he'd ever taken. Instead, he asked, "So what bar are we going to?"

Apparently, all the stories he'd sat through in AA hadn't stuck. Because, as predictably as if he'd been the subject of an after-school special, Nate had let one drink become two, and two become ten. When Dev finally did call him back the next morning, he'd slept through it, passed out facedown on his couch next to a puddle of his own vomit, dead asleep.

NATE RUBBED HIS TEMPLES AND SAT DOWN AT HIS DESK. THIS year would not be a repeat of the last, he promised himself. He had come close to another stumble last summer, when he'd seen Rachel's wedding photos on Instagram and Facebook, a digital parade of her happiness that did not, could not, ever include him. But he'd stayed on the path, and he planned to do the same today.

The box, though. It sat before him labeled with Dev's distinctive, disheveled handwriting, which could contain anything from old college mementos to a set of signed books to a note telling him to go fuck himself.

Or maybe it was a genuinely kind birthday gift? Could it be an appeal to make their friendship more than one of occasional texts and empty promises that Dev would visit him in Chicago?

After deliberating for a long time, Nate decided that he simply couldn't run the risk. He threw the box in the trash, unopened, and, heart thundering, dialed his sponsor.

HE AND JIM MET AFTER WORK AT A DINER ON ROOSEVELT, THE sort of place where a character in a play might meet his sponsor, so perfect did the old red booths and twenty-four-hour neon lights serve as a *Nighthawks*-like set. It reminded him of Rachel taking him to see a Hopper retrospective at the Met. He remembered when his life had been a series of curated adventures, Rachel dragging him by the hand into this museum, that theater.

He said this out loud to Jim. It was nice to be able to share his emotions freely with someone he knew could be just as ruinous as him. It was good to have a place at last where coolness couldn't buy you anything. Earnestness was the currency of AA, and if the old Nate would have scoffed at that, well, the old Nate was the one who'd gotten him into this mess to begin with.

Jim spilled a drop of black coffee onto his old jean shirt as he raised his mug off the Formica table to clink with Nate's. He let loose a predictable stream of muttered curse words in response, and Nate smiled.

"Well, happy birthday, kid," Jim toasted him. "Probably not how you wish you were spending it, but hey. Life's full of surprises. Not all of them bad."

"Dev sent me a box," Nate said. "Maybe for my birthday, maybe a coincidence. I threw it away."

"Hmm. Why'd you do that?"

Nate thought about it. He thought about admitting what had happened last year, when Dev calling him back eighteen hours late led to him taking his first drink in eighteen months. He could tell Jim that he feared the package would be disappointing. He could shrug and say that he didn't want to revisit the past. Instead, he took his time and found something he thought might be truer.

"He's the last person on my list. I haven't . . . made amends."

Step 8. Make a list of all persons we have harmed and become willing to make amends to them all. "It's one of those cases where I'm not sure if I need to or not."

"Well, you know what I think about that. If you're not sure, then you probably do."

"I don't really know what to say." He sipped his coffee. Unlike with Clarissa and Rachel, Nate and Dev had texted, even talked on the phone since his relocation to Chicago. He had told Dev he was getting sober—met with a genuine-sounding "good for you, man"—but he had to confront the fact that even before his arrest, even before the disastrous weekend in Steamboat, he and Dev had not been as close as they once were. He'd drifted away, working longer, partying harder, spending time with tools like Jake Matthews over his real friends. He thought that Dev's success had played a role, too. He'd seen the trailers for Dev's movie, which had come out a few years before, and he'd texted his congrats but hadn't been able to make himself watch the whole thing. Thinking of Dev on the red carpet, picturing him bringing Rachel or Clarissa or even some beautiful young actress to the premiere—all while he sat watching it alone, in a Chicago theater down the street from his one-bedroom apartment? It bummed him out in a way he was not yet prepared to handle. But maybe he could, one day. Maybe one day he would see it, and he would call Dev, and he could tell him, in a deep, genuine way he had always avoided with his male friends, not wanting to seem "soft," that he was proud of him. That he was sorry for the fact that he'd never said it before. He had been, by turns, oblivious and envious when it came to Dev's life, but that was over now. Or at least he wanted for it to be.

One day at a time.

"I like that you've moved forward at your own pace," Jim said. "That said, here's a place where I'm going to push you a little."

"Oh, really?"

"Yes," Jim said, full chest. "Write something. A letter, like you did for Rachel. You don't have to send it, just write it. Whatever comes to your mind. And then you can decide what you want to do with it."

"That sounds fair," Nate said, finishing his coffee. "But before I go, I have something better to tell you. I have a date."

"All right, Nate, I see you. Tell me more."

"I don't know if I'm really supposed to be dating . . ."

"You know I'm not the sole authority on that. Just not in the first year, is what I say. But if it's because you're still making a few amends? My view's that we're bound to be doing that for life. Keep making 'em, stay humble."

Nate nodded. For several months now, Nate had seen the same woman at the gym every Thursday morning. Blond, though not his typical type. Incredibly strong, maybe an athlete. He'd admired her form on box jumps, but he hadn't wanted to bother her during a workout, so he just minded his own business, hoping one day they'd run into each other more naturally. It had finally happened when, through pure luck—one of the earlier steps had been to admit that he was powerless over his own life—one of his sneakers had fallen out of his unzipped gym bag after he left the locker room. She'd run up behind him to return it.

"I don't think you'd want to lose this," she said, proffering one of his new Nikes.

"Thanks. Wow, I should be more careful. I think I'm still half-asleep."

She looked at him appraisingly, and he noticed her light blue eyes. "You are always here early, aren't you? I'm an early bird, too, and I noticed."

"Nate." He stuck out his hand as they walked to the elevator, feeling bolder than he had in a while. "It's nice to meet you."

"Steph." She smiled, and by the time the elevator deposited them in the lobby, he had a date.

He recounted this to Jim, who nodded approvingly. "And what are you doing for this date?"

"A walk through Lincoln Park, if it isn't too cold, and then brunch. I'm planning on telling her I'm sober, if you were wondering."

"I don't judge, and I try not to worry. But I'm glad to hear it." Jim heaved himself up out of the booth and reached for his coat, ending their meeting without fanfare, as he always did. "You let me know how it goes."

"I will," Nate said, and he realized that he looked forward to it. More than he had looked forward to anything in a long time. Church bells chimed in the distance, audible as the diner door swung open. He walked through it and out onto the street, and for just that moment, Nate knew he could take any route home, could pass any bar he wanted, and temptation would not get the better of him that night.

CLARISSA

2018

Are you ready," Rebecca said into the bedroom mirror as she clipped in her earrings. Her tone made Clarissa realize that it wasn't a question at all, but a reminder, because of course Rebecca knew, after all these years, that Clarissa would be the one running late. She looked down at her unwashed overalls.

"Um." She smiled. "Almost."

Rebecca turned around to appraise her. "I guess you *could* just wear that. It is our anniversary, and *that* is the embodiment of the woman I fell in love with—underdressed, running late, and so absolutely fucking gorgeous it doesn't matter." Rebecca pecked her cheek.

"Sadly, three years is not the overalls anniversary, I've heard. Which one is that, fifteen?"

"That's crystal, hon."

"How do you know these things?"

"I thought you accepted this by now." Rebecca smiled,

slipping on her heels and walking out of the bedroom. "I know everything."

"I'll change," Clarissa called after her. "Be there in a minute."

She strode to her closet to pull out a pair of suit pants, the same ones she'd worn the night before, for a fundraiser for a local progressive candidate for the midterms. Ever since the presidential election, Clarissa had been attending more rallies and events than ever but simultaneously feeling more powerless every time. She remembered campaigning with Rebecca almost a decade ago, running around Chicago talking about "hope" and "change," which would feel as though they had been—that her very *rights* had been—repudiated a mere eight years later. Had she really been so naïve? Or was there still a place inside her that could believe in those things, who could do the work to make the world safer, better for herself, for her wife, for everyone like her?

But she would not think about that anymore tonight. She pulled out a white blouse, one she knew Rebecca liked, one where she could leave several buttons undone without revealing too much. Tonight, she would celebrate the fact that three years ago that day, she had married the woman she loved.

THE PROPOSAL HAD BEEN SIMPLE. NO GRAND PLANS, NO rings. Clarissa had bought one and reproposed later—because she knew Rebecca would like it, that grand gestures, when Clarissa could remember to initiate them, made her happy—but in the moment it had been perfectly, intimately them.

They had been in their living room, sitting on the sofa with Rebecca's feet in Clarissa's lap, both of them reading. Rebecca spoke up to read aloud to Clarissa from her book of poetry. Clarissa consumed poetry only through Rebecca, and she often pretended to roll her eyes at its sentimentality, but in truth she had started to enjoy it. Rebecca read:

> *In truth, we had married,*
> *that first night, in bed, we had been*
> *married by our bodies, but now we stood*
> *in history—what our bodies had said,*
> *mouth to mouth, we now said publicly,*
> gathered together, death.

"So do I need to say it?" had been Clarissa's response.

"Say what?"

"That it's about us. That I . . . that I've felt married to you for a long time, actually."

"I've felt married to you since the day we met." Rebecca had smiled her irresistible smile, both rows of bright teeth showing, like she was on the verge of laughter. "Even with all the . . . years in between."

"Well, we did move right back in together in about two minutes."

"Yes," Rebecca had said. "But I also mean that you are my family. You always felt like family—and, you know, family is always fraught, but fraught can be because of how much feeling there is, rather than how bad things are."

Then, suddenly, Clarissa had been unable to stop herself. "I want to be a family. With you. Officially, legally, let's do it. If that's still something that you want."

"That"—Rebecca had leaned in close, their noses almost touching, her smell intoxicating—"is the only thing I want."

"Other than this, I hope." And Clarissa had lifted her shirt over her head, and Rebecca had murmured, "Yes, God, yes." An agreement, an invocation.

IT HAD BEEN A PERFECT DAY. SIMPLE, INTIMATE. SHE TOLD DEV and a few other trusted friends right away, but she and Rebecca had waited a while to announce the news to their wider circle. Which meant, of course, Clarissa's YouTube followers. All two million of them and counting.

She realized she had been right to wait: As soon as she made one of her regular "life update" videos that shared the news, thousands of comments poured in. From messages on YouTube to DMs on Instagram (which she now had to cultivate a presence on, much to her chagrin), all her followers had wanted to hear details of the proposal.

Clarissa understood why. First, she had deliberately cultivated an interest in her personal life through the faux-intimate nature of the platform, and thus her followers felt she was talking *to* them in her videos. Second, there were fewer scripts for queer women regarding proposals and marriage, and the representation mattered. And finally, the "life update" video had featured a rare joint appearance, with Rebecca, and it had unintentionally been uploaded at a pivotal time: Three days later, the Supreme Court issued its transformational ruling, which had made same-sex marriage the law of the land at last.

On that day in June, Clarissa's cynical side had almost won

out for just a moment—the ruling was so far overdue, the notion of legal equality something that she thought should feel more like an obvious fact than a dramatic victory—but she had to admit that she had ended up moved beyond words, that it had really *felt* like something. She and Rebecca had run downstairs from their apartment out onto East Fifth Street and heard horns blaring, watched rainbow flags flying from windows and fire escapes.

When she looked up at the flags, she thought of childhood. In the windows of the shops near her home, she had seen Poland's flag nearly every day—but the first pride flag she had ever seen was at Northwestern. The first openly gay person she'd ever met had been there, in college. She thought about the first time she had ever closed her eyes at night and imagined a girl next to her, all the way back in her childhood home, and slipped her hand down under her grandma's old quilt. She remembered the way she had bolted upright, forcing her eyes back open. She had tried to delay admitting, even to herself, what it meant that she looked forward to seeing her biology lab partner, Dalia, every single day, excitement burning like a crush. She tried to deny herself for years.

Now she looked up at the windows, and then higher, to the rooftops, and she realized that she wanted to shout something, as if the scared young girl she had been so long ago might somehow hear her across time and know that it was all headed here, today.

"This is my wife!" Clarissa shouted, wrapping her arm around Rebecca's waist. "My wife!"

A horn honked, a voice called, *Hell, yeah*, from somewhere, New York City roaring back its approval, and her wife—her wife!—just laughed, then whispered, "I love you," into her ear.

That day had signified, consecrated, something for both of them. But it had also marked something else: the first moment Clarissa had doubted if she wanted to continue living a life where she had to record a video announcing every important occasion in her life and broadcast it to millions of people. Clarissa had sat at her desk in their home office, the old window AC unit blowing directly into her face but still failing to cut through the fetid summer humidity, and she wondered how to record a video that did justice to that moment on the day of the ruling between her and Rebecca. If she even could or wanted to. Not even if it would win her awards, not even if it would get her more (incredibly lucrative) brand deals. She wondered, in earnest for the first time, if it was time to leave this part of her career behind.

It wasn't as if she had ever wanted to be a YouTuber, as they were now called. When she started, there hadn't even been a name for what she did, and sharing digital videos seemed like a free and efficient way to distribute her comedy. But while many of her videos did include jokes or start from a premise that she had explored in a separate stand-up set, there existed a clear distinction between what her subscribers liked best about her videos and what kind of art she wanted to create. There was something so personal in nature about the platform. Her You-Tube audience remained younger teens and twentysomethings who wanted her advice, or who were curious about her life, or who self-identified as "Clarissa fans," but more because of her now "iconic"—yes, it had made a *BuzzFeed* listicle—coming-out video, which had first gone viral, than because of her comedy or her writing. Shooting and editing videos now took up most of her time. It also made her the most money. She had ever more frequent requests for videos of her "routine," of her "day in the life." It seemed strange to her, this growing desire people had to look through a screen at how someone else washed their face, how they organized their morning.

I want to quit! the voice in her head had shouted.

And then three more years went by. In the lead-up to the 2016 election, Clarissa had *wanted* to be an influencer. She had wanted to use YouTube to inspire people to vote. But the platform had also swirled with conspiracy theories, and then wedged up against that, inane videos of "what I eat in a day" that seemed doomed to promote eating disorders. The whole thing was a melee.

But it was a circus that had paid the bills—and then some—as Rebecca had finished school to become a therapist. It had paid for the East Village apartment in full, and then a honeymoon in Italy. It had paid for Joey's private school tuition in Chicago. It had paid for Clarissa to continue to occasionally drop in on the bill at comedy hangouts that were high on prestige but low on paychecks.

But now, tonight, Clarissa was thinking differently.

As she held open the door to Dirty French, the swanky Lower East Side spot where she and Rebecca were celebrating their anniversary, she realized—with both a touch of pride and a flush of shame—that she could afford to pay for this dinner many, many times over. Thousands. And she was thirty-three. She had to wonder how long she could keep posting on YouTube. For how long could she adapt to the new platforms, the Instagrams, now the TikToks, the whatever was bound to come next?

I'm going to quit, she thought as they sat down at their private corner table. *For real this time.*

The decision swelled inside her chest like a balloon. The sensation floated to her head, which buzzed with excitement. Why not quit? The fame? While the event invitations and the awards shows had first served as affirmation that she had arrived, she had tired of the posturing, the people striving to have their picture taken in the right place, to position themselves around just the right people. But where was the satisfaction? Work as an adolescent therapist truly fulfilled Rebecca; Clarissa's volunteer work with New Dawn Treatment Center and GLAAD did the same for her. Although she did not know what the future might bring, she had always known one thing about herself: She had decided long ago not to be bound by the milestones society expected—and while that could be frightening, the hidden underbelly of that fear was relief. When there is no script, you can write your own. *What do I want out of life, truly?* she could afford to ask herself. What would fill her days?

"Rebecca, I just decided something," she blurted, no sooner than they had clinked their complimentary glass of celebratory champagne. Her wife—her beautiful, smiling wife—just laughed. "Sorry, maybe I should have saved this for a different moment. But I have to tell you."

"Why doesn't that surprise me?"

"Because you know me?"

"That I do."

"Well, I'm going to quit YouTube. I'm going to stop making videos."

Rebecca just nodded, humoring her, because of course this was not the first time Clarissa had mentioned this.

"You don't say."

"No, it's different this time." Clarissa took her hand. "I've thought it through. I want to start writing—more material for shows, but maybe even something longer. A TV series? Turn back to the screenplay."

"The one you started last year?" Rebecca asked, remembering. Like she always did.

"Yes."

"Well, then." Rebecca raised her glass. "It looks like we have two things to celebrate tonight."

They touched their glasses. The high-pitched *clink* rang out, the noise of a bell sounding as the door of her new life swung open.

There would be much more to talk about, she knew. Their marriage was a partnership, after all, and they'd need to understand and agree on the new shape their lives would take. The hours. The clients Rebecca might take on in her private practice, the status of the investment accounts, the weighing of this charity or that trip. What would be next for both of them, individually, and also as a couple, three different entities that needed to balance, to live in harmony. But they both knew as they looked in each other's eyes that night, Clarissa was sure, that it was the start of a new chapter. For real, this time.

THE ENSUING VIDEO WOULD BE CALLED "WRITING MY OWN Script, Literally and Figuratively: A Goodbye to YouTube." When it was finally posted three months later, it would spark hundreds of thousands of views, thousands of comments, two panicked calls from Clarissa's agent, and a thundering congratulations from Rebecca and Dev, who took her out for too many margaritas that very night. They toasted her new projects. They toasted the deal for a TV adaptation of Dev's second book, on HBO, though who knew when *Variety* would get around to making the announcement. And they toasted something else, too, something private that, so far, Clarissa and Rebecca had only admitted to each other. Clarissa was on the precipice of something new, again. Something secret, but that felt exactly right.

But she was also possessed by a strange feeling, that in the narrative arc of her life, something was missing, even if it didn't make complete sense.

She wanted to call her family, back in Chicago, and tell them, too. Whether or not they would understand. Whether or not it would disrupt the fragile progress between them since she had married Rebecca.

And, without fully understanding why, she wanted to tell Rachel.

RACHEL

At least they still had snow days.

On Tuesday afternoon, Rachel got a text from Dev, predicting an early snowstorm on Friday. He would be stocking up on their favorite supplies—wine, salt-and-vinegar chips—and she had to come over, per tradition.

Her phone had buzzed with this text during work, while she was finishing a round of particularly satisfying edits for a young author's debut, a pitch-perfect work of autofiction with a timely storyline. She had gotten lost in reading it, hoping to distract herself from the frustrating news of the day from D.C. It seemed like a waste of time to keep repeating and reposting what everyone else in New York had to say about the administration, disbelieving the latest news or getting outraged at the latest tweet; the island of Manhattan had become an echo chamber of disgust that (apparently) betrayed just how out of touch most New Yorkers were with the entirety of a divided nation. Still, it was hard to stop herself from engaging, even when it could do no good.

It wasn't everyone, of course; Rachel and Aaron knew several people who condemned the president (was he really the *president*?) and his behavior in public, but then confided in private that even if they didn't like his demeanor, they were willing to overlook it for the right tax breaks, the right judges, the right support for Israel. But for Rachel it was different. It felt personal in a way she had only started to be able to verbalize.

Why? Because of that damn phrase, "locker room talk." *Because do you know who actually speaks like that in locker rooms?* Rachel sometimes wanted to yell. *And who's proud of it? Misogynists. Abusers.* Rachel believed she knew how abusers sounded; she knew how they behaved, how they ran their hands over women, over their money, over their fancy cars, indiscriminately, all three of those things the same to them, just tools they could boast about, objects to make them proud, pieces of machinery that existed to serve them. They were a class of men who had always been excused no matter what they did or said, their full measure never taken because they were either too charming or too powerful or just plain too *useful*, too likely to trade your stocks or lower your fucking taxes. People liked to bicker over whether Trump was "actually guilty" of sexual assault or whether he just liked to brag about being technically able to get away with it, just using it to inflate his own dominance, his own appeal, as if that were somehow better, as if the fact that he would *hopefully, maybe* stop just short of actually committing the crime made it all okay.

Years later than she should have, perhaps, Rachel knew the truth. It was not, and had never been, okay. A part of her felt embarrassed that it had taken so many other women doing the hard work—that it had taken the rising swell of #MeToo—but she had finally told her therapist the full truth about what Cody had done that night more than a decade ago: how he had deliberately gotten her drunker, how she knew he had held her down in bed when she tried to stop him. That he had raped her. Acknowledging it had dredged the pain to the surface at first, but then lifted it off her like a weight. The pain had been transmuted into something . . . else.

Her phone buzzed again. Dev. "And by the way, this is your daily reminder to take a break from the news. You've been obsessing."

He wasn't wrong.

She remembered how, years ago, they had teased Clarissa, calling her "the political one" of the group. Now it seemed like an immense privilege—as well as an embarrassment—that she had been able to ignore so much for so long.

It was frightening, the world. She did not want to admit it. The hacking, the election, the uncertain future. Global fucking warming. Was the world getting worse? she wondered, only to remember something her father had told her a long time ago, after 9/11.

"This is tragic, horrific, but it isn't new," he'd said. "The world has always been terrifying. You just weren't old enough to know it yet."

It shouldn't have been comforting, especially not to a teenager, but it was. It still was, somehow.

Rachel inhaled deeply, then exhaled. She texted Dev back with a thank-you, and she told him that she would come over on

Friday night, whether it was a true snow day or not (she was betting on not). It would be just her, she told him. Aaron was away on a work trip to San Francisco for the week, and she felt a little unmoored, eager for him to be home. She knew it would be good to see a friend.

ON FRIDAY NIGHT, RACHEL WEAVED HER WAY THROUGH THE unplowed streets of Soho with a baguette under one arm and a wheel of Brie under the other, carefully stepping through deep car tracks and snowdrifts that reached up to her knees. The normally ten-minute walk took her almost half an hour.

"'The newspapers were right. Snow was general all over Ireland,'" Dev quoted as he swung open the door.

James Joyce. She remembered the Joyce seminar they'd taken together, in college.

"I love 'The Dead,'" she said, handing Dev her coat and the baguette. "It's such a haunting love story at the end."

Dev shook his head. "You are the only person in the world who thinks 'The Dead' is a love story."

"But it *is*. Because it all leads up to the moment where Gabriel is heartbroken to find out that there's so much about his wife, whom he clearly loves, that he didn't know—about Michael Furey, and what he represents—and then Gabriel's just watching the snow fall as his wife sleeps, and thinking—"

"'The Dead' is not about Gabriel's relationship with his wife. It's about paralysis, stagnancy. It's about Irish politics."

"It's about both. It's also about jealousy and male pride, come to think of it." Rachel raised an eyebrow, baiting him.

"Touché. You always were smarter than me." Dev closed the door behind her, then snatched the cheese out of her hands. "Is this Saint André?"

"Hello, by the way." She elbowed him.

"Remember when we used to eat bread with that gross block of Colby Jack back in college?"

"I never did that," she said. "That was all you and . . . Nate."

"Well, I blame you for ruining me with your expensive taste."

"You probably should. I mean, look at this place." She gestured at the apartment's open kitchen and expansive living room. Dev had finally gotten rid of his framed soccer posters, and the sprawling sofa and nesting coffee tables under new modern fixtures looked straight out of *Architectural Digest*. She felt an unexpected pang of nostalgia, of longing, for the Dev who had sourced most of his furniture from street corners and had once asked her "Who's Tom Ford? Was he in our dorm?" But that had been before the film adaptation, the TV deal. The bestseller lists.

Evaluating the changes in the apartment, she realized it had probably been a few months since she'd seen it. She remembered a time that seemed not so long ago when they had all practically lived out of each other's apartments. She used to see her friends three, four, five nights a week, eating dinner off their coffee tables, using their products in the bathroom, crashing in their beds and on their couches after a long night out. What had happened? Life, she guessed. She still came over to Dev's apartment, sometimes with Aaron, sometimes alone, but mostly for group dinner parties, or so they could take an Uber to an event together. But now here she was, tonight. It was nice to be with someone for no reason. She made a mental note to do it more often.

Behind her, Dev splashed something into a glass. "Okay, Bergen," he said, pointedly using her maiden name. "You're not getting out of the most important snow-day tradition: the shot ski."

She whipped her head around and saw him pouring clear liquid into two shot glasses glued to a ski on his kitchen counter. *The* shot ski.

"No way. Absolutely not. That is disgusting."

"Yes way."

"Why do you still have that?" She laughed. "This is a grown-up's apartment, not a fraternity house."

Dev mimed looking over both his shoulders. "I don't see any grown-ups, so . . ."

She groaned and shook her head. She remembered the four of them lifting the ski in tandem, coordinated at first, and then getting out of sync and spilling vodka down their shirts as the night went on, their inebriation increasing. During the snowstorm in '05 they had set a record, hadn't they? Ten rounds of the shot ski without anyone throwing up. She grimaced. Had they ever really been that young? Clarissa had made a notch on a beam in the house's basement for every shot they took, writing down their record for posterity. It was probably still there, carved into the woodwork.

"How is Clarissa, by the way?" she asked, a non sequitur that she knew Dev would follow completely, because how could they get out the shot ski without thinking about her? She liked how many memories they shared, how easily their minds could travel wordlessly down the same pathways.

"She's good," he said. "Actually, I meant to tell you: She mentioned all of us getting together for dinner, sometime soon."

It embarrassed Rachel how much this moved her. She crossed her arms in front of her chest, not wanting to give away too much. "If she really did want to get together, she could call me, you know." A pause. "She has my number. We like each other's posts on Instagram."

"Oh, come on, Rach, this isn't college anymore. You drifted apart, yeah, but you can also . . . drift back together."

"Poetic phrasing. I see why we gave you another two-book deal."

"And thank you for that, by the way," Dev said, although she wasn't his editor directly, she appreciated being credited that way, as an important part of the imprint that published his books. She liked it, feeling a thrill when a book she had worked on received a rave review, or when she helped an author launch their career. It felt like what she had imagined seeing her own book in print one day would feel like.

Almost.

"You're welcome," she said. "Anyway, when will this important dinner be taking place?"

"Soon. I think it's past time that we all catch up."

"I saw she stopped doing the YouTube thing."

"Exactly, lots to catch up on. See, things change, people grow, there's no . . . no bad blood anymore. She's just busy, you're busy, these things don't happen on their own. So, I'm making it happen. Let's say next weekend, dinner?"

Unable to hide her feelings anymore, or maybe even not wanting to, Rachel grinned. "Fine. It really will be great to see her."

"Now stop stalling and come take this shot so we can move on to the good stuff," he said, and they raised the ski hesitantly to their lips. For a moment she thought they would spill it completely, but then muscle memory took over and they flipped it smoothly, downing the shots together; some things you didn't forget.

AN HOUR LATER, THEY WERE SPRAWLED OUT ON DEV'S SECtional sofa, a quarter of the baguette and an empty bottle of wine before them, full and happy and definitely buzzed. Snow fell gently out the window. A Joni Mitchell album played on Dev's turntable, which they had finally agreed on after arguing about Radiohead, whom Dev still dearly loved. The night stretched in front of them, and Rachel realized that she wasn't worrying about what might happen or trying to make something happen. She spent so much of her time organizing things—planning the dinner party, presenting sales numbers, ushering people from one room to the next. It was a relief to just *be*. She wondered if she could learn how to channel this feeling into the other areas of her life; it felt most possible around Dev, but maybe it wasn't about their relationship as much as it was about the fact that he knew her from a time when everything had seemed simpler, from the last time she had truly felt young, relaxed, at ease.

She said a version of this out loud to Dev.

"That makes sense, but I have to tell you, I don't really remember you being that laid-back in college, either." He smirked, standing up to open a new bottle of wine and refill his glass. "I mean, it was a comparatively simpler time for a lot of us, sure, but you were wound pretty tight back then, too."

"Ouch."

"I mean it as a compliment, actually." Dev looked down at his lap, like he was making a confession. "To be honest with you, I think I admired that intensity, that control, in a way. There are a lot of things I've just sort of . . . let happen to me."

"I don't think that's true at all," she said. She thought about the opportunities Dev had seized: coming to New York when his parents discouraged it; setting a deadline for finishing his first book and working hard enough to actually meet it. "Sometimes you took charge of things more than I did. In a way, I think I used things that happened to me—you know, my mom getting sick again—as an excuse. But really, I think I was just too scared to go get my MFA and fail. How's that for embarrassing?" But she wasn't embarrassed, not really. It just felt good to voice that thought at long last.

"Well, for what it's worth, I think you did the right thing. Staying."

"And so do I, now! Look at the time I had with my parents; look at Aaron. I have a job I love, a life that's stable and that makes sense for me. But it's true that you made certain things happen for yourself, creatively speaking, when I . . . just didn't." She shrugged, then sipped her wine. It didn't hurt so much anymore. She still felt twinges of insecurity, or professional jealousy, from time to time, but not as often, and never the way she had when Dev had first sold his book. Now it was more like the way you might feel an old injury, something that flared up only in certain types of weather. "But I do think you and I have opposite problems with life, actually."

Dev raised his eyebrows and sipped his wine. "Oh really? And what are these problems?"

"Well, you've always had the drive, even when I didn't. But what you don't have is the ability to just, I don't know, settle down now and let things be good." She meant enjoying his success, rather than constantly striving for the next accomplishment. She also meant his relationships. Cleo. Dev had ended things with Cleo not long after the wedding, a vague excuse about how he was "not ready for the next step" and needed to "see what else is out there."

Dev stayed quiet for a minute, his mind seeming far away. He stared down at the rug, avoiding eye contact. "No, that I haven't. You're right. I have . . . not known a good thing when it was staring me right in the face. Many times."

She felt a little deflated then, like she had been too harsh. She hadn't meant to criticize him, though it *was* unlike Dev to take a comment like that personally anyway. She had expected a joke, a retort. Its absence felt strange.

"But maybe I've settled a little too much, so what do I know," she offered, backpedaling. It was at least partially true, she noted, thinking about her work, about the fact that she'd had the same editor title for years without planning her next move. She was happy enough, but maybe she could get motivated again, start some creative writing projects on the side just for fun, something like that.

She thought Dev might be evaluating her the same way she was auditing herself. But when she glanced up and saw him looking at her, it became clear in a shuddering thundercrack of a moment that he was thinking something else entirely. That he was thinking about her, Rachel, *like that*. That he thought, when she said *settling*, that perhaps she had meant that she settled in marrying Aaron.

She tried to open her mouth to tell him that he was wrong, to stop him before he could embarrass himself, embarrass both of them. But the wine had somehow turned into an anesthetic in her veins and she felt herself numbed, unable to act decisively. She found herself sitting still on the couch, just looking at Dev's mouth, watching his crooked half smile starting to break across his face, lighting him up. Somehow, she couldn't look away. *That smile, God*, she thought. It could freeze time. Or maybe even reverse it, leave her feeling like a twenty-two-year-old girl on a rooftop, with a boy, his gaze burning her up from the inside out.

Dev moved closer to her on the couch, the few remaining inches between them vibrating with possibility, electric.

"Rachel, look. I've had a lot of wine, and I'm just going to say the damn thing we're never supposed to say. Why wasn't it us?"

There was a time in Rachel's life when Dev uttering those words would have made her drop her wineglass. She would have watched it shatter and then leaned right over the shards to take his head in her hands and kiss him. She would have told him that it could be them, had always been them.

Now, though. Things were different.

She didn't gasp. She didn't fall toward him; she also didn't slap him. For one flash of a moment, his words lit her up inside, a match igniting, and she thought, *Oh, finally*. But then just as quickly as the match had lit, it snuffed out, and she found herself wishing that he hadn't spoken at all. She was in love with some- one else now; she had been for years. Didn't he understand? She had chosen Aaron, she had *married* Aaron, and she and Dev had their friendship, a peace and closeness between them that finally felt solid, at last. She didn't want his words to upend that. Not after everything. She sighed.

"Because, Dev." She covered his hand with hers compassionately and shook her head, choosing her words with care. "Because when you wake up here tomorrow, and your head is clear because you haven't been drinking out of a *shot ski*, you will remember that I'm just a friend, your old friend, your *married* friend—"

"You weren't always married, and you know that's not what I'm asking. I'm not asking about now. I'm asking—"

"And if that's not enough, you'll also remember that I, unlike you, am the kind of person who likes to go to bed at ten p.m., and that I like to schedule every single minute of my day, and that I absolutely refuse to fly certain airlines, even if it will save me money, and that we . . . we just work best as friends, Dev. That has always been true. Otherwise, something"—she threw her hands up, gesticulating at nothing—"otherwise something more would have happened, wouldn't it? And not tonight, not with me married and you just feeling drunk and lonely, but years ago, when it could have. But it was always going to be like this. Okay?"

"It's not because I'm drunk or lonely."

"Dev."

"Okay. Right, okay, you're right. Shit. Sorry."

"Don't be sorry," Rachel said, though part of her meant, *Good, you should be.* She drew in a deep breath, and even though she still felt unsettled, she breathed in the knowledge that this would pass. This was just a moment, one small, strange moment in a relationship full of strange moments, some behind them, and many more still ahead.

"Well. More wine, so I can get over the embarrassment of having said that?"

"I think I'm going to go." She drained the last sip of her glass. "But not because I'm upset, I promise. Just because . . . I don't think anything good is going to come out of us getting any drunker tonight. I really think it's better if we just get some sleep and let it go away on its own. Because it will, I swear."

"Yeah. Yeah, you're right."

"And I think that's the first time I've ever heard you say that, so this was all worth it," she said, and he laughed.

They hugged goodbye at the door, and Dev seemed a bit chastened, but not upset. It would all be fine.

"I'll call you about next weekend," she promised. "Thanks for a great snow day."

"Night, Bergen," he said, and her heart dropped a little bit as the door slammed shut between them, but she told herself it was nothing.

SHE WALKED HOME SO SHE COULD HAVE TIME TO THINK, although calling an Uber would have been a better choice between the treacherous streets and her dizzying wine haze. What should she have done? she wondered. Why did everything feel so wrong? She missed being in the apartment with Dev already, even though that seemed impossible, and even though she wanted to be angry at him for ruining an otherwise perfect night.

But she remembered Dev next to her, talking to her through her fear back in college, the night she had first found out her mom was sick. She thought about the secrets of hers he knew, and everything she knew about him. She thought about the long-ago nights dancing on the Lower East Side, the nights in East Hampton, Dev reciting a poem at her wedding, the two of them bantering back and forth, her reading and editing his work. She held all these things in her mind, and then she knew what she could have said to him instead.

"Our lives are entwined in so many ways," she should have told him. "Why is it some kind of tragedy that we didn't 'get together'? Why did there have to be sex? We have everything we need from each other; we always have."

She paused at the corner of Leroy Street. She wanted to turn around, to run back and tell him: The very premise of his question was flawed. "Because in every way that matters, Dev," she could say, "it already is us." What she had with Aaron meant the world to her; he was who she had chosen as her partner, forever, and nothing could change that. She would never risk what they had, would never give up their love for anything, and tonight had proven it. But that didn't make it the only important story of her life.

She could tell Dev tomorrow, she decided, when they were both clearheaded, when she could be sure he would hear it as a friend, the way she intended. And after—she smiled—they would reach out to Clarissa, too. It was all still there, she thought, the bulwark of her life that she had forgotten she needed. She pulled her coat tighter around her and made her way home.

WHAT SHE COULD NOT KNOW WAS THAT, AT THE VERY SAME moment, wine drunk, lonely, and angry with himself, Dev decided that he needed something to clear his head and calm him down. He needed cigarettes.

He bounded downstairs with just his sweatshirt and shorts and gym shoes on; the bodega was just around the corner. The weather was worse than he'd thought, but it was nothing compared to Chicago. He was determined not to get soft. And because of that, because he was looking down, looking for the best way to clear the snowdrift at the curb, he didn't see the car careening through the stop sign on Howard Street.

The driver did not see him, either.

A flash of light, and Dev snapped his head up over his shoulder and thought, *Oh, shit*, but his reflexes were too slow, and he didn't move, and then with a crunch of metal, everything Dev thought disappeared forever.

CODA: CLARISSA, NATE, RACHEL

ow about a walk?" Rebecca's bell-clear voice called into Clarissa's study.

"No," Clarissa snapped. "I'm busy. I'm working."

She registered Rebecca padding into the room gently in her slippers. She felt a flash of annoyance followed quickly by the warmth of certainty that someone cared. That Rebecca always cared. She peered over Clarissa's shoulder at the computer screen, and she did not comment on the fact that it displayed only a completely blank Word document.

"Just around the block, just five minutes," Rebecca said. "Take your mind off things."

"Nothing takes my mind off of it."

"Of course not. Poor choice of words. But let's think about it outside, in the fresh air."

Even though this did not lessen the ache inside her even one bit, Clarissa knew she was right, and she knew, somewhere inside her, in a place currently overwhelmed by grief, she did feel grateful, too.

CLARISSA HAD KNOWN SOMETHING TERRIBLE HAD HAPPENED the minute she unlocked the front door on that December night and saw Rebecca still awake. She had been at a friend's gig in Brooklyn, down in Gowanus, and trekking home on the F train had been a mistake. She unlocked the front door quietly, mindful of Rebecca's asleep-at-ten routine.

But there Rebecca sat, stiff and upright in a corner chair in low light, like a detective lying in wait for a suspect.

"What?" Clarissa had barked immediately. "What's wrong?" She prayed Rebecca would say that she just couldn't sleep, but somehow, she knew better.

Rebecca stood and stepped toward her, eyes red-rimmed and puffy. She wrapped a blanket around Clarissa's shoulders. "Honey," she said.

Rebecca's dad? He'd had heart surgery the previous year, and they now talked on the phone almost every day.

"You're scaring me."

"Honey," Rebecca repeated. "I'm so sorry, come sit down."

"I don't want to sit down." *Her sister? Her parents? God, if they died now, without her getting the chance to see them one more time, to really fix things . . .*

"I don't want to sit down," she repeated. "I want you to tell me what's going on."

"Okay." Rebecca took a deep breath and slipped an arm around her. "It's Dev. There was a freak pedestrian accident; he got hit crossing the street. They took him to Langone, but he—he didn't make it. He died. Love, I'm so sorry."

Clarissa had not thought that words could break a person. As a writer and performer, she had always believed in their power, but she had prided herself on being able to hear anything, take anything. She had been bullied, called horrible names. She had faced the trolls in the comments and laughed; she'd taken rejection. She'd withstood the judgment of her family. But those words. *He died. Dev died.* It took her a moment to put them together, to force them to make sense, the way she had felt thirty years ago, in preschool, when she had first learned English.

On umarł. *He died.*

Once she truly understood them, something collapsed inside her rib cage, her lungs. She made a guttural wail, a noise she heard like a stranger, wondering if it had really come from her. She sank to the floor, pulling Rebecca with her, while the pain roiled inside her, an unholy storm she couldn't exorcise.

"I'm here," Rebecca said. "I'm here."

Clarissa stayed on the floor in the foyer all night, her cheek pressed to the matted rug. Rebecca brought her a pillow. When the sun streamed in the next morning, light falling on her cheek, she brought her a tea. Finally, twelve hours later, Clarissa stood up wordlessly and began to make calls. To phone back Dev's family, to ask if she could help to plan a New York memorial. She spoke to Rachel. They chose the Angel Orensanz Foundation, and they began to work to put together a "celebration," as they called it, of Dev's life, even though it did not feel like one at all.

With every word, every decision, the unthinkable became real.

Clarissa did not cry again, because people needed her. Because Dev's family needed her. Because someone would always need her. But a part of her, she feared, was still and would always be there in that doorway, frozen in time, lost to the last moments when the beating heart of her chosen family still existed, the last moment that her soul felt intact.

THE WIND PRICKED CLARISSA'S EARS AS SHE AND REBECCA started out on their walk. Rebecca slipped an arm around her. Clarissa leaned into her touch, a welcome protection against the crisp spring air.

Spring, a new season. The first without Dev. As every new thing would be, forever.

"So, the new project you're working on," Rebecca said. "It's a pilot, right? A TV series?"

"I haven't made much progress." In the three months since Dev's death, Clarissa had worked with Rachel to draft an obituary, which ran in *The New York Times*. She had not written anything else.

"That's okay," Rebecca said. "I just want to hear the idea."

"It's going to be a show. About four friends who meet in college, and what happens when one of them becomes famous."

Rebecca smiled. "Now, that doesn't sound familiar at all."

"They do say to write what you know." Clarissa shrugged. "But I don't know. It's supposed to be funny, but I don't want an avatar for myself in there. No comedians. The famous one is the guy, the writer."

"Ah," Rebecca said, understanding. "I think Dev would love

that he's a character. I can just see it." They turned the corner near their bodega, their strides matching, and headed back toward home in wordless agreement.

Clarissa nodded. She hated the narrative that the dead could live on through art, or through children, or through any act of the living. They were gone, and anything else was delusional sentimentality. She chafed against the idea that loss had a "point," that it should inspire her somehow at every turn. She did not want to start a charity in Dev's honor, or put his name on a plaque, or even announce that he had inspired a character in her newest work. But the fact was that he *had* inspired her, whether she gave voice to it or not.

"Yes, he would like it. Of everyone I know, Dev would stupidly, smugly, like it the most."

Rebecca slid the key into the lock on their door. *Their home, together.* "You can always talk about him, you know. After months, after years. Grief isn't linear; it doesn't have a shelf life. It isn't something you root out and throw away after three weeks."

"Every once in a while, it does pay to be married to a therapist. Though not necessarily financially, of course," she joked, and Rebecca gave her a playful shove.

"Humor as a defense mechanism, your favorite," she responded, and Clarissa felt the buoyancy of the comment, not of its humor, but of its normalcy. Things had been heavier between them since Dev's death. Of course they were. There were plans they had put on hold, subjects they were afraid to touch. They stepped around them like they were broken glass. But she could feel Rebecca waiting, patiently and kindly, for Clarissa to come back to herself. Maybe it was happening now, only a little bit, drop by drop.

Clarissa's phone buzzed as they walked into the apartment.

"Let's get that drink soon," the text from Rachel read. "If you're up for it."

RACHEL WOULD NEVER, EVER ADMIT IT TO ANYONE, BUT WHEN it happened, the second emotion she'd felt was a kind of relief.

The first was the gut punch of pain, a blunt force that left her gasping, unable to sob, just sucking in air.

"Is this Rachel? This is Sumeet. Dev's brother. You were the last person he messaged."

Dev's brother?

"Rachel, sit down. There was an accident. Dev he . . . didn't make it. He died." A piercing cry, animal, then nothing.

Those words. The punch. The sinking to the floor of her apartment, phone still in her hand. The shouting for Aaron even though he was gone, wouldn't be home until the next day. The pain vibrating through her, unbearable, she thought she might be sick with it.

Then, inexplicably, relief. Because Rachel had lived her entire life fearing that the worst was just around the corner. She had been an anxious child, then an anxious adult. It felt as if she had been waiting for it, somehow, the one big thing. Every time something bad happened, her fear constricted, tightened: when her mom was diagnosed, then the morning after Cody, then when she heard Nate had been arrested. Each time, the voice in her head would ask, *Is this it? Is this it? Is this the worst it can get?*

Now she knew. She did not need to make any comparisons, analyze, future-project. *What if? What if?* What if nothing. The worst had happened. She could not change it.

AFTER WORK ONE THURSDAY, RACHEL TOOK AN UBER DOWN to the East Village. The days were getting longer, the sun shining across Broadway at five thirty in the evening. Spring had come without her notice.

As she rounded the corner on Fifth Street she saw Clarissa waiting outside the bar. Her pulse sped up, an old feeling she remembered from the seconds before meeting a blind date. But this was Clarissa, who had seen her vomit in a dorm bathroom, who had heard her have sex, who knew the way her voice sounded when she was trying not to cry. They were not strangers, even if it felt like they could be.

"It's good to see you," Rachel said, her voice cracking as she took in Clarissa's close-cropped hair, her red lips, her trench coat worn open over a pair of painter's overalls. "And look, we're matching." She gestured to her own trench coat.

"I'd guess that what's under yours is a little more J.Crew than Johnson's Plumbing, but yes." Clarissa flashed a small smile. "And it's good to see you, too. Thanks for texting."

Clarissa swung open the door, and they took two seats at the bar. Old leather stools, with dust-covered bottles on the wall behind. A signature Clarissa spot.

"Of course," Rachel said. "When we were together at the memorial and we promised to stay in better touch . . . I just, well, you know how those things are. But I didn't want that to be it. I've been meaning to see you for a long time. I'm sorry."

"Me, too," Clarissa said. "I had just told Dev that the three of us should get together sometime. Right before . . . you know. And then I saw you."

She did know. On the day of Dev's funeral—would those words ever sound right together? every time she heard them, she processed them as Dev's funeral *scene*, as in something he wrote, or something he directed—she and Clarissa had seen each other in person for the first time outside the Angel Orensanz Foundation on the Lower East Side, where they had decided with his family to hold a New York memorial service. They had not run into each other on the way in: They had bumped into each other, physically, in an alley around the back. Clarissa held a coffee, Rachel an illicit cigarette. Clarissa was probably trying not to be recognized, Rachel guessed, trying to enter without photos or attention. Rachel was just hiding, unable to deal with her emotions, unable to face anyone, especially with the knowledge, the hanging guilt, of the last conversation she and Dev had ever had. The overpowering grief that if she'd only loved him more, or differently, or at least enough to stay, he'd still be alive. She had sent Aaron inside alone.

She looked at Clarissa with tears and snot running down her face. She wanted to say something, but she couldn't think of anything, and then suddenly they were hugging, wordlessly, her arms slipped all the way inside Clarissa's coat. They stayed like that for a minute, or an hour, and then they walked into the building together.

They had sat in the back row despite having done a good chunk of the organizing, listening quietly to the speeches. Rachel had wanted to find them moving, but too many of the words of the eulogies felt like they could have been applied to anyone. She wondered if Clarissa thought the same. But then she started imagining Dev evaluating this whole scene, wishing he could just write all the damn eulogies himself so he could get the tone right, could immortalize himself as the charming, revered, just-a-tiny-bit-tortured artist he fancied himself to be, and at *that* thought she had to stifle a laugh. When was she going to stop pinging wildly between inconsolable and inappropriately amused? she wondered. But she suspected that this was what grief *was*, an unending series of shifting emotions that couldn't be predicted or rearranged.

Rachel and Clarissa stood in the doorway after the service, having exchanged no words about their relationship directly, but she could feel the gravity between them shift. They greeted Nate, who had flown in, for the first time in years, but none of them seemed up for much more than exchanging pleasantries. Then, just when she had thought she was all right, Rachel had fallen to her knees in tears in front of everyone, right there at the exit. It had taken almost an hour before she could steel herself to go over to Dev's parents, where they planted kisses on his mother's cheeks as tears washed down them. They promised to call her soon, that they would never lose touch, and they meant it as much as they possibly could while now possessing the knowledge that it is quite difficult to promise anything of that sort at the distance of years and possibly decades. They hoped, though. Hope was good.

"Please call me sometime," Clarissa said, almost whispered, as they walked down the steps to the street, she arm in arm with Rebecca, Rachel with Aaron. "Not now, but, you know."

"Sure," she'd said, the tears threatening again. "We can get a drink sometime. When things are . . . better."

THINGS WERE NOT BETTER. OR MAYBE THEY WERE, OR AT LEAST they were not measurably worse. In any case, four months had passed. Time ticked on in perpetual motion.

"So, is this your neighborhood spot?" Rachel gestured around at the room, meaning to indicate its obvious Clarissaness, and eager to turn the conversation away from Dev. "You live nearby now, right? How do you like it?"

She nodded. "Yes, it's my local, but not for long. We're moving to Brooklyn. Shocking, right?"

"I'm only shocked that you didn't already live in Brooklyn."

"Only because of my beautiful wife. But she has finally agreed that we could indeed use more space for the money. Maybe a yard. Full domestic." She paused, and then her features rearranged subtly, turning like a kaleidoscope. Rachel wondered what this meant.

"You?" she asked. "'Domestic'? Maybe marriage really does change people."

"We're, um. Maybe I shouldn't say, but it would be good to tell someone other than Dev, actually, so fuck it."

"What?"

"We're trying to have a kid. When Dev died . . . well, we delayed things a little bit, but we're on several adoption lists.

And Rebecca is planning to start IVF. She thinks she wants the experience of being pregnant, and God knows I don't. Anyway, we might end up with two kids. Or none! But it's exciting, actually. In a way I wouldn't ever have expected."

"Clarissa! It's so exciting," Rachel gushed. "Congratulations. And I know it isn't easy, per se"—she knew multiple couples starting IVF—"but it's a journey, and an adventure, and I'm so happy for you."

"Thank you," Clarissa said, taking a sip of the draft beer that had shown up in front of her like magic, no order necessary. "I'm nervous, but I am very, genuinely excited about it. Not in the same way that I am about the TV project I'm working on, and not the way I feel before I go onstage, but in a very specific, new way. It's its own thing. I never guessed that."

"How do you mean?"

"I mean, you know I've always loved my sister, and Joey. But 'having a family'? Having kids? Not something I ever dreamed about or planned for. Not like you did. But the dreams you go in with aren't always the only ones you end up with, it turns out. Something like that."

Rachel stayed quiet, not sure exactly what to say. Because the truth was that, at the moment, she, Rachel, the woman who had picked out baby names at age eighteen (Ava and Sarah), did not know when or if she wanted to have children with her husband. She didn't know if it was because of her grief over Dev, or simply because she felt so much *younger* than she had always imagined she would at thirty-four. She wanted to say these things to Clarissa, these things she had not yet found a way to say to Isabelle or Nicole, whose first children had been born like dominoes in March and April of the previous year. But she did not want to take this moment and make it hers. Not yet, anyway.

"I'm actually not as sure about when to have kids as I used to be," she ventured. "So, you're right. The plans you have when you're young aren't always as ironclad as they seem. But tell me more. Where in Brooklyn? When? Can I babysit?"

Clarissa rolled her eyes at her exaggerated enthusiasm, but Rachel could see that she liked it. That something about it made her happy more than it annoyed her. Clarissa answered, and the words began to flow easily between them, water over a dam.

They spoke about work and marriage, compromise and grief. Then, finally, they spoke about Dev, because how could they not?

"I keep having these memories," Rachel said, echoing something she had so far only confided to Aaron. "I dream about him, probably more than I should, and it's all things that really happened. But that I couldn't remember until after he died." So many thoughts kept coming back to her, unbidden, that had been buried somewhere in her unconscious. It was as if Dev's death had unlocked a hidden compartment in her mind—but one that was, ironically, of no real use or enjoyment without him. She needed someone who remembered the same things.

"I feel the same way." Clarissa nodded. "Tell me one."

Rachel thought for a moment, and then realized the moment she wanted to share.

"It was right before his first book came out," Rachel started, and Clarissa watched her with rapt attention.

Right before the publication of his first book, Dev's

mother—sweetly, Rachel added—had asked him with grave concern if the story had a happy ending. She was proud of him, so proud, she said, but she just didn't like books that were sad, wasn't sure she could read it if it ended tragically.

"So, what did you say?" Rachel had asked him, knowing full well that the book certainly did not end happily, at least not in the traditional sense.

"I lied." Dev winked.

"Your poor mom."

"But you know." Dev leaned forward from his perch on the edge of the sofa, like he sometimes did when he wanted them all to know he had a serious and important point. "No book has a happy ending, really."

"Is this a derivative, pseudo-intellectual lecture about how there's no such thing as 'happily ever after,' because if so, please, please spare us." Clarissa rolled her eyes.

Dev elbowed her jokily. "Come on, Clare, as if. No, if there aren't any happy endings, it's not because nothing's happy. It's because nothing ends. I technically think of Damian in the present tense, I guess. We just only saw this one part of his life in the book, you know?"

"Yep, okay, that's worse." Nate groaned. "That's some literary bullshit. Fiction is made up. Books end. Period. And so do conversations. Like this one."

Everyone had laughed, and they all stood up and left the apartment, her old one on Cornelia Street, and they had ambled off to a bar to get day drunk and celebrate Dev's good fortune, oblivious to everything that lay ahead of them.

"I don't think it means anything," Rachel said to Clarissa,

concluding the story. Clarissa sipped her drink, quiet. "But it helps me, a bit. 'It's not because nothing's happy. It's because nothing ends.'"

"It is a little trite. I think Dev probably thought it was profound when he was twenty-five, and it would have made him cringe later."

"Probably."

"But to hell with it. Maybe he was right."

Rachel nodded. Because, she had to admit that, despite everyone's platitudes, despite all the statements of faith, nothing else had helped; she couldn't imagine Dev as *being* anywhere. The Jewish concept of the afterlife from her childhood was far too nebulous and mysterious, something that maybe didn't really exist at all. Nor could she see him reincarnated, reborn, no matter how much of a comfort it might offer to his mother. No, she thought, he was just gone. It was all over. Her chest felt like it was caving in on itself, the loss of Dev digging up every other loss she had ever experienced, the hole inside her growing exponentially.

But Dev's words, though. They made some kind of sense, not in the way that life never ends because there's a heaven you can go to, but because there was no one moment when everything that had comprised Dev's life, everything he had touched, would be truly over. It was better not to decide, she thought.

"To no endings, then. Whether happy or not." Rachel raised her wineglass.

"Fuck it. To no endings," Clarissa agreed, and then they stayed like that, close on their two bar stools, talking far past happy hour and long into the night.

THE INVITATION ARRIVED IN NATE'S INBOX ON A SUNDAY, unexpectedly, in between a bulletin from the Ultimate Frisbee co-rec team he had joined to stave off weekend boredom and a reminder to check his May American Express statement. He almost deleted it before he registered what it was.

You're invited to: Aaron's 40th birthday bash! the header of the Paperless Post invitation read. Nate blinked, running through his mental Rolodex to place an "Aaron," until the sender's email address caught his attention: Rachel.Berstein02@gmail.com.

Did this mean that, in Rachel-speak, he had finally been forgiven? Did he even care to be, want to be? He set his iPad down on the couch next to him, then shouted into the next room for his girlfriend.

"Steph? I'm going out for a run."

"Okay, babe," she called back, and the term of endearment, which he usually liked, grated on him. He knew he needed to clear his head before he could do or say something he'd regret. His relationship with Steph was by far the best thing in his life: He loved her downy blond hair, her strong shoulders. He adored the way they sang together in the car, their shared passion for indie bands of the '90s, the fact that they both wanted to get married someday but didn't want kids.

Yes, he needed to leave before he could snap and take his frustration out on Steph. He grabbed his headphones and bounded down the condo stairs, heading for Lake Shore Drive.

After the first quarter of a mile, Nate inhaled deeply and picked up the pace. His thoughts were a storm, a dark cloud swirling in his brain. *If it hadn't been for the funeral, I probably would never have seen them again*, he kept thinking. *Even after the letters, nothing. If Dev hadn't died . . .*

If Dev hadn't died. That thought choked him up, and he pushed himself harder, determined to press through it, to outrun it. Rachel had been the one to call him, to tell him through tears that she "thought maybe you should know" before word hit social media. That had pissed him off, her acting like the gatekeeper of the news, deciding who should be informed, and that Nate had just barely made the cut—as if Dev hadn't been his best friend, too, for most of his adult life. His anger had been misplaced, of course; therapy and AA and Jim had taught him about that. In truth, he was angry at the universe, devastated that Dev was gone. He'd hung up the phone. Alone, he had wept. It was the first time he had cried since his arrest.

He had also felt guilty. He wondered how Dev could be dead when he, Nate, was the one who deserved to be. After all, Dev had never driven drunk. Dev had never been to rehab, devastated his parents, torpedoed his career, relapsed in secret. He was just trying to cross the fucking street. Nate hated the asshole who hit him with a burning passion, one he expected to last forever, even though he knew that hating someone was like drinking poison and then waiting for the other guy to die. (Jim's advice, again.) But after Dev had died, Nate had not been much in the mood for words of wisdom.

He would not have been able to go to the New York memorial if it hadn't been for Steph. They had been officially a couple for less than a year, and he had been hesitant to lean on her, but she had stepped up for him in every way: She had booked flights to

New York, flown with him, then graciously sent him to the memorial service alone, just waiting for him to come back to the hotel. It was there that he had seen Rachel and Clarissa for the first time in more than five years.

They didn't speak until after the service. Rachel hugged him, but they hadn't exchanged many words beyond confirming that neither of them was okay, and repeating, futilely, how shocked and sad and sorry they were.

"I was with Dev that night. The night he . . . I had just seen him," Nate remembered her saying through tears, and he had wanted to ask about that. Had she been with Dev right before he went out, inexplicably, in shorts in the middle of the night? Did she know why? Could she make any of this make sense? But then Dev's mom had come up next to them and they were kissing her cheeks and promising to stay in touch, and he ended up saying goodbye and wandering back to his hotel as if in a fugue state. Dev, gone. Him, still here. It couldn't be possible. It didn't make sense.

Five months later, it still didn't, though he had accepted it as much as he possibly could. He would never see Dev again. As for Rachel and Clarissa? They had texted just briefly after the service—he let them know when he made it back to Chicago, and Rachel had said he could call if he needed them—but that had been it. For months he had been torn about whether he should contact Rachel. He missed her, or he missed the way he had once felt inhabiting his life, a more exciting life, back when they had been friends. But he had also made his amends, and said what he needed to say, and he had other relationships now, with his family, with Steph, and he knew those were the ones he should invest in. He had decided not to call.

But he was sure as hell going to call now, he decided. He slowed to a trot, then stopped, plunking down on a bench along the running path overlooking Lake Michigan. Because where, exactly, did Rachel get off, contacting him only with this email event invite for a party for her husband? Nate had loved her for years in New York, and she had to have known that. Didn't she? Had she gotten his apology letter, the one where he'd poured his heart out? After everything, she was going to drop back into his life like this, with a *Paperless Post party email*?

This was not his better self talking. But Nate was getting tired of having to be his better self all the time. Before he could think better of it, he clicked on Rachel's name in his contacts and called her.

"Hello? This is Rachel," she answered on the third ring.

No sign that she knew who was calling. He wondered if she had deleted his number.

"Hi, it's Nate," he choked out. After multiple amends, hundreds of hours with Jim, years of therapy, he wondered if he should be better at this by now. He still found it difficult to cold call someone sober, afraid he would say the wrong thing.

"Nate, wow," she said. "It's . . . a surprise to hear from you. But a good one. How are you?"

"Fine, fine." A strong breeze blew up off the lake, whistling. A thunderstorm loomed; he covered his ear. "Listen, I'm calling because I got the invite to Aaron's party? Ha, Aaron's party. I just heard it."

"What?"

"You know, like the song? 'People all around you got to come get it,'" Nate sang, and then he cursed under his breath. How had he called with the intention of getting some answers, of letting Rachel know that she needed to be intentional if she wanted to be back in his life, and then ended up off-key singing the chorus to . . . "Aaron's Party"?

"Right. The invite." A pause. Nate realized for the first time, suddenly and with a feeling of queasiness, that it was quite possible that she had sent him the invitation by mistake. Maybe she'd meant to invite a Natalie or a Nell or even a different Nate, and a typo or an autocorrect mistake had simply filled in his address.

"Sorry if this is awkward," he said, determined to push through. *Just be straightforward, and honest.* "I don't know if you sent it to me by mistake, or if you wanted me to come. Either way, I should say I was happy to hear from you. Mostly, anyway."

He waited.

"I'm glad you got the invitation," she said at last. He still couldn't tell if this meant it had been intentional; it would be just like Rachel to act as if this was what she had wanted all along. "No pressure to fly in, of course. But it would be good to see you. The last time you were in New York, well. I wasn't in my right mind."

Yes, the invite had been a mistake. He'd put money on it.

"I don't think any of us were." This, at least, was true. "I'd like to talk more, though. Properly, this time. Not on the phone, or in a letter, or . . . at a funeral."

"Sure, yes." She sounded distracted for a minute, and Nate wondered what she was doing. He'd heard she'd become an editor—at Doubleday, Dev's publisher. He remembered the days before he got updates about her secondhand, when he had known every detail of Rachel's routine, the nuances of work drama, how she spent her weekends. They had emailed and BBM'd all day long. Now she existed for him only as a social media avatar. A name in an email.

But maybe they could have a friendship that wasn't so . . . intense. Or end things on better terms, at least. She had Aaron, and he had Steph now. He had a life, a different one than he had imagined maybe, smaller in some ways, but bigger in others. A life that was all his own, that did not hinge on who thought he was cool, or who promoted him, or whether he could get into a certain members-only club. (Soho House, as far as he knew, was still holding his application somewhere in its years-long wait-list purgatory.)

"Sorry about that, I'm back," Rachel's voice returned. "Anyway, I did want to tell you, too, that I got your apology letter. Maybe we can talk about it while you're here? I'm not going to say I'm sorry I didn't respond, because I wasn't ready, and I . . . I need that to be okay, Nate. But I am happy for you, for where you are now, and I would like to hear about it."

"Thank you," he said, and if he had learned anything in the past four years it was that he was not due Rachel's forgiveness, nor did he need her acknowledgment in order to move on with his life. But damn it if he wasn't happy to hear it anyway.

"So, if you're able to come, let me know when you get into town," she said. "Maybe we can get a coffee?"

"That sounds good," he replied. "It will be good to be back in the city. And to show my girlfriend around for the first time.

Steph, that's her name. She came with me for the memorial, but I'd like her to see it under, you know. Better circumstances."

"Steph," Rachel said, and he thought he could hear a smile in her voice. "I can't wait to meet her."

"Be in touch soon, then," Nate said, and he hung up. He shook his head, a "what can you do?" style gesture.

He pushed off from the bench and broke into a run, sprinting back toward home.

Home. He looked up at the low brick buildings of Lincoln Park, the oak trees, feeble compared to those in his Ohio suburb but far lusher than the sad, chained trees in Manhattan. Hardly anyone was on the sidewalk, and only one car cruised down the street, slowly.

Did he miss the noise, the chaos, the sensation that wherever he was must be the very center of everything? Yes, he did. Often. There was no point in refusing to admit this to himself. For every moment that he relished the comparative quiet, there was one where he felt like he had failed, somehow. Washed out. For every time he felt stronger, healthier, with all the running, and the Frisbee in the park that Steph loved to play with her charming, hippieish friends, there was a moment when he was certain he had never felt more alive, more vital than when he had been young in New York, pushing hard and fast in a world of late nights and early mornings with hustles and accomplishments ahead of him. Had he grown up, grown into the life that was right for him? Was there something to be won in being just a little healthier, a little saner? Or had he lost something after all, something that he had been able to effectively ignore until he heard the echo of its voice on the phone?

The residential street gave way to a busier avenue. On the corner stood an old bar, nameless, cozy, discreet. Nate slowed, then came to a halt in front of the doorway.

One day at a time.

I like who I am now.

No, I miss who I used to be.

You don't.

I do. Parts of it, anyway.

One day at a time.

Nate stood there on the corner, gazing into the bar's darkness, teetering on a fulcrum.

At the end of the summer of 2019, they finally went back. To Evanston, for a weekend visit that Clarissa had billed as a "class of 2006 reunion, but without all the people we wouldn't want to see."

"So . . . just the two of us?" Rachel asked. She wished, deeply, with a tugging in her heart, that Dev could come with them—the irony being, of course, that if he were alive, he would never have wanted to, anyway. Campus nostalgia had never been his thing.

"Nate can join us for a campus tour if he still wants," Clarissa acquiesced, referring to a conversation they had all had at Aaron's fortieth birthday party, about revisiting Northwestern's campus. They were back in touch, the three of them, though the bond felt tentative, like a construction in progress, not yet ready to bear weight. Privately, Rachel did not expect Clarissa and

Nate to be friends ever again, and that was fine. For her part, she wasn't sure where she stood.

That, too, would have to be fine.

It was the week after Rachel's thirty-fifth birthday. After a day of fielding calls from family and friends—she and Clarissa had talked for an hour, finally finding something like a rhythm—Rachel and Aaron had spent a quiet but perfect evening celebrating alone, just the two of them. They had dinner in the bloom-filled backyard garden at Palma, one of her favorite neighborhood spots, and then when they got home, he gave her a simple but beautiful pair of jade earrings that suited her perfectly. She put them on right away, even though she was already in her pajamas, and then it was her turn to give *both* of them a gift: She told him that she had made an appointment to have her IUD removed.

"Are you sure?" Aaron asked.

"Yes," she said, and it was mostly true, true in a way she couldn't have imagined just six months before. She now had a sense that there was this huge part of her life that was waiting for her to come find it, people and places she had yet to be introduced to. *A person*, specifically. An as-yet-unknown individual who would be part Aaron, part her, their two selves balanced in some kind of alchemy that she found herself excited to discover. She still did not know how she would be as a mother, but Aaron would be a wonderful father; she knew this in her bones. More than good enough to make up for her.

As they boarded the flight to Chicago, Rachel thought about the sum of her choices that had led her to this point: choosing Northwestern, moving back to New York. Meeting Aaron, not going for her MFA. Somehow all of that had led her *here*, to a seat on a plane bound for Chicago next to a man with whom she had decided to create a new life. A person was going to come into existence because she had forced herself to go on yet another first date to a West Village wine bar almost a decade ago. She wasn't foolish; she knew a pregnancy wasn't a foregone conclusion. Every day it seemed like another acquaintance opted to start IVF. And she *was* thirty-five, she reminded herself. But if that life—the life of biological parenthood—didn't come to fruition? That would be fine, too. She would find a way, because she always did.

It seemed to Rachel then that maybe there were an infinite number of lives she could have lived, but this, by sheer chance, was the one she had ended up with. If, say, she and Dev had somehow gotten together for real—there he was in her thoughts again; he always would be—she probably wouldn't have had children. Dev had never wanted them, and Rachel's desire might not have been strong enough to serve as an animating force on its own. With Aaron, now she would have children. But neither of those lives was inherently the *right* one for her. They just sort of . . . were. Like flipping a coin, a mere result of mathematical probability. A coin landing on heads wasn't inherently better or worse than a coin landing on tails, just like Rachel having children wasn't, in her mind, inherently better in the abstract than her not having them. Before they happened, outcomes were, to an extent, equal and arbitrary. But a result of heads *did* create a particular series of events and put them into motion. Once her children came into being, she knew not only that they would be perfect and beloved, but that they would feel like they had been inevitable. Choices created other choices, which created a set of parameters that then became the one and only truth. *Her* truth. Her life. How strange, how mysterious. How limiting, how beautiful. She remembered her younger self, who had always asked, "What if I had never come here?" Now she knew the answer: It didn't matter because she *had* come here. Her life had happened the way that it did, whether for a million reasons or for a few. That was all she needed to know.

Dev would have understood what she meant by all this, she thought. She could have said her stream of consciousness out loud to him, verbatim, and he would have heard it exactly as it was intended, would have known that it was a thought exercise and not a pointed commentary on her happiness with the life she had ended up with due to her own series of coin flips. She turned to Aaron, who was sipping a mineral water and flicking through *The Economist*, and she almost told him. But she knew him, and so she knew how he would hear it. He would hear a critique, an idea that they possibly could have—should have?—ended up with people other than each other, and it would have seemed unkind, even if that wasn't how she meant it. What would be the point of implying that they were only together, that they would only have a family, as a result of random chance? Rachel stayed silent.

But before that could make her sad, she realized something else, too: She and Aaron didn't think the same way, no. Their minds didn't work in perfect sync. But they *did* know each other. She knew him well enough to intuit how he would interpret her thoughts, and she knew how to then act on those thoughts in a way that would be kinder to him. He knew how to do the same thing for her in return. And that was not nothing. It was an achievement, actually: It spoke to persistence and knowledge and patience and dedication, rather than something so change-able and ethereal as "chemistry." She was lucky, actually. So in-credibly lucky. Just in a different way than her younger self might have hoped to be.

"I love you," she said to Aaron.

He peered over his magazine and turned to her, looking at her as if she had just come home from somewhere very far away, after a very long time.

"I love you, too," he said. "Did you know that?"

"Actually, yes." She laced her fingers with his. The pain in her heart, the pain that had been there since the morning she got the call that Dev was gone, still lingered. It throbbed; it ached. It would last for a long time, maybe forever. But there was something else inside her, too, a feeling of warmth, of safety, and it grew the longer she held his hand, just soaking in his presence next to her. "Today, I do know."

She felt the landing gear come down. The plane dipped slowly, inching closer to the earth.

THE SIX OF THEM MET UNDER THE NORTHWESTERN ARCH, THE official entrance to campus: she and Aaron, Clarissa and Re-becca, Nate and Steph. Rachel surprised herself by hugging both Nate and Steph, but it did not feel like a reunion between old friends. Nor did it feel passive aggressive, or like they were enemies. Nate reminded her of an acquaintance, someone she didn't really know. He smiled at her, deeper lines than she re-membered visible around his eyes and mouth.

They walked down the path to Deering Library, the start of their tour. The sun shone through gaps in the robust leaves that shaded the walk, warming Rachel's shoulders.

"God, was it always this beautiful?" she asked, gazing across the sun-dappled quad.

"No." Clarissa snorted. "We were never here in the summer. It was, like, twenty-five degrees the other nine months of the year."

"The memory is always better than the real thing, huh?" Nate said.

"I don't think so," Rachel disagreed, suddenly warmer, more nostalgic than she thought she'd be. "I think the real thing was actually pretty great."

THEY CONTINUED THEIR WALK FOR SEVERAL HOURS, POINT-ing out landmarks and reveling in telling old stories to their partners. Then, as the sun started to set, the buildings of their youth—Elder Hall, the Allison dorm—began to cast long shadows over the streets of Evanston, and they picked up the pace, knowing without any discussion where they were going. Before long, they found themselves in front of the old house, on the doorstep of 2102 Maple.

Rebecca spoke first. "So, this is it, huh? The famous house."

Clarissa nodded. "I almost can't believe it's still here."

"Dev's and my room probably should've been demolished after we moved out." Nate shook his head. Steph laughed.

Rachel looked up at her old bedroom window, remembering the last night there, before graduation, and then all the many nights prior to it. She remembered the promises they had made, the people they had hoped to become. She wondered what twenty-two-year-old Rachel would think of her now. Would she be impressed by her editor title, or disappointed that she hadn't published a novel? Would she think herself ordinary? Old? But then again, it wasn't as if young Rachel had been so admirable herself: She had been ambitious but anxious, posturing and superior, yet still secretly insecure. Rachel liked herself better now, she decided. She did. Or was that just what people said to make peace with themselves, to placate the creative dreams within them that had never come to fruition? She hoped not.

The six of them stood there in reverent silence, watching as the sun set behind the rooftops and it started to grow dark. A warm glow began to leak from the old house's windows as it lit up with all the young life it contained inside that had nothing to do with them anymore. Rachel took Aaron's hand on one side, Clarissa's on the other. She breathed in the knowledge that she was exactly where she was supposed to be.

Suddenly, the front door to the house swung open.

"Um." A college student dressed in leggings and an oversize NU hoodie stood there leaning against the doorframe, arms crossed, staring at them curiously. "We saw you through the window. Can we . . . like, help you?"

They all looked at one another, wide-eyed and panicked, and then simultaneously started to laugh. Rachel's sides heaved until they hurt. Clarissa laughed so hard that she sank to her knees on the front steps.

"No, no, sorry," Rachel told the girl through bursts of laughter, waving a hand. "Don't mind us. We're just some old alums who used to live here. A million years ago."

The girl cocked her head and then nodded. "Uh, cool. Well, bye," she said, and closed the door, leaving them to their moment.

But the spell had been broken, and now the door was just a door.

"Okay, enough," Clarissa said finally, and it was enough, Rachel thought, and together they turned their backs on the house and walked away into the darkness, heading back toward all the other places that were waiting for them.

ACKNOWLEDGMENTS

A resounding thank-you, first and foremost, to my brilliant editor, Cassidy Sachs. You saw this book right away, far more clearly than I could, and I am so bowled-over grateful for your vision. Thanks, too, to our phenomenal marketing and publicity teams, and to everyone at Dutton.

Thank you to Allison Hunter, my fabulous agent who (somehow) kept me sane through the nerve-racking process that is writing a second book. I don't know how you do it all, but you always do. Thanks to everyone at Trellis Literary.

On to the friends and family section, because it truly does take a village. With deepest gratitude:

To Arvin, who got the dedication on this one and certainly deserves it. Instead of listing off all our inside jokes here, I will simply write: Thank you, which is, of course, wholly inadequate, but what can I even say? Some people are just meant for each other. I think I started believing in fate the day I met you.

To Ashley, who always asks to read the earliest chapters and then raves about them—no matter how jumbled and nonsensical they may be. Your belief and loyalty are unmatched, and I think somehow I knew it from the first time I saw you across the circle in Deering Field. In my heart, we'll always be those lanyard-wearing Northwestern freshmen with a lifetime of adventures ahead of us. (Special thanks as well to Alberto, who has been taking care of us since we were those students and has known us almost all along.)

To Meredith, Anna, and Holly, with love—and Maria and Diana, too. Thank you for the real Maple house and all the memories.

To David and Catherine, always. Special thanks as well to Mark and Wendy, who are not only friends but lovely interview subjects and important sources of detail on the scenes relating to Lehman Brothers in 2008.

To Kendra, who also spoke on background, and whose insights and experiences were invaluable.

To all of my friends. When I wrote *Friends from Home*, I felt so privileged to be able to list out the dozens of people who have supported me for years—and I thank them all, resoundingly, again (you know who you are). But when I wrote that list in 2020, I never imagined how much it would continue to grow. So, now, a special thanks to my Toronto family, in no particular order: Emily, Jeff, Max, Neetu, Audrey, Andrew, Taryn, Adam, Casie, Matt, Ashley, and even more of you than I have the space to name. Thank you for seeing me through the pandemic, for cheering me on through book two, and for making me a home up here when I didn't think I needed or wanted one.

To Tom and Joanne, for the Howe Island writer's retreat (and lots more).

To all of my family, and especially to my parents, Deb, Bert, and Todd. I thank you every time, but of course I do: I'm here—literally and metaphorically—only because of you. Thank you for your unwavering support and for your love, for every day of my life. Special thanks as well, of course, to my grandma, Marge.

To the city of New York: then, now, forever. The setting of my books, the source of so much of my inspiration. I'm coming back for you, baby.

And finally, to James: In many ways, this is a book about the *Sliding Doors* moments of life, of which we all have many. It is natural to wonder about our decisions, to second-guess, to consider what might have been. But every once in a great while, we might choose something that feels so innately, purely right that we never imagine, not even once, that it could have been otherwise. For me, that has always been you. They could run a simulation a hundred times, and we'd be together in all one hundred. Our life is at once my greatest choice and an absolute inevitability.

ABOUT THE AUTHOR

LAURYN CHAMBERLAIN was born and raised in Michigan. She studied journalism and French at Northwestern University and then moved to New York City, where she worked for several years as a journalist, freelance writer, and content strategist (sometimes simultaneously). She currently lives in Toronto.